Fossil Lake IV:

SHARKASAURUS!

Edited by

Christine Morgan

Published by
Sabledrake Enterprises
www.sabledrake.com

A Fossil Lake Anthology
https://fossillake.wordpress.com/

For ordering information, contact
christinemariemorgan@gmail.com or visit us online.

ISBN-13: 978-0-9844032-8-8

10 9 8 7 6 5 4 3 2 1

"You're gonna need a bigger boat." -- God, to Noah.

"Let those curse it who curse the day, who are prepared to rouse Leviathan." -- Jeff Goldblum in some movie, probably.

"Din-o-SAUR, din-o-SAUR, ancient enemy of Man!" -- *Reptar On Ice.*

"With a great big hug and a kiss from me to you, won't you say you love me too?" -- Bruce the Shark

"Calm is the bottom of my sea: who would guess that it hides droll monsters!" -- Nietzsche

"Dah-dun ... dah-dun dah-dun ..." -- Sue the T.Rex

Table of Contents

About the Contributors

Lost Import

Tim Meyer

290 Million Years Ago

From the murky bottom, she rises.

The surrounding water vibrates, overloading her sensory system. She senses food, something plentiful, somewhere near the coast. Her tail propels her toward the meal. As she moves, something sweet makes its way into her nostrils. Something palatable, something delicious. Something she craves.

Blood.

Lots of it.

Fully titillated, she glides through the cloudy waters, lugging power and the desire for violence toward the coast.

Today

The scissors slice through the yellow tape and the celebration is so loud, Dr. Patrick Hammond can hardly hear his own thoughts.

He's smiling, but only because he has to. If he doesn't, Dr. Curry will chew his ear off later in private. Hammond slaps his hands together over and over again listlessly, making nice-nice with Curry and the rest of the public. The watch on his wrist rattles with each applause. He checks the time, the countdown to doomsday.

This is bad, he thinks. *Very bad.*

Curry smiles for the flurry of flashes that follow. He waves at the crowd as they toss questions at the stage. There will be plenty of time for a press conference later, once the demonstration is complete. He ignores them for now and continues to flap his hand at the media like a pigeon wing. A foolish grin pulls his face taut.

Hammond knocks his knuckles against his mentor's shoulder. "We need to reconsider this."

Curry shakes him off, continuing to address the crowd as they shower him with deafening praise.

"I'm not messing around, Kristoph."

Curry, refusing to let go of his happy charade, leans back and whispers to his protege, "Not now."

"Yes. Now." Hammond's lips practically kiss his ear as he speaks. "You know I haven't finished testing the circuits. The transistor was acting funny just yesterday."

"No time!" Curry shouts, but pleasantly so. He keeps his face trained on the reporters, accepting their congratulatory noise for an uncompleted job.

"But, Kristoph, the engineers haven't finished signing off on–"

Curry twists around once more, giving the crowd his back. His face contorts, the bone white of his teeth filling up his open mouth. His lips zig and zag as his rough voice trembles. "Do what I say. Now!" His words are barely heard over the applause and the barrage of questions. "Prep the room. Power on the Omega Transit and for Christ's sake, get your shit together, man. We have history to make."

The big boss rotates back to facing the crowd, wearing his smile like it never left. The cameras roll on, blinding flashes of light flicker, and the public's display of affection carries on.

Hammond retreats, ducking behind the Omega Transit, wishing he could disappear, run away, get as far away from the lab as he possibly can. He knows the dangers a throw of the switch might bring. During the long and punishing process, failures haunted them every step of the way. How Curry can sign off on something so elementary in progress, so apt to flounder, he'll never know. This isn't a demonstration of a finished product – it's advanced trial and error.

And the margin for error is infinite.

She shimmies through the brown, billowing cloud of lake dust. Light flits on the surface, bouncing in and out of her eyes. The smell of blood is bold here. She's getting close; she can taste the coppery flavor on her tongue. The phantom tang almost nourishes her. Her belly grows warm with bloody prospect.

She wonders what's ahead. What's hurt? What's bleeding? Why is there so much of it? Perhaps it's coming from one of her own. She contemplates whether she'll eat her brethren. Figures she might. Flesh is flesh, blood is blood. It's all the same once devoured.

She whips her tail rapidly, the idea of muscle, flesh, and blood too influential to slow her down. She sails forth, craving the slaughter.

Hammond pulls down on the lever. The Omega Transit erupts with life. Bright, eye-stabbing light casts the room in a heavenly glow. Hammond looks away. He finds Dr. Curry, who's staring straight into the LEDs, that stupid grin continuing to occupy real estate on his face. His eyes balloon with joy, mad with power.

I have to stop him, Hammond thinks. *He can't possibly predict what will happen.*

Curry spins, faces the crowd. They're over clapping now, finished chatting over each other. They stand in silence and witness the Omega Transit buzz with life. A few cameras flash off, but otherwise, Curry has their undivided attention.

"Ladies and gentlemen," he says like a circus entertainer. Hammond thinks that's what he's become. "I give you the Omega Transit. The very first portal into another world. Into another time."

Oohs and aahs circulate the crowd.

An animated Curry paces the stage. "Today will go down in history as science's greatest accomplishment. Today, we will attempt to draw a beast that once lived almost 300 million years ago into our world."

Incredulous gasps. Nervous laughter.

"No joke, ladies and gentlemen. No parlor trickery. This is the real deal. One-hundred percent scientific breakthrough."

Hammond eyes the machine. It's about six feet tall, constructed of solid steel. Ten feet wide. Its frame is circular, moon-shaped, but hollow in the center where the wall between worlds stands. The bright lights are embedded in the frame. In the center of the portal, where things come through, a hazy veil exists, the only barrier between a different place and time. The barrier looks like a liquid curtain. It sparkles with shades of purple and blue, always moving like the waves of a busy bay. Hammond focuses on the control panel where a million switches and dials sit, unprotected. He wonders how many he can smash with his fist before Curry's handpicked security squad rushes over and stops him. Not many, he thinks. He can feel the brutes' eyes settling on him, reading his thoughts.

"How does it work?" a member of the press shouts from the crowd.

Curry laughs and most of the crowd joins him. "A magician never reveals his secrets. If I divulge such secret information, what's to stop other corporations from replicating our design and profiting off our discovery?"

That answer satisfies only a small portion of the curious

gathering.

"How *does* your company plan on profiting from reintroducing extinct creatures?" a woman asks, raising her pencil in the air. "I mean, do you plan on opening an amusement park or something?"

This tease gets the majority to chuckle.

"No, no," Curry says, slowing his giggles. "Nothing like that. We plan on selling off our discoveries to labs around the world who can research these beasts. Maybe by learning about the past we can better serve our future."

It sounds like bullshit, but no one questions him.

Another reporter raises his hand in the air. Curry calls on him. "What do you plan on bringing back for us today?"

Curry smiles. The crowd grows completely silent. "Today," he says, "we're going to bring back one of the first sharks to ever stalk the prehistoric waters. Xenacanthus."

"Xena-what?" someone asks.

"Xenacanthus." He directs the crowd's attention to a projection screen. There's an audible click and an illustration appears, depicting something that resembles a combination of modern day shark and an eel. "Relatively small in size. Not dangerous. At least not to us air-breathers." No one laughs at that joke. They're too entranced by the possibilities. "Right. Well, there you have it. They don't grow longer than six feet. They feed on smaller fish. If things go according to plan, the Xenacanthus will be our first successful import."

There's a dragging silence, and it feels like forever until someone speaks again.

"You mean ..." the woman reporter says curiously, keeping her pencil raised, "you've never actually done this before?"

Curry loses a piece of his smile. He narrows his eyes. "Well, no. Not exactly."

"But what if ... something goes wrong?"

He acts like the idea never occurred to him. "Nothing can go wrong, my dear. You will witness the most wondrous scientific advancement history has ever seen. I assure you."

The crowd shrinks back, feeling less confident, less jovial. Curry's overconfidence has sucked every drop of excited energy from the room.

Hammond knows his chance to stop this is now. He plots.

She enters the sector of violence. Burgundy clouds explode around her like fireworks. Ragged chunks of muscle and meat float by. She snatches what she can in her jaws as she passes. The small gobbets are not enough. She needs her fill.

She pushes through the bloody curtain and bursts into a clearing. Ahead, she spots her own kind, five of them, thrashing within another rolling fog of crimson. There's another creature there, a larger creature. In its mouth, wriggles one of her sisters. The creature bites down, tearing through cartilage with ease. Her sister's head detaches from her body and floats toward the surface, a trail of rusty nebula following in its wake.

She dives forward, joining the fray. The creature snaps at another shark, missing by the length of its tooth. The shark goes for the neck and sinks its mouthy daggers in. It comes away with a chunk of flesh, but it's nothing. The dinosaur reacts by clamping its jaws around the shark's tail, severing it in one bite. In its last moments of distress, the shark dives to the sandy bottom of the lake, seeking safety. It can't out swim death and in minutes, the poor fish floats belly-up, towards the sky.

The vision of watching the slaughter of her own kind unexpectedly infuriates her. She lunges forth, burying her teeth in the dinosaur's back, just below where a giant, fan-like fin rests along its spine. She makes sure her teeth are good and sunk before tearing away a mass of meat. The finned dinosaur screams in agony as a ruddy smaze blankets the visibility factor. She lets the meat float away as she readies herself for seconds; this isn't about food or nourishment any more – it's a territorial war.

As she and the rest of her army strike again, their campaign of death is cut short by a blinding flash of light. It blinds her. She can see again. But there's more flashing. More blindness. Next, there's black. Then, something else.

A burning sensation in her eye sockets. A different kind of light infiltrates her.

She can't breathe.

"Shut it down!" Hammond pleads. "Shut it down now!"

Curry jockeys for control of the switchboard. Hammond shoves him aside. Behind the mad scientist, he spots the security squad rushing toward them.

"Stop! You fool! You'll mess this all up!" Curry throws an elbow and connects with Hammond's jaw. The force of the blow knocks the young doctor backwards, sends him falling on his ass. The security squad reaches him and it takes the three of them to corral the eager fool. "Do you have any idea how much damage you've possibly done!"

The audience looks on in shock. Some of them, non-media attendees, search for the exit, wishing themselves far away from this public relations nightmare. Curry notices this and confronts them.

"Please! Don't be alarmed. Everything is under control." He turns to the machine, twirls a few dials and pokes a few buttons. A loud sound that reminds him of an air conditioner condenser kicking on fills the silence. The lights on Omega Transit dim and dance with operational readiness. "Ah! Yes! Just as we predicted. See these heat patterns!" He points to the control panel. The five dots on the monitor pulse and glow red. "It's a heat map. We've set the directional navigation coordinates 290 million years in the past, focusing on a portion of the earth indigenous to Xenacanthus. Those must be them!"

"What's that larger dot?" the pesky female reporter asks. Curry wants to snap her pencil in half. "Is that a Xena-camu-thesis, too?"

Not wanting to admit a certain degree of incompetence, he simply replies, "Yes." No one asks for him to elaborate, but he feels the need to add, "Must be the mother of the group, the leader of the pack."

Hammond yells from the floor, "Shut it down, Curry! You don't know what you're doing!"

Curry grimaces. "Guards – remove this man. Kick him out of the building and have his level ten access revoked."

"Are you firing me?"

"Goddamn right." Curry spins back to the machine. "Ladies and gentlemen," he tells the gathered, "Let's explore the past in the future."

He throws the switch and the portal begins to crackle and sizzle, and the room smells like fire.

More light.
It hurts. It burns.
She feels herself change. Her body feels like a wet rag being wrung out. She has no concept of this and starts to panic. Her lateral line twists and wrinkles, feels like someone is bending her body in half. She hates this feeling. Survival mode kicks in and she starts to thrash. Unable to breathe, she bites the fleeting shadows, attacks the bright

pulses of light.

There's one final flash before she wakes up in an alien world, no longer herself. Now she's part of something bigger.

Something unnatural.

In the center of the room sits what the Omega Transit brought forth through time. Curry can't believe the images his eyes convey to his brain, thinks it must be some mistake. He checks the screen and sees all five heat patterns are gone.

"Oh, dear God," he says, realizing what has happened.

"I told you," Hammond says. He marches forward, away from the guards, all of whom had let go of their prisoner when the portal brought through the giant monstrosity. "I goddamn told you."

"We can send it back," Curry says. As he speaks, the Omega Transit barks and hisses. Dusty-brown smoke unfurls from the top of the control panel. Electric glitter fires off, explodes like handheld sparklers on the Fourth-of-July.

"I warned you about the transistor!" Hammond grabs his boss by his white collar. He shoves him against the control panel. Sparks continue to flare around them, dancing in the air like festive pixies. "You overconfident fuck, I warned you!"

Curry shakes his head. "We spent years perfecting it. I don't understand."

Hammond opens his mouth to hammer home another *I-told-you-so*, but his words mean nothing and he knows it. Together, they turn and face what Curry's carelessness has brought upon them.

In the center of the room, a dinosaur-like creature with an enormous sail on its back, at least twenty feet long, thrashes around, snapping its powerful jaws at the crowd of frightened onlookers. Eel-like creatures with dome-shaped snouts protrude from its midsection as if they belong to the creature's body, like its arms and legs. They snap at the air, wildly whipping around like speared snakes. They wheeze as they struggle to breathe, their bodies not built for land. The shark-like eels bite its carrier body, removing chunks of flesh with each strike. This instigates the dinosaur-like creature, enraging it, causing it to charge the collected crowd.

The audience shrieks in unison as they realize the thing is coming for them, and they've backed themselves into a corner. They start to panic and run, bowling into one another, knocking each other to the ground. They trample the fallen, colleagues and strangers alike, frantically searching for an exit.

"What is it?" Hammond asks, from his zone of safety, near the edge of the stage.

"It's a Dimetrodon. A land predator of that time period."

"And its friends?" He points to the shark-like eels. "Are those our Xenacanthus?"

Curry nods and looks back at the map, where the heat patterns glowed only moments ago. "They must have been too close together. We drew them through at the same time. They must have amalgamated."

"How do we fix it?"

The switchboard fizzles and pukes smoke.

Curry swallows a rush of sadness. "We don't." He grips Hammond's shoulder. *"We run."*

She can't breathe, but she can snap her jaws. She bites her host, rips away flesh and blood, but it gives her no satisfaction. The alien world will kill her, this she knows. Her objective: eviscerate her host, whatever the cost. It's the least she can do.

As she lashes out to accomplish this, other creatures scurry past her. She has no sense of what they are and doesn't care. She snaps at them as if they threaten her very existence. Her sisters nip at them too. The sister on her left catches an alien in her mouth, bites down, watches hot streams of blood spurt like a volcanic explosion of lava. The thing cries out and scarlet erupts from the open hole in its face. She enjoys watching this and lunges at the next alien she sees. She grabs a female (she can smell its sex) by her leg and chomps down. She feels its bones break under the force, and tastes coppery liquid in her mouth.

Blood is blood, she thinks. Flesh is flesh.

The carnage continues.

The crowd tries to rush past the creature, but the monster is deceptively fast, not as cumbersome as its body suggests. The head matching the rest of its lizard-like body does most of the damage; it's able to bite and shred through flesh, targeting anyone who enters its attack zone, its range of motion. It backs a small group of survivors into the corner of the lab and selects its prey, not wasting time on being too choosy. If it has its way, everyone will meet the teeth.

One man dodges its jaws and ducks under its arm, but finds himself in the maw of one of the shark-like eels. His death is quick, but not without pain. The bite tears out most of his stomach, and before the man enters an unconscious afterlife, he sees his tangled mess of innards slop on the floor before him. The female reporter discards her pad and pencil and attempts to escape, but the Dimetrodon fills his mouth with her head, bites down across her shoulders. It swallows her neck and cranium whole, and a crimson geyser erupts, showering the rest of the throng in scarlet.

Screams ripple across the room. Some are silenced as the creatures continue their onslaught. A red lake takes shape on the floor, spilling toward the stage.

Hammond grabs his mentor's collar. "You're not going anywhere. You're fixing this."

"Try to stop me," Curry barks.

Hammond reaches back with his fist before flinging it forwards, knuckles connecting with the center of Curry's face. The floodgates in his nasal passages open, releasing a crimson waterfall down his lips and chin. The impact knocks Curry on his back.

"Fix this," Hammond says, reaching back with another fist.

"All right!" Curry struggles to his feet. "The Omega Transit is technically still open. If we can lure it close enough, maybe we can draw it into the portal and send it back."

"Got it." Hammond turns, faces the creature.

Each one of the shark-like eels has their faces stuffed with human parts. The Dimetrodon whips its head back and forth, slinging a prominent member of the Channel 7 News team into the air. Ribbons of blood follow the sailing body. The man lands twenty feet away, hits the ground like a stuffed doll, and never moves again.

Hammond cups his hands over his mouth and yells. "Hey!"

It takes several minutes before the Dimetrodon grows bored with killing media folk and sets its sights on the stage. It sneers, puffs of wet air exploding from its nostrils. It licks its bloody maw, savoring every drop of human flavor.

Then, it charges the stage.

"Do it now."

Nothing happens. Hammond locks eyes with the creature's.

"Curry, do it now!"

The Dimetrodon leaps into the air, crashes on stage. It shakes its body, launching droplets of sweat and blood into the air, a fine, almost magical mist. Its spiny sail moves with a certain fluidity.

Hammond knows it's ready to attack.

"Curry, what are you waiting for!" Hammond turns, faces the control panel.

No Curry.

Out of the corner of his eye, he watches the emergency exit door close behind his mentor.

"I don't believe it." But in truth, he can.

Without thinking, he runs over to the mouth of the Omega Transit and faces it. Behind him, the Dimetrodon's claws scratch the stage. It's on the move. Scurrying toward him.

"Here goes nothing."

Hammond jumps into the sparkling portal, and he feels the teeth of space and time chew him apart and the belly of the universe digest whatever remains.

Ten Years Later

"And that's how string theory works. Mostly." Professor Campo gives the class of two hundred the thumbs up, the way he ends every lecture. The students scrape themselves up from their seats. Over the hustle, he tells them, "We'll continue this discussion on Thursday."

The auditorium empties, except for one lone student. The student hops down the stairs, toward Campo's desk with a budding confidence that unsettles his professor.

"How's it hanging, Professor Campo?" the student asks as he reaches the area around the professor's desk.

Campo looks up from his papers. He sees the young man's eyes, knows exactly where the conversation is going before it gets there. "Can I help you?"

"Oh, I believe you can, Campo. Or is it ... *Curry?*"

Hearing his previous surname cuts him deep. He tries to play it cool, acting confused, but his silence betrays him. "I don't understand."

"Don't give me that shit." The student folds his arms across his chest. A pain-strained expression overtakes his features. His cocky attitude has been erased, replaced by a trembling fury. "I know who you are."

Curry swallows the cottony feeling in his mouth. He figures it was only a matter of time before he faced this moment. Ten years is a long time to get away with such a thing. In a way, he's almost glad the time has come. He thinks this moment will unburden him, release the guilt. "What is it you want?"

The student's eyes water. "I want you to bring him back."

"Who?"

"My father."

Curry shakes his head. He doesn't understand.

"My father. Doctor Patrick Hammond."

The name brings back the worst memories. "Son, your father ..."

"He's alive."

Curry shakes his head. "No. There's no way."

The student disagrees. "They never found his body."

"Even if he made it through the portal, he wouldn't have survived. The atmosphere 290 million years ago – it was different. The air was different. His lungs wouldn't have acclimated. His skin wouldn't have handled the severe temperature change."

"Maybe he adapted."

Curry bores into him with a hard gaze. "No," he says. "No, that's not possible."

"Bring him back," the student says. Droplets leak from the corners of his eyes. "Bring him back, goddammit, or I'll out you. I'll tell the authorities. I'll tell the entire world who you really are."

Curry sighs. His options are few. Killing the kid might be easier than trying to resurrect a dead man. "I'm sorry for what happened to your father."

"No, you're not. You left him there. Whatever happened that day, you left him there to die. With all those people." He pounds the desk with his fists, rattling the coffee mug and scattered notebooks. "What was it? What killed all those people. A fucking dinosaur? I've read the reports. They said those people were eaten by sharks."

"I don't know what happened."

"Liar!"

"Shhh," he says in a whisper. *"Keep your voice down."*

"Help me go back and find him. I know he's alive. I ... I know it."

"You don't know a damned thing."

"I see him."

Curry tilts his head to the side. The kid is clearly disturbed. Another result of what happened ten years ago, a byproduct of his impetuous mistake. "You see him?"

"In my dreams. He's still alive. Living in the past. He comes to me. Talks to me. Tells me to come find him."

"Uh-huh."

"He has a big, bushy beard. He's always naked. But alive. He eats ... dinosaur meat. Prehistoric fish. Whatever it takes. Some days, he doesn't eat at all."

"Dreams."

"I see him."

"Right."

Another fist shakes the table. The coffee mug shimmies near the edge. It teeters, then falls. Smashes into several pieces.

"That was my favorite mug," Curry says.

"Help me. Or I tell everyone."

Curry closes his eyes. "Fine. Two weeks. That's all I'll give you. After that, if we don't find him, we part ways and we never see each other again. Deal?"

"Two weeks? It'll take us years to build another Omega Transit!"

Curry smiles. "No. It won't."

The student squints. He doesn't understand.

Curry rolls his eyes. "Because I already have a replica." The smile never leaves his face. "And she's fully operational."

290 Million Years Ago

The water pours over him. He scrubs his beard, washes it out with cleansing oils he extracted from indigenous plants. Once clean, he uses the oil to coat his body. It's been weeks since his last bath. He doesn't know when he'll get another. He's been hunting a pack of herbivores. One of their corpses will provide him with a week's worth of meat, an opportunity not to be missed.

Once showered, he removes himself from the small lake with the crystal clear waterfall. He dries himself off in the heat and grabs his watch, the only remnant from his home world. It no longer tells time, but the compass still works, and that sometimes comes in handy, especially at night. During the day he doesn't need it. He knows where north is according to the position of the sun. He glances down at the watch, sees the compass is off. It's no longer pointing north. Now, it directs him east.

Strange, he thinks. Why would it suddenly stop working?

As he tracks the vagrant herbivores, the idea eats at him. East? Why east? It doesn't add up. Soon the idea overtakes his brain. He even becomes less hungry until his appetite fully dissolves and there's nothing but the want – no, the need – to explore the east. He needs to know why the compass is directing him there. He doesn't believe in a higher power, but the event appears divine.

As he treks east, leaving the herbivores behind, he realizes what it could mean. He thinks back to his old world. He thinks back to his experiments. He thinks of how compasses operate.

It's following an electromagnetic pull.

He runs as an idea hits him. A theory. A sound hypothesis. What makes such a pull that would draw his compass east?

A portal, he thinks. A big one.

He storms hills, crosses rivers, dodges carnivores, and climbs over mountainous terrain. Finally, in the middle of a grassy field, he sees it. It stands alone, tall and shiny, just like he remembers. He drifts ahead as if trapped in some hypnotic trance, tears in his eyes, hoping it's no dream, hoping everything he sees is real.

He reaches the portal and puts his fingers through the glassy barrier, purple and blue sparkles shimmering on his flesh. He smiles as the cold sensation flows over him, freezing his blood. It feels like an angel wrapping its arms around him, bringing him home.

Home. It's where he goes.

My Body Lies Over Sharkzilla

David W. Barbee

Every god promises eternal paradise.

Sharkzilla just eats you.

For Mad Matt, runner-up for the World Surfing Championship qualifiers from nineteen-eighty-one to nineteen-eighty-seven, eternity turned out to be a skyscraper-sized fish.

It was painless, at least. Before he'd even noticed the shadow in the waters beneath him, the beast emerged, encircling Mad Matt's board with a wall of pale gums sprouting rows upon rows of teeth. The jagged maw snapped shut and Mad Matt's existence on earth ended in darkness and a rush of water. In a way, it was a good death for a surfer.

When consciousness returned, he stood just a few blood cells tall. He and his board shorts were made of translucent blue goop, like a cartoon ghost. In life Mad Matt hadn't been religious. The only praying he did was to the next wave that might kill him. But it was Sharkzilla who'd killed him, and so as he haunted the colossal creature's body, watching the functions of its ancient organs, he determined that God was surely this giant shark.

And there were benefits. Eventually all the ghosts adapted to Sharkzilla. Millions of men from throughout history haunted its flesh and blood. The ghosts of innumerable sea creatures swam through its veins. There were ancient kings and monsters of antiquity, yet Sharkzilla was older and mightier than them all. In the darkness of its guts, they lived in a world made of cold luminous meat. The ghosts trapped inside were forced to make new lives in this surreal landscape.

Mad Matt's favorite pastime was surfing Sharkzilla's blood vessels. He found relaxation in the rushing red tubes, surrounded by the traffic of other souls. He cut angles around other travelers on a board made from his own gooey essence. Ghostly catamarans and yachts raced through the cold blood, trailing bubbles in their wake.

Ships and swimmers tumbled through the current, yet they were vastly outnumbered by the creatures of the sea. Schools of dead fish filled the veins along with whales and giant squid. He cut through packs of barracudas and eels. Orcas tried to bully him against the arterial wall but on a board Mad Matt was untouchable.

As he made his way through traffic, Mad Matt gazed through the arterial lining to see some of the beast's organs passing below. He beheld the ruin of Sharkzilla's stadium-sized genitals, tucked up inside its body, shriveled like rotten fruit.

He slipped away through a capillary and came to a stop at a vast field of dense meat. The tail was Sharkzilla's most powerful muscle. Mad Matt fell against it and sank inside as if it were a soft pillow. The meat squeezed shut over his gooey blue spirit. Inside the muscle, it almost felt like he had a body again. Massive sensations flowed through him, like a million sparks on his skin, warming him in the coldest place on earth. Mad Matt heard the ominous rhythm of the beast's tail beating against the ocean itself, an ominous lullaby with the power of a god. It felt like a hurricane whispering in his ear, and he could almost make out what it was saying.

He lay there for days until the vicarious high of Sharkzilla's power began to wear off. It was always that way with the beast's gifts. There were wonders to be had in this body, but with enough time they all lost their lustre. Mad Matt pulled his spirit from the dense musculature, groaning as his blue goop oozed out into the open. Hungover and weary, Mad Matt slipped into a capillary and flowed into the bloodstream again. He declined to surf the traffic and instead dog-paddled with the strongest currents, crossing back over the beast's continent-sized gut sack.

The arteries grew larger as he approached the heart. Sharkzilla's heart was a mainline of naked prehistoric savagery. There the essence of the beast boiled, built pressure, and pumped like the tides of hell. Mad Matt approached the titanic structure through the rapidly rushing blood. It gave him the impression of a cathedral made of pulsing meat, glowing bright red. Mad Matt entered through an enormous valve and swam through a series of chambers. The walls of muscle were so dense that even the spirits couldn't pass through them. They throbbed in time with the organ's thudding beat. Blood gushed through the chambers like tribal drums.

Ghosts clogged the gigantic rooms. Many flowed in and out of the heart, but scores of spirits had made the organ their permanent home. Their blue essences flickered in time with the heartbeat, and their expressions had warped into an odd mixture of ecstasy and hatred. The thud of the walls and the heat of the blood had driven them to madness. They'd been made addicts to its ancient murderous power.

But Mad Matt was just visiting.

He swam into the deepest chamber, a red room where the oldest sea gods and mightiest ocean monsters swam along the walls, gigantic fins and tentacles and tails undulating together in a monstrous mass. In the center of the room was a boiling red star made of blood and shadow. Mad Matt joined the spirits in their orbit around the red star. He did his best not to look at it, instead focusing on riding the waves of twisting bodies.

Leviathans slithered beneath him. A storm deity roared past, driving a chariot and throwing lightning. Fangs and claws slashed all around, glowing crimson from the room's influence. Mad Matt dodged the barbed tongues and spines that stabbed for him. He leapt over the gaping maws of undead kraken with a spray of boiling blood. He kept his eyes on the waves, resisting the lure of the red star. Surfing a storm of sea monsters was enough excitement without falling for Sharkzilla's murderous siren song.

Outside the heart, some said the red star was Sharkzilla's soul. It radiated malevolence, which was why the biggest and worst monsters were attracted to it. Mad Matt surfed along quivering scales and humpbacked spines. Every few moments one of the creatures broke off from the wall and swam to the center of the room, roaring, laughing, raging for the red star as if they would have it all to themselves.

They burned to nothing.

Mad Matt didn't bother to watch. He knew that these ghosts had been tricked. The red star filled them with aggression and arrogance, converting them to its evil mindset. It fooled them into believing that they were the ultimate predator, worthy of possessing Sharkzilla's shadowy essence for themselves. When they built up the courage to take what was theirs, they became nothing. Being eaten by Sharkzilla was death, but being consumed by the red star was death for the dead. That was part of the thrill for Mad Matt. He could surf amongst the monsters and not fall prey to insanity.

He rode the ridge of a prehistoric crocodile and let its curvature shoot him towards an exit valve. His ghostly goop glowed bright, especially his feet, where the blue had bled into dark pink. He poured his spirit like steaming sludge into colder bloodstreams, and drifted toward the jugular vein as quicker ghosts rushed all around him. Mad Matt wiped itchy sleepiness from his eyes as he floated up the beast's tongue and poked his head up through a taste bud to watch the show.

Surrounding him was a mountain range of teeth, growing from both the ground and the sky. The monumental jaws bobbed ever so slightly in the current. Millions more ghosts had camped out on the tongue or in the gums, watching the black water rushing into the beast's mouth. They'd come to watch Sharkzilla kill.

The jaw muscles began to clench and a cheer rose from the crowd. The black water surged in as Sharkzilla burst forward and the jaws stretched wide. Mad Matt watched the upper teeth rise and disappear into the darkness, then crash back down in a great furious gulp. Twelve sea lions slipped into Sharkzilla's mouth, each as big as a city, and were eviscerated by the teeth. Blood billowed through the water like fireworks in the night sky, and Mad Matt lifted his hands and let the hot fluid trail between his ghostly fingers as it flowed past. The last of the meat rushed down the beast's throat and Sharkzilla's great maw returned to its stationary position. The water cleared away the blood and the ghosts gave one last cheer of appreciation before beginning the wait for the next kill.

Mad Matt climbed out of his perch on the tongue and swam down Sharkzilla's throat, ready to head back to the tail for another nap in the muscles. He bypassed the gills and phased through the esophagus into the spinal column, where a river of glowing fibers ran the length of the beast's body. Mad Matt had surfed the spinal cord several times. The glowing stream made for a leisurely trip. He touched down on the river's surface, which undulated like millions of intertwined worms. Downriver he could see haggard ghosts camped along the banks, using strings of their own blue essence to fish the river, hoping to catch stray thoughts that might be swimming in the beast's subconscious. They fished for Sharkzilla's ideas, but there was nothing there. Nothing traveled through these nerves. A gigantic fish god from antiquity was beyond such trivialities. Mad Matt turned his attention from the ghost fishermen and looked upriver.

Some vague impulse caught hold and Mad Matt surfed upriver. He passed under vertebrae arches as he approached Sharkzilla's massive skull. Mad Matt came to a stop at the brainpan and was met by more ghosts, these even older and more ragged than the fishermen down the river. Their blue essence had been warped into hunched over hulks, their faces frozen in a mask of slack, resigned terror. They meandered around a wall of cartilage, pale and smooth like a mirror. Mad Matt drifted through the crowd for a closer look.

As long as he'd lived in Sharkzilla, he'd never visited the beast's brain. Somehow he'd never even thought of it. Finally, a chance to see something new. Mad Matt saw his reflection in the wall of cartilage and closed his eyes. He phased through and opened his eyes to the void of Sharkzilla's brain.

Nothingness spread out as far as he could see, and yet in the infinite distance there was a horizon. It felt like he was standing on a barren black planet, and above him was a black sky without stars.

Mad Matt looked down at his hands. He could still see himself, the bright blue goop in the shape of a body he'd once had so long ago. Looking around, he couldn't see the wall of cartilage. There was no skull to phase back through, and as the terror of an eternity in Sharkzilla's brain matter began to dawn upon him, he saw the light.

Neurons sparked inside the black planet and filled it like electric roots. The planet lit up with the same blue color as Mad Matt's ghostly essence. The darkness melted away as bolts of energy rose up from the ground and spread into the black sky, crosshatching into an intricate moving mosaic. Mad Matt made the mistake of looking into the dancing lights in the sky, and he saw the names all the other ghosts had given to Sharkzilla. He saw the prey swimming just out of reach of its jaws. He felt the monsters sacrificing themselves in the depths of its heart. He felt the black water against his skin as he swam not just through oceans, but through reality. He trawled every plane of existence, eating and swimming without end. He even moved past the barrier between life and death, and by existing as both he was neither.

Mad Matt saw the reality in which he'd spent his two-and-a-half decades of life. It was miniscule, like a grain of sand on the ocean floor. His brief and primitive life was just another hunting ground. As Mad Matt's mind tumbled over its own insignificance, the glowing mosaic in the sky caught flame. Before the explosion blinded him he glimpsed the walls of cartilage and ran for it.

He phased through and opened his eyes to see the red terrain of Sharkzilla's insides. Mad Matt leaned against the skull and held his head in his hands. He felt a million existences pressing against each other, none of them real but each begging him for validation. It was too much for his tiny human brain to hold together, and that was assuming that Mad Matt himself existed, which he began to doubt as well.

He looked up to see an old ghost standing before him, a bearded sailor covered in seaweed. Like the others his back hunched over and his eyes had been stretched wide with shock. He stared at Mad Matt and never blinked. Mad Matt returned his stare, and found himself hoping against hope that this could all be explained. After what felt like an eternity, the old man's wrinkled blue lips parted. He said, "It's just another way the Fisher King eats you."

Mad Matt watched the old man shuffle away, then he looked over his shoulder at his reflection in the wall of shiny cartilage.

His eyes were enormous, and he never blinked.

The Beauty Of Mount Sagitta

Sheryl Normandeau

Kent has been dreaming about *Melanocarpa spectabilis.*

He awakens in his tent with a shout, startled by the noises outside. Sweat is slick on his brow despite the ice sheeting the woollen blankets, and he knows he's been grinding his teeth. He can feel the Beauty of Mount Sagitta within his grasp. He cannot let her get away from him this time.

He does not want to ponder the darkness, and instead strikes a match to the oil lamp. Snow has drifted in the flap of the doorway, spilling across the floor. He brushes at his frozen eyelashes and stares beyond the flame. He ignores the sounds on the mountain, the shrieks of a pack of wild animals echoing off the walls in the bowl of the cirque. He recalls the first time he came to the mountain seeking flowers for Van Gelder, the rich man who is his employer. He delights in the memories of his first sighting of *Melanocarpa spectabilis* in the Valley of the Stones, and relives his elation at finding something so rare and valuable, and the rewards it would bring.

There is no longer a need to dwell on the destruction of the specimen case during the return trip, the dismemberment and partial consumption of the pack horses in the middle of the night, and the disappearances of several of the men. It did not help that one of the boys who had been on the expedition leaked information about the flower to a fellow collector, the deep-pocketed Van de Vorte. Van Gelder was incensed: spurred by his lust for the plant and the desperation to outmaneuver his rival, he ordered Kent on a second expedition, to race Van de Vorte's outfit to the Valley of the Stones and claim the treasured plant. Kent knows this is his final chance to redeem himself. The Beauty of Mount Sagitta is all that matters now.

Kent cannot occupy his mind with the stories the packers had whispered about, the ones about *de Mortuis*, the flying flesheaters. He prefers to worry about the unpredictability of spring weather on

Mount Sagitta, the precious time it will take to dig out of the snow and make the descent into the Valley. His stomach churns with the sickening feeling that Van de Vorte's men will get to the flower before him.

His thoughts drift to his wife in Amsterdam, her belly swollen with their first child. He wonders how he will break the news to his family if he cannot claim *Melanocarpa spectabilis* for Van Gelder.

He hears a shuffle at the entrance of his tent and the flap of the door is raised. DeWaal, the sharpshooter, crawls inside. He pulls back the woollen muffler that obscures his face and removes his goggles. "Saw your lamp," he says. "Talked with the packers last night. They want to go home. They say there are too many signs."

Kent is outraged. "Signs? Of what? A bit of work? Surely they aren't prattling on about those creatures –"

"I know what I saw on the first expedition," DeWaal says quietly. Kent knows, too, but there is the flower to consider. Always the flower.

"And yet here you are," Kent says. DeWaal is only in it for the money, of course. He doesn't give a damn about the greatest botanical find of the century. "I will not be deterred."

DeWaal doesn't have an answer for this. He goes out.

It takes more than a week to get through the pass, a task that would have been accomplished in three days, but for the defection of most of the packers. Even the cook takes up a shovel. Kent is frantic, fearing his rival is making an approach from the opposite side. The timing of the crossing is bad; how were they to know that the snow pack would linger this year?

On the fourth day, they come upon the half-frozen carcasses of a pack of wolves, twelve strong. The snow is dark with blood and pulped entrails. DeWaal moves among the furred bodies and looks to the sky. They press on silently.

It is snowing heavily when they finally break into the Valley of the Stones. Although it is mid-day, the clouds strangle the exhausted group. They cannot see the attack coming, only hear the throbbing wingbeats as the creatures descend from the skies above.

De Mortuis! The packers scream, knowing their enemy. The flying flesheaters cut them down with gaping jaws, teeth flashing in and out of the fog. It is difficult to tell how many there are – six or ten, perhaps. Kent has never seen anything such as these creatures: obscene narrow heads with golden reptilian eyes, sleek bodies with long, feathery tails. They have wingspans larger than any bird he knows, both from literature and his travels – twenty feet, at least. Clawed feet twist the men's bodies upwards, breaking bones and giving the fanged maws purchase.

DeWaal fires into the melee, but he cannot take the flesheaters down. They seem impervious to his volleys, and screech their annoyances to the wind.

Kent is clipped with a wingtip and hurled face-first into the snow. Something is crushed in his lower back. He cranks his head upwards and gulps air. That's when he sees it.

The flower. More exquisite than the most treasured jewel, the gold of a thousand kingdoms, even the baby his wife will bear without him. *Melanocarpa spectabilis*, shining there in the snow, only a few feet from his nose.

Kent can no longer hear DeWaal – either the man has run out of bullets or the creatures have killed him. Kent doesn't care either way. His only goal is to get to the flower. He begins to crawl.

His half-eaten face sports a gleeful grin and he is still holding the shredded remnants of the Beauty of Mount Sagitta – the only specimen in existence – when Van de Vorte and his men make their descent into the Valley of the Stones a few hours later.

A Line In The Sand

Kevin Holton

My grandfather left me his Victorian estate by the sea, and god *damn* if I wasn't going to throw a little party to celebrate my new home.

I led our parade of cars, with Jodi, my girlfriend, next to me, and my best friend Hansen in the backseat. Some thought it wasn't fair that I only took two guests, but we brought most of the food and half the booze, so the other cars could eat it. Besides, as their most gracious and humble host, I didn't think it fair if I picked up all the slack.

Our celebration came late in the summer of 2008. We no doubt looked like a typical bunch of rowdy college students, wasting our days on drinking, but the economy had crashed, taking all of the available work along for the ride. All the jobs we'd been promised we'd have after college were gone, leaving us unemployed with mountains of student loan debt. What else were we supposed to do, if not try to forget our troubles?

We arrived mid-afternoon after a few hours of driving. Grandpa lived in Ivy's Path, Massachusetts, a town older than America itself, though relatively unknown. Created around the same time as Plymouth, the locals joked the Witch Trials overshadowed their existence, leading to a sprawling, beautiful town undisturbed by tourism, even today. Others suggested dark forces at work, so the town that only accepted those allowed to enter, unconsciously driving all others away.

Grandpa's house stood at the edge of the sea, proud and undaunted by the crashing surf, and unshaken by the salty Atlantic winds. A spacious front yard led to a wide stone staircase to the sands, while a large backyard separated the three-story structure from the woods. A thirty-minute walk through those woods took you to town, but there was no direct, drivable path.

As a child, I'd always found the house drafty and cold. Warm memories fought those chills away. Whenever Mom and Dad got busy traveling for work, they dropped me off, and sometimes, my cousins would come down too. We'd have barbeques, stay up late playing games, and tell scary stories by the fire. I came to associate those oceanic winds with good times. Now, I can't stand rooms with no breeze. Modern homes are built so tight they might as well be hermetically sealed.

When I stepped out of my car and stared up at the house, with its rustic reddish paint, wrap-around porch, corner spire, and small viewing platform off a door in the attic, I couldn't have felt more free. "Here she is!" I yelled out, pointing.

"She?" Jodi said. Her voice bore a hint of her parents' Irish lilt. She'd been raised somewhere in northern New Jersey, but never specified where. "Is there another woman in your life?"

Hansen hopped out of the car behind me and put an arm around my shoulders. "This old lug? He's such a prude, he couldn't cheat if he tried. The first thought of *deviant behavior*," he said, shaking his hands to mimic fear, "and he'd get the world's first de-rection."

My girlfriend snorted, covering her mouth, and I couldn't help but grin. It was true. I'm fairly conservative, not at all ashamed of that. Such qualities became part of why I made such a great boyfriend, or so Jodi said. I'd been raised to know there are certain boundaries, guidelines to behavior that all should follow. No matter the teasing or insults, I didn't cross those lines.

The other two cars held an assorted crew of our closer friends, including Davey, Justine, Larry, "The Bird" (a *really* nice guy who'd gotten an unfortunate nickname after getting very publicly attacked by a pigeon), Samantha, Sam – another girl, but we couldn't call them both Samantha – Daniel, Danielle, Mark and Michelle. Their complaints made it clear how cramped the long drive had been, but an array of aching smiles and glassy eyes showed they'd been laughing for a long while. Or maybe lighting up. I wasn't so old-world that I would've begrudged them a little weed to take the edge off long distance driving.

Before we entered, I made a show of stepping up onto the porch, holding my hands up to draw attention before we entered. "Folks, if I could say a few words," I said, speaking up as best I could. The breaking waves were overpowering my voice, and half of my wanting to speak to the group was satisfying a primal need to show I was stronger than the natural world around me. Despite my urge, I refrained from shouting. The ocean didn't mean me harm, after all.

"I just wanted to thank you all for coming." On that porch, I felt like Gatsby, or an old-time Congressional candidate giving a stump speech to all thirty of his constituents, like I'd become one with the age and austerity of my family's home. "And, as much as I'd hate to start a party off with rules," they groaned at this, "I'd be remiss if I didn't lay down one or two.

"First: I'll need a little help getting the place in order. I want to move what we can down to the basement to avoid anything getting smashed or trashed during the night.

"Two: no drinking games inside. I don't want beer on the original hardwood floors.

"Three: If you puke, you clean it up, no matter how hungover you are.

"Four: We're almost real-world adults, so be responsible and don't drink too heavily.

"But five," I grinned, "we're not adults *yet,* so let's have a good time!" They cheered, and I unlocked the front door, waving everyone inside.

Did part of me feel a little guilty about using Grandpa's house for a college party? Sure. But, in fairness, I knew my friends pretty well, and none of us were the type to get smashed. Only one of us–Daniel– had been in a Greek organization, and he was pretty vocal about hating his fraternity. Danielle, Samantha, and The Bird all had a thing for old houses, so I knew they'd treat this one with respect. Jodi and Hansen would do the same, out of respect for me.

And, as far as the law cared, it wasn't Grandpa's house anymore. I owned the house now. The rest of our group didn't need to know about the letter.

I couldn't stop thinking about it. It had come with the home, as part of his will. The last words he'd ever say to me. We set about removing all the expensive, breakable items, all the antiques, the statuette of Edgar Allan Poe (for whom my grandpa had been named), the paintings, and I thought about the brief note he'd included for me.

Dear William,
If you're reading this, I've passed on, and left you our ancestral home. After seeing how your mother has handled herself, I don't believe it should go to her. A place like this, an old place set among the elements, has power. It, and the land around it, deserve respect.
Should you choose to stay here, I know you'll make a fine

God damn was I stupid not to pay attention to his note. Or maybe I wasn't. Maybe I knew what was going to happen.

None of us drank too hard, nor partied too heavily. The loudest we got wouldn't have woken the neighbors, if there had been any. This house stood alone for a few miles in each direction, so we were generally free to do as we wished. At our rowdiest, Michelle chucked a beer can into the woods behind the house. Mark wandered out front and pissed on the sand. Casual, goofy little acts of rebellion. Youth's dying gasp before the harsh realities of adulthood set in. I did my best to clean up after them and curtail our impact on the area. Besides, this was my property, so I'd have to do the clean up anyway.

The fact that we were all asleep by midnight testified to how lame we'd become, but I didn't mind. Really, I'd always been an early bird, preferring to rise with the sun and knock out around ten or eleven at the latest. College forced me to change a little bit. Not much. My roommates had always been heavy sleepers. Staying up late, whether for studying or celebrating, just meant sleep would feel that much better the next day.

When I went to sleep, Jodi stayed up talking to Mark and Michelle. Davey, Larry, and Hansen were out back, kicking a soccer ball around. Justine sat on the front porch, practically shouting down her cell phone about whether or not her internship would turn into a full time position. I doubted she wanted to use her business degree to work as a *Hertz* phone operator, but in this economy, who could afford to pass up a job? Either way, I pitied the soul she'd called.

Grandpa's house was just as I remembered it, and I slept in my old room, out of habit. I couldn't bring myself to lay in his bed. It felt disrespectful, like I hadn't earned the right to the house yet. I wasn't its master, so no master bedroom. That's why it was odd when I woke up. The house itself slumbered, cool and quiet. I heard little sound at all – some snoring from nearby rooms, the lull of waves on the cool sand – but nothing to have actually made me wake.

The bed next to me lay empty. Jodi must've slept elsewhere. We often laughed about how she'd wake me up all the time. People could be talking five feet from my head, a fire alarm could go off, hell, someone could probably detonate a bomb without waking me, but as soon as I felt that mattress shift, I was wide awake. Even when she stayed the night, she made sure not to drink anything an hour or two before bed out of courtesy, knowing that just getting up to pee could ruin my night.

There came a dull thump from the porch. I dimly recalled Justine asking if she could sleep on the porch swing, and I'd said, "Knock yourself out." If she'd fallen off, she might very well have.

I got out of bed, pulling on the underwear and jeans I'd left bunched on the floor. I couldn't leave a guest potentially injured.

Then came another sound. A creak of floorboards, followed by a wet, rumbling dragging, a soggy carpet being hauled over loose stones. My gut churned. Through the open window came the sea-scented breeze, tinged with the briny waft of marine life and a copper undertone getting stronger by the second. It was the same smell from the time Hansen broke his leg and I'd taken him to the hospital. The bone stuck through his skin and he bled all over my car. The backseat still had a faint hint of that telltale odor.

Someone very close by was bleeding. A lot.

I crept to the bedroom door just in time to hear the front door open. A figure moved stealthily below, but Grandpa's house had been built so you could see down to the foyer from every floor, almost like an old hotel, as if it had always been meant for guests–not that we had many bedrooms. Peering down from between the wood posts in the railing, I saw a truly massive figure enter. It looked like The Mountain, from *Game of Thrones,* except even bigger. And … wrong. Darkness obscured its form. My sleeping brain tried figuring out what danger we might have been in. Maybe we'd left the door unlocked and this person had stumbled in, hurt, looking for assistance.

It turned toward the living room, where Sam and Samantha were sleeping. As it stepped into a beam of moonlight coming through one of the windows, I caught sight of why it looked so horrible. This wasn't a man. It wasn't even human. It was a massive shark's head on a ripped, bluish-gray human torso, walking on two legs, and had four sets of arms.

No. I rubbed my eyes, not believing. When I looked again, the image had grown worse, still a shark-man, except the top two 'arms,' which jutted out from where shoulders should've been, were *more sharks.* Two powerful upper bodies jutted forward, mouths gnashing. They writhed in the air, sniffing for something.

Copper wind filled Grandpa's home. Sniffing for prey.

"Sam! Samantha! Everybody!" I screamed, praying I was dreaming so that I could wake up, praying that I was dead wrong and everyone would laugh at me, because complete public humiliation would be better than what I'd seen. "Get up! There's – there's something in the house!" A lame finish, stolen from a movie I saw years ago. It did the trick.

A couple disgruntled groans came from the rooms nearby. The shark creature whirled back, only for an instant, to look at me. Then Samantha shrieked and the creature lunged out of sight into the room beyond. Her scream cut short. My stomach wanted to empty, I wouldn't let it, no, I had to run to help them. My feet hit the floor hard as I cut into a sprint, grabbed the banister for support as I turned onto the stairs, and pounded down two at a time.

People were awake now, streaming out of the woodwork, popping out of all sorts of rooms, and one even thought to do what I'd neglected in my haste: turn on the lights. I almost wished they hadn't. When I slid into the living room, Sam was already dead too. The King, because there could be no other name for such a creature, turned to face me.

Its central head was bent toward me, like a human's, but its neck was wide, as a shark's head slopes into its body. The two other sharks jutting out from its upper body were built from the middle to the head, and each of those heads had fastened around the stump of one of my friend's necks, guzzling their blood. The King's two actual arms were thicker than my torso, rippling with muscles a thousand experts couldn't have named.

In this direct light, I could see it stood easily nine, maybe ten feet tall. My blood cooled, trying to turn me to stone so that this creature might not target me. It didn't work. The King turned its abyss-black eyes on me and, with the wet, creaking voice of a shipwreck dredging itself up from the depths to sail the seas again, said, "Hello, William."

I'd mocked people in old stories for fainting at the slightest provocation, but my legs gave out and my head spun. Hell, I'd wanted to pass out. Cruel consciousness continued, forcing me to acknowledge what I saw, this sentient mutant beast who could casually devour my friends then address me in perfect English, and by name, no less. Even as I watched, the two smaller sharks twisted upward, levering the girls into their mouths, gulping them down almost without swallowing.

"Will, what's going ..." Daniel said as he reached the bottom. His eyes widened for a moment before he cried out, "Oh, *hell no!*" Hands grabbed me under the arms, yanking me away from the scene. Took a second to realize Hansen ran with him. They were carrying me toward the kitchen.

"The hell is that thing?" Hansen sputtered, his normal, overly-macho tone replaced by the same shrill whine I'd heard at the ER, before they doped him up and reset his broken bone.

I shook my head, looked back, shrugged, almost puked, managed not to, and saw Daniel heading for the knives, set nicely in a butcher's block. "What do you think those are going to do?"

"It's better than having nothing!" he shouted.

From upstairs, The Bird yelled, "What's going OH MY GOD!"

The King lumbered into the foyer, still apparently unsated. It turned slowly, looking at the upper floors, then turned its gaze back to us three. The center head made this motion again, turning up and down again, then started upstairs.

Hansen grabbed a bread knife and a meat hammer, yelling, "It's going for the girls!"

It wasn't just women up there. That wasn't the point. He took off for the hall, but I grabbed him, shaking my head. "No. No, another stairwell. Here," I said, stumbling toward a secret panel in the kitchen wall. It opened on well-oiled hinges to a dark, but dust-free staircase, lit by a single bulb that turned on automatically when the doors opened.

I'd first discovered that old secret when I was very young. While playing, I bumped into the panel hard enough to jostle it open. Grandpa explained about secret doors, for when you really needed to use them, "just in case." That got me interested. Kids love testing their elders, and that's what I did, asking why it had been made so easy to open if designed for secrets and hiding.

He wagged his finger. "Never for hiding, William. It's a staircase – not meant to keep things safe. Stairs are for when you need to get somewhere. *These* stairs are for when you need to get somewhere quickly."

Daniel ran up first, then me, and Hansen followed up at the rear. That didn't surprise me.

We emerged into one of the unused rooms on the second floor, which had always been labeled as more of a supply closet. I saw now that Grandpa kept it carefully organized so the secret panel was always accessible. The Bird stumbled backward into the room and slammed the door behind him, his curly hair matted down with sweat.

"What the hell?" Daniel barked, prompting The Bird to scream. "You left them?"

"Where did you come from?" he squealed.

"Move!"

He didn't need to be told twice. Daniel's always been a big guy. Combine that with high anxiety and a large cleaver, and The Bird didn't stand in the way for long. We stumbled out onto the second floor in time to see The King casually push the door open to Mark and Michelle's room. They screamed for help, and we rushed in.

Daniel, running in first, drove the cleaver at its back. The blade snapped uselessly off its handle. He stopped, rage frozen by shock, as the massive beast turned and said, "I'll get to you in a minute."

Unlike me, he actually *did* faint. He must not have heard it speak before. I just stared, even as Hansen hauled ass outside. A dark, wet stain spread over the bedspread.

That's when I realized where we were. The master bedroom. This room was *sacred* and they'd probably spent the night screwing, making it their little love nest, and now, literally soiling it. I thought of the nights I'd come knocking on Grandpa's door, scared of monsters only loosely bound by the edges of my dreams, and how he'd let me scoot up on the sheets as he told me a story. He'd carry me back to my room, already fading into a more peaceful slumber, and I knew nothing could hurt me as long as he stood by me.

And now, watching Mark piss the bed, piss *Grandpa's* bed, I'd never felt my hero more distant.

"You defile this house," The King growled, moving forward. He didn't even use the shark arms. They stayed away, leaving my 'friends' unbitten even as his humanoid hands coiled tight, one around each throat. I stood watch, no longer scared, keeping vigil over some rite I had to witness.

When their bodies fell limp, The King turned back to me, still carrying the two corpses. My heart didn't race or skip, just stayed the course, beating with steady strength. All six of its eyes surveyed me, the two shark bodies arcing to face me. My eyes stayed focused on his central head.

"You no longer fear me," came the shipwreck voice.

"No," I replied.

"Your grandfather didn't either."

Wind began to blow against the house, forcing sea-scent into the room, masking the ripe stink of urine. "I know."

The King cocked his main head as a car outside rumbled to life and peeled out along the dirt road. "It seems the little bird has flown away."

"He's not exactly a fighter," I shrugged. "The kid knew better than to try to take you on."

It flashed a row of pointed teeth as it grinned, momentarily. A memory flashed in its dark eyes and the smile fell. With a more somber face, the being said, "My condolences." All three heads bowed in respect.

I bowed too. My heart told me I wasn't the only one in the room to have lost someone. "And mine, to you."

We had no other business in the bedroom, so we walked back out into the hall. I glanced around to see where everyone else went–the house had fallen deathly silent–when The King spoke up that they'd evacuated, but that Jodi, Hansen, and Davey were nearby. Larry had left with The Bird. Daniel lay there, unconscious, likely to be asleep for hours.

When I asked him about how he knew this, he replied, "I've walked this earth for eons. I know many things, and I know how to do many things. Perhaps, since it appears I cannot die, my body learned to evolve so that I was not left some vestigial behemoth of days passed. Reading into the hearts and minds of other beings is just one of my talents."

I had to ask. "So ... can you speak other languages? Like Spanish?"

"No hagas preguntas tontas a menos que desee respuestas tontas."

"Okay then," I said as we walked outside, not bothering to turn on the porch light. The wind felt different now. There were red stains on the ground in front of the house, and large, inhuman footprints leading up from the waves, but the cool ocean air told me autumn was closer than I thought. It would be time to rake leaves, soon. Time to prepare for snow, gather firewood, pack supplies away in case of emergency. The house might need a caretaker.

"The others ... they disrespected the land. This is sacred ground, you see. It's why your great-great-grandfather built this home himself, using only material that the woods and sea saw fit to give him." The King looked stern, yet his eyes – all of them – were far away, lost in reminiscence. "I am a bit of an expert in knowing what lines aren't meant to be crossed."

A tall wave crashed down against a nearby jetty, moonlit spray filling the air. That pale lunar sphere floated high above us, almost disappearing behind the roof of the house, not quite ready to cast us into darkness. "I'll make sure the others leave. The land ..." I paused, thinking of the letter my grandfather wrote to me. "This whole town is sacred. A type of old magic most aren't ready to deal with, isn't it?"

The King nodded, then started off toward the ocean. "I'll get rid of these," he said, holding them aloft like cans of beer. He continued across the lawn, not looking back until a bright shape hurtled out of the darkness, smashing into him. Fire exploded across his body, the grass, and Mark and Michelle's bodies.

Hansen jumped out from the side yard. "Take that, you freak!" Jodi trembled a few feet behind him, looking scared, her hair and clothes disheveled, makeup smeared.

"Hansen, what the hell are you doing?" I yelled.

His face, upon whirling toward me, showed both surprise and anger at my presence, eyes darting between us. "What the hell are *you* doing?"

"Damn it, Will, don't get involved! Hansen knows what he's doing!" Jodi shrieked.

A matte red smear on Hansen's collar caught my eye, cluing me into yet another fact I'd suspected, but had not confirmed. The King turned toward me. The fires on him were already out, but the grass burned. "You know the trust they broke. The boundary they crossed. But that is your boundary, not nature's. Would you have me act on your behalf?"

I'll admit, I was angry. I wanted to break Hansen's nose. I wanted to scream at Jodi for cheating on me, with my best friend, no less. Making The King hurt them wouldn't have helped me. Nor would hurting them myself have helped. "No. They made their mistakes. They can live with the guilt, or die with it. Their choice."

"What are you talking about?" Hansen yelled. Jodi chimed in with, "Will, you prick, stop talking to that ... that ... thing!"

The King walked toward the ocean once again. This time, Hansen pulled out his father's fishing knife. "Hey, asshole!" he yelled. "Maybe I can't kill you, but this here was my dad's, and he used it to filet fish, but me? I think I'm just gonna find every last shark I can and cut their fins off, Japanese style. I'm gonna film their stupid, limbless bodies sinking to the ocean floor as they try to breathe, then laugh when they die. I'll put it on YouTube so the whole world can laugh with me! How you gonna like being all alone, freak?"

Hansen waved his stupid knife in the air, reflecting the last glint of light as the moon dipped behind cover, blanketing the lawn in shadow. The King turned, dragging the bodies as he walked toward my ex-best friend, who laughed maniacally. I could hear that his tiny mind had snapped in half. Jodi didn't look far off from that fate. "What are you gonna do, punish me for something I haven't done? It's not like I've killed any yet!"

Watching from the edge of the porch, I saw Jodi back away. Smart move. Hansen was a few feet away when The King said, "No ..." The two humanoid arms grabbed his collar as the shark-arms lunged forward, ripping Hansen's arms from his body. Hansen had just enough time to whimper before the center head opened its mouth wide, closing over Hansen's head and tearing it from his body.

Despite the gore, I felt nothing. Not anger, not sadness, not disgust. I watched with cold calculation, just a scholar, observing the first of many strange phenomena.

Jodi screamed, but the sound didn't mask The King saying, "But you would've."

Davey came hurtling out of the other side yard, feet crunching on the crisp, cool dirt as he dove into his car, cranking the engine. We'd all whipped around. Jodi ran, streaking past the being that had just killed her lover, jumping into the backseat. Davey yelled for me to get in; I waved him off, watching horror spread across his face as he realized what I meant. They reversed, then sped away into the dark.

The festivities were truly over now. I walked with The King to the ocean. He dragged all three bodies with one huge arm. "You're not afraid they'll talk about you?"

"Others have seen me and lived to tell," he said, stepping into the now-calm water. Moonlight still danced on its surface, unobstructed by the forest and house behind us. "They've gone mad. Those who haven't spoke of me and were thought so anyway."

"And the few that don't do either?" I said, thinking of Grandpa.

The King just looked back, smiled, and disappeared into the sea.

I needed time to process the night's events, so I put a pot of coffee on, then sat in Grandpa's favorite armchair, clutching my mug, lost in thought. When Daniel finally roused himself from unconsciousness, he came down, walking slowly, eyes wide, trying to see as much as he could of the new world into which he'd been tossed. I gestured to the coffee pot, visible through the doorway to the kitchen. He joined me in thought, sitting quietly on the loveseat, elbows braced against his knees as he sat hunched forward.

Eventually, we got around to talking. Daniel didn't go insane. He knew better than to talk about what we'd seen. I asked what he planned to do next. He had a simple plan: go back to his house, eat a sandwich, get some sleep, then maybe see about real estate listings in Ivy's Path.

"Maybe it's crazy, but ... I feel like I belong here," he said. Edgar Allan Poe's bust loomed above him, both the legacy of a great writer and a symbol of my grandfather, staying with us and tending to the land even after he had gone.

"Me too," I said, turning my head to look out at the ocean, each little ripple catching the moonlight, capturing a hint of light before sinking back into a vast darkness.

Finding Megalodon

Richard King Perkins II

One never knows
when a giant tentacle will reach up
from out of the sea –

like that object that crept up from water
which might be bleak discovery;

quite out of place in the arid world,
so that if we didn't know better,
we might call it archaic hammerhead,
or plesiosaur or even megalodon –

but we know it cannot be these things,
so we rename our find, calling it *cryptozoic.*

Seen against the illicit horizon,
its appearance changes with each
slashing grasp of water –

and our conviction wavers as well,
so we rename our passenger,
calling it *hateful* and *vile.*

Looking for another existence
and the remainder of the world,
we found something flourishing
at the bottom of a decayed, thieving ocean –

the fossil-lives of recognizable creatures
kept in the immutable state
which we would likely call *horrific.*

Hunted Origins

Mike West

As the waves crash above their heads, Mother Plesiosaur and her infant dive beyond the maelstrom.

Her child moves in for shelter, her ancient body scarred and weathered, her giant flippers crusted with barnacles. Mother nuzzles her offspring as they descend, unconditional love unspoken and understood. The infant begins to purr as he moves under her flipper, nowhere safer than with Mother.

A silent shadow flickers past their periphery and they instinctively know they are not alone. Scanning the murky waters, Mother can just make out a monolithic shape diving deeper in the distance.

As old as the sea, Mother knows the determined movements of a predator and begins to swim faster towards the distant coast, her little one trying to keep up, her immense tail propelling them quicker. Panic sets in over him as he realises for the first time that his mother is not the biggest in the ocean.

Frantically searching below, he sees the gargantuan. A primordial fear rising, he instinctively knows what is hunting them.

Megalodon.

Mother knows the same and has witnessed the ancient evil that has decimated her kind since the dawn of time. The shark glides underneath them, its massive body effortlessly keeping pace with the two, mouth agape as the water rushes over rows of serrated, razor teeth.

Twisting her long neck to track their hunter, Mother sees the colossal tail fin disappear into darker depths and knows there is not much time. She scoops her young one to her front with one flipper and holds him there, knowing speed is the only advantage they have.

A panicked squeak from her child tells her what she has been waiting for. It's coming.

Water rushes up as the monster attacks, its enormous mouth

wide with anticipation. The force of the assault wrenches Mother away from child, both narrowly missing the megalodon's teeth as they spiral into the thrashing water. The velocity of the attack catapults the shark out of the ocean, a surreal vision of power and fury before it crashes back into the waves.

Mother calls as she breaks the surface, her long neck whipping left and right as she searches. A response echoes across the heaving waves as she sees her infant, relief pouring over her before freezing as a dorsal fin slices through the water between them.

She dives down to see their hunter circling. She roars over the ocean to her child to head for land to escape. With a frantic splash, he takes off towards the coast as fast as he can. Mother's heart sinks as the fin twists and gives chase.

With all her might, Mother furiously swims to reach them. The gargantuan comes into view as she drives her teeth into the tip of the tail fin. The monster doesn't even flinch as a trickle of blood oozes from the bite.

Mother tries again to no avail. Making her way alongside it, she continues to nip at the pectoral fins, her small teeth doing little damage to the battle-worn behemoth. In her frustration, she dives into the side of the megalodon's head, biting at its gills. With a roar the shark thrashes, sending her sprawling through the waves. As she spirals, she sees her child reach the rocky shore and relief overwhelms her.

The megalodon continues along the shoreline, waiting for its prey to return to the ocean. Mother heads for land herself, when she sees Man appear over the beach. Man, moving towards her child, hollering and waving flaming torches and sticks. As the rocks and sticks of Man crash down, she roars. Panicking, the child dives back to the sea and heads inland along the river mouth, away from Man.

The giant dorsal fin of the megalodon slices through the waves and towards the river mouth.

Mother also races towards the river mouth, intercepting the shark. Using her momentum, she drives into the side of the massive predator, its coarse skin scraping as she pushes it off course into the banks of the river.

It thrashes, dislodging earth and rock from the river bed, turning the water into an opaque mist. In the turmoil, as Mother continues to slam into its side, biting at its fins, blood swirling into the murky water. A searing pain echoes through her body as the megalodon's teeth find her tail, severing it.

Pain emanates from her stump as she continues to charge the hurricane of fin and tooth, battling up the river as the shark gives chase. She breaks the water's surface in the chaos, and sees her baby reaching the opening of the river into a giant lake, terror and panic across its young face. As blood gushes from her wound and darkness begins to ebb into her periphery, she notices a crop of boulders and rocks near the water.

Using the last of her strength, she dives deep into the river and propels out, narrowly missing the shark's jaws. She slams into the boulders, shovelling earth and rock down across the river, creating a shallower pass.

The megalodon, frenzied and hungry, charges the gap to reach the child, the rocks scraping its sides as it jams itself. Mother lands on top of the giant shark and with her last efforts, tears at its gills and eyes, turning the murky water crimson.

The child calls out for Mother as it swims through the huge lake, through the rubble and carnage.

Mother whimpers as she sees her child safe, no predators in sight. Dying, she knows her son will survive until the end of time. As she draws her last breath, her child cries in vain.

And a tribe of hunters see the strange creature in the lake. They drop to their knees, praying to their Gods to protect them. Protect their Loch Ness.

The Lost Island Of The Sharkasaurus

T. W. Garland

It won't be long. I can hear it move. It sounds like teeth being dragged along metal pipes, ending with an unholy crunch of a bite. In the small dark places that I hide, my only comfort is knowing my family are far away and know nothing of the nightmare that is the Sharkasaurus.

As I write this last record of all that has happened, I can see my happiness reflected in my family's faces as they asked me about my big adventure. A paleontological expedition into the Pacific Ocean isn't exactly the same as climbing Everest, unless you remember sitting in the movies watching *Jurassic Park* with a small plastic dinosaur in your hands. I went into finance when I grew up, but I kept the plastic dinosaur. I didn't need much convincing when I heard about the expedition. The promise of living for a month on a Pacific island while taking part in the discoveries of a lifetime, what could go wrong? A three-week ocean voyage on a shipping tanker brought us to our destination. It wasn't what I expected. The diameter of the island was under five miles and was shaped like a ring donut with a freshwater lake in the centre. Standing on the beach where we landed, I could see a beach on the other side.

The crew of the tanker had warned us about the inhabitants. Essentially an ancient tribe, their numbers had been increased by the survivors of the occasional shipwreck or plane crash who showed no interest in leaving. Saying a lack of interest in being rescued wasn't the oddest thing about them wasn't saying much. Their primitive mud huts formed a single row of sprinkles on a flat donut, all looking into the centre of nothing. They didn't have a leader as much as a guy who wandered around in a wicker headdress that made him look like the high priest of the basket people.

The inhabitants were all very friendly and we were all busy heading towards the lake. Even now, after everything that has happened, the sight of the fully formed dinosaur fossils assembled around the lake in a gigantic naturally created outdoor museum was more than the special effects of any summer blockbuster could produce.

There were more fossils than the dozen amateur palaeontologists and couple of professionals could handle. We each picked our favourite dinosaur and spent our days scraping, chipping, brushing, cataloguing and photographing. Given the size and scale of the fossils, the professionals abandoned us and we indulged our own appetites for whichever dinosaur took our fancy.

In the evening, the locals would gather in a large clearing like some kind of Central Park or Trafalgar Square of the primitive world. An enormous Triceratops horn was positioned at the far end. No one went near it. Instead, the congregation told stories around a large fire that smouldered with a heavy red smoke.

The high priest in his wicker hat turned out to be a car salesman from the Midwest. He wasn't specific and we didn't ask, because he told the most amazing stories of prehistoric creatures. He had a knack for making it sound like he had just seen them, and gave each of them a distinct personality. To return to the fossils the next day left us surprised that the dinosaurs were dead and, with each passing day, they became more real.

In those early days, I kept hearing odd mutterings from the other amateur palaeontologists. My allergies were playing up so I couldn't sit with the others near the fire. I stayed as far away from the red smoke coming out of the fire pit as I could while still listening to the stories.

The one the high priest most enjoyed telling, and no one tired of hearing, was about the final dinosaur to walk the island. She was the last carnivore and by definition the most powerful. After all of the herbivores and omnivores were eaten, the carnivores turned on each other until only she remained. The survival instincts of an apex predator were more than a little impressive. She increased the time between eating, surviving for weeks without food. Pushed on by the impulse to survive, she understood the salt water preserved her meat and strayed from the freshwater of the lake. She watched the ocean, its rhythm called to her, luring her with the measured pulse of oblivion.

The lack of hunting and absence of all other lifeforms deteriorated her mind and she grew weary. Her muscles grew lethargic and a void expanded from the empty depths of her existence. In a final purposeless desperation, she walked into the ocean.

Despair drove her into deeper and deeper water until the power of the sea left her as helpless as her prey. The need to endure wiped away all other concerns until she realised she was fighting a force she could not conquer.

Struggling for a moment to keep her head above the water, she released her need for life as she slipped into the depths of the ocean. She bared her teeth against her inevitable extinction, only to be faced with rows of unfolding teeth poised to rend flesh. Her own power to crush bone and destroy was held in limbo against a set of teeth sharp enough to shred through even the toughest hide.

The supreme carnivore from the land was face to face with fiercest creature of the ocean. Rarely had any lifeform survived a confrontation with either of these monsters.

An unimaginable moment passed between the two creatures.

A spark of the divine ignited. Many would have considered it an aberration of nature, others would have identified it as the moment in which love first existed.

Regardless of how the moment was described, it changed everything. The shark nurtured and tended to the dinosaur. He brought food when she needed to eat. He lifted her to the surface when she needed oxygen. He carried her through storms. Her life depended on him and he cared for her completely.

The two creatures were inseparable and at some point, possibly repeatedly and in many different ways, they shared the physical union reserved for the continuation of the species.

Such interbreeding would usually require a little explanation or be the subject of ridicule. All the high priest said was "Love will find a way." The comment prompted agreeing nods from his audience. The calm acceptance seemed to disregard the inevitable violence involved in the copulation of two apex predators.

As she became large with child, the dinosaur returned once again to her island. Her shark lover sensed her revived will to live and understood her need to protect her young in an environment she knew. Although it broke his heart, he guided her back to the island from which she originated. Leaving her in the shallows of her beach, he wanted nothing more than to live on land by her side. She took one last look and, carrying the love child of a shark and dinosaur, she returned to her nest with contentment and purpose. Barely a month later, the child of the two predators ripped through its mother's stomach, leaving her for dead as it pulled itself towards the fresh water lake.

The high priest told the story with wonder and excitement. Repetition did nothing to lessen the impact. The tale was equal parts a heart-warming love story, the trials of a dysfunctional family, and the macabre warning about the power of nature. Swirled together, it was difficult to sort out my feelings. Utter disbelief lingered at the furthest edges of my comprehension. Fear mingled with awe and respect was followed by a desire to serve.

On more than one occasion, I heard whisperings that had all the pace and intent of prayers directed towards the prehistoric monster. Even my closest neighbour on the beach of fossil lake began to spend long hours in positions of supplication.

The unusual became so normal, it was only just under a month after we had arrived that our long abandoned radio crackled to life. The tanker was about to return and very few people were interested. My relief was not shared by my colleagues. They had moved closer and closer to the red smoke of the fire, arriving earlier and earlier to the arms of the tribe. As I spoke about the arrival of the tanker, I got the feeling my colleagues would not be leaving.

I waited alone on the beach. The tanker was only hours away. I watched the waves crashing against the shore and thought about my family. I regret to say they had been absent from my thoughts. In the cool air of the evening, hopeful feelings filled me with an optimistic view of my life. I had seen wonderful places and experienced a different way of life. I wanted nothing more than to share all I had seen with those dearest to me and yet furthest away. Little did I know that the most astounding and terrifying experience was ahead.

When the great horn thundered its call across the island, it was the beginning of the nightmare from which there seems no end. I was under no misconception that the horn in the central meeting place had been blown. Its sound shook the ground and gripped the island with a feeling of anticipation.

I turned to look towards the fossil lake, but its waters remained still. I began to notice the members of the tribe. They had stepped from their huts and were standing with arms raised in praise with joyful expressions.

The horn thundered once more. This time the vibrations continued after the sound had dwindled. I would have easily believed it was an earthquake until I saw the water of the lake part.

My mind scrambled for understanding as an enormous dorsal fin broke the surface of the lake. I felt like I was looking at a joke shark fin in a paddling pool, but I knew it to be so much more dangerous.

After the fin came the skull, with black eyes and a bone-crushing jaw. The head hunched forward, its pointed nose casting a shadow over a row of teeth as large as surfboards.

It shifted forward and drew its body up out of the water. Under its hunched shoulders it had sinuous arms with long talons for hands. Digging deep into the shore, its talons pulled it forward as the monster's long tail pushed it upright and onto its feet.

The Sharkasaurus overshadowed the gigantic fossils littering the shore of the lake. It cared little for the remains of the deceased dinosaurs. It scanned the ring of huts circling the island, where each member of the tribe stood with arms outstretched. Some had been reduced to sobbing, reaching up towards the monster. It surveyed the shore like a discerning diner at a smorgasbord. The people were offering themselves, their shouts and calls for attention rising to a hysteria.

I can understand the joy of being released from the squalid conditions of the island, but this was more of a religious experience. I was terrified, but I understood. I could feel their need, and a small part of me wanted to go and be picked as if I was in a life or death selection by the most popular kid in school for the dodgeball team.

The ground shook as Sharkasaurus moved towards the huts to make its selection. A man jumped up, reaching towards those horrific teeth. The monster paused. It leant forward and swiped at the man, grabbing him in its mouth. His screams of pain were silenced with a bone-crunching snap. His body sagged in its mouth, teeth shredding his flesh. Its claws gripped either side of his torso, pulling him apart. His remains dropped to the ground and the beast bent to continue its meal. When it lifted its head, its nose and jaw were smeared with blood.

Looking up and down the row of huts, it was greeted with enthusiastic waves, and stepped towards its next victim.

I staggered backwards, splashing into the ocean, unsure where to go or what to do. The sound of the monster snapping and crunching its victims continued uninterrupted, like Friday night wings at an all you can eat buffet.

It consumed two more of the tribe and waded into the lake. The water turned red as blood washed from pale scales.

I dropped down into the surf, my chest heaving at the effort of breathing. My hands shook and I laughed. I don't know whether it was relief or the onset of lunacy. The combination of seeing people ripped apart with vicious intent, alongside the joyful nature with which such a horrible death was received, made my head spin.

Little did I know that the nightmare had barely started.

The monster's head had almost submerged as the horn of the tanker spun me around. My salvation had arrived, or so I thought. I glanced back, expecting to see still waters, and instead saw the Sharkasaurus rise again, caught in a moment of hesitation, the flesh of its victims still hanging from its teeth. The second call of the tanker's horn sparked it into action.

I scrambled to the small boat that had been anchored since our arrival. Its motor burst into life as the monster re-emerged from the lake. It thundered across the beach, making straight for the tanker. I pushed the boat to its limits. Skipping over waves, I thought I might flip it sending me into the charging monster's path.

I didn't dare look back for fear of what I might see.

Barely slowing, I crashed the boat into the side of the tanker, launching myself towards the ladder. I scrambled on board, shouting warnings at anyone I could see. I swung my arms violently, trying to get the sailors to start the engines and get moving. Expecting to collect over a dozen passengers, they gave me confused looks. I ran towards the bridge. I had covered half the distance when a thud echoed against the hull. The tanker shifted, the deck listing at a forty-five degree angle. I held on for dear life as I saw a couple of sailors swept overboard. They might have been lucky, because the next moment a massive claw swung onto the deck. Talons ripped through the steel, tearing violent gashes in the hull, as the Sharkasaurus pulled itself on board.

The tanker, for all its size, fared poorly.

Its arrival destroyed the prow, ripping away the anchor. Staggering aboard the rocking vessel, it clawed away metal containers and crushed a number of the lifeboats.

Armed sailors attacked with weapons reserved to dissuade pirates. The Sharkasaurus barely noticed, snapping and crushing the pests underfoot.

Screams of panic rose to a higher pitch and sailors ran for the remaining lifeboats, motors bursting into life as the men attempted to flee. The Sharkasaurus sprang into the sea, its massive jaw of teeth bearing down. The sailors who weren't immediately killed became the playthings of the giant beast. It nipped at them, removing an arm or leg. It left them swimming for a moment and then pulled them under, allowing their remains to float back to the surface. It had no further interest in eating.

After the lifeboats had become a sinking graveyard and only chum floated in the sea, the Sharkasaurus returned to the tanker. It seemed pleased. Spreading itself out on the deck, it stretched its limbs as if embracing the stricken ship.

The few remaining sailors made no attempt to fend off the monster and instead fled below decks. The deepest bowels of the tanker became a place where the struggle for survival took over.

All the lifeboats were destroyed. The radio masts were crushed and most of the electrical systems were ruined. We drifted until there was no land in sight. Not a single sailor can figure out our location. We may be only a mile away from the island, but we might as well be on a different planet.

With almost clockwork regularity, the Sharkasaurus launches itself into the sea. The entire tanker shakes as it dives, and it can be heard knocking occasionally against the hull as it swims around. Then it claws its way back on board, and for the next couple of days, the creature is quiet.

I can only speculate, and yet, the monster's behaviour seems unusual. Even if it is a freshwater creature, the way it stays close to the tanker and touches it is almost affectionate. If I could consider myself anything less than delirious, I would say that the Sharkasaurus was in love.

After the massive destruction we've sustained, I wonder how we stay afloat. I have spent hours in worried silence considering whether drowning would be preferable to becoming the next meal. And yet I am powerless. I cannot sink the tanker any more than I can escape the monster.

It has been nearly four weeks since the Sharkasaurus rose from the lake and ended up on the tanker. Unless it feeds when it swims, it must be getting hungry. I have heard its teeth grind in the darkness and its claws scratch on the deck like a child attempting to open a chocolate bar. I fear that its hunger will motivate a search for the remaining sailors, so I hide.

In the darkness, I think of my family and hope for a quick death.

Transition

Sara Codair

"I don't think gender reassignment surgery will make you happy," said Dr. Feck in a voice as plain as cardboard.

"Excuse me?" asked Julia.

Dr. Feck scratched his shit-colored mustache as he read his notes. "You complain about fragile fingers and fat-padded hips, but frankly, you'll be just as miserable as a man."

Julia crossed her arms so she wouldn't punch him. "And why is that?"

His burnt-bacon hair twitched as he shook his head. "You just don't like being human."

"Your ass is fired." Julia stormed out of his office and slammed the door behind her. She stomped down the sidewalk until a lime green flier caught her attention. It was a rectangular beacon of hope among a sea of warped staples:

Volunteers needed for human enhancement experiment.
Email <u>Fank C@XLab.gov</u>
Visit our office on 66 Main Street between 9 a.m. and 4 p.m.

Julia's fingers fluttered. It was 3:34 and Main Street was just a couple blocks away. A vortex of butterflies erupted inside her stomach. This was her chance to be something more.

She ran.

Fifteen minutes later, she was standing in front of a black door marked with the two lime green sixes.

She gave it a push.

It opened.

A wave of cool air and antiseptic blew on her face as she stepped into a waiting room.

"Can I help you?" asked a blocky man with bulging biceps.

"I'm here for the experiment," said Julia as she struggled to catch her breath.

"I'm sorry. This is an IRS office."

"Bullshit." Julia stormed towards the plain desk. "I saw the flier with your address. You number is even painted the same color."

"I'm sorry, but I think you're confused."

"I know it's real. I want in."

He leaned closer. "Where did you see this flier?"

"Outside my shrink's office. The third telephone pole on fifth."

"Damn. I'm going to kill Jackson." The man stepped away from the desk and took her by the arm. "You're going to leave and never come back. For your own safety."

The butterflies in Julia's stomach morphed into wasps. This was her chance to finally be rid of her useless body.

"I don't need safety. I need change."

"You're leaving. Forget you ever saw this place."

"No." Julia stomped on the man's foot, elbowed him in the gut, and ran. She leapt over the desk, pulled the door open, and found herself in a lab with a frazzled, gray-haired man clad in a stained lab coat.

"You shouldn't be in here," he stammered before placing a cork on a steaming vial.

Julia smiled. Just across the room was a glass case full of needles. They were filled with glowing blue liquid and labeled "Sharkasaurus Serum."

"Miss, you really should leave."

She snatched one and jammed it into her thigh.

"Dammit, why'd you do that?" He grabbed her arm. Her head spun and her limbs felt heavier than ever. She tried to answer him, but all that came out was a jumbled moan.

She heard the thud of boots on tile.

"Did it work?" asked a familiar voice. "Did she get it?"

"Yes," said the scientist. "Now help me get her into tank. I'd appreciate a warning next time you send me one of these crazies."

Large hands seized her legs. They swung. She flew for a few splendid seconds before hitting the water and sinking like a mooring ball.

The voices vanished.

Pain shot through her body like heroin in a junkie. Her muscles exploded like smashed pumpkins. Her spine stretched and popped. She twisted, screamed and laughed as her body broke apart and remade itself.

She clung to consciousness as hard as she could, not wanting to miss a moment of her transition. She weathered the pain like the loss and depression that had plagued her since childhood. She savored every moment of her rebirth.

It was over as quickly as it started.

She opened her eyes. Even though she was underwater, her reflection appeared crisp in the mirrored floor.

Her massive body was covered in shiny, blue scales. Her head was shaped like a shark's, complete with beady black eyes and gleaming white teeth.

She pushed her body up, realizing she had bowed legs and clawed feet. She flicked a serpentine tail as she took her first steps across the tank's mirrored floor.

She tried swimming next. She pushed and swished through the water like a rocket. It rushed over her gills, filling her lungs with moist oxygen until her snout broke the surface and she was able to suck dry air in through her nose.

"I'm amphibious," she said, but it came out as a roar. She laughed, and it sounded like a bark.

"Julia, how are you feeling?" asked a familiar voice. Julia turned towards the sound and saw her therapist taking baby steps into the cavernous lab.

She smiled, showing him the hundreds of teeth she longed to test out. Her stomach growled. She swam towards the edge of the tank.

"Julia, are you in there?" he asked slowly.

She nodded when she got to the edge of the pool.

His shoulders dropped. "Nod twice if you can hear and understand me."

She nodded twice then used her short arms to haul her body out of the pool. She felt heavy on land, but stronger than her human body had ever been.

"Do you like your new form?" He took a step closer to her.

She nodded.

"Do you have full control of your limbs?"

She nodded again and charged. He stumbled towards the door. She sank her teeth into his leg as his hand closed around the doorknob. Blood squirted from his arteries into her mouth, sweet and metallic. His muscles were stringy but satisfying. His organs were like chocolate pudding and his bones crunched like a graham cracker crust.

Julia roared. Her new body was glorious.

And male, she thought as she noticed the large dick dangling between her legs.

Bite Marks

Amy Fontaine

A memory of your smile
tears through my mind
like a shark:
consuming everything,
making the waters run red.
<u>RED</u>!
All I see is red,
a sheet of red beneath my eyes.
Now I know how blinded beasts feel
in the depths of the sea,
alone and mad and wanting to kill everyone.

Oh, the wounds
we have to live with:
a dead humpback whale
stewing in the sand.
A dolphin making love
to the male who killed her calf.
Mountainous elephant seals
with chunks ripped out of their sides,
lying on the beach
as if nothing happened.

The Mermaid's Purse

Em Dehaney

"I've had enough of this shit."

The rock-pooling trip was not going well. She had spent the last half-hour rolling her eyes and tapping away on her phone. He had found nothing more than a single, pitiful crab.

"I'm bored," she said. "I'm going to the pub."

Mikey watched his mother stomp back to the beach, shouting over her shoulder.

"Why can't you just play in the penny arcade like a normal kid?"

She was right. He wasn't like other kids. He picked his way after her, jumping between the shallow pools. The crab in the bottom of his bucket bobbed about as seawater slopped over his trainers. They were a size too small and molten blisters made him wince with every step. With a mind to give up and head to the pub garden, where he hoped a packet of crisps and a can of warm pop would be waiting, Mikey spotted a black jewel glinting in the sunlight. It was oblong and about the size of his hand, with a shiny bubble in the centre. A curved tendril sprouted from each corner giving it an alien, beetle-like quality. He knew what it was. Better than any crab. Better than pirate treasure even.

It was a mermaid's purse.

Holding it up to the light, Mikey could just make out the shape of a baby shark, smaller than his little finger and flicking its minuscule tail against the confines of the egg case. He dumped the crab without a second thought and carefully placed the mermaid's purse in the bucket with a covering of fresh seawater and few fronds of seaweed.

That night, lying under a scratchy sheet trying not to hear his mum's headboard banging on the wall next door, Mikey couldn't stop thinking about the baby shark. He had hidden it under his fold-out bed when they got back from the pub. Mum hadn't noticed. She was too busy with the sweaty slob who had been plying her with cider all night. He pulled the plastic bucket out and stared at the floating black sac. He imagined the shark growing inside. He imagined it tearing through the leathery skin of the purse with its teeth, ripping a hole in the side of the bucket and sending a torrent of sea-water cascading through the corridors of the B&B. Naked holiday-makers running screaming from their rooms, struggling to breathe as the flood pulled them under. His mother and the greasy pig on top of her washed away, spinning and tumbling, bones smashing as the tide dragged them down the stairs, through the door, along the beach and out to the ocean, never to be seen again.

Mikey had quite an imagination.

The next morning, Mum was still asleep when he got up, quietly packed his rucksack and tiptoed downstairs for some breakfast. When he asked the landlady if he could make himself a bacon sandwich to take away, she looked down at him with a frown.

"It's for my mum. She's not feeling too well and ..."

"Where did you get that bruise, love?"

Mikey's hand instinctively went up to his left cheek, where a yellow ghost lingered from the week before.

"Fell over," he mumbled.

The landlady pursed her lips and hurried off to the kitchen, returning with the bacon sandwich plus a packed lunch in a Tupperware box.

"There you go, love. Safe journey."

It will be now, thought Mikey. He shoved the sandwiches into his rucksack, scoffed the slice of sponge cake and launched the apple into the bushes. Then he tenderly poured the mermaid's purse and seawater into the lunchbox, closed the lid and waited for his mother to surface so they could catch the train home.

Mikey rushed to his bedroom when they got back to the flat, slammed the door and ripped the lid off the Tupperware, releasing a thick, fishy odour. He breathed in deeply. The smell of the sea, so out of place twelve floors up, made his tummy flip over. The shark had grown on the journey, he was sure of it. Tiny fins strained against the edges of the bubble. No fluid could be seen inside the egg case now. It was all shark.

Mum went out as soon as she had unpacked and re-applied her make-up, leaving Mikey to scavenge whatever he could find for dinner. He was just sitting down to a cold tin of out of date ravioli when he heard a splash from his bedroom. Bounding through the door, he found his little friend thrashing and snapping its way out of the tattered egg case. The flapping of the distressed baby shark had displaced most of the water from the lunchbox. Mikey panicked, only now worrying how he was going to keep the fish alive so far from the sea. He ran to the kitchen and found a huge saucepan, filled it with tap water and dumped in all the salt from the shaker on the table. Mikey carried the pan back to his room, his matchstick arms wobbling with the strain. Gently transferring the shark to the pan with both hands, he could sense the coiled potential within its smooth flanks.

"Don't worry," Mikey whispered as he placed the shark gently in the saucepan. "I'll look after you."

The shark circled his new territory, prowling the edges of the pan with a flicking tail. Mikey sat up and watched him swimming round until midnight, when he heard his mum's key in the front door. He jumped into bed and pretended to be asleep. She didn't check in on him.

Every morning, while Mum was sleeping off her hangover, Mikey rushed to his wardrobe where he had hidden the shark. He was feeding him on dried goldfish flakes he found under the sink. The goldfish had been a gift from Dad, back when he still used to visit once in a while. He had proudly named him Frank. Mum had come home with a man one night, and Mikey heard her laughing and shouting, "No! You can't do that" but giggling all the while. In the morning, six-year-old Mikey found Frank floating belly-up in a tank filled with stale lager and cigarette butts.

He sprinkled a handful of flakes into the water. The shark, now a sleek grey bullet with black tips on each fin, ignored the food. He had bright, beady eyes, not dead black ones like the shark in Jaws, and he stared out from the pan with a malevolent glare. Mikey didn't need to speak shark to understand the message.

No more flakes, Mikey.

Tentatively opening a dusty can of tuna he had found at the back of the cupboard, Mikey dropped a few crumbs into the pan. The shark greedily hoovered it up, champing his ragged razor-wire teeth up and down. After that, he fed the shark a spoonful in the morning and a spoonful at night. Instead of smelling like crusty tissues and stale armpits, his bedroom now reeked of fish, both dead and alive. He was soon shoplifting two cans of tuna a day from the corner shop, as well as his usual chocolate bars and penny chews.

The shark was now almost a foot long. He had outgrown the pan and needed a new home. The only thing Mikey could think of was his old paddling pool. He remembered splashing about on the balcony, naked and happy, with his parents smiling and laughing together. The paddling pool had been crumpled into a ball and shoved in the outside cupboard when Dad left. He opened the door and reached into the dark. Spiders dropped down onto his bare arm and unknown creatures tickled his fingers. Fighting every urge to recoil, he rooted around blindly until he made contact with the cold rubber of the pool. It was covered in mildew. He dragged it through the house leaving streaks of grime on the bare boarded floor. Mikey was seeing stars after blowing the thing up, with a mouth full of dust. The shark could sense change was afoot and he swam in eager circles, his teeth bared in a snaggle-toothed grin. Plucking him gently out of the cooking pot, Mikey held the shark up level with his face. The shark calmly stared back.

"This is your new home, but please don't bite it or you might die."

Silent and inscrutable though the shark was, Mikey was sure he gave a solemn nod as he released him into the paddling pool. He remembered hearing something about fish growing to the size of their surroundings and hoped it was true. The shark became sleeker and more sinister with every inch he grew.

One morning, up before dawn feed the shark his breakfast, Mikey cut his finger on the tuna can. A single drop of blood fell into the water. The shark flicked around and pointed his long snout at the blood, now slowly sinking in the water like a wisp of red smoke. He orbited the dot, making Mikey feel dizzy. Another spot dripped from his finger, and the shark went into a snapping, thrashing frenzy. Dirty water soaked into the carpet. The next day when he threw half a tin of tuna into the pool, the shark swam underneath and tossed it up in the air with a splash before swimming away in disgust.

There were only three more days of summer left, and Mikey didn't have any of the necessary equipment that he needed for his first day of secondary school. No uniform. No pencil case. No shiny black shoes. No scientific calculator. At midday, he knocked lightly on her bedroom door.

"Mum ... Mum."

No answer.

"Mum. I need some money to buy things for school."

"Fuck off. I'm asleep."

"But Mum, I need ..."

"I told you, I'm asleep. Leave a list on the table and I'll see what I can do. Now, piss off."

Knowing that was the best he was going to get, Mikey popped his head round his bedroom door.

"I'll get you some real food, don't worry," he cooed to the shark.

I know you will, Mikey, came the reply in his head. *You're a good boy.*

Sneaking through the back alleys of the nearby new-build estate, Mikey popped his head over garden fences and through hedges, trying to decide whether a shark would rather eat rabbit or guinea pig. He came to a garden with a high gate. Pushing his eye up to a knot in the wood he saw lily pad flowers in bloom, bright white and bubble-gum pink against the black water of the pond, too beautiful to look at.

Luckily, Mikey was a scrawny kid and he easily squeezed himself through the thin opening between gate and fence. Staying close to the shadows, he crept closer to the house. Satisfied that all windows and doors were shut, and not seeing or hearing anyone, Mikey pulled the plastic bags from his pocket and got to work.

It was past dinner time when he got home. There was a note on the kitchen table.

Here's your school stuff. Gone for a curry,
Mum

In a pile on the chair were a two greying shirts, a single threadbare jumper and a pair of grey trousers with a hole in the knee. On closer inspection, all had labels sewn in them bearing different names. A couple of biros stolen from the bookies instead of the fountain pen he asked for. And the final insult; not a brand new rucksack, but a battered old briefcase. He had finished primary school as the weird kid who smelled of piss and never had new trainers. Now he was starting secondary school as the weird kid who smelled of fish and carried a briefcase.

Throwing the clothes across the room and kicking the briefcase so hard he hurt his foot, Mikey scooped up the two plastic bags he had left by the front door and made his way to the bathroom.

The thunder of the taps filling the bath filled Mikey's ears, drowning out the lightning inside his head. How could she do this to him? Why did she hate him so much? Mikey already knew the answer. The older he got, the more he reminded her of Dad, and for this he had to be punished. Once the bath was full, Mikey upended the first plastic bag. A black and orange koi carp plopped into the water, followed by a second, dazzling and silvery-white, both stunned and still.

Entering his room, Mikey was intoxicated with the stench of rotting fish. He reverently picked the shark up, stroking the sleek flanks. He put his face to the dorsal fin, rubbing his cheek along its edge.

"Time for dinner," he whispered.

The shark demolished the koi in a rabid frenzy of ripping scales and flesh. The skeletons of the fish revealed, blood and fish guts filled the tub. When the orgy of feeding was done the shark was happy and full. Mikey was hungry and tired. Tired of it all.

He heard his mum stumble through the door in the early hours, tripping over her feet as she made for the toilet.

When the sound of her screams had died down, Mikey crept into bathroom. Through the gloom he could see blood splattered up the tiles and soaking the shower curtain. He climbed into the tub, letting the delicious warmth surround him. He put his arms around the shark and slept.

The first responders found the boy clinging to his mother's brutally ripped and ragged corpse in a bath full of coagulating blood. The attending detectives hypothesised a crazed partner, or even pimp, had committed the horrific crime. No murder weapon was ever found and the post mortem was inconclusive. The final reports painted a tragic picture of abuse, with all the usual hallmarks of neglect – no food in the cupboards, filth on the floors and walls, evidence of heavy drinking and drug use.

All depressingly common, and despite the initial horror of the bloody murder scene, the case was soon forgotten.

Forgotten by everyone apart from a young Crime Scene Investigator, straight out of college, who knew how it felt to be a hungry child.

Tasked with sweeping the house from top to bottom for any evidence of a murder weapon, she found a desiccated but intact shark egg case, hidden under the boy's bed. When the CSI held it up to the light she saw the tiny, unmistakeable shadow of a dead baby shark inside.

Poor little guy, she thought, *he never stood a chance.*

Jurassic Snack

Frank Roger

Adrian had been driving for hours and was growing hungry like hell. When he saw a Jurassic Snack, he pulled over and parked his car.

Jurassic Snack? Wasn't that a new fast food chain opening outlets all over the country, and becoming wildly popular with kids? Anything that had dinosaurs was a big hit these days. He had seen those funny commercials on TV, complete with dino hunting crews that traveled back in time to get supplies. Although the dino craze left him cold, he went in anyway. He'd be happy to have a good meal.

He cast a glance at the menu: T-Rex Burgers, Skewered Trilobites, Megatherium Stew, Velociraptor Legs ... No wonder this was popular with kids.

He ordered a T-Rex Burger and a Fossil Coke, took a seat and started eating. Halfway through his burger – very richly flavored; he wondered what kind of meat this was – he suddenly bit on something hard and for one moment he was afraid he had broken a tooth. Fortunately he hadn't, but it had been close. He took the hard bit out of his mouth and found it was a coin. A coin? How had this thing wound up in his burger?

He studied it and saw it was not an American coin. It was foreign. Wait a bit. He peered at it more closely. This was no ordinary coin. He remembered this from his history courses. This thing looked like an ancient Roman coin. That was totally incredible.

He got up, walked to the counter, showed the coin to the cashier and said: "I found this in my burger. I almost broke a tooth. This is unacceptable. I want my money back."

The girl looked at the coin and said: "I'm afraid that's impossible, sir. These things do happen. Did you read the small print on the menu?"

"No, I didn't, but I don't accept this," he said. "How can this happen?"

The girl sighed, clearly bored with the situation. "Our crews go back in time for our supplies, but every now and then something goes wrong."

"What the hell are you talking about?" he said, losing his patience. "Time travel? Cut the crap. That's a marketing ploy for kids. It may work well in commercials, but don't try it on me."

"No, sir, this is serious. It's called collateral sweepings."

"I beg your pardon?"

"The constant traveling in time back and forth creates a vortex, which generates time-space anomalies. All sorts of stuff may be swept along to the present. That explains the coin. Occasionally we've had bigger stuff turning up too. I'm sorry for the inconvenience, sir."

"I don't believe a word of what you're saying. I just want my money back."

"That's impossible, sir. A coupon with a ten percent reduction off your next meal is all I can offer you. You may apply for one on our website."

"I want my money back now. Am I making myself perfectly clear?"

They were still arguing when the gigantic meteor appeared and crushed the Jurassic Snack, along with its staff, its customers and the entire neighborhood, thus ending the discussion prematurely.

The Swimming Pool

Trevor Tolliver

There is nothing in the swimming pool.

Randall Gleason ran the mantra over and over again in his mind like an emergency Morse code delivered from a sinking warship. It was ridiculous, this wild, unchecked terror of the water that forbade him from going any deeper than the top step in the shallow end.

There is nothing in the swimming pool.

He didn't even want the damned pool, but when you made it into his tax bracket, and when his maximum budget with which to purchase a home could safely sustain a village in some impoverished country, it came with the territory ("A slice of paradise," the realtor had said with a dramatic sweep of her chubby arm. "The finest resort in the neighborhood is right outside your back door!").

And it was a gorgeous pool, designed to appear as if it were a natural, tropical lagoon the rest of the property had just somehow been constructed around. A waterfall splashed over a grotto of stacked boulders that emptied, chuckling, into the deep end of the pool's wide, bean-shaped body. Imperious palm trees swayed and rustled in a ring around the back yard, and emerald fronds grew dense and lush from between the mounds of low, sparkling rocks that encrusted the rim of the pool like unmined diamonds. And the water, clean and cool and turquoise, was a beacon in the summer heat.

Yet here he was, standing on the top step like a child afraid to venture further without the security of his floaties puffed around his biceps, a forty year-old stockbroker clutching to a fraying, yellowed message of fabricated courage–

There is nothing in the swimming pool.

Randall straddled the inflatable raft he bought the day before. He might spend the first summer in his new home sitting on the patio, hiding behind his sunglasses and burning himself to a lethal shade of red, or he could join his wife and son paddling around in the water.

The fact was, Randall wasn't a confident swimmer; he could have been, if it weren't for the summer of his seventh year, when he and Gerald spent those blistering months at their grandmother's house in Houston. She tried teaching Randall to churn his little hands and kick out his legs ("Jes like a little bull-frowg," she told him in her thick, warm drawl) so he could tread water and stay afloat. Suddenly from the sidelines, Gerald sprung up from his patio chair, pointed with a dramatic, quivering finger to the forbidden deep end, and shrieked in his girly ten year-old falsetto, "Shark! Get outta the water, Randy! *Shark! Shaaarrrrk!*"

So Randall churned and kicked like hell, mustering all the strength his scrawny limbs could muster. He didn't look back – didn't need to – the animal was behind him, slowly closing in, relishing the hunt, its tail swishing lazily back and forth. Its unsanded, blunt snout was at Randall's feet, he was certain. He was sure the shark could smell his terror, as sweet to the monster as the scent of a sirloin steak, its wicked, black eyes rolling up into its head in an orgasmic rush of hunger-lust. Randall tried grabbing handfuls of water as if it could give him purchase, as if it might somehow drag him forward like a knotted rope, but his exhausted limbs stopped pumping as the solid, safe edge of the pool seemed to be retracting, sliding further away from his grasp.

As water filled his lungs and the blackness swept over him like midnight, he could hear Gerald's frantic screaming, the sound of it gurgling as Randall's ears dipped below the surface of the water: "Swim, Randy! *It's right behind you!*"

Grandma had plucked him from the water, wrapped him in a towel, showed him the empty pool and explained in her cozy-quilt tone that a shark couldn't possibly pop up in a concrete pond in a family's backyard (*there is nothing in the swimming pool*), and that it was the lifetime career of all big brothers to torment the little ones. He was too busy sobbing to laugh.

As adults, Randall would forgive Gerald for the multiple loans he never repaid, forgive him for nearly costing Randall his life's savings in a shady business scheme, could forgive him for missing their grandmother's funeral but taking a front row-center seat when it was time to spoon out dollops of the inheritance she'd left them. But Randall would never forgive his big brother for the gift of a crippling fear of deep water that tore through the next thirty-three years of his life like ugly scar tissue.

He stayed on the shore when he and Rachel took Brian to the beach on summer vacations. He avoided fishing weekends with his colleagues and eavesdropped with sickening jealousy as they recounted their drunken escapades the following Monday morning. Hell, he even stopped taking baths when he was seven and converted permanently to showers. No sharks in a shower stall.

He fooled himself into thinking he was conquering his fear each time he merely circumvented it. He may have been afraid of the vast and endless sea, but he would go on to spill an abundance of bravery (and blood) on dry land. The trophy room in the house was a testament to his masculinity, a toast to his prowess with a weapon: a menagerie of species–a cheetah, a boar with curved tusks, a young male lion with a fuzzy mane, an assortment of crania with antlers and gnarled racks of horns–glared down with glassy eyes from their plaques on the paneled walls (unimpressed, Brian just rolled his eyes, quipped that his father's den look like Noah had gone on a shooting massacre on the Ark). And when the prizes were too large or too risky to transport across international borders, Randall displayed photographs in gilded frames that served as alibis for his unbelievable tales of adventure–crouching in his khakis beside a lifeless giraffe, or a rhinoceros, or an elephant, great beasts felled by nature's most dangerous, cunning animal.

There is nothing in the swimming pool.

Randall's trim body fit perfectly on the narrow yellow raft, but when he flopped backwards onto the slippery plastic, he gave himself too much of a push, and he shot across the water like a torpedo. He flailed his arms, trying to reach for the edge before he rocketed too far away from it, but he was skimming fast over the placid surface like a skipped stone. He listed to his left, nearly capsizing, and he grasped the sides of the raft so tightly that he flattened a couple of its inflated ribs. He wobbled until he was level again. Behind his head, the sound of the waterfall cascading out of the grotto was rising; he was sailing into the deep.

The raft slowed and turned a half-arc, then just bobbed over the white disc of the drain that seemed to look miles below the top of the water, like peeping down the wrong end of a telescope. Randall was motionless, as stiff as a corpse in a casket, clutching the raft and balancing himself with his jutting elbows. He lay still. The mild current churning from the base of the waterfall gently nudged the raft away from the grotto toward one of the curved edges of the pool, and Randall leaned slightly to help his trajectory along.

From under him, something hard, something sharpened into a pointed nub, rubbed against the bottom of the raft, pressing into the plastic along Randall's spine. He gasped and froze. His racing heartbeat sloshed in his ears.

There is nothing –

A large mass drifted beneath him, and another hard, sharp nub caught the end of the raft at Randall's feet –

– in the swimming pool.

– and spun him one full revolution. He dipped his chin to his chest and peered down the length of his body, his feet pointing to the waterfall. In the bubbling wake of whatever was moving below the surface, he saw it. Only a fleeting glimpse, but enough for his screaming mind to identify the gray, triangular fin cutting through the surface of the water just before it slid beneath the grotto, into the deep.

At dinner, Rachel loaded a tray with condiments, a basket of sesame seed buns, and a platter of raw hamburger patties. She had changed into her bathing suit and covered herself with a crochet tunic and wedged her daisy-patterned flip-flops between her bright pink painted toes. She had been waiting for summer–Memorial Day couldn't come fast enough–and she wanted Randall to fire up the barbeque so they could welcome in the season with open, sunburned arms.

Brian moseyed into the kitchen, picking at the pickles and slices of cheese on Rachel's tray. She slapped his hand away and he grinned back. He shuffled across the tile in his sandals, lifting the bottom of his tee shirt to scratch his flat, hairless belly. "So, Andrew and Luke might come over tomorrow to swim, if that's okay." His voice was as dull as a shingle, registering the perpetual, epic boredom of a sixteen year-old boy.

"Fine with me," Rachel said. "If they come early enough, I can make some lunch for you guys."

"Sweet," he tried to say without yawning. "I'm gonna take a dip before dinner."

"Hold up," Randall said, a bit sharper than he had intended. Even Rachel flicked her eyes up as she counted out silverware. "The water's not very good right now."

"It isn't?" Rachel leaned over to glance at the pool through the glass slider. "Looks beautiful from here."

"No, something's off. I went in earlier, and there –" *there is something in the swimming pool* "– there's something dirty about the water. Looks a little murky. I think we need to adjust the chemicals a bit."

"I'll keep my head above water," Brian droned, popping in his earbuds and turning away from his parents. He flipped his towel over his shoulder.

"No," Randall said, grabbing an end of the boy's towel like the reins on a horse and stopping him in midstride. "No, I think we need to stay out of it. Just a little longer. Just until we can get someone to come check it out."

As if the muscles keeping it up snapped like rubber bands, Brian's head flopped back and he half sighed, half groaned into the air. "So *lame*, Dad. Like, it's not a big deal."

"Well, you know how it is," Randall said. "My day isn't complete without ruining your life. But do me this for me, pal. Stay out of the water until I can get it looked at. I promise I'll call on Tuesday."

"Awesome," Brian mumbled. "There goes the entire holiday weekend."

As the teenager skulked out of the kitchen, his thumbs clicking ferociously over his phone's keypad (no doubt, slaughtering his father to sympathetic friends), Rachel cocked an eyebrow. "What's going on?"

"Nothing," Randall said with a chuckle. *Nothing at all. Thought I saw a dorsal fin in the swimming pool, is all. Damn near drowned pulling myself out of the water. Heard my awful brother in the back of my mind screaming for me to get out of there, not to look back, don't look back.* "You do me a favor, too, will you? Stay clear of the pool?"

The next morning, Randall found the seal.

He was holding his coffee mug under the faucet to rinse it out when he glanced out the bay window that overlooked the backyard and saw the brown blob beached by the side of the pool. He crept to the sliding door, watching for the animal to move, but from this new angle Randall could see a chunk was missing from its side, exposing layers of blubbery fat and spilled coils of intestine. He recognized the muzzle of the animal, the whiskers, the limp flipper resting on its bulk.

He slid the door open and stepped outside, heard the buzzing hum from the plume of blowflies swarming the open wound. The water in the pool was clouded and rosy, and patches of the seal's leathery flesh mottled the surface.

A squeaky gasp from behind him made him jump. Rachel stood in the doorway, both of her hands cupped over her mouth. "Oh my God, Randall, is that–"

"Yep." He squinted his eyes against the morning sunlight glinting off the crimson water. "But I want to know *how . . .*"

"I can't tell you how he got here," the animal control officer said. He was down on his haunches, peering into the seal's gory flank. "The closest beach is almost eighty miles from here. Two, three hour drive. He never could have made it this far inland on his own. Could have dropped off a truck in transport?"

Randall shrugged. He wanted answers, not to surmise his own.

"Something got him," the officer said, nodding to the polluted pool.

"A bear?"

"Here? No, I shouldn't think so. My best guess might be a coyote, but one good slap from this flipper tail and he'd knock a dog out." He straightened up, snapped off his smeared rubber gloves. "Big lacerations. They go deep, took a good slice out of him. I'm not a marine biologist, but whatever got him–" he held his hands several feet apart "–seems to have a pretty wide bite radius with lots of sharp teeth. Something big took a nice, juicy bite out of him and tossed the carcass up out of the water."

Randall tried to swallow, but it stuck in his throat like a billiard ball. "Something like what?"

"Sounds crazy," the officer said, shaking his head at his own hypothesis, "and I know it's not possible, but my best guess is a shark."

"Of course there isn't a shark," Randall said. *There is nothing in the swimming pool.* "But whatever happened, it left a mess. I'm going to drain it, clean out the filter, and we'll get it good as new for the summer."

Animal control sent a larger truck and a hoist, and a small throng of curious neighbors stood along fences and gathered at the curb to watch the mutilated seal be hauled away. They all asked the same questions, and Randall and Rachel could only give the same pat, empty answers that they'd been given, the same answers they had no choice but to give each other in private. Nope, don't know how it got here; nope, have no idea what in hell happened to it, why it was so–*ravaged.*

Once the corpse was gone, Randall hosed down the patio and shoveled up whatever couldn't be absorbed in the grass beltway along the cinderblock wall. Then he maneuvered the net over the surface to scoop up the debris of animal flotsam. Staring into its murky depths, Randall dipped the net into the water, stirring in slow, broad circles.

Maybe the movement would attract the great fish. Maybe swirling and spreading what was left of the chum might entice the monster out of wherever it was lurking to break through the red water, flash its stony jaws, roll those blank, evil eyes. Maybe the shark –

A hand pressed against his back, and he shouted and whirled around. Rachel flinched and giggled. "Sorry, sorry. I thought you heard me. What are you doing?"

"Nothing, just ... tidying. Got to get the big pieces out before we drain it."

"What happened yesterday when you went into the water?"

"I told you. Nothing."

She got behind him and wrapped her arms around his chest, rested her cheek against the back of his neck. "And I'm telling you, I don't believe you. I've never seen you swim in twenty years, so what got you in there yesterday?"

"I was practicing for you," he said, smiling. "But . . ."

"But *what*, Randall?"

But there was a fin, and a tail, and I swear to God it touched me, swam beneath me, has found a way to swim and feed and escape again, he gibbered in his mind. He imagined the concern that would cloud her face, the doubt that would flash in her eyes like summertime lightning, and he couldn't stand the thought of her thinking he was (*say it, it's fine, you're thinking it*) insane.

He sighed, pulled the net out of the pool. "But the water was just ... bad."

The pool drain hummed and gurgled merrily, and as imperceptibly as the hands spin around the face of a clock, the water level began its slow decline. The shallow end was foggy with dark pink water, but the floor of the deep end was obscured by the heavier scarlet of the seal's blood.

Randall refused lunch and sat in a vinyl patio chair beside the pool, his elbows on his knees, scanning the water like a vigilant lifeguard in a watchtower. Chomping on a sandwich and picking at the bread crumbs that flaked his shirt, Brian sauntered into the backyard and pulled up a chair beside his dad. "Spot anything yet, Ahab?"

"Hardy-har," Randall said. He wasn't in the mood to be made fun of, but Brian's reliably snarky commentary never failed to get a wry smile out of him.

"What are you looking for?"

"I'm not sure," Randall said. "Just want to see if there's a way these animals are somehow finding a way into the swimming pool."

"Well, just the seal," Brian corrected. "What other animals are you talking about?"

"The seal, and ... whatever got him."

"Is that why you have *that* out?"

Randall's hunting rifle, a sleek Remington .700, stood at attention and was poised for duty next to him, leaning against the tiled outdoor table. "Maybe. Just in case."

"And if you see something, you're gonna blow it in half and mount the head in your den?"

Randall blew air out his nose and shook his head. His son had never approved of his father's hobby, avoided strolling into the den as much as possible, wouldn't cross the threshold even when he was summoned. He never asked questions about the hunts, showed no interest in the process of tracking a target, stalking it, firing off a single bullet for a quick, clean kill. But Brian had never been haunted by fear, he was never a kid who shouted for his dad in the middle of the night because of perceived monsters under the bed, or the heavy presence of a perceived great white shark circling in the water below.

He's steadfast in his opinions, I'll give him that much, Randall thought. *No one's going to make that kid do anything he doesn't want to do.*

"There's probably nothing," Randall said. "But I'd feel better if I knew we were safe."

Brian dragged himself to the edge of the pool; Randall wanted to warn him to be careful, but he'd already been served up ample helpings of sideways glances and eye rolls the last couple of days. The boy planted his fists on his hips, then crouched down on the heels of his Converse sneakers, honing in on something. "Hey, Dad, come here. Have you seen this?"

In the shallow end where there was less water and greater, but not much, visibility, long, squiggly slashes burrowed into either side of the pool as if someone had taken a spear to the plaster walls and made several passes back and forth. Randall stuck his arm into the water and felt the raised, jagged ridges.

"It's all scraped up," Brian said in a tone that passed for reluctant acceptance. "It's like ... something huge caused some damage when it tried to turn itself around over here."

A vise clamped around Randall's chest and squeezed. He could picture the scarred belly of the enormous predator grazing the bottom of the pool, its firm pectoral fins jutting out from its trunk like airplane wings, digging into the walls as it finished its regular prowl of the swimming pool and made its clunky, awkward rotation to return to the grotto end.

He was jarred back from his horrific daydream by Brian's voice coming from the center section of the pool where the bottom made a sharp drop into its maximum depth. "Dad," he said, dipping his gangly arm into the opaque red water, "I can feel the scrapes over here, too."

"Brian! Move away from–"

Brian fumbled to rise, and between being too close to the edge and not having stabilized himself before straightening up, his stomach curved forward, his arms twirled like pinwheels, and the boy pitched forward and disappeared below the surface.

"*Brian!*"

The sliding door slammed open and Rachel bounded out like a grizzly. "Randall! What's happening?"

Brian popped up and jerked his head to flip his long wet bangs out of his eyes. "Feels good in here!"

"Brian! Grab my hand!" Randall dropped to his knees and extended his arms. He'd get a strong hold of his son's hands and fling him out like a slingshot in reverse.

"Chill, Dad," Brian said, paddling to the edge.

Randall glanced over at the grotto, and from the darkest, most crimson-dyed depths behind the waterfall, the gray fin punctured the water, carved forward, and descended below the surface again. "Oh God, oh Jesus, Brian, *get out of there!*"

Randall got on all fours, pounded the concrete with one frustrated fist, hurled himself into the water. He swam with the grace of a one-legged pig, but he managed to lurch his way to his son, snatched a handful of Brian's collar, and dragged him to the side. "Rachel, hurry!" He hefted the boy the best he could; the center of the pool was too deep for Randall's feet to find leverage. Rachel took Brian's hands and hoisted him out. Neither one was laughing now.

Randall's frantic kicking and splashing drew him further away from the side of the pool and he realized as he gasped for breath and fought to keep his head above water that he was thrusting himself further out to sea. From the corner of his eye, he saw the dorsal fin stab the air and slice an incision through the water like a stainless steel scalpel.

Rachel shrieked and circled the pool to the shallow end where the draining water exposed the top step. "Randall, listen to me. Swim to me! Swim this way!"

Randall punched the water, his arms rowing like clumsy oars. He swallowed water and gagged, spit it out.

"Don't turn around, Randall. Just swim to me. *Just kick, Randall, hurry!*" Her eyes, always so tender, so mild, now blazed with white, searing terror at whatever was trailing him in the water.

He was seven again, his limbs weighted down with exhaustion and clothing. His legs pumped ("*like a bull-frowg*," shrieked his grandmother's voice) but failed to give him any speed, just enough to keep his nostrils above the choppy water. He extended a toe, hoping to feel a rise in the floor to give himself a boost. Nothing. Still out too deep.

"Randall, Jesus Christ, *swim!*"

On the patio, Brian grabbed the rifle and knelt by the side of the pool. He brought the barrel up to his chin, stared through the scope, and pulled the trigger, yanked it over and over, but nothing was happening. Confused, Brian stared down at the weapon, studied it, tried to spot a magic button that would make it fire. Looked so easy in movies–aim and shoot. But cowboys didn't have safeties set on their pistols, and Brian, who had never held a gun in his whole life, had no idea how to disengage the lock.

"Almost, Randall. Almost!" Rachel dropped to her knees and reached her arms forward, her fingers splayed like starfishes. "Don't turn back! Just keep going."

Finally Randall reached a point in the pool's undersea shelf where his foot made contact with the floor, the cliff where it plunged into the abyss. He used his leg like a pogo stick, staggering forward through the water, stretching his hands out to Rachel.

Behind him, water rushed and roared as something immense

burst through the ceiling of the shallows. Brian wailed from the shadows of the patio, and Rachel shrieked and tumbled away from the edge. Randall made one final push to make it to the steps and glanced over his shoulder.

Massive jaws closed around his ribcage and pelvis, stabbing him with rows of butcher knife teeth. The great white's lips curled up, exposing rocky gray gums. Its breath was hot and putrid. Inside his head, Randall heard the crunch of his bones breaking, felt parts of him being shorn off his torso in fleshy ribbons. The shark dragged Randall away from the steps, whipping him from side to side to disorient him.

Water filled his ears, muffling his wife's shrill screams, and before he disappeared into the murky, red depths, Randall stared into the beast's black marble eye as it rolled back into its head with sublime ecstasy.

The Bumblesaurs

Sara Wilson

That first flush of pollen
to dust the muzzle of a T-rex
stained his scales and
changed the very air.

Atmospheres thickened
with the floating fluff
and musth of flowers,
were heavy with the scent
of sex and sprouts that piqued
the interest of all dinosaurs.

But Ceratops and Stegoceras
and all the others would wilt,
wither beneath the weight
of pollen, a will
for flowers to flourish,

for the bumbling
beasts failed to flit
between florets. Blossoms
were crushed. The flowers
the avid had flocked to fell
amidst the ferns, beneath
the fumbling fossils:

to the floral crave and itch,
slaves to nectared thirsts and urges,
and stuck beneath the tickle
of insects, new and perverted,
the dinosaurs would slump, lost
and buried beneath the sweetened
feet of bees just born.

Hides to hives.

Tarantulasaurus Rex!

Jeffrey Blevins

Who would've thought this would happen?
Nobody thought it *could* happen.
Yet it is ...

Bones are spread across the rocky embankment of its lair, littered over the stony ledge like parmesan cheese over spaghetti. Stringy, sinisterly strung layers of silk serve as protection for the entrance of its den of decay – draping as tapestries of death inside the hollows of Thompson Peak.

Janesville, California's once hospitable mountainous retreat, is now a cesspool of carnage. Bodily debris lies scattered along the trails of monstrously sized prints left in the mud – this eight-legged creature, enhanced from a bizarre genetic mutation, has been haunting the town for three days; and already one third of neighboring Susanville's dismally small population has either been consumed, or spun into a silken cocoon to satiate the creature's massive appetite at later feeding times. Call it a doggie bag for the doomed, where saving leftovers isn't considered trendy but necessary for secluded mountain living; for a monster to snack during times of daylight relaxation.

This abomination will not stop until all of Janesville, California, and its neighbor Susanville are decimated. It doesn't fear, it doesn't stop, and it will not surrender. Retreating into its den of the already damned, it waits for the moon's full cooperation to utilize its preternaturally-enhanced nocturnal vision.

Then it will hunt. It will stockpile and savor – existing only for the thrill of inflicting terror...lurking, waiting beneath the rocky terrain, thirsting for blood. In just seven hours, Susanville will once again be rampaged by this ninety-foot tall beast. It will ransack our town and snatch our loved ones, just as it has mine.

Against all reasoning and scientific explanations, the remote mountain populations have recently been acquainted with the destruction of ... a Tarantulasaurus Rex!

I, Matthew Steinbeck, stand beside the glowing embers of our town's smoldering City Hall. A council has been called. Where we once rallied, sitting in leatherback chairs, sipping a hipster concoction of fruits and kale, and formulated the town's monthly agendas. September the 19th, today, there will be no sipping of chic drinks; there will be no sitting in leatherback chairs, unless a person wanted to singe their backside; nor is there to be lengthy discussions regarding monthly agendas. Pioneer Days are obviously cancelled and Mrs. McCleary won't be baking her award winning Pumpkin Dandy – not because she lacks the will or the resources, but because she lacks the 'life' that's associated with completing any given task.

The Tarantulasaurus Rex claimed her as its 'award winning' treat. If it was capable of tangible thought, it would've pinned a blue ribbon upon her chest and served *her* to local judges.

In the aftermath of its destruction, we, the survivors of three brutal nights, gather here today to discuss a matter of absolute importance – and that's how we're going to kill a ninety foot tall, carnivorous Spider Dinosaur. Sound absurd? Walk through the rubble of smoking houses, grocery stores and schools, then tell me it sounds ridiculous.

Of course it sounds ridiculous – that goes without saying. Yet it doesn't keep it from being true. By virtue, this creature is categorically improbable; I mean really, at nearly one hundred feet tall, eight scaly legs and a dinosaur-infused facial construction, it doesn't sound probable to me either, dagger teeth and all ... until it captured my dearest Jezalinda.

She was, and still is my girlfriend: a symbolic crossbreed of Jezebel and Linda all her own. Yes, technically she was a transient, never having one place to call home. But she worked her way into my heart. Professionally, she was a solicitor of 'womanly delights,' whatever that means – where she seemed to only find customers by the name of John. Still, she was mine. More beautiful than an autumn pathway, clusters of orange-brown leaves twirling in wisps, the aroma of freshly burned cedar.

But now she's gone, vanished, into the creature's lair. Presumably, she's dead ...that's what the town tells me. Yet my heart informs me that she's alive – somehow, someway, she's alive. She's always been resilient and clever. I know this for a fact. Her friends would always disclose that she was the best at turning tricks; therefore, she's a trickster; capable of pulling one of the creature's eight legs; a survivor.

Therefore we gather here in this ashy monument to discuss the insidious nature of the monster.

Mayor Kenzy, who would theoretically count as three people if the beast consumed him, due to a unique dietary condition called *overindulgence*, begins to speak. "People, I understand this tragedy is demoralizing to our home lives. But we must stand united!"

Thus far, his opening statement is spoken like a true politician, and does little more than enrage my frustration – it's obvious we need to stand united. It took more than one Neanderthal to bring down a Mammoth.

He continues between bites of last night's left over barbeque chicken, broiled over the flames of his crumbling home, "It's with great unease that I inform you," He tosses the devoured bone (I don't know why he didn't just swallow it whole), licks his pudgy fingers and goes on, "There's significant reason to believe that the creature will attack … again."

Those in attendance, nearly all of the remaining three hundred, gasp in rapid succession.

What a shock? Are these people as ignorant as they portray? Of course it's going to attack. It's done so on all three consecutive occasions: the first night, the second night and then last night.

But I heard him announce earlier that an explanation for the creature's creation had been discovered and that it will be revealed today. Any information about it is worth my time. If I'm to save my beloved Jezalinda, I must be knowledgeable about this eight-legged atrocity.

"Listen, my loyal constituents, listen here. Discovered in the vaults of our community college's scientific research facility, a decoded document may shed some light on the origin of our dangerous enemy."

He certainly tests my patience. Only a politician would take the time to describe an enemy as dangerous. Has there ever been a harmless enemy? And what leads him to believe that it's dangerous – maybe that it's a ninety foot tall tarantula genetically infused with a Tyrannosaurus Rex? I literally can't imagine a more threatening enemy. The two are already horrifying animals when standing alone, the latter of the two being extinct – or so we thought.

Still, I give the mayor a chance, who now spoons through a tub of refrigerated macaroni salad, almost as if it's compulsively comforting. "I call upon Doctor Neal Frederickson to detail his analysis of these documents."

A professional-looking man steps up the crumbled stairs of our pitiful Hall Podium, never mind not having a ceiling to enclose it. He dons a traditional white coat, smeared with both charcoal and blood. A silver stethoscope must've been salvaged from the ruins for it hangs over his right shoulder, "My friends," he begins with a low, experienced voice, "I am but a simple doctor who holds degrees in the psychological field."

Why on Earth would a psychologist wear a veterinarian's coat and carry a medical doctor's stethoscope? His doctoral dissertation must've been on the lapse of sanity brought on by traumatic events. Then again, the entire town's gone a little whacky since these attacks – myself included. I've always been a staunch advocate of being fair.

Regardless, he's more knowledgeable than myself on the subject and I will withstand the torment of listening if it might help me save my Jezalinda.

"In deciphering the text, it's of my belief that explorative studies were being conducted against our knowledge. Experiments that focused around the drainage lines leading from nearby High Desert State Prison. Evidence shows that the constant flow of contamination excreted from inmate cells was carrying a strange and undocumented gene. Bear with the initial stupidity of this statement, but it's being proven in these texts that an 'evil' gene could enter a living entity's permeable exterior, such as that of the desert tarantula who often burrows their quarters inside those remote foothills."

I can accept the concept of a hidden gene being excreted from 'evil' beings. I can even humor the idea of this gene seeping through a tarantula's membrane. But if they expect me to believe that High Desert State Prison was caging criminally-prosecuted dinosaurs, then wrap me in a white restraint jacket and toss my body into a rubber room.

Despite the absurdity of these 'scientific' facts, I must continue listening for my beloved's sake.

"Furthermore, I believe that local researches integrated an extracted chromosome from a prehistorical excavation with that of our native tarantula. It stands to reason that when properly applied and with aid from external conditions, the creature that terrorizes us is entirely possible."

This time I nearly explode with undiluted anger. My normally calm demeanor erupts with a spewing volcano of criticisms. "Gee, Doctor, what makes you think it's possible? The fact that it smashes through our humble homes every night? Does that make it *entirely possible*?"

Rather than react, he maintains a collected disposition and sighs. "Young Steinbeck, I sympathize with your brazen efforts in wanting to retrieve Miss Jezalinda. Your actions are commendable – you've no shortage of courage. I myself routinely employed services from your girlfriend and can attest to her quality – it's the same quality that nobly flows through your blood. But you must understand. This monster, this…mutation, shouldn't fog your judgment. Perhaps this is all hogwash. Maybe genetic researchers locked away falsified, if not completely fabricated, documents to spare us the grisly truth. But this is all we have towards a direction. The creature has disabled our ill-prepared lines of communication. Outside entities will not be rendering aid. Therefore we must understand the monstrosity's origin with whatever resources become available – only then, do we stand a chance of stopping it."

In an instant, my emotional whirlwind slows to a gentle spin. "Forgive my rashness," I announce. "I just can't stand by idly knowing she's up there."

He frowns with acknowledgment. There's no convincing a twenty-year old tanner's apprentice that he can't successfully execute a task.

Love is stronger than fear…and often twice as foolish.

And while the concept of this crossbreed seems insane, the scientific community has long been blending the genetic structures of one species to another. We live in the ages where cloning other lifeforms has become a mundane topic, and where synthesizing human intelligence into the mind of sheep isn't a matter of possibility but of morality.

Is it really so unreasonable for researchers to attempt such a shameless experiment?

I've been caught up in the lineage of this creature's existence and have forgotten my primary purpose. It doesn't matter where it came from or how it was conceived. In this case, knowledge necessitates a plan of patience – but I must operate on blind rapidity; being swift is my only chance at sparing Jezalinda the horrors of being consumed.

The meeting continues but I deviate from its communal hearing. My needs are different from those who protect their loved ones. They can discuss defensive strategies until the impending attack actually comes but it won't yield results in my particular dilemma. Where they can stand ground in the fortified fortresses of remaining homes, my loved one already resides inside the cave's mouth – hopefully not in that of the creature's.

I navigate behind the podium, evading the cascading remnants of devoured appetizers. I must remain vigilant if I'm to avoid cranial collisions with the mayor's discarded corn cobs. For a man of power, he sure does have impulsive control issues. Obesity must be an issue of status – where the bigger the abdomen, the higher they climb on the social ladder; one would think they'd eventually snap an aluminum rung.

Ultimately, his accelerated consumption habits aren't of my concern.

After stepping into the murky concrete heaps of our former library, I thumb through the Dewey decimal system in search of tarantulas. Know thy enemy. Be swift, but be well-informed. According to the labeled cards, the edition of *WildLife* regarding spiders is located somewhere between the corpse of Mrs. Reese, librarian volunteer extraordinaire, and that of an upturned Ford Ranger that's replaced the public computer room.

My perpetual dig through various volumes of forgotten lore avails minimal prosperity. My graying fingers sift through the charred ashes of what's probably the remaining staff, desperately looking for more informative material than, "Crickets, the Thinking Man's Chirp."

Unless our Tarantulasaurus Rex breeds with a cricket, this burnt periodical will have little relevant information. Not to mention questioning the procedure for impregnation given the hybrid's endowment. On a more fortunate note, I do stumble across an issue of *Nature Weekly*, which by chance, features an article that explains incredible facts about tarantulas.

It really is quite the windfall.

Of note, females traditionally live longer than males. This of course, isn't of much concern being that the town's totality will be engorged upon matter of days, let alone years. Next, tarantulas tend not to bite humans, given the weak potency of their venom. In terms of toxicity, it doesn't warrant medical attention in the rare occurrence of a bite – regardless, I know another predator who does bite, a T-Rex! Moving forward in accordance, a tarantula actually defends itself by retrieving needle-like hairs from its abdomen and hurling them at potential enemies.

That immediately places the hostility level significantly higher. It would be as if nature allowed gorillas to pitch javelins. Whereby an already intimidating creature becomes even more dangerous. What were these genetic scientists thinking?

To my relief, the detailed article informs me that a tarantula's abdomen is the most vulnerable portion of their exoskeleton, therefore, teaching me where to strike should I face the mighty beast. Unfortunately, through the molting process, (where it can regenerate lost limbs), the maiming process isn't enough. To disable it won't stop the series of nightly rampages. Also of notable merit, tarantulas prefer to hunt their prey at night, creeping stealthily before pouncing – where, with each leg capable of using retractable claws, climbing redwoods has never been easier. Giving it an advantageous spot to leap from.

While this is all very interesting, and disturbing, I do find one shred of confidence-building material. Mere inches from being burned away, an unusual fact appears: even the slightest fall for a tarantula can be fatal, causing a rupture in the spider's exoskeleton – this is no doubt, the reason behind its impressive leg span: the largest species exhibiting the dimensions of a dinner plate. Enlarge its body by, oh, let's say...a thousand (that's a generously low estimate) and we're dealing with a fantastic animal that spews dread from every orifice. Combine that with the hunting fluency of an extinct carnivore, and we have a creature that should discourage me from futile searching.

Let's reevaluate my opponent for a moment: Canyon-stretching legs, hair-like projectiles, spinnerets capable of stringing endless amounts of silk, enhanced nocturnal vision, venomous due to proportion, fangs in conjunction with enormous teeth and the ability to climb trees.

Yes, it certainly does make the monster a daunting rival.

If I had any sense, I'd take cover under the nearest bridge and pretend I was homeless. Transients seem to survive the longest in most horror-genre cinematic tales – stereotypically, they're overlooked altogether. In many examples, the groups of dumpster dwelling degenerates are disregarded by an assortment of creatures: engineered sewer crocodiles, sludge monsters, even aliens, all seemingly ignoring the alley of vagrants while pursuing the story's protagonist.

I have the *grimy* part down being that available bathing water is in short supply – but I don't necessarily want the substance dependencies that are typically associated with chronic homelessness.

My only hope is, tripping-up the beast and hoping it falls on its stomach. Or avoiding it entirely. My skills in stealth are limited but they'll have to prevail. Because tonight, I'm going into its lair and retrieving what's mine. I just have to continue believing that she's alive. She must be. She always remarked upon her keen ability to 'spot a sting' so I'm assuming the needle-like projectiles won't affect her.

Interestingly enough, and in my favor, a tarantula's spinneret-generated silk isn't spun with the intent to capture prey; they use it merely as an alarm system: to alert them of potential predators or to signal that a meal is nearby.

Being that this Tarantulasaurus Rex is largely without a contender, preparation for a predator isn't required – therefore avoidance of its silky alarm must take precedence. Finally I know how Bilbo Baggins felt when preparing to sneak into Smaug's mountainous lair.

When leaving the library I'm joined by lifelong friend, Jeremy Knox.

"Jeremy! Over here, buddy!" I exclaim with jubilation, thrilled that he wasn't devoured in last night's raid. "You have no idea how excited I am that you weren't killed in the feedings."

He struggles to hike over the metal carnage of an annihilated school bus and rises to the top as victor. "Matt, is that you? You made it!" He elates, "You freakin' made it, buddy! I heard about your girlfriend – that's going to make Valentine's Day a difficult holiday to celebrate, what with you being alone and all. But don't worry, *we* can swap cards!"

My heart warms from his condolences. He never fails to uplift my spirits during periods of emotional turmoil – he's Vicodin for the soul.

Stumbling down the molten remnants of our past civilization, he embraces me with a hearty fist pound. It's our own unique way of displaying friendship – only the strongest of relationships are worthy of 'the bump'.

"Man, Matt, I seen your place and thought you were a goner. Did your parents make it?"

"Tragically, they were swept up in the initial surge," I reply sadly. In truth, I've been gainfully distracting myself from their absence. When the town is restored, life is going to be exceedingly difficult without them. Meal preparation and laundry services will have to be attained elsewhere; yet another reason I must retrieve Jezalinda! "I'm going in tonight, Jeremy," I state with a solemn gravity, giving no indication of the capacity to be reasoned with. "I'm going to save her. She means the world to me, and now, other than you…she's all I have."

"Had," he corrects. "You *had* her until the spider dino took her."

"Thank you," I express sincerely, fortunate to have a friend who will repair my poor use of grammar even in times of stress. I study his weathered appearance. Like myself, standing at six feet tall, his face is also smeared with the soot of memories past.

At some point he's managed to swipe one of Mr. Henry's vintage World War I commemorative rifles. They served the man as an artistic antique, displaying a tenacity for his fondness of firearms from the tomes of time. This, however, marks a day when the historical collectibles of yesterday become our primary tools of victory today. "Jeremy," I say aloud, "You have a rifle, I have a mission, what are you doing tonight?"

He actively navigates through an iPad's cracked screen and announces, "My calendar is pretty much free. I was going to rummage through Ted Lancer's garage and see if I couldn't pilfer any of his adult cassette tapes. Found an old VHS player in my grandmother's barn – was fixing on entertaining some company."

He shows me a screenshot of a should-be-mortally wounded Cassie Lake. Both arms have been amputated by our local veterinarian and thick bandages are covering surgical lacerations around her skull.

"She wouldn't be able to do much anyway," he says, "But she's always good for a listen."

I sigh with understanding – if my Jezalinda were here and not in the dark expanses of the creature's chasm, I too would relax under the glowing veil of an adult VHS tape. "Well my friend, I'm sorry but I must depart…There's work to be done and no time to waste. Your company has been most cheerful in a world that's enveloping gloom threatens to strangle."

Jeremy pauses with the brevity of thought and then exuberates, "Ya know what, buddy, I'm going to move my appointment with her to tomorrow. She's still technically comatose and her husband still doesn't recognize my position as the runner up lover should he be eaten. Tonight, I'm going to help you because, as a love-longing soul myself, I can spot genuine adoration. You have that ethereal gleam that travels alongside a relationship's sovereignty. Believe me, buddy, if she's alive, which I doubt, she's definitely waiting."

On some unlikely facet of life, I'd been blessed with an admirable friendship. His selfless service to my quest will never be forgotten. With him and me at the helm, this Tarantulasaurus Rex will never know what's coming… at least that's my hope.

Jeremy pauses moments into departure and questions with interest, "When we do get inside the cave, there's going to be a lot of people crying out for help, can we differentiate them from her?"

Actually, that's a valuable question. I never considered the proposition. With all the screaming and toiling, it'll be impossible weaving through them all without interference. "Well, Jeremy, from what I've heard, we are creatures of habit – we stick to routine affairs as a means of preventing change. Therefore, she'll likely be in the furthest part of its alcove; probably wedged deep inside a corner. She often said that her workplace was situated on the corner, of what corporate building I don't know, but it's safe to say that's where she'll be, tucked away in the corner."

"Works for me," he replies with satisfaction. "I'm really overjoyed that fate has aligned our paths. I wanted to talk to you about those recipe books my mother borrowed from yours. I guess she won't be needing them huh?"

I suppose she won't …

We get lost in idle conversation as we travel across the apocalyptic wasteland known as California's Highway 395. The black-topped road is riddled with monstrous indentations, appearing as if a giant were attempting to aerate it. In several of them we find indicators that the beast had used this route; mangy fibers of fuzz follicles, broken scales, needle-like hairs that have impaled an assortment of unsuspecting drivers, nothing unusual given the circumstances.

The mountain draws nearer with every fateful step.

Janesville's territorial boundary lays just *yonder*, a clodhopping term used by the locals to describe any particular segment of distance or direction. In our case, *yonder* is five miles away. With the sun beginning to set, we must make haste in our expeditionary movements before we're pinned out here during nightfall.

Judging from the dismembered bodies, turning that interesting shade of purplish-blue that correlates with every unattended death, this isn't the safest path to tread when the sun gives way to the dominance of darkness.

Still, we travel gaily, whistling tunes of forgotten times – kicking aluminum cans over the railroad tracks where heaps of digested bones would make passage for cargo trains rather inconvenient.

Between recitations of classics such as: Lollipop, Earth Angel, Hound Dog and Down With the Sickness, Jeremy glances toward me and says with an educated air, "Did you know that tarantulas actually belong to the family of spiders known as Hairy Mygalomorphs?"

"No, I didn't know that."

"Let's play the funny-word-when-used-entirely-out-of-context-game..." Before I can say game on, he chimes, "If my girlfriend Cassie had a Hairy Mygalomorph, I'd make her shave it or I would leave her."

For one, his girlfriend is somebody's wife, and two, "If my girlfriend Jezalinda had a Hairy Mygalomorph, I'd make her keep it, I like the natural look."

"Ewwwww!"

We laugh with the simultaneous splendor of two young men embarking upon a journey that will forever bind them in the tides of companionship. Never will life be the same.

As the sun sinks deeper into the mountainous horizon, granting way for the awakening of our insidious adversary, we stride toward Janesville's miniature food mart. It's the very convenient store that parallels 395 and marks our entrance into the town of Janesville – thus concluding that we have arrived at Thompson Peak's base.

The store, unlike its employees, remains virtually undisturbed save for the cavernous hole through the ceiling that's directly above the cash register's area – add commercial burglary to the monster's mounting infractions. When we approach the register, two blue-rotting hands lay upon the checkout keys. Tendrils of ligaments and tendons drape over the side, leading to a splatter-pattern circle of dried blood atop the cement flooring. The body itself remains a mystery as to where it went. Given the state of distress and recent attacks, it's fair to assume he's *checking out* the Tarantulasaurus Rex's stomach contents.

Jeremy, the genius that he is, uses the mostly missing employee's fingers to open the register.

"What are you doing?" I ask with a bewildered expression. "Why do you need money?"

He grins with all-knowing lips. "The County may be habitually attacked by a monster, but the rest of the world isn't. When this thing is finally brought down, money's still going to spend and I'm going to be seventy five dollars wealthier from it."

He makes an adequate point – stealing is against my moral code, but being that the creature has been the biggest thief of them all, I'm willing to overlook Jeremy's minor character flaw.

Hunkering down for a moment's rest, we both look out the storefront's massive window and watch the twilight of early dusk. The mountainous lair is precisely five miles up an ever-winding road, making foot travel a tedious task.

"Look what I found here," he says after twenty minutes of looting the convenient store for various *supplies* (amounting to a bag full of energy drinks and candy bars). "It's the shop attendant's car keys."

"How do you know?" I ask, seeing the blood-stained loop of keys.

Between the motor oil aisle and that of the boxed goods, he elevates the left thigh of a male gas station clerk. "Seems pretty fair in assessment, can't imagine this leg belonging to anybody else. I wouldn't expect somebody else to carry the building's keys. I think it will be more convenient to borrow his vehicle."

Unfortunately, I agree – it won't do the clerk much good; certainly not without a left leg to operate the clutch pedal. Now we have a *leg* up on our competition.

In the spirit of this untimely and remote apocalypse, Jeremy opens the refrigerating unit that holds alcoholic beverages, such as beer and boxed wines. "Since we're going into the mouth of the devil, we may as well indulge in his libations."

A focused mind and logical thoughts are what's needed for the success of this daring operation – but in light of the circumstances, I can't refuse. "All right, just one … we need our full level of thinking on this trip."

Several hours later we stumble through the abandoned aisles, flinging bags of individually packaged chips and guzzling 40 oz. bottles of anything considered 'illegal' by our age standards. I'm almost of the legal age, give or take several months … that's my justification at least.

We're like two tipsy kids in a candy store – where instead of consuming sugary 'delectables', we gulp down calorically dense splendors of the adult world, without heed towards moderation.

At one particular point Jeremy even wrestles with an industrial strength floor buffer and goes careening into an end cap of packaged cookies.

I can't help but state, "That's the way the cookie crumbles." Cliché, yes; corny, perhaps. But I'd rather he toss those cookies than have us toss ours.

Through our drunken merriment and overall conduct of

unruliness, we quickly neglect the fact that our mission is to take precedence and embrace the anarchy that only a monster's tirade can bring. 2 liter soda bottles are smashed without worry of cleanup or damage. Entire racks of cheap sunglasses are knocked over, (you know the kind: where they're purchased for 11.95 yet we tell our friends they're designer.)

The pointless demolition we cause is proof that somewhere in the land of monsters and myths, there exists somewhere in the middle, man. But we are of youth and an adolescent's mind will take advantage of chaos. A person wouldn't place two bulls in a red-colored 49ers stadium without expecting a little destruction.

So distracted we become by our own commotion that we don't instantaneously notice the ten massive eyes preying upon us through the building's damaged roof.

Jeremy, the first to notice, asks quietly, "Hey Matt, how many eyes did that magazine say a tarantula has?"

Trying to remember through this cloud of inebriation, I say with confidence, "I believe eight."

"And a Tyrannosaurus Rex?"

"That's common knowledge, Jeremy, two. Why do you ask such questions?"

He cautiously walks towards me and shows me his cracked iPad, previously set in 'selfie' mode. I see his grinning face from an upward angle, where above him stares a ten-eyed monster: Eight of these peering eyes are set in grotesquely unconventional locations, surrounding two centralized eyes that resemble a crocodile's. Hairy fangs protrude from the creature's lips, which are embedded with teeth resembling sabers.

I look up slowly. Its eyes, jaundice-yellow and terminally glowing, gaze down upon our merry transgressions. This hybrid, said to have been eliminated in the Cretaceous-Paleogene extinction event that caused the dinosaur's disappearance, stands ninety feet above us. But this version, this cross-species, is entirely different: hair like fibers mold into scales, covering its body. Its face, sculpted like a dinosaur's, with an elongated jaw, is fierce.

Upon our discovery of its interest in our activities, it hovers over the massive hole to reveal a tarantula-like body. Eight tremendous legs stretch over the expanse of store like a dome. Its hair-covered tail projects streams of silk into the night air as if for demonstration purposes only – as if to intimidate us.

Jeremy's first thought is to aim his rifle directly beneath the creature's underbelly. It's unlikely we will ever gain such an opportune positioning again. Not taking this shot would be like flying over Nagasaki and failing to detonate the atom bomb. Strategically, placement will never get better than this.

In a drunken stupor, induced by countless 24 oz. cans of high-gravity beer, he fires twice but doesn't even come close to his intended target – instead, he shoots out the remaining light fixtures on opposite ends of the hole.

I gaze at him with a profound look. "You mean to tell me, that with *it* only ten feet above, you miss twice?"

"Hey, Matt, I'm not a fighter okay? I'm more of the loving type." He admits, covering his pride's double folly, "It was bright, and I didn't want the lights to blind my third and final shot!"

Unfortunately for us, that shot will have to wait.

Provoked, long slivers of hair are flung toward our location. Several pierce through an adjacent table and embed themselves like giant quills, making the area look as if a porcupine exploded.

Together we sprint through the aisles, narrowly avoiding the onslaught of lined projectiles. If it wasn't for being startled and intoxicated, we may have exhibited the common sense to split our paths. Yet we continue running side by side until Jeremy climactically falls to the ground. His right knee scrapes against the polished cement floor and I watch the trail of hair-like projectiles lead towards his collapsed body.

"Go, Matthew, save yourself!" he exclaims. "If you're a coward that's what you'll do!"

By description of physical characteristics, I'm not what anybody would call 'hero potential'. But when my best friend is in peril, my relatively small frame takes on a rush of adrenaline that challenges even that of the attacking monster.

Quickly I grab him by the shoulder and pull him to his feet. His knees are scraped but no worse for the wear. He begins running towards the store's back end faster than I do. "Are you even injured?" I shout angrily, watching his athletic prowess come to life.

"No, I just wanted to see if you'd leave me!" He acknowledges while leaping into the emergency exit's narrow hallway. In turn, I leap with movielike agility and narrowly escape being impaled with arrow-like hairs.

Together we have two options when preparing the vehicle keys for use. We can wait until we're under an extreme time constraint outside, being chased by the Tarantulasaurus Rex. And fumble around with them near the truck. Or we can give ourselves easy access by readying them in the safety of this hallway.

"Let's go!" Jeremy shouts. "We can deal with those at the truck."

We crash through the rear exit into a littered back alley. Reeking dumpsters and empty bottles of miniature liquor shots line our path to freedom.

After dashing to the truck, lungs blazing and panic reaching at the furthest depths of our souls, Jeremy hurls the keys while stating, "You drive! I don't have my license on me!"

I can understand wanting to practice safe driving techniques and following all regulations of the roads, but that doesn't explain why he hurled them as if throwing a football. Forty yards away I dash towards the charging creature, dodging its preternatural javelins.

When my body slides over the keys, both of my legs seize as sharp claws dig in for keeps. The truck is so close yet I'm completely captured, pinned down by an animal twenty times my size.

Jeremy, displaying genuine heroics, leaps from behind the parked truck and runs down Highway 395 back toward Susanville.

My body forces me to turn and confront the opponent. I'll be damned if my end is met hiding in a pronated cower.

"Fine you cursed monster!" I shout, accepting my death by the claws of this formidable foe, "You win! Eat me already! You've taken everything else from me! My parents, my girlfriend and my best friend!" (Who technically fled but that's irrelevant).

A long, stretching leg looms from behind me and deploys its specialized pincers. As I struggle, the pinching claws grab ahold of my undergarment's elastic band. Only when it lifts me towards a level view of its eyes do I wish I hadn't worn a red thong tonight – poor planning on my part: then again, I didn't quite suspect I'd be given a wedgie by a cross-genetic spider lizard.

"Do your worst!" I spit, dangling from its grip, the T- like backing of my unmentionables pulled skyward.

Ten intermittently blinking eyes study me. They seem to know that I'm not afraid of it.

"Come on! Kill me already!" I curse, watching its unbelievable flinch of grief, as if my insults hurt its esteem.

Then, despite all that's contrary to this creature's makeup, I witness sadness in these round, starring yellow mirrors. There's a sense of hurting, of longing. Call me absolutely crazy, but I sense loneliness – the same I often express when left without my Jezalinda.

My inner-fight ceases as I'm suspended without struggle, "You don't want to hurt me do you?"

Something inside of me relates to this monster, sympathizes if you will. It lowers me to the oil-stained asphalt and continues starring.

Against reason, I reach out to touch the monster's fuzzy, scaly leg. It recoils but inevitably allows my caress. "You must get lonely up there in the mountain huh?" I question, unknowing if the creature's capable of comprehending human conversation.

Without speaking, obviously, it leans down and nudges me in the abdomen with one of its furry fangs. It's not a piercing push nor one that's aimed at spearing, but a playful one – like when a cat bumps into your feet.

I'm completely baffled – this whole time, my impression of the Tarantulasaurus Rex has been eschewed. The town's people fear it, even abhor its presence, boiling in a culvert of bubbling hatred … yet never once have we considered how this isolated monster feels? What is *its* emotional state?

Its bizarrely timed affection causes me conflicting thoughts: on one hand, it destroyed everything I held dear. But on the other, it seems to take comfort from my accompaniment. Am I betraying my family and friends by taking comfort in its? Shouldn't I vow for vengeance, sinking a stake into its abdomen at the first chance?

Revenge, or compassion – retaliation, or adoration?

I consider the possibilities before coming upon an enlightening revelation: What exactly is a ten-thousand pound, ninety-foot tall Tarantulasaurus Rex supposed to do? It was engineered, by the very species it terrorizes, to be a tyrant. The name Tyrannosaurus Rex in Greek means Tyrant Lizard – combine that with the animal kingdom's largest spider and what was supposed to happen? Surely it wasn't designed to be somebody's harmless pet. It was constructed to kill, to eat and to survive.

Still, I have to voice aloud my inner-doubts. "Tranchy," I call him/her by this more personalized salutation instead of *beast* or *monster*, "Everything inside me wants to fully sympathize with your creation but you took my mother and father – you stole my Jezalinda."

The Creation blinks towards me with resound compassion, as if it, against all odds, cares about me.

Tears begin streaming from my eyes, torn between what is right and what is wrong – a portion of me feels as if I'm collaborating with the enemy; yet a larger portion feels that by condemning this being's friendship I would be reflecting the inhumanity it's been shown thus far. I may be mankind's only hope of understanding this beautiful Creation's heart – maybe even its soul.

Upon looking up, I can actually detect pain in its perpetually blinking eyes; each closing at different rates to create an alternating pattern. When it arches eight legs in order to crouch, a long tongue retracts and I stand not in terror, but in anticipation when it licks my arm. A layer of green slime, viscous and gelatinous, covers the wholeness of my hand.

Some would exclaim, "Gross!" but it's really no different than when a canine licks its owner. It's merely a display of affection given from one species to another.

As if analyzing, Tranchy lifts me atop its fuzz-covered, scaly head and begins crawling up the mountain at supernatural speeds. Tree tops brush its underside as if the tallest are but a bump in its path. What should take hours to scale the summit takes us only two minutes. Both of my clenched fists are forced to wrap around an improvised mane in order to keep from falling into the rocky canyons below. Though I don't think this increasingly gentle Creation would allow for that to occur.

Upon reaching the top, Tranchy permits me to dismount before entering his enormous cave. This subterranean mouth is colossal, with stalagmite teeth descending from the top, nocturnal bats flapping around above. Piles of skeletons litter the entrance's rocky bottom; some decaying, some decomposed, and most literally stripped to the bone. Though horrifying, something tells me this Creation hasn't harmed my beloved Jezalinda.

Memories of her warm embrace flood through the overflowing rivers of my mind. One such memory comes to life before my thoughts: it was a hot summer day, therefore my beautiful girlfriend went to work wearing a form-fitting top and bikini bottoms – that summer she had been some sort of a telecommunication operator because she maintained a work area within close proximity to a payphone; I believe her official title was a call girl, so it makes sense to be near an outdoor phone. I had driven up and handed her a home cooked meal through my window. She was extremely appreciative even though her boss ran up and said, *"Are you blind? This piece don't work for food."* Ah, those were the days of our early romance. She must've excelled to be titled as a *piece*. He was probably referring to a 'timepiece' or a real 'piece' of extravagance.

Yes, she was my piece. Hopefully she'll bring me peace if still alive.

Tranchy urges me along, waiting for me to follow in its precise steps so as not to get strung up in large threads of silk.

Upon entrance, the walls are covered in strung bones, white synthetic ropes from the Creation's spinnerets holding them as decoration. Surprisingly, there's minimal blood spilled about the cave flooring but I suspect that Tranchy uses it all for nutrients – it's a beautifully large being and undoubtedly has a large appetite – one third of Susanville could attest to that, if they could speak as the digestive waste of their consumer of course.

I'm guided through the underground tomb. Snowy, silky cocoons hang from the ceiling like strings of decoration – resembling ivory-colored Christmas lights used during seasonal celebrations. Each pulsates slightly, indicating that there's life behind each body tight prisons.

Any one could be that of my dear Jezalinda, or my parents if we get around to it.

When we approach a dark corner, presumably where my Sweetheart is located, Tranchy beckons for me to stop. At this point, I'm guided only by touch and cling to its leg for navigation. The lightlessness is unbearable – but for a large Creation like this one, it's the perfect burrow for safekeeping.

Tranchy lowers its glowing yellow eyes, no longer snarling as I once envisioned it but expressing an unmistaken appearance of regret, as if warning me. "What is it Tranchy?" I question, "What's wrong? Is there something you don't want me to see?"

All eyes light up as a response that's indicative of confirmation.

Still I pursue, "Show me Tranchy, please, I must know."

The structurally sound Creation reaches towards the ceiling with one of its left legs, retrieving a strung white bundle.

Only when the cocoon is placed alongside my feet can I see it with Tranchy's illuminating eyes. There she is, Jezalinda … alive and well apparently.

Her golden-haired head is uncovered – unfortunately, so is his.

She's been cheating on me since the abduction – this is what my newfound friend, Tranchy, didn't want me to see.

"I came, despite inherent danger, and this is how I find you?" I begin feeling every emotion associated with betrayal, "In the arms of another, lips locked with those of Pizza Rally's delivery boy?"

She glances skyward, shocked by my presence. Rather than question how I've come to endeavor this distance and befriend 'the beast', she says dryly, "Sorry, in so many words, I've become *hung* up with him." I'll give her credit on the clever use of words but nothing more.

"You have betrayed me, Jezalinda – you've broken my heart." Once again tears begin leaking from my very soul. "I loved you."

"Matthew you don't understand!" she claims between kisses with Ronald Hagermath, the pimple-faced arm candy of Janesville's greasiest pizza company. "This isn't what you think…I realized you would rescue me and I knew we'd need a new start – I'm only with him for the money."

For the money? Why could being with another individual produce financial gains?

Suddenly it makes sense.

I've been naïve for so long: the unaccounted hours of absence, the sweat-soaked tank tops upon arrival, disheveled hair and always having loose bills. "Jezalinda, I know what you've been doing! Making money on 'tips' huh? You're … you're … you're a delivery girl! For Pizza Rally!"

Her questioning eyes look up toward mine. "Uh, sure. That's exactly what I am."

Today I have finally lost everything. A childhood friend. Parents. A home. And now, my girlfriend.

"Goodbye, Jezalinda," I say with grief.

My emotional aura signals Tranchy to respond to my distress and it pierces the betraying Jezalinda through the heart with both fangs. I watch as her life drains away; years of love, thrown away for this well-to-do young stud.

Tranchy does for me what nobody ever could. It showed me what my girlfriend was really about.

When she's sucked dry of her deceitful blood, I gain a sense of strange satisfaction. I somehow knew that her blood was tainted – with all of her claims that it was H-Ivy positive – any woman who has plant toxins coursing through her veins surely must be poisonous … not so much as to deter Tranchy.

Under the commotion of flesh being eaten, I hear Ronald Hagermath's squeaky voice of manliness. "Does this mean I won't have to pay her?"

With only my nod, Tranchy does the same to him – Her infidelity will be forever remembered by their discarded remains here in the dark corner; exactly where she belongs.

Unaware to even myself, a grappling emotion takes over my body and I reach to hug Tranchy's powerful leg, "For the last three days I've fallen for the deception that you were evil – and as it turns out, you're my best friend."

In a world where a man has almost nothing – he can find genuine solace in the heart of a scientific Creation gone terribly right.

Some call it a derivative of Stockholm syndrome, where an abducted person can actually learn to rely upon their captor, but I call it true love. In the face of treachery, the terrorizer in this case wasn't who I thought it would be.

"Please take me to the gas station," I say with a saddened sense of relief, "I need a drink and you can pick me up on your way back from town. We'll hang out tonight, buddy."

With nowhere to go, the small town gas station, source of my short-lived merriment, will be my transitional estate between visiting my only friend. I will find everlasting comfort in seeing the bones of Jezalinda stacked atop all of those whom she probably served in the past – rumor has it, she's served many of Susanville's residents … a delivery girl all this time and I was too blind to see it.

When Tranchy guides me out of the cave, careful not to crush me in the process, we both hear the sound of engines roaring up the steep grade.

"What on Earth is that?" I shout with alarm, fearing for my newfound friend's safety. "Tranchy, somebody's coming. They're coming for you!"

It pushes me to the rear with a fur-covered leg. My heart is touched by the endearing display of protection but the impending trouble won't stop unless I obstruct advancement – my only chance will be by explaining Tranchy's gentle nature and that it can be nurtured without violence or death.

Nobody would amass in vehicular procession and travel up the near vertical slope just for a sightseeing trip – these people, barreling upward, maybe by the tens maybe by the hundreds, mean absolute destruction for my friend.

But why now? How have they accumulated the courage to initiate a counterattack?

The town's people must've learned of a weakness – it's unusual for them to rise above the safety of their fortifications and mount a retributory strike.

How can they have summoned the intestinal fortitude? What manner of information has given them the freedom to strike? What weakness have they discovered?

Then it hits me like the Titanic hit an iceberg ... Jeremy.

He must've hitched a ride back into town and informed them of what I learned about tarantulas – exposing their vulnerability.

Seven trucks roar to an idling halt when merely one hundred yards away from Tranchy and myself. Each is manned with four shotgun-toting hillbillies and large, front mounted pipes that have been ground into spears.

They're going to harpoon Tranchy, skewering my friend in its singular place of susceptibility.

Spearheading this assault is no other than Jeremy. "I'm coming, buddy!" He rumbles through the midnight air. Revving engines sound as a precursor to battle, like the insistent drumming of warring tribes.

"No!" I scream. "You don't understand! It isn't evil!" My flailing arms appear only as a signal of distress.

When I begin dashing forward, weaving between eight massive legs, Tranchy pushes me to the rear once again. He/she doesn't want me in harm's way.

Against my pleas, Tranchy initiates the charge and the trucks respond accordingly. This is a classic example of adopting a ram's style of fighting – head on and full force.

"No, Tranchy! They'll kill you!" I beg, watching my friend stampede towards the trucks, utilizing only a fraction of its true speed.

Missiles of blade-sharp hairs are slung in volleys. Two of the badly welded trucks are hit in the tires and begin a long voyage down the mountain head-over-head.

Jeremy's crew leads the incoming convoy – spitting bullets of every caliber. Each direct shot serves only to enhance my new friend's rage.

Aggression ignites an inner fire inside Tranchy. Moments before they make impact, shrieks of pain resonate through the mayhem's clamor.

My pain ...

A stray bullet has lodged its way into my chest cavity, barely avoiding the puncture of my vital organs.

Tranchy stalls for a rearward glance, ever-protective of my well-being.

My tears are not of pain but of grief when I watch the beautiful Creation stutter into an earth-shattering fall. Its softer underbelly is bayoneted by the improvised lance mounted on Jeremy's vehicle. The truck is forced to a screeching halt and its members are ejected from their seats into the night sky – like pole vaulters without the volunteered leap.

Overhead, I stare wildly as Jeremy's body glides toward a pile of jagged rocks.

His words will be immortalized in the tribute of my mind. "Sorry, buddy! I should tell you it took ten allowances to hire Jezalinda's services too!" Then he's splattered onto the side of a particularly craggy rock formation.

In life he wasn't much to admire, but in death, his straightforward confession is praiseworthy. She must've served him a helluva pizza for the price of ten allowances.

My legs can't carry me fast enough to the scene of carnage – metal components mesh with living tissue. Blood, gasoline and oil mix together to create red-tinged grease spots. This ordeal only demonstrates the necessity for proper application of safety restraint systems; nobody was wearing their seat belt.

Them, I care little about: not the mayor who technically died from choking on a chicken bone. Not the doctor/psychologist/veterinarian who helped forge the assault. Not even of the seven lifelong acquaintances that paralleled my growth throughout childhood.

What does concern me is Tranchy. "No," I cry in despair, caressing its leg as if it'll restore vitality to a dying energy, "Don't let this be so! Not like this! Not now!"

It blinks in its normal intermittent pattern, starring at my harrowing accompaniment with softened eyes. If it could form perceptible words I know it would say, *"You so quickly became my friend in life, during my dying breaths you remain as such."*

To think, Jeremy and I were raised as neighbors, spending every waking hour learning of each other's interests, caring for one another, and yet when embarking upon his great journey in the sky, I don't pain for his loss – yet with Tranchy, in a matter of minutes we became impossible friends; where its death will hollow an emptiness into my heart that nothing will ever fill.

I reach out to touch its hairy fang. "Go to a better place Tranchy, filled with unending amounts of people to trample on. No matter how short of a period we knew each other, I will always love you."

Each eye blinks successively until only one more remains open. With every bit of conjured strength, its arching leg creeps over and the tip places a mild amount of pressure against my outstretched knuckles – a farewell fist bump from two unlikely friends.

The light goes out in its eye and I close its eyelid laboriously; we'll call it a labor.

With the rain theatrically extinguishing the flames of this vehicular massacre – of this senseless bloodshed, I look up to the heavens and exclaim, "Why? Why take this loving Creation?"

In the land of monsters and myths, there exists somewhere in the middle, a creature known as man.

Upon final consideration, I ask myself who the real monsters were in this epic ordeal. Was it Jezalinda for her hidden *trick*eries against my heart? Was it Jeremy who betrayed my trust and friendship? Or was it a town in crisis, clenching to the fabric of conceptual victory?

The answer my dear friends is ... well, it's still Tranchy for terrorizing and rampaging the town.

Yet, in that cave, if an adventurous individual were to explore the furthest recesses of its hidden world, there waits an egg ... this of course is a metaphorical egg and has absolutely no capability of hatching an offspring for a sequel story – but an egg of concept, regarding a young man and his Tarantulasaurus Rex.

The Shark That Ate Everything

Amber Fallon

The global warming alarmists warned us of the damage we were doing to the planet and the dire consequences that would result, but they never said anything about the sharks…

The first incident was just off the coast of Barrow, Alaska. Some Undiscovered Channel nature documentary was filming a pod of killer whales for one of their *Predators of the Sea* specials. I don't remember which one it was, exactly, but that isn't important. What's important is what they caught on camera.

The narrator/host of the show, some famous Brit, was going on and on about the mating rituals of orca while his crew filmed several angles of the animals in the ocean below from their special camera-equipped helicopter when one of the cameramen cried out "HOLY FUCKING SHIT! WHAT THE FUCK IS THAT?!"

At first, the host looks annoyed that one of his crewmen has ruined the take, and then he looks down. His eyes open so wide that even watching the video is enough to cause sympathy pains. His wrinkled hand goes to his mouth. "God save us," he mutters.

Thankfully, the cameraman (the one who did the initial swearing, I think) had the presence of mind to keep filming, but even if he hadn't, one of the robotic cameras on the outside of the helicopter would've caught at least some of the action on film.

The scene starts out exactly like you'd expect; five or six of the black and white whales swimming together in a pack, occasionally breaking the surface with their majestic fins pointing skyward. Then the ocean just beyond them darkens, almost like a shadow was passing over it.

For a second or two, it looks like a large cloud moved in front of the sun or something, no big deal. But then the whales make a sharp turn away from the shadow, towards land, which is completely uncharacteristic of them. The shadow darkens. One of the whales is a little slower than the others; it lags a bit as the pack surges forward.

Suddenly an enormous creature emerges from the shadow – no, it *is* the shadow! A set of impossibly large jaws filled with teeth that must easily be two or three feet long clamps around the whale, biting it in half.

"What the fuck was that?" someone asks.

"Did that thing just eat a fucking killer whale?" asks someone else as the shadow recedes once more into the depths of the ocean, leaving bloody water and bits of whale backwash in its wake.

The video of course went viral, but there were too many detractors, too many people insisting it was fake for anyone to pay much notice. Until the next time the creature surfaced.

About a week after the first sighting of the creature up near Alaska, a group of 'disaster tourists' had just disembarked from their medium sized luxury boat, *The Intrepid,* and were making their way inland along what used to be Route 11 just outside of Volcanoes National Park near Hilo, Hawaii.

Disaster tourism had become something of a pastime for the rich, those unimpacted by the rising of the oceans, and there were plenty of desperate residents of Hawaii, California, what remained of Florida, and other affected states that were only too happy to oblige the whims of the elite by taking them on tours of their own flooded homes, some of those tour guides still living in them despite the risks. It was sad and awful but at the same time, it was a living.

There were seven tourists in all, led by a husband and wife team of tour guides who had lived on the island all their lives. They pointed out landmarks as they went and talked about the native wildlife. It's amazing how much life changed when the oceans really started to rise. Less than a foot of water had displaced hundreds of thousands of people, practically destroyed the economy of dozens of countries, depleted the food supply, killed thousands of people and animals, and created the perfect conditions to spread disease to anyone close enough. And it was about to get a whole lot worse.

As you might expect, the tourists all had their smartphones out and were snapping pictures all over the place; resorts in the distance that had been rendered useless and uninhabitable after a foot of water took over the first floor, submerged roads, signs, debris and other artifacts of the island's previous life, a few of them even took shots of bloated corpses, human and animal, as they floated by. The water was only up to everyone's knees at best and they were all wearing fishing waders, but still. It was worrying how few of them seemed to care about the death and disease all around them, like they were insulated from it or protected somehow, just because they had enough money to move further inland as the oceans encroached.

One of the guides turned back towards the ocean and the boat, which had been anchored a mile off shore so it wouldn't scrape up the hull on what used to be the beach. The little motorboat they'd taken ashore was tied to a pair of palm trees off to the side.

The guide was herding her group of tourists, making sure no one fell too far behind. She was in the middle of explaining to an older gentleman and his female companion that taking selfies with a bloated corpse wasn't a good idea when something caught her attention. She stopped mid-sentence, mouth agape, as the largest shark she had ever seen – wait, that couldn't be a shark, could it? No shark was that big! – surfaced underneath *The Intrepid* and bit the front half of the vessel clean off. Four of the tourists took pictures, capturing the terrifying creature in all of its awful glory. Two of them took video. One managed to capture the entire event. With so many eye witness accounts, so much photographic evidence, it was much harder to deny the existence of the monster shark this time.

It wasn't long before the scientific community caught wind of the gigantic shark sightings and became interested enough to tear themselves away from efforts related to global warming and the rising seas. As it turns out, though, the two were actually related.

It seemed like the entire world, suffering though it was, stopped and turned its collective attention away from the heat, humidity, and the rising ocean level and towards the gigantic shark/creature. Those naval vessels left in operation began patrolling the areas where it had been sighted, looking for any trace of the massive beast. Everyone anywhere near the coast kept their eyes peeled for an enormous fin or monstrous head or tail appearing from beneath the waves. Politicians and government officials of all sorts began offering bounties on the thing (although it wasn't exactly like anything short of a nuke would be able to take out a being of that size, at least the people were reassured that SOMETHING was being done about the threat). Some industrious entrepreneurs began printing t-shirts and hats with slogans like "I survived MONSTER SHARK!" and a silly caricature of the massive animal. The whole world watched as the attacks continued, and as the unforeseen side effects of introducing a monstrous predator into the already fragile, damaged ocean ecosystem presented themselves.

What happens to an alpha predator like, say, a great white shark, when it's no longer the big fish, so to speak? When a bigger, badder fish invades its territory, maybe even decides that ol' greaty looks like a nice snack?

I'll tell you what, because I saw it first hand: The entire prey/predator table shifts drastically and sharks start appearing in places they shouldn't. Places like home.

Venice was the site of the first disaster. As a city already besieged by some of the worst flooding, due to the waterways, and worst contamination, due to the pollution and garbage already prevalent in said waterways, Venice was hardly prepared for yet another blow when it came. And it came, all right. In the form of an influx of sharks.

Now I'm not talking about that great mythic shark, I mean the *other* sharks. The ones he or she had displaced from their standing on the food chain. Everything from threshers and hammerheads to nurse sharks and, yes, even a great white or two found their way into Venice proper. And once inside the city, they did what came natural to them; they hunted and they ate. Anything and everything they could get their pointy little teeth into was on the menu: humans, pets like dogs and cats, even other sharks. The waters of Venice ran red with blood and video of the carnage flooded the remaining news outlets much the same way.

It wasn't long, though, before attention turned away from Venice. A bigger story had broken out to the north.

A Russian research sub had located the colossal shark just south of the Arctic Circle and of course, they had gone to investigate. The foolhardy investigators never stood a chance, even if their sub had been equipped with weaponry of any kind. The shark swallowed the vessel whole. The crew continued broadcasting for nearly nine hours after they'd been eaten. But before the transmissions ceased, they had revealed the awful truth about our enormous new attraction's origin ... and its friends.

The Russians hadn't originally been looking for the shark, surprisingly. They were actually gathering samples of ice from the underside of a great glacier, trying to do futile research on the whole global warming thing. How passé.

What they'd found in that glacier wasn't an answer to the melting of the polar ice caps, however. It was a hole. A hole just a little bit bigger than the enormous shark that had been causing all the trouble.

And it wasn't alone. There were three more holes of a similar size and shape nearby, of which one was still occupied.

The grainy submarine camera footage clearly shows an enormous, shadowy shape encased within the ice. The ship moves closer, the dark shape taking up almost the entire frame, and then the shape *moves.*

It shifts within the ice, giving a shuddering little jerk not unlike a chick hatching from an egg. A few minutes and several more tremory little convulsions later, chunks of ice larger than the submarine itself start to break free, releasing that enormous beast into the water, directly in front of the sub.

Now, I imagine that being trapped inside a giant chunk of ice for thousands and thousands of years might make you hungry. I don't know personally, but I think it's a pretty safe bet. So it was hardly a shocker when the shark opened up a mouth easily the size of an airplane hangar and just sort of engulfed the submarine, crew and all.

They were absolutely terrified. I don't speak Russian, but that was evident from the gasps and panicked screams that could clearly be heard over this odd throbbing sound on the video. Eventually, after several viewings, I realized that the throbbing sound was the creature's heart beating in its cavernous chest. Yikes.

If you watch all nine hours of the footage, you'll see that the crew eventually gets bored before going totally batshit crazy. I guess I would lose my marbles, too.

The shark attacks – regular sharks, I mean, not the giant ones – continued. The new coastal regions – places like central Pennsylvania, West Virginia, and Arkansas – had it bad enough with all the plague-carrying dead bodies floating around and the flooding and all, but after wave upon wave of hungry, terrified predators began showing up, things went from bad to worse to fucking nightmare level real quick.

News outlets started disappearing one by one as the waters began to rise more rapidly. You see, those giant sharks escaping their icy containment had broken at least one MAJOR glacier into smaller chunks, and smaller chunks of ice melt faster than large ones. Something about having more surface area, I think. I don't know, thermodynamics was never really my thing. Maybe the oceans were just warming up faster than predicted. Whatever the case, the sea continued to eat up the land like that giant shark had eaten up that killer whale in its first appearance. It was closing in faster than we could evacuate, even if there was anywhere left to evacuate to.

The news outlets might have been just about the only thing on earth that was drying up. Print and television ones, anyway. But the internet was alive and well. Plenty of people lost power as the nearest power plants became flooded, but as long as they had a charge on their smartphones or at least a spare battery, they could still watch videos of people being eaten by sharks big and small all over the world.

The next sighting of one of the mammoth sharks was off the coast of what remained of Northern Texas. An offshore oil rig that had been converted to hold refugees, but was abandoned when the waters overtook it, somehow still had working security cameras. Maybe they were special because the rig they were monitoring was out in the ocean, I don't know. What I do know is that those cameras picked up something big, and I mean BIG, headed inland towards the U.S. As soon as someone reviewed the tape and saw what was headed for us, helicopters were dispatched.

The choppers flew for miles before they found anything unusual. Unless you counted the bloated corpses of the former inhabitants of the Frank Buck Zoo in Gainesville, Texas as unusual. Perhaps the helicopters should have stayed at a higher altitude instead of dipping down to investigate the bodies of giraffes and rhinos. After all, sharks are attracted by the scent of death. Or so I've been told.

At any rate, the helicopters were all equipped with gyroscopic cameras. One or the other of them must've decided to get closer to the corpses for a better look, or maybe they saw something or someone worth rescuing. Whatever the reason, one helicopter in specific sunk very low, the dead animals floating in the ocean beneath it coming into stark detailed clarity as the wind from the blades whipped the water into a foamy froth the shape of a circle around them. Maybe that's what did it. Sharks are attracted to movement like splashing water, aren't they?

The helicopter zooms in on the body of a dead lion for some reason and you're so focused on that that you fail to notice the enormous black shadow beneath it. There's a second, maybe less, to react before an unfathomably large mouth appears, growing quickly larger, until it fills the entire frame, then static.

The film from the cameras on the other choppers is just as dramatic. In it, you see that lone red helicopter swoop gracefully towards the decomposing lion and then hover there like a red and white hummingbird. That shadow appears, faint at first, then darkening moments before that monumental creature, that ancient and savage beast, leaps from the water and swallows it in one bite.

I'd like to tell you more, but that's the last news story I saw. The power went out here last night and my cell phone died not long after. I wanted to write all of this down in case anyone survives, so they'll know what happened to us. Sharpies are waterproof, right? And it's not like anyone is going to care if I vandalize the gym wall of a high school in Barton County, Kansas, anyway. Everyone here has bigger problems to worry about.

Like the sharks I saw swimming down what used to be Main Street not too long ago.

But I guess that's okay. It's their home now.

Falling Stars

Jonah Buck

"Hi, I'm Sylvia, and I'm a wereshark."

"Hi, Sylvia," the other members of Shifters Anonymous said in unison. They opened every weekly meeting with the little ritual of stating their name and shifter identity. It helped build a sense of openness and community.

Ever since Sylvia took over as the head of the local Chicago branch of Shifters Anonymous, she'd worked on giving members a sense of belonging to something. Some members, especially the lycanthropes, really needed to belong to a pack to feel comfortable.

Everyone sat in a circle in the middle of the room. The space had been a dance studio before Sylvia started renting it for the meetings. The rest of the Mickelthorpe Building housed offices for second-rate lawyers, radio repairmen, and a florist.

A table sat in front of the window. Earlier, Sylvia had set out a couple of pitchers of cool lemonade as well as a platter of crackers, meats, and cheeses. The meats were all gone. Most of the crackers and cheese lay undisturbed.

Outside the window, the bustle of downtown Chicago flowed past. Horns honked. People hustled in and out of the Attican Detective Agency building across the street. Newsies hawked the latest edition of the day's paper, the Washington Park Beast still the top headline.

It was the week before the full moon, their most important meeting of the month. Everyone felt the most anxious around this time and needed the most support. Some of the newest members didn't know how to handle the shift yet and needed extra care until they learned how to cope with the changes in their lives.

And with news of the Beast still in the public's mind, men with hard faces and briefcases full of holy water, silver bullets, and blessed artifacts were almost certainly prowling Chicago already. The members of Shifters Anonymous were nervous, and rightly so.

"It's been a pretty good week for me," Sylvia said. "I got a promotion at the shirt factory, and in a couple of days it will officially be seven years since I mauled any swimmers to death."

Scattered applause followed. This too was part of the ritual. Everyone shared their successes and failures since the last meeting. Sylvia had learned the hard way that it was important to enforce openness among the group.

If someone was quietly losing control, and no one noticed, the results could be disastrous. People had fallen off the wagon before and gone completely feral. The resulting deaths always brought professional monster hunters to town, and their community suffered when that happened. Her predecessor hadn't enforced the rules as strictly, and he and half the other shifters in Chicago caught a silver bullet because of it.

"I don't have a whole lot else to report, so I'm going to grab a seat and turn the floor over to all of you," she said.

Suddenly, there was a knock at the door. Sylvia twisted around, unsure she'd heard anything at first. The knock came again, hesitant and timid. She walked over to the door and pressed her eye to the peep hole.

A young blond woman stood on the other side of the door, uncertainty etched across her pretty features. She clutched her purse against the front of her dress, looking as if she was trying to decide whether or not to bolt.

Sylvia undid the deadbolts keeping the door closed. There were four of them. The door also had a solid steel core hidden under the cheap wood finish. She didn't unlatch the security chain, which was thick enough to serve as the anchor line for a small boat, but she opened the door a crack.

"Can I help you?" Sylvia asked. She didn't recognize the blond woman, and that was always dangerous. Society had hunted shifters down until they only lived in the shadows. As far as most of the industrial world was concerned, they were just myths to frighten naughty children. That didn't mean there weren't still plenty of dangers out there, though.

"I ... I hope so," the woman stammered. She didn't act like a fearless werewolf hunter, here to slaughter them all in cold blood, but that didn't necessarily mean anything. "May I come in?"

"Just a moment," Sylvia said. She took a deep whiff of the air in the hallway, testing it. During the full moon, she could smell the mice nesting in her neighbors' attic. Hell, as a wereshark, she could sense the electrical fields living creatures gave off. In her day-to-day life, she didn't have any special senses. But she didn't need them right now.

The woman was wearing a lot of perfume, but it couldn't completely mask a heavy, musky smell. All shifters had a deep and often offensive bodily funk. There was no getting rid of it. A scented bath might whisk some of the odor away for an hour, but a certain level always remained.

Sylvia knew what most of her community smelled like. The pack of werewolves always smelled like wet dog, no matter what. Depending on what they shifted to, some members of Shifters Anonymous smelled earthy or briny or even like rotten eggs.

She didn't recognize the smell on this woman, though. Under her perfume, the petite blond smelled like rotting meat and burnt ozone and something Sylvia couldn't quite put her finger on.

Still, it was enough to convince her to undo the security chain on the door. The woman was definitely one of them, even if she wasn't like anything else in their little community. "Please, come on it. It's always nice to welcome a new face. There's lemonade and some cheese and crackers, if you'd like. What's your name?"

"I'm Rosemary. Thank you, but I'm all right. Listen, I think I need help."

Sylvia took the young woman by the shoulder and guided her toward the circle. "So do we all. Here, come sit next to me over here. I'll show you how we do things, and then you can introduce yourself to the group."

"But–"

"Over here, Rosemary." Sylvia didn't want to derail the meeting. New people always brought drama, and they didn't need a major disruption right at the beginning of their meeting. Even if she was a wereshark, sometimes she needed to be the pack leader if she wanted things to run smoothly. Showing Rosemary a calm, structured environment full of people with the same sorts of problems would probably do a lot to unknot her emotions.

Everyone came in confused and alone, convinced that their problems were unique and unsolvable. This new one would be the same. If she had to, Sylvia could schedule some one-on-one time with her before the full moon at the end of the week. She remembered the nervousness and discomfort of coming to her own first meeting.

The session continued as planned. They went around the circle, discussing problems and achievements. Sylvia had to push the conversation along a couple of times to steer some of the more chatter-prone members.

Beside her, the new woman fidgeted and squirmed the entire time. The poor thing. She must have butterflies careening around her stomach like barnstorming stunt pilots. As the meeting went on, Rosemary only seemed to become more agitated, not less. Outside, the sky started to tinge red as sunset drew closer.

Sylvia was trying to urge the meeting along when Rosemary stood up. "I can't wait any longer. I'm going to transform tonight, and I don't have anywhere to go. You have to help me."

A second of confused silence hung over the group.

"Tonight? The full moon isn't for another week," Sylvia said.

"I don't transform with the full moon," Rosemary responded. Flustered, she reached into her purse and pulled out a copy of the morning's paper. She ripped it open to the seventh page, well past the furor given to the Washington Park Beast, and pointed to a short article. It was little more than a stub.

Amateur Astronomers Excited for Pons-Winnicke Comet. The paper only spared a couple of paragraphs on the minor celestial event. Like its more famous cousin, Halley's Comet, the Pons-Winnicke Comet passed by the earth every few decades. Unlike Halley's Comet, the Pons-Winnicke would be little more than a smudge of light in the night sky. Anyone who wanted to view it with any detail would need a telescope.

"I don't understand," Sylvia said.

"The full moon doesn't have any effect on me. Meteors, asteroids, any significant space debris. That's what causes me to change. It's going to happen tonight with this comet." Rosemary's voice cracked as she spoke.

"Okay, okay," Sylvia said, trying to calm Rosemary. The young woman was shaking, and Sylvia put an arm around her shoulders. "I believe you. I've just never heard of this before. This is all brand new to me. Let's start from the beginning. What do you shift to when these conditions are happening?"

Sylvia's mind whirred. She'd heard of ... anomalies before from other Shifter Anonymous groups spread around the country. One man in Los Angeles vanished altogether on nights when there was no moon, reappearing in the morning with no memory of what happened. There was a woman in Memphis who shifted during solar flares. Usually anomalous members didn't live very long because their cycles were less predictable, but they were very rare to begin with.

"I don't know what I become, exactly. I have my suspicions, but I'm not actually sure. After I transform, I can only remember little flashes and brief impressions."

"We call it 'shifting' here, not transforming. It's a reminder that we're still human inside, where it really counts." Sylvia automatically handed some Shifters Anonymous literature to Rosemary. The pamphlet was full of such happy platitudes.

"Fine, fine. When I shift. I don't know what happens to me."

"What originally attacked you? How did you become a shifter? Let's start there. It'll help me understand."

"I was eighteen years old, living on my family's farm out in the countryside. I remember the evening very clearly. There was a meteor shower that night, and I stayed up late wishing on every single falling star. It was absolutely beautiful.

"But then the cows started bellowing from the barn. They were making horrible noises, noises I'd never heard before. That's when I heard the splintering wood, the barn doors bashing open. The cows just kept screaming louder and louder. There was something in there with them, attacking them. I could hear other noises, too. Ripping. Tearing. Crunching.

"My whole family ran out. My father and brother both had shotguns. The cows had gone silent by then. Even from the front porch, we could smell the blood.

"I never got a good look at the thing as it emerged from the barn. I just remember seeing two glowing red cinders, a pair of eyes in the darkness. My father fired at it, and that's when it charged us. It knocked me into a post when it came after my father, and the porch collapsed on top of me. The blow must have knocked me unconscious.

"In the morning, our neighbors found me under the debris. Our whole herd had been torn apart. My family was all gone. And I had this." Rosemary raised her left hand to show where a couple of fingers were missing at the first knuckle.

Aside from the events taking place under a meteor shower instead of the full moon, Rosemary's story wasn't so very different from some of the other members' in the group. A few of them nodded in sympathy.

"I think we can help you," Sylvia said. She walked to the far side of the room and opened a door.

A series of closet-sized spaces stood behind the door. Each was made from the same battleship-grade steel plate that reinforced the front entry. For each little room, there was another door made of solid metal with a small sliding plate to peer through. Rebar blocked anything so large as a hand from fitting through the slot. Chains and restraints hung from the walls, anchored to the walls by massive clamps.

"I realize they may not look very friendly," Sylvia said. In fact, they looked like something out of the Marquis de Sade's private romper room. "But we use these in case of emergencies. They're mostly for new members who haven't built a sufficient safe place to confine themselves to during the full moon yet, but you'd be welcome to use one tonight."

"Thank you, but I don't think this will work."

"Why not?" Sylvia asked. She glanced out the window. The sun crept closer to the horizon, marching ever closer to darkness.

"When I trans–, err, shift, I get big. Really big."

"How big are we talking, exactly?"

"I could probably peek through your window there." Rosemary gestured.

"But ... but we're on the third story." Sylvia felt her heart beat a little faster. No, that couldn't be possible unless, well, maybe. "Are you a weregiraffe?"

Rosemary gave a sad little smile. "I think I'm something a lot more ... ancient. The last thing I ever remember right before I shift is a taste in my mouth. It's the taste of ashes and decaying flesh. It's the taste of extinction. I'm not anything of this era."

Sylvia tried to puzzle out what Rosemary said. Suddenly, the pieces fell into place. She didn't even want to ask the next question because it sounded so insane, so outlandish that her tongue refused to form the words. "Surely you're not suggesting that you're a weredinosaur? How would that even be possible?"

"I don't know how, but that's right." Rosemary said. "An asteroid annihilated the dinosaurs. The impact sent billions of tons of vaporized space rock, deep earth metals, and the cremated remains of a hundred thousand instantly extinguished species billowing into the air on a tidal wave of fire. The sun was blotted out for months. Maybe that combination allowed some virus or bacteria to briefly evolve or mutate and infect a few of the prehistoric shrews that inherited the earth that day. Maybe it's some sort of blood curse or something. Like how haunted houses often have a brutal murder somewhere in their history except on a scale that wiped out most of the life on earth. I don't know. When meteors and asteroids come close though, it triggers the change. For one short night, it throws the world back a hundred million years."

"Why are you only coming to us now? You've been a shifter for years. Did you try to seek help on your own?"

"Comets and meteor showers don't happen that often. Most of the time, I can lead a perfectly ordinary life. I rent a flat just outside the city and run a little accounting operation. I keep track of specialty astronomy periodicals and charts, so I know when I'm in danger of shifting. I thought I could keep things under control, and it would just be my shameful little secret. I was wrong, though. Listen, I really need your help. It'll be dark soon, and when that happens …"

"Right. I think we can help you. We rent a warehouse on the docks, a werehouse if you prefer. Our group used to have a werehippo before a monster hunter gunned him down. We couldn't keep him in a normal containment room, so we rigged up the walls of the warehouse with reinforced plating and ran some wire around it. When we turn on a generator, it runs a current through the wire, like a big electric fence. We still use it for emergencies sometimes."

"This is an emergency," Rosemary said. Outside, the sun waned closer to the horizon, sending shafts of amber light between Chicago's towering buildings.

Sylvia nodded. This woman needed their help, and her options were closing.

"Jerry, bring your car around and meet us out front. The remainder of tonight's meeting is canceled." She pointed at one of the older, more trusted members of her group.

A few minutes later, Sylvia bundled Rosemary into the back of Jerry's puttering Model T. Rosemary wore a grim look as she looked up at the red-tinged sky, rapidly fading darker and darker.

"We'll have you to the warehouse in five minutes," Sylvia said, forcing herself to sound confident. In actuality, their schedule very much depended on what Chicago's traffic was doing.

"That would be good," Rosemary said, her eyes watching the setting sun. Her voice sounded like her mind was very far away.

"So I take it you just recently heard about our support group?" Sylvia asked, trying to distract the woman from the light leeching out of the sky. The Model T farted away from the curb, leaving a trail of blue smoke in its wake.

"Oh, no. I'd heard about it before. I simply thought I had things under control. I thought I'd learned to cope with this. For the most part, I had." Rosemary's fingers kneaded her purse.

"How did you deal with this before? What was your safety plan?"

"I always checked my astronomy charts, so I always knew when the next shift would come. I'd drive out to the most barren, uninhabited stretch of countryside I could find well beforehand. The next morning, I'd always wake up naked in some unknown place. One time I woke up near the remains of about eighteen sheep. But I always found my way back to my car and a spare set of clothes. It wasn't pleasant, but it was manageable. I mostly work at home for my accounting services, so it's not as if I have a boss who will fire me if I walk in late and covered in sheep entrails."

"But you said you'd heard of our support group before? What changed? Why did you come today?"

"There was an incident a couple of weeks ago." Rosemary's expression turned sour.

"The Washington Park Beast? That was you?"

Rosemary nodded. "That was me."

The papers had dubbed the killings the work of the Washington Park Beast. Five people were torn to bits. A few people reported seeing a huge creature in the area, so the police were working under the assumption that there was an escaped circus elephant loose somewhere near Chicago. Animal control experts had been called in to track the creature down, even though no circuses reported any of their animals missing. So far, so one had found any sign of the Washington Park Beast, but the papers couldn't push ink fast enough to speculate about it.

Just like everyone else, Sylvia read the lurid stories in the newspapers. She hadn't thought much about it at the time. To her relief, the events didn't occur during a full moon, so she knew none of her people were involved. Pausing, Sylvia strained her memory.

"I don't remember a comet or anything that night."

"There was a meteor shower. It was just a tiny one. In fact, it was so tiny that the newspapers didn't bother to report it. If you happened to be awake in the incredibly early morning, you would have seen as few quick streaks of light as a patch of dust burned up in the atmosphere, and that's it. It was so tiny that no one noticed it was going to happen. It didn't make it onto my astronomy charts. No one predicted it in advance."

"I see," Sylvia said.

"Exactly. You and your group have to deal with the full moon more often than my celestial events, but it's routine. It's regular. It's predictable. You can set your watch by the phases of the moon. Sometimes, I'm taken completely by surprise."

"We have a problem," Jerry said from the front seat. Ahead, traffic was slowing into a tangle. Off in the distance, Sylvia could see a fire truck and ambulance dealing with an accident, but they were nowhere close to clearing it.

"Cut through downtown," Sylvia said, eyeing the stopped cars ahead.

"That'll take a while to loop back to the docks," Rosemary said. "We don't have much light."

"I know," Sylvia said. She was gambling, but their main route was blocked. Even if everything went smoothly from here on out to the docks, they would still be cutting the timing close. The path ahead was jammed solid, though.

Overhead, the first pinprick of light appeared in the darkening sky. It was Venus, brighter than a mere star. So far, it was the only thing visible in the gathering gloom, but soon there would be more lights, including the faint glow of a distant comet.

Jerry cut over to a new street, marking their new course. Sylvia peered out the window, hoping traffic was moving at a brisk pace. Her heart sank as she saw the sea of stopped vehicles ahead of them. They needed a bulldozer, not a Model T, to clear their way through the mess.

Rosemary gave a quiet moan. "I can feel it getting ready to happen." Sweat beaded on her brow, mushing her curly blond hair to her head. Her eyes shone with feverish intensity.

Sylvia had seen that look plenty of times in the past. Nothing good ever followed it. She put a hand on Jerry's shoulder. "We need to get to the docks. Right now. Kick us up on the sidewalk and go as fast as you can."

Jerry turned around and started to protest, but then he got a look at Rosemary. "Right," he said, his jaw clicking shut.

The Model T veered out of its lane and bounced up onto the curb. A legion of horns blared at them, and the pedestrians on the sidewalk scattered as Jerry gunned the car forward. They blew past a fruit stand selling apples and oranges, the proprietor shaking a fist at them as they passed.

A traffic cop blew his whistle at them. Jerry kept going, wading into cross-traffic like an explorer macheteing his way through jungle underbrush. Cars snarled in both directions as their little Ford zipped through. They bashed their way back up onto the street on the other side of the intersection. Furious whistling rang out behind them from the traffic officer.

Rosemary groaned and slumped over in her seat, resting her head on Sylvia's lap. Sylvia put a hand on the woman's shoulder. Her skin was colder than an Arctic grave, but covered in torrents of hot sweat. Her breath came in hitching gasps, and she quivered like a broken windup toy. They didn't have much time.

Sirens howled behind them. Sylvia looked over her shoulder and saw a couple of police vehicles swing into place a few blocks back. The flashing lights shunted some of the traffic off to the sides of the road, allowing the police cars to claw their way closer.

"Keep going," Sylvia said.

"But –"

"I said, keep going," Sylvia commanded, her voice like iced steel. Jerry obeyed.

The Model T swerved back into the street, using some of the space the police sirens had cleared. Jerry pushed the car harder, moving as fast as he dared down the middle of the cramped street.

Sylvia could feel Rosemary's muscles bunching and clenching up under her skin. She struggled to hold the woman down as she started to contort and writhe.

There was a cracking noise, seemingly loud as a rifle shot in the confined space of the Model T. It was the sound of a bone snapping, rearranging itself into a new configuration inside Rosemary's body.

Sylvia held her tight as more bones popped and separated. The noise sounded like an enormous kettle of popcorn reaching critical temperatures. Rosemary's body felt like a sack filled with squirming kittens all trying to get out.

The stars were fully visible in the sky now. Not far from the bright light of Venus, there was a dimmer light. Little more than a smudge against the darkness, the Pons-Winnicke Comet hung above their heads like the sword of Damocles.

They weren't going to make it to the docks in time. Even with the clear route ahead, they were still more than a mile off from their destination.

At the next intersection, the light turned red. Unable to see the police cars barreling forward, a heavy stakebed truck lumbered into the crossing. Grimy letters declared that the truck belonged to Kelly's Hog Farm.

Jerry jammed the brakes, but it was too late. The Model T skidded headlong into the side of the truck. The impact flung Sylvia against the rear of Jerry's seat. She lost her grip on Rosemary, who tumbled onto the floor.

Fumbling with the door handle, Sylvia fell out of the Model T onto the pavement. Jerry lurched out after her. A cut on his forehead oozed as he staggered away. Steam billowed out from under the car's crumpled hood.

The first police cruiser crunched to a halt, its tire coming to rest a few feet away from Sylvia's face. Gravel sprayed her cheek, drawing blood.

Car doors slammed as Sylvia tried to stand up. She made it a few yards before she fell down again, her senses rattling from the accident.

"Freeze," a voice shouted. Sylvia caught a glimpse of shined black shoes pounding over the pavement toward her before she tried to pull herself up again. One of the officers tackled her when she was halfway up, and then she was on the blacktop again, her face mashed into the asphalt next to a squashed cigarette butt. From her new perspective she could see another officer slam into Jerry as he tried to wobble away.

"Run," Sylvia yelled. An arm pressed into her back, preventing her from struggling further. The police thought she was yelling to Jerry, already on the ground and being slapped into handcuffs. They thought she and Jerry were trying to run away from *them*. No, she was trying to warn the officers to run. To run for their lives.

Sylvia twisted around in the police officer's grip. He grunted a curse as she managed to flip over onto her back and look back in the direction of the vehicle.

The Model T bulged like a snake that had swallowed a meal far too large for its belly. Its thin metal frame creaked and groaned. A rivet shot out like a bullet, starring the windshield of one of the police cruisers.

Pressed against the Model T's window was a great, baleful eye. The rest of the car was filled with twisting, expanding flesh. Inside, the shape was growing and growing, pressing against the sides of the Model T like a chick ready to hatch from an egg.

The eye locked onto Sylvia.

With a noise like someone crushing the world's largest beer can, the Model T split apart. It blossomed in a burst of metal and glass, falling away as a massive shape rose out of the wreckage.

The cop holding Sylvia twisted around to see what the

commotion was. Before he could react, a pair of massive jaws clamped on top of him and lifted him up into the air. There was a scream and a meaty crunch. Warm spray rained down on Sylvia.

Rubberneckers who had come to gawp at the road accident fled, screams pouring from their throats. Service revolvers spat lead as the other officers fired at the creature, but the gunshots were drowned out by the noise of a gigantic roar.

Huge, scaly feet pounded away from Sylvia, leaving impact craters in the blacktop where they landed. A long, muscular tail whipped past over her head as the massive shape rounded the corner.

Sylvia could hear cars flipping over, knocked away like toys. She had already turned to run, scampering away with the rest of the panicked crowd.

An electrical pole crashed to the ground amid a volley of sparks, and the street lights flickered out.

Behind her, another unearthly roar echoed up to the only source of illumination, the stars and the comet above.

The Feast

Jennifer Crow

She passes, pale shadow,
through ragged curtains
of blood and flesh. Tattered
fins, splinters of bone, shreds
of cartilage streak the waters
and she parts it all with a sweep
of her sickle tail.
In some distant age, landwalkers
will build idols in her shape,
steal her guise for killing machines
and tremble at her memory.
But for now, she glides
and the pulse of life flows
across her skin, and the future
gushes through teeth like blades.

This Is The Way The World Ends, Not With A Bang But With Wizard-Sharks

Jarod K. Anderson

The sharks drifted toward the inlet in slow, serpentine courses. The first to arrive was an old bull shark with a scarred snout. At fifteen feet, she was a record-setter, but nobody had ever had the chance to measure her. Two blacktip sharks and a young hammerhead followed. More were coming. They could smell magic and it called to them just as strongly as blood in the water.

Josiah sat on the fiberglass deck of The Wizard Clem's pontoon boat and tried to remember why he had ever wanted to be an apprentice to the fat, old redneck passed out in the deck chair. The boat was anchored by the mouth of an inlet just off the coast of Alligator Point, Florida. "Tail-Chaser" was painted on the back of the boat in fading blue script.

Josiah had begged to be an apprentice and more than begged. He had given Clem the entirety of the federal loan money that was supposed to be paying for his living expenses spring semester at Florida State. More than that, Josiah had walked away from all his plans, studies, friends, and family for the opportunity to study magic under Clem.

"Why?" Josiah said to the rising moon. "Why did I ask for any of this?"

Clem farted, made a whimpering noise, then mumbled something that Josiah guessed was a scrap of Old Norse.

"Because he is a goddamned wizard," Josiah said under his breath. "That's why."

He sighed and ran a thin, knob-knuckled hand through his hair.

It was true. Clem was a legitimate Wizard. The things Josiah had seen the man do were nothing short of miracles. Sure, Josiah had been full of skepticism when he'd followed a tip to Clem's shithole trailer next to a swampy estuary a mile from the Gulf Coast, but after ten minutes with the man there was no room for doubt. Clem worked miracles. He just also happened to be a complete asshole.

It was impossible not to entertain thoughts of abandoning Clem for all the petty, mean bullshit the man loved to inflict. Clem forced Josiah to sleep on an old food-stained recliner out on the dock for the first week of his apprenticeship. Josiah guessed he'd lost about two pints of blood to mosquitoes and he developed a hacking cough that left a sour taste on his tongue. Clem said it was all part of the process and then laughed like a clogged drain.

"Ain't gonna learn fuckall about magic 'til you become butt-buddies with nature, fella," Clem said.

Even with all Clem's nonsense, leaving was out of the question. Josiah had been haunted by a quest to find real magic in the world ever since he had burned down Roosevelt Middle School with a wish when he was twelve years old. He had no doubt that magic existed, but he had no control, no system for harnessing or understanding the power. He needed a teacher. Besides, he had learned more from Clem in the first three months of his apprenticeship than he would have guessed possible.

In fewer than ninety days, Josiah had learned to talk to animals, to command the elements, to levitate objects, and to share his mind and experiences with a fellow practitioner the way you might loan a book to a friend.

"If he were pulling out my fingernails with pliers and feeding me live cockroaches it would still be worth it. Anything would be worth it. Get the knowledge and then get the hell out."

Josiah looked over his shoulder at his sleeping master. Clem's "Federal Boob Inspector" tank top had ridden up and his pale beer gut looked luminous in the glow from the battery-powered string of Christmas lights dangling from the ragged canopy. The thick black hairs around Clem's bellybutton waved like seagrass and began arranging themselves into arcane symbols. Josiah gagged and looked away.

"Worth it," he repeated to himself.

Earlier, when Clem had still been sober enough to talk, he told Josiah they were going to anchor here for the fishing. There had been no fishing. Clem drank two six packs of Coors by himself and went lights out. Josiah didn't dare to start up the engine and head back without Clem's permission, and he knew it would be a couple hours before the drunk old wizard woke up enough to give permission for anything. So, Josiah decided to use the time to practice his craft. There were no other boats around and it wasn't likely that anybody could sneak up on the pontoon without being spotted a long way off.

Clem always stressed the importance of secrecy.

"You ever got your bell-head stuck in your zipper, shit-stain? Well, you get seen doin' magic an' I'll do that ta yer whole body, I shit you not," Clem said shortly after beginning Josiah's training.

Josiah walked over and swung open the little door next to the swim ladder. He sat on the edge of the deck with his legs crossed. He didn't dangle his feet in the black water because he was more than a little afraid of the ocean. He'd never admit it to Clem, of course (he didn't like to think what the old bastard would do with such knowledge), but his imagination always conjured up hungry monsters just beneath the surface of the waves.

Above the water, humans sat comfortably at the top of the food chain. Beneath the water was another story entirely. Josiah had grown up watching *Shark Week* and other TV shows about the hunters of the deep, feeding his fears and his fascination.

Josiah pushed his fears aside and concentrated. The boat drifted in a slow waltz, circling around its anchor. He stared at the milky streak the moon painted on the water and thought about his lessons. He took a deep breath, silenced his thoughts, and reached for his magic.

"Okay, listen up shit-for-brains," Clem said in Josiah's memory of his first real lesson. "You ain't magic. Magic comes outta ol' Mama Earth and the critters that run around on her. You're just the pecker. She's the balls. Got me, cock-knocker?"

Josiah blew out a breath and felt for the magic around him. The salty smell of the water filled his mind. The moonlight became a tangible thing, a weight draped around his shoulders like a heavy jacket. The sound of the waves lapping at the pontoons sent a vibration through his limbs that sang in his bones like an extended note from a violin. Josiah's hair began to stand on end and he felt the pop and buzz of static sparks arcing between his fingers.

Turning his eyes to the dark water, Josiah sensed the animal presence there and the magic in him was too strong to permit any fear.

"Come, animal. We are kin, you and I," Josiah said.

They weren't quite the words Clem used for the spell. Clem just said, "get the fuck over here critters," but Josiah found it was the meaning more than the words that mattered.

Clem farted again in his sleep and then, in answer, giggled to himself before returning instantly to a steady, buzzsaw snore. Josiah ignored him.

"Come to me, animal. We will talk as old friends."

He could feel another mind deep in the water, deep, but coming steadily closer. No, not one mind. More than one. These minds were unlike the other animals with which Josiah had communed. He had known the bright, frantic minds of squirrels and nuthatches, the buzzing electric minds of bees, the green, sun-warmed minds of anoles. The minds beneath the water were different. They were stark, polished things like sharp-edged hunks of volcanic glass. Josiah hesitated for a moment, but he knew that growing as a wizard meant moving beyond his comfort zone, pushing his boundaries.

"Come forth. Share yourself with me. Speak to me."

There was a tug at Josiah's mind. He froze. It was a familiar sort of tug, but different. At first, he couldn't place the sensation, and then it came to him. It was the magic of mind-sharing that one practitioner might use to commune with another. It was the way Clem had poured understanding into Josiah without the need for words or explanation. It was wholly different from the spell for communicating with animals.

"Ah, you wish me to share my mind with you ... my knowledge. Well ..."

Clem hadn't told him this kind of mental sharing could take place with an animal. Simple communication, yes, but not this. Certainly, Josiah had never felt such a sensation during his time among the birds, small mammals, and reptiles of the Florida backwoods. Josiah had thought that only human wizards could share knowledge this way, but of course Clem hadn't told him everything.

A sudden greed to learn something on his own filled Josiah's mind, images of swimming like a fish or breathing water. If he could become his own teacher, if he could take the lessons directly from nature, then maybe he had a chance of leaving the asshole Wizard Clem and seeing to his own magical education. Nature. Perhaps nature was the best teacher, after all.

"If that is your wish, so be it. Let's learn from one another," Josiah said to the dark water and the strange presences beneath the boat.

As he called forth the magic to link his mind to the strange visitors', a sudden, instinctual dread uncoiled in the pit of his stomach, but before Josiah could analyze the feeling, the mental barriers were lifted and his mind was naked before the alien intelligence below.

Josiah felt cold, an absolute, penetrating cold that had no use for warmth. The cold filled him, but it wasn't alone. There were other sensations. There was a hunger and a mechanical certainty of purpose that felt simultaneously freeing and confining. There were no nagging questions of identity or self-esteem or social status. There was just the cold and the hunger and the eons-old instincts as powerful and irresistible as continental drift.

Josiah gasped, his mouth opening and closing spasmodically like a fish out of water. He toppled backwards on the deck and felt the link to his mind become two links. Three. A dozen. He felt those minds link to others until he was just a speck in the center of a vast web of inhuman consciousness, a web woven out to the open sea.

Secrets were flowing out of Josiah, flowing out and down the web of linked minds. He could see the knowledge pulsing out of him like blood from a cut vein. He made an effort to stop the bleeding of ideas and experience, to break the links. It was like trying to stop the flow of a river with a single hand. He didn't have the strength.

A moment later, it was done. Josiah was sprawled on the deck and the other minds were gone. He was alone in his own head once more. He was back, back from huge distances and crushing depths, back from vistas of understanding, vast and blue and beyond human reckoning.

Josiah coughed and pressed his palms against his eyes. His head was on fire and his throat felt battered, as if he had been screaming.

"Whuzzat … What … What the fuck ya playin' at? The fuck?"

Clem was pulling himself to a standing position, swaying back and forth as if the boat were traveling choppy seas and not anchored in a calm inlet.

"It's okay, Master Clem," Josiah said in a hoarse croak. "You can go back to sleep."

"You was screamin' bloody murder, dumbass. What did you get yer dick-skinners on this time? What did you do? Summpin feels… feels… all bass-ackward."

Josiah pushed himself to a sitting position and looked up at Clem.

"I don't know. I was practicing. I was talking to the animals and…"

Josiah trailed off. Clem's eyes had gone wide and he took a stumbling step toward Josiah.

"Talkin' to what animals? What ANIMALS? You dumb sombitch…"

"I'm not sure, I just …"

There was a sighing rumble behind Josiah like the roar of blood heard in a conch shell pressed against the ear. The sound brought with it an aquamarine glow that lit Clem's face. Clem looked instantly old and instantly sober.

"You fuckin' did it now, junior. Christ on a cracker, boy. You taught fuckin' magic to fuckin' sharks."

Clem's features hardened and he brought up his hands to chest level. Arcane energy trailed his fingers and created ghostly afterimages. He slashed his left hand downward and a wide tear appeared in thin air while a white-hot ball of fire swelled and blossomed above his right palm. There was a sound like huge sheets flapping on a clothesline and a massive pterodactyl emerged from the tear in nothing. Josiah had never seen magic like it.

Josiah's jaw hung open at Clem's display of raw magical power and then there was a green blur and Josiah saw what had made the light and the roar. He saw the creature that had carried his mind and his secrets away into the deep waters.

The bull shark was a luminous thing now, encased in a shimmering oval of suspended water. Its eyes shown like green stars and its teeth were the impossible white of freshly fallen snow. It shot over Josiah's head, trailing a spray of seawater that hissed on the deck like rain.

Josiah wiped saltwater from his eyes and looked up in time to see the headless stump of Clem's neck shoot jets of arterial blood against the pontoon boat's weathered canopy. The force of the blood spray made a sound like tearing burlap as it struck the canvas. A bib of blood cascaded down Clem's chest, blotting out the cartoon bikini model on his tank top. His body stayed upright for a terrible second that seemed to Josiah to stretch on forever before it finally tumbled forward.

The old bull shark flicked its tail and turned in midair, closing on Clem's body with no apparent hurry. Its jaw worked and Josiah saw the last of Clem's salt and pepper scalp disappear behind rows of serrated teeth. The pterodactyl and the portal from which it had emerged both vanished from existence in a shower of yellow sparks now that the wizard who had summoned them was dead. The pterodactyl gave a ringing cry as it vanished, and a smell like ozone mingled with the copper smell of blood.

"Jesus Christ," said Josiah. "Jesus Christ, Jesus Christ, Jesus Christ."

The bull shark stopped advancing and shifted a dorsal fin. Josiah could feel the force of magic radiating out from the shark. Clem's body rose from the deck, limbs swinging like a marionette, and floated toward the shark's open mouth.

Josiah turned his head, unable to watch the rest of the bull shark's meal. He looked out to sea and what he saw there drove the last rational thoughts from his mind. A constellation of lights had kindled beneath the waves for as far as Josiah could see. The lights grew, rising up from the water, cresting and hovering above the foam. The sharks were rising. They had spread the magic down the genetic pathways. They had shared the hidden knowledge selflessly, thoughtlessly, and now the entire family tree of shark-kind was flowering with new power and purpose.

For an endless, weightless moment, all of the sharks Josiah could see simply hung in the air, glistening spheroids of water like jewels shimmering above the black ocean. Then, as one, the sharks began moving. They swam through the air, diverse shapes and sizes beyond count.

They swam toward the land, toward the unwary food that walked there.

Belly Of The Beast

Courtney Cullinan

The creek next to Lydia's house only ran wet after heavy rains, but those torrents brought new treasures every time. When the town flooded and the streets became seas, her parents feared for their twice-mortgaged home and fretted over the days they could not make it into the office, but Lydia thought only of what precious mysteries she would unearth when the rain stopped and the creek drained bare.

The sun glared too bright, as if to prove it still had its mojo after such a long absence, and the creekbed mud squished beneath her sneakers when she clambered down into its wilderness on the first day that her mother allowed her to play outside again. She ignored the broken amber beer bottles among the rocks and the blue plastic bags that clung to the trees, turned over every rock and explored every cranny until she thought that, for once, the creek would disappoint her – but then she saw it, playing innocent in a sea of stones, an imposter –not another stone, but a shiny black tooth, larger than her head.

Her parents dismissed it – it could not be anything more than a funny looking rock, or perhaps even some ancient construction debris. But she knew what it was, and she moved the other treasures on her bookshelf aside to give it a place of honor. This was no broken arrowhead or half an imprint of a leaf – she'd found a true relic of the mysterious past.

She flipped through her illustrated book of dinosaurs until she found the one she sought – a *megalodon,* a word that felt more like something the Power Rangers would fight than a monster that once swam where she now stood. She begged her father for a ride to the library and read everything she could about the beast – marveled over its incredible jaws, tried to imagine a creature that dwarfed even the humpback whales she had seen projected at the IMAX on a school trip.

She tucked the fossil beneath her pillow like an offering to a prehistoric tooth fairy. She dreamt each night of the ocean, but not the clear emerald waters she had seen on her family's trip to the Panhandle. This feral ocean spanned planets. She hung in the water, bubbled, surrounded by blue above and black below. She pedaled her feet so she did not sink further, although she was not so sure there was more to fear beneath her than there was above. For a week she spent her dreams frozen in terror, suspended in that vast and vacant ocean.

One night she fell asleep and knew she was not dreaming when she felt her clothes grow heavy with seawater. Once again the ocean suspended her, but this time, it did not gift her an immunity to its power. Her lungs filled with water and the salt burned her eyes, but she could not look away from the leviathan that stared her down.

It outsized the megalodons of her library books by so many magnitudes that she knew at once that those beasts had just been charming fairy tales. When it bared its spindly smile, she realized that the fossil she had found must be little more than a baby tooth, a mere warning of the skyscraper-sized incisors to come.

However, the leviathan did not need to use its teeth to consume her – it swallowed her with a gulp of ocean, and she found herself drowning in the black galaxy of its esophagus, flushed down into its cavernous stomach. She saw such wonders as the current dragged her along – whole cities lining the folds of its innards, a graveyard of skeletons larger than warships, even a submarine with green lights still glowing. She stretched a pale arm out towards the vessel, but though she could see its alien inhabitants laughing and drinking inside, they did not spare a look her way.

She descended into the ocean of slime in the pit of its belly and wished to drown before she felt her flesh digested – but the leviathan showed her no mercy.

When her mother went to wake her for school the next day, she found neither Lydia nor the fossil. She found only bedsheets sopping with seawater.

Junior

Gary Couzens

So, there I was, babysitting Olivia, the eight-year-old girl down the road, and as soon as she'd gone to bed I called my boyfriend round. And there he was, lying half on top of me on the lounge, me with my arms in the air as he tugged off my T-shirt over my head, when Olivia came back in. I didn't notice for a couple of seconds but there she was, standing in the doorway in her pyjamas.

"Hey, *what*?" I said.

"It's too hot. I can't sleep."

Boyfriend only had his shorts on. He had a cushion pressed to his lap to hide his hard-on. My lippy was all over his mouth and cheeks.

"Oh for *God's sake,* Olivia," I said.

"Nice bra." My best one. Just as well boyfriend hadn't taken it off yet. "Hey, *dinosaurs.* Cool."

The TV was still on behind us, the sound turned down low. Animated DNA and a baby dinosaur hatching from an egg. For real.

Olivia sat cross-legged on the floor and turned the volume up.

The first dinosaurs I ever saw were the fossil skeletons in the museum. I held Dad's hand and gave a little shiver, awed and just a little bit scared by this huge assembly of bones towering over us. And, though I couldn't have put a name to it, something else stirred inside me for the first time.

Jurassic Park was my favourite old movie as a kid. I watched it over and over and I wrote my own fanfics. I – pear-shaped, blonde Bronwyn – was always the one who sacrificed herself so the others could escape. And then the T-Rex would eat me. It was always a T-Rex. Somehow I stayed alive as it bit off parts of me at a time – a foot here, a whole arm there, a chunk of flesh out of my side – and ate them, taking its time chewing before moving on to the next part. Finally it would lower its mouth over me, its teeth digging into my neck before it bit off my head.

When Dinoworld South opened, billions of dollars' worth in a large tract of reclaimed Great Victoria Desert, I'd just finished college. There was no way I wasn't going to apply for a job there. But so did everyone else. I kept trying and eventually succeeded. I moved near to the park, into a single room with a dunny you had to lift up to check a redback wasn't sitting there, looking forward to biting me on the arse. It was a big enough target. I watched as the Prime Minister of Australia and the King of England opened the park to the public, giving thanks to the traditional owners of the land. I did maid work at several of the hotels in the complex and the purpose-built airport, from the almost posh to the downright daggy, then finally got a job inside the park. I sold T-shirts, baseball caps, fridge magnets and all sorts of souvenir crap.

I bought myself a T-shirt with the park's star attraction on it: Junior the boy T-Rex. I got a size too small so that, the way his image was printed, my boobs made him look fatter than he actually was. At the end of my shift I'd go to his enclosure to watch him.

"You're beautiful," I said.

At that moment, he looked up and our eyes met. He let out a gurgling, guttural growl from the back of his throat.

"Yes you are, Junior. You're beautiful."

Sometimes I was lucky and could get to the enclosure at feeding time, when a whole cow – pre-killed, of course – was lowered in. I'm sure Junior drooled as it was let go, landing on its side with a thump. And then he pounced on it, his huge teeth ripping at the cow's flesh. I couldn't look away as he tore open its belly with his powerful clawed legs and teeth, the animal's insides spilling out onto the grass. I let out a sigh.

At the end of the day I'd spend my time in the bar with my mates. If I had a boyfriend I'd go back to his place, or else go home, trying to sleep in forty-degree heat and shitty aircon.

One afternoon, I was watching Junior feed when a pair of hands clamped themselves over my eyes.

"Tranh, piss off," I said.

He removed his hands. "Thought you'd be here." He kissed me on the cheek, slipped his arm about my shoulders.

"I'll be his keeper one day," he said.

"Okay, don't brag." At the moment he was a keeper for the brontosauruses and the other herbivores.

Junior seemed bored of his cow leg and dropped it. No doubt he'd return to it while it was still edible. He stood upright, stretching his shoulders. Then he stepped away into the middle of the clearing. His legs bowed as he squatted ... and took a sizeable shit.

"Ewww," I said. "I bet it really stinks in there."

"That's our job," said Tranh. "Clearing up dino shit. You should see how big a dump the brontos take." He leaned forward, pointed. "It's all in there. Dinosaurs have cloaca, like birds do. Their boy parts or girl parts are inside. If they need to piss or shit, that's where it comes out of. And if they want to fuck, they rub their cloaca together and go at it."

"Do you think he wants to have sex? Thinks about it all the time?"

"Well, he is a boy ... If he starts rubbing himself against a rock, you'll know. There's a baby girl T-Rex at Dinoworld China. When she's old enough they're going to try to mate them. Make more dinos the natural way."

I said nothing. That would mean that Junior would go, once they'd sorted out transportation and quarantine and all that. There was no way I could follow him to China. Who knows if he'd ever come back?

I must have looked sad. Tranh kissed me on the forehead. "Come on, let's go for a drink. Get something to eat. Catch a movie."

One day, I came in early, my uniform in my backpack. I took the long way round, past Junior's enclosure. I guessed there wouldn't be anyone there as the park wasn't open yet. Junior was awake. I tapped on the thick glass and he looked up.

"Hey, Junior," I said. And I lifted up my top. I wasn't wearing a bra underneath: I'd packed that in with my uniform.

Junior turned his head, almost cocking it to one side as he watched me. He stepped forward, surprisingly delicately ... one, two ... I held up my top as his huge head leaned forward, almost touching the glass.

"This is all for you, Junior. You know you want it."

Junior's head was almost as tall from jaw to forehead as I was. He was so close now that when he breathed out, he misted the glass.

There was a sound behind me, and I dropped my top back into place. I glanced around hurriedly. "Hi, Bron." It was one of the vets. "You're in early," she said.

Losing interest, Junior had turned away, striding to the water pool to drink.

Tranh gave me a surprise present for my birthday.

By then he had been promoted and was one of Junior's keepers. So, in the evening, he took me with him into the enclosure.

There would have been no problem with the herbivores. They barely noticed you and the most danger you'd be in was that one of them would step on you by accident. But with a dangerous carnivore like Junior, things were different.

Tranh had checked out a pair of uniform dungarees for me. I wore a T-shirt under them. "It's tough enough to keep away the smaller critters," he said, "but if Junior really wanted to bite you in half, it wouldn't really stop him."

With his security badge and password, he let us in to the enclosure. It was dark, with a flashlight trained on Junior. He was lying on his side. His mouth was wide open, and a small indigenous woman was standing between his jaws, checking between his teeth. I thought that Junior would just have to wake up and snap his jaws shut and she would be dead.

"Hi, Angie," said Tranh. "This is Bronwyn."

Angie stood up. "Hi, Bronwyn. As you can see, I'm Junior's dentist for tonight. He does keep his teeth in good shape." She tugged at something between two of his molars, a lump of meat the size of her hand, which she dropped to the ground. "No fillings yet."

"That'll be fun when he gets toothache."

"Hopefully when I'm not around." She took off her gloves and wiped her forehead with the back of her arm.

I wandered over to Junior's side. I glanced around to see if anyone was watching me then leaned forward and rested one gloved hand on his flank. Strong muscles, built to walk the Earth millions of years ago, now able to do that again. The thin layer of fur, not really feathers but not hair either, the firm flesh underneath.

"Take your time, Bron," said Tranh. "Make the most of it. Don't tell anyone I told you, but he won't be here much longer."

I stood up. I wished he hadn't chosen that moment to tell me, had left me alone with Junior.

"So they're breeding him with that Chinese girl T-Rex?"

"No, Dinoworld West have bought him. So he's off to California. They probably will try to breed him, then we'll get a baby one instead."

"They *can't*. Not Junior."

"They will. They just haven't announced it yet."

There were tears in my eyes. "Can't they stop them?"

"Too late. Contracts already signed."

"It's not fair."

He slipped his arm about my shoulders.

I shrugged him off. "*Don't*, Tranh."

He moved away, leaving me with Junior.

I knew I didn't have much time if I was going to do it.

At the end of the week, the night before Tranh's day off, we went out for dinner at the poshest restaurant we could afford, then after a few drinks, okay, *quite* a few drinks, we went back to his place. He had aircon that worked properly and his dunny was ensuite, so no checking for redbacks. One day, maybe, if Tranh and I stayed together, I might move in here fulltime.

We rooted. He was enthusiastic, I was preoccupied, but I don't think he noticed. He was soon asleep. He'd stay that way for a good eight hours, I guessed. While he hadn't been looking, I'd mixed a crumbled-up pair of sleeping pills into his wine.

Because it had been a night out, I'd come here in my best dress and heels. Best undies, too. I put the undies back on but slipped one of Tranh's T-shirts over my head. It was too big for me, but that didn't matter. The same went for his uniform dungarees, but I tightened the belt more than Tranh would. Hair, quickly tied back. I put on the gloves, boots and hard hat, and took his security pass with me, locking the apartment door behind me.

No one bat an eyelid as I walked though the complex late at night towards the enclosures. The park itself was shut now, with the business being done in the hotels, clubs and casinos. I knew that if anyone took a good look at the pass I'd be arrested, as it had the name and picture of a Vietnamese man and I was a white Australian woman.

It was a long walk, but eventually I was outside Junior's enclosure. I'd watched closely as Tranh had entered his password to let me in. Not that it wasn't hard to guess: *Bronwyn16*. The digits were my year of birth.

"Hey, Junior," I whispered. Then, bolder, "Junior!"

The enclosure was soundproofed. During the day, Junior's roars were filtered though to the audiences in the viewing galleries. But he could be really loud and they didn't want him disturbing the dinosaurs next door. The night watch had a baby monitor, but I knew they mostly turned it down while they played games. So no one should be able to hear us.

There was a guttural, back-of-throat rumble from the other side of the enclosure. In the semi-darkness, Junior scrambled to his feet.

I'd planned this for a long time. From those mornings and afternoons before and after my shifts, I'd memorised the entire layout of Junior's enclosure. So I knew where the ideal spot for me was: a flat rock pushing out of the grass like a bald man's scalp from what was left of his hair. It was also about as long as I was tall.

Thump ... thump ... Junior's tread as he approached.

If I'd got this wrong, I was in the last few minutes of my life.

He leaned forward, sniffing the air.

"You know you want it," I said.

I jumped up onto the flat rock.

"You're beautiful. I've loved you ever since I saw you."

His head moved from side to side. He opened his mouth and exhaled.

I laughed. "Pity they don't give you some of the breath mints."

Junior leaned forward still, his nose just a foot away from me.

I dropped the hard hat, which rolled away into the grass, and kicked off the boots. My eyes meeting his, I slipped off the dungarees and the T-shirt soon followed.

"This is just for you, Junior."

I was standing there in my undies for several minutes. Then Junior lifted his right hand, one of the two arms so small in proportion to the rest of him. I leaned forward. The end of one claw touched me just above the navel. I lowered myself so I could slip the band of my bra around his claw, then stood slowly upright so that it stretched, finally being cut in two. Junior had nicked my skin in several places, trickles of blood running down my front.

I stepped out of my knickers, kicking them away. I lay down on the rock, flat on my back.

Junior leaned forward, sniffing at me. I knew he relied more on his other senses than his sight, but I wondered what those big black eyes could see.

I slid my legs apart, as far as I could. I was so wet.

"Oh, Junior ..."

He stepped forward. *He's getting it. He knows.* He moved aside a little, lifting one leg over me so that my right leg was between both of his. The muscles strained in his legs as he lowered himself into position.

He pushed further forward. It hurt intensely, as if he was about to split me like a wishbone.

"Junior ..."

He was pressing down on me, so that I couldn't move anything below my waist. I could hardly breathe. My heart was beating so fast I was afraid I'd faint. How much more pressure before he ruptured me?

"Junior ... *fuck me.*"

And he entered me.

I screamed out loud, my head leaning back, my back slamming against the rock. Junior's hands skittered over me, one digging into my arm so that blood ran down it, the other scoring a thin line below my boob.

"Go on ... fill my cunt ... you want it ... fuck me."

He thrust again, huge, only just large enough to be accommodated by me.

"Junior ... do it ... do it to me ... you can do it ... fuck me hard as you can ..."

He thrust a third time. He opened his mouth. It was like he was smiling. His face was all I could see.

I let out a gasp, my back arching, my head leaning back.

I was almost passing out, stars filling my vision.

His hips tensed for another thrust, then he paused.

"You can do it," I whispered.

And then he thrust again, deeper still. He leaned his head back and let out a deafening roar.

He pulled himself out of me, a gout of his semen and my blood pouring down my legs, onto the rock to drip onto the grass.

I pulled myself up the face of the rock. Resting on one hand, I tried to raise myself up, but a shaft of pain went through me. I screamed, and fell back, supine on the rock.

Junior lowered his head level with me. A low sound like a grunt.

I reached up and stroked him under the chin, up his cheek as far as I could reach. He lowered his head still further, turning it so that his cheek was level with my face, near enough for me to kiss him.

Scales Of Injustice

G. H. Finn

There's a lot more money in fossils than most people imagine.
Not enough to die for.
But enough to make murder a serious temptation…

It began when I read an article in *National Geographic*. They were talking about how fossils were big business. At the top of the range, a complete T-Rex skeleton could sell for over $8millon. But even fossilized shark-teeth, leaves, fish, dinosaur egg-shells, scales and claws were worth good money. Easily $100,000 per-ton on the black market. High-quality specimens could fetch a lot more.

What put me off was the physical labor it would take. Hunting fossils can be back-breaking. It relied on hard graft, expert knowledge and a good measure of luck. It could take years to get rich. I almost gave up on the idea. There was no way I'd be doing that amount of work, no matter how much money was involved.

But then an old man bought the house at the edge of the lake. I didn't know who he was. Just some long-in-the-tooth ancient mariner. A retired sailor or something. He brought with him a van-load of antiques, boxes of books … and several crates of fossils.

I asked around about him. Discreetly. No-one knew anything much. He lived alone. He had no visitors. No family. No friends. No-one locally had ever stepped foot inside his house. He had his groceries delivered. It seemed he never left the house. If he had, I might have tried to rob him while he was out, even though that would have been risky. But he never went anywhere. So I decided to kill him. No-one would know if anything was missing after the old man was dead.

There's one sure way to get away with murder. Make certain no-one realizes a crime has been committed. I thought about that …

I'd ruled-out fake-suicide. It'd raise questions … Why'd he want to kill himself? Was there a suicide-note? If not, why? How could I forge one? Nope. Too complicated.

"Accidental" death was appealing. Car brakes failing ... Falling off a roof ... Electrocuted by a faulty appliance ... All perfectly reasonable, but hard to actually pull-off.

I needed something *better.* I had an idea.

Over the past weeks I'd secretly searched the old man's trash. I was lucky. It always contained empty rum bottles.

I went and bought dark rum. Not the same brand the old man drank, so that he wouldn't be too surprised if the flavor was a tad "different."

I went to a drug-store. Not the local one, they'd be sure to recognize me. They knew me too well. They'd notice what drugs I was buying.

I bought pain-killers and antihistamine tablets. The sort you take for hay-fever. Then I went to *another* drug-store, and bought more. Antihistamines cause drowsiness. Many people can't stay awake when they take them.

The next week I bought sleeping-tablets.

At home, I put on gloves and wiped fingerprints from everything I'd touched. I opened both bottles of rum, crushed antihistamines, pain-killers and sleeping-tablets then added them to the first bottle. I resealed and wrapped it. I tipped about one-third from the second bottle, then put it and the remaining medicines into a backpack. I removed my gloves.

I was sure the drugs mixed in the rum wouldn't be enough to kill someone, but I was certain even one small glass would knock anyone unconscious. Any tox-screen during an autopsy would show alcohol, sedatives, pain-killers and antihistamines. An unwise mix. *But not enough to be fatal.* It'd just look like he didn't pay attention to what he was taking. It wouldn't be drugs and alcohol that would kill him. Not directly.

I live alone so I didn't need to worry about anyone seeing me drug the rum. But this also meant I couldn't claim to have been at home with someone at the time the old man died.

... It used to be me and Dad living in the decrepit house near the lake. Dad had been depressed. Ever since Mom had left. Probably even before that. He used to complain she'd changed. That she wasn't the girl he'd fallen in love with. She was no longer the woman he'd married. So he got drunk. A lot. Too much. She went away. Neither of us knew where she went. In the end the drinking killed him. Or maybe the sense of loss, after she finally left. Whatever. In any event, it meant

I was alone ...

My alibi was simply going to be that I'd been home watching TV. I'd already checked the TV guide and found some films I'd seen. If it became necessary I could tell the police their plots.

I walked to the old man's door and knocked.

As I waited, I couldn't help thinking about why I was doing this. It wasn't for fun. Not greed either. It was the drugs. I needed them. I had to buy more drugs. As soon as possible. I still had a small supply, but I was getting desperate. Terrified I'd run out before I had the money to buy more.

That's why I needed the money. You can't imagine how it felt.

But I've not explained this very well.

You probably think I'm on crack. Or heroin. Or crystal-meth.

But those aren't the kind of drugs I'm talking about.

I mean medicine. I need it. For my condition. I'm ill. My doctor had never seen anything like this before. Whatever I've got is rare. There aren't any recognized treatments. The only drugs are experimental and unapproved. Which means my medical insurance refuses to cover them. I can still buy them, from a clinic in Switzerland where they're doing research into genetic disorders. But I have to pay for the drugs myself. And they cost a fortune.

I'd used up all the money Dad had left me after he died. I'd mortgaged the house already. Twice. And every day my body was getting worse. I could feel it ... it was changing. It felt like my bones were twisting. It hurt to have the sun on me. I got out of breath easily. That's why I knew I'd never be any good at hunting for fossils.

Maybe it wasn't just my body that was changing, though. My brain was being affected too. Before the illness started, I'd never have dreamt of committing a murder. Now ... Somehow, killing didn't bother me the way it should have ... Or maybe I was just shit-scared of dying and would do anything to survive.

I knocked on the door again. He opened it.

He was a very odd-looking old man. His ears were tiny but his eyes were large, bulging out beneath his narrow, bald head. His stare was unnerving. He never seemed to blink.

This would be the hardest part ... not the killing, but making normal, polite conversation.

I smiled. "Hello! I'm Belinda."

He looked surprised. This was the first time I'd spoken to him.

"This is for you." I said, thrusting the bottle toward him.

The old man looked at the gift, puzzled. After a moment he took the present, saying, "You're the girl from the house at the end of the road? This is ... unexpected. Thanks."

He looked unsure what to do next. I stood there, knowing what would inevitably happen. I'd given him a present and wasn't hurrying away. What choice did he have?

"Would you like to come in?" he asked.

"That'd be lovely," I said, stepping inside, talking quickly. "We've lived so close to each other and never spoken. I figured I'd come and test the waters. Someone has to take the plunge. Please, go on, open it."

He seemed taken-aback when he unwrapped the bottle, mistrust creeping across his face. Suddenly the old man didn't look friendly or feeble. "How did you know I drink rum? Who are you? Who sent you?" he muttered, his croaking voice sounding dangerous.

"What's wrong? Don't you like it?" I asked, trying not to panic. "I didn't mean to offend you."

I probably sounded upset.

His face softened. "No," he said, "I'm the one who should apologize. Sorry. I'm a foolish old man who's lived alone so long I forget my manners."

"Don't worry about it," I replied, smiling. "Try some," I suggested, innocently, pointing at the rum. He hesitated but didn't want to upset me by refusing.

"Let's share it," he said, "Please, go through."

I was about to open the nearest door when his hand slammed on top of mine. He said firmly, "Not *that* room."

I snatched my hand back. He pointed to the next door along.

I shivered. I'd been so busy planning how to kill the old man, I hadn't considered what might happen if I failed. What might he do if this didn't work ...? At the very least he'd call the police and I'd be facing an attempted murder charge. But if he guessed what I was planning ...

It was too late to worry about that now. Far too late.

He led me into the parlor and invited me to sit. I felt like a fly visiting a spider. I couldn't understand why. I was the one planning on killing him. But somehow he unnerved me.

He crossed to an ornate cupboard that looked like it may once have graced the captain's cabin on a sailing ship, removed two glasses, opened the rum and poured generous measures. He passed me a drink.

I put the glass to my lips, pretending to swallow but barely tasting it. I couldn't detect the drugs. I put my rum down, waiting, like I was being polite. The old man took a sip, then knocked the rest back. Inwardly I sighed with relief.

I needed to distract him. I looked around the room for something to talk about. His wall was decorated with antiques from the fishing and whaling industries, glass-floats, marlin-spikes, flensing knives, hurricane lamps, fishing-nets, harpoons, tridents and all kinds of nautical paraphernalia. Some of it looked local, maybe nineteenth-century, but other things looked seriously antique, medieval or even maybe Roman or Greek. I noticed oil paintings and sepia-tinted photographs of people, all with similar odd features, the same weirdly distinctive prominent eyes, receding hair, large lips, loose jowls. They were probably his relatives. I asked about them. He turned to stare at the portraits.

"They're my kin," he said, in a far-off voice. "Some are my ancestors, others are my descendants." He finished his rum then began to pour more. I studied his face. His eyelids were drooping over his bulging eyes ... Were the drugs working already? I wanted to keep him talking while the sedatives took effect.

"I don't know much about you," I said "Someone told me your surname's Marsh?"

"Yes. But don't hold that against me. Call me Ahab." He sounded sleepy.

Ahab's head was nodding, his eyes closing, mouth hanging open, half-snoring. Saliva dribbled down his chin. He slipped into unconsciousness. I waited, impatient, nervous, until I was certain Marsh was so drugged he wouldn't notice anything. I spoke to him, shook him. Nothing.

I put on my gloves, went upstairs to the bathroom and turned on the bath-taps, then came back to the parlor.

I put my arms under his, hoisting him up, struggling. I half-carried-half-walked him upstairs and into the bathroom.

The next part wasn't easy. I had to remove his clothes. In the past I'd helped my Dad get undressed when he'd been stone-cold drunk and puked everywhere, but that'd just meant getting off his shirt and jeans. With old man Marsh I had to remove everything. I never realized how hard it is to take underpants off an unconscious man. Especially one as weird as Ahab. He must've had some skin-disease because everywhere I looked his flesh was an unhealthy grayish-color, mottled, covered in scabs. I shuddered. As if it wasn't unpleasant enough having to handle his body, bits of his scaly-skin kept flaking off.

Once undressed I hauled him up and slid him into the bath. It was just about full of water. I turned off the taps.

I felt … strange … I didn't like this. Physically, killing Ahab was going to be easy. Psychologically …

But my mind was set.

Marsh wouldn't wake up. Ever. The medication and alcohol would keep him unconscious … but it wouldn't kill him.

The water would do that.

Gritting my teeth for the most horrible part of my plan, I got hold of Ahab's ankles and pulled him down. I didn't want to look at his face so I stared at his feet. They were huge. He had the condition people called "webbed toes." It must be more common than I realized. My mother had it too. I looked away. *I shouldn't have thought about how he reminded me of my mother.* I needed to be cold-blooded. I didn't want to think of him as a person. His body slid further into the water … covering his neck, with its loose, flabby, rolls of flesh. Then his chin … mouth … nose … until his whole head was submerged.

He didn't wake-up. He didn't struggle. He just slipped beneath the surface.

A few bubbles escaped his lips.

I turned away. I didn't want to see any more.

I took the other bottle of rum from my backpack and left it near the bath. I went downstairs and got the glasses we'd used, leaving sleeping-tablets on the parlor table. I took my glass to the kitchen, washed it, left the pain-killers by the sink, then returned my glass to the cupboard in the parlor. I took Ahab's glass up to the bathroom, rinsed it, splashed fresh rum inside and left the antihistamines on the bathroom shelf. I closed the bathroom-door behind me and went downstairs.

It would be judged an accidental death. Just an old man who'd mixed his medications, had a few drinks then fallen asleep in the bath. It wouldn't be treated as foul-play. Even if it were, who'd suspect *me*? I had no grudge against the man. No motive anyone knew about. Whatever happened, I would be fine. No one knew exactly what he had in his house. I could take any fossils. Maybe even some of the antiques, if they looked valuable and were small enough to carry. I'd sell them online, use the money to pay for my medicine, and no-one would suspect a thing.

I heard a scraping-scratching noise coming from somewhere.

I almost panicked, imagining it was Ahab crawling from his watery grave to scratch at the bathroom door. I went back to check, even though I *knew* he'd have drowned by now.

I opened the door ... I could see his body beneath the water, his huge feet sticking over the end of the bath. He must've been underwater for fifteen-minutes. He was definitely dead. I sighed with relief.

I heard the scratching again.

Did Ahab have a dog? Or a cat? I hadn't seen one ... but if he never let it outside ... Had I seen pet-food cans in his garbage? He'd seemed to eat a lot of fish, the bins were always full of their remains ... but maybe they had been for his cat?

If he had a pet, could I leave it? With no food or water ...?

I went downstairs. Killing Marsh was one thing. He was old. I was desperate. I needed the money and I couldn't see any other way. It was a matter of survival. But there was still some part of me that couldn't leave an innocent animal to starve to death.

The scraping-scratching sounded again. It came from behind the door Ahab hadn't wanted me to open. Maybe his cat was inside?

I opened the door. It was dark. I heard scratching, like nails scraping down a blackboard. Was the animal trapped?

"Here kitty-kitty!" I said, flicking on the light-switch.

I saw a desk piled with books. The top one had a bizarre illustration of some ancient human-fish monster. I scan-read a page:

"Adapa was the foremost Mesopotamian 'Abgallu' (Wise-Man). In Sumerian, literally Ab=water, Gal=great, Lu=man."

A handwritten note in the margin read:

"Ab-Gal"="Great-Water"="Wise"="Deep"

"Lu"="Man"="One"

I read more:

"... Adapa refused the gift of immortality. The story is recorded in the Kassite-period (14th-century BC), and on tablet-fragments from the late-second-millennium BC.

Adapa, also known as Uan / Oannes, and his fellow 'sages' are described in Mesopotamian literature as 'Holy-Fish-People.'

"Adapa was a fisherman portrayed as a fish-man composite. The Armenian translations of Eusebius and Syncellus (Chronicon and Ecloga Chronographica) record the Babylonian scribe Berossus' account (circa 300BC) of the Sea-Creature known as Oannes, or Dagon in Eastern-Mesopotamian-Semitic.

'The whole body was like that of a fish; and had under a fish's head

another head and also feet below, similar to those of a man ...'

'... it was his custom to plunge into the sea and abide all night in the deep for he was amphibious.'

"*Oannes taught mankind writing, arts and sciences, being far wiser and more knowledgeable than humans' ...*"

Boring. Meaningless mythology. I moved on.

There was a work-table in the middle of the room. It held glass-jars, vials, test-tubes, pestles-and-mortars, Bunsen-burners, microscopes, weighing-scales and a state-of-the-art PC. It made the room look like a cross between a wizard's workshop and a mad-scientist's laboratory.

On the table were weird medieval woodcut illustrations of heavily-scaled half-man-half-fish creatures called 'Sea-Bishops.' One was labelled "from Johann Zahn's *Specula physico-mathematico-historica notabilium ac mirabilium sciendorum,* 1696;" another as being "from Conrad Gesner's *Historiae animalium, 1551–58."*

I wondered if they might be worth something if I auctioned them on eBay.

I glanced at some hand-written notes, which read:

"*Near Orford in Suffolk, certain fishermen caught in their nets a fish having the shape of a man. The fish was kept by Barlemew de Glanwille, custodian of the castle of Orforde, for six months. The fish-man did not speak a single word but happily ate all kinds of meat but none more greedily than raw fish, after he had crushed out all of the moisture. He was often taken to church but he showed no inclination to pray. Eventually, when he was viewed unfavourably, he stole away back to the sea and was never seen again. (Translation from 'Stow's Annals', 1187AD)."*

Worthless. I ignored it.

On the floor was a heavy-looking old sea-chest. I heard the scraping-scratching again. Could the cat have got inside?

I reached out to open the antique chest.

There was a thump from inside.

I nearly jumped out of my skin.

Pulling myself together, I opened the lid.

Inside the box was a ... *thing.*

It was pallid. White. As if it belonged lurking at the bottom of the deepest, darkest ocean, thousands of leagues below the sea. Yet it looked bone-dry. Wizened. Mummified. All the water in its body had evaporated.

At first I thought it was a fish. It had a huge gaping mouth, like a great white shark. Then I saw it had legs. Scaled and ending in huge claws like those of a dinosaur. Its body was translucent, emitting a dull sickly glow. Its hideous mouth was full of many rows of vicious triangular teeth. Around its mouth, I saw the protrusion of stubby tentacles, covered in suckers tipped with barbs. They dripped a pus-like yellow liquid. I felt sick. This wasn't natural …

It opened its eyes and looked at me. With hatred.

I screamed. Pulsing, the thing tried to use its teeth to chew through the sides to get out. They made a scratching-scrabbling sound but couldn't bite the wood. It was trapped. For now. I could feel panic rising in me. I had to get out.

I ran from the room.

Then I saw him.

Ahab had risen from the water. His face was gray and deathly-pale. He was naked, dripping water onto the smooth, polished floor. His flesh glistened like a toad. He stared at me with cold, fishlike eyes.

He raised an antique harpoon.

I turned toward the front-door and tried to run but slipped on the wet floor. I hit my head. Hard.

The world went black.

I felt like I was deep below the water, struggling to swim upwards, trying to reach the surface.

With a shock I regained consciousness. I was tied to a chair in the parlor.

It all came back to me. The room. The *thing*.

No! I'd imagined that. *It couldn't be true* …

Ahab sat next to me. How could he be alive? He should've drowned. No-one could go without air for that long …

He smiled at me.

It wasn't a nice smile.

His teeth were sharp … sharklike …

He spoke. "You thought you could drown *me*? Didn't they tell you what I am?"

I glared at him. "I've no idea what you're talking about." But I was curious … "Why aren't you dead?" I asked. "Why didn't you drown?"

He laughed. "As if water could harm my kind." Then he looked puzzled. "You really don't know?" he asked.

He was crazy.

I kept talking, while trying to get free from the ropes. "Why did you come here?"

He paused, thoughtful, remembering ...

"It is a long story ... I used to live in Innsmouth. My family name, Marsh, is infamous there. My father Obed was a sea-captain. And the founder of the Esoteric Order of Dagon. He died in 1878. I had a sister named Alice ... and relations living throughout the town. But my kin prefer not to speak of me. I'm the black-sheep of the family."

I wasn't surprised. If he thought his dad died in 1878, Ahab would be about one-hundred-and-fifty-years-old. He was clearly mad.

Ahab continued, "My mother's still alive of course. Dwelling down in Y'ha-nthlei. Brooding beneath the sea, near Devil's Reef. She's not human. She's one of the Deep Ones. A race of amphibious fish-people.

"My father first met them in the Indies. They struck a deal. The Deep Ones would provide fish and gold in return for human sacrifices. And human mates.

"The offspring of such unholy couplings appear like normal people when young. But we slowly metamorphose into Deep Ones. The completed transformation is welcomed by most, for it brings eternal life, dwelling in ancient cities under the ocean."

I stared at Ahab. "You're telling me that you're an immortal-fishy-frog-thing?" I didn't sound convinced.

He shook his head. "I hope not," he said. "The taint is in my blood. I cannot alter that. We cannot choose our parents. I hope we can choose our futures.

"Unlike most of my kin, I don't relish immortality. Not at the cost of my humanity. I've struggled against the change. I've delayed my ... alteration ... I've studied chemistry, biology and alchemy. I pioneered discoveries in genetics. I hope to halt my metamorphosis and reverse the effects of the transformation."

I needed to keep him distracted. I asked, "What's the problem?"

He shook his head. "My ... *relatives* ... want to stop my research. At first they didn't take me seriously, dismissing my potions and elixirs as unimportant. But, when they realized I'd fought-off the transformation for over a century, the Deep Ones became worried. If I developed a way of permanently resisting or reversing the metamorphosis, and if I shared this knowledge, they feared their own existence might be in jeopardy.

"They ordered me to stop my researches. I told them to go back to the watery hell they'd crawled from. I moved here. Even though I now despise the sea, I cannot bear to be far from water. So I bought a house near a lake. I chose this place because once I had a great-grandchild who lived nearby. I hoped my elixir could help. But I was too late. Her transformation had gone too far. She had already joined the Deep Ones. I discovered she'd left to take her place beneath the waves before I'd even moved here.

"I thought the Deep Ones would forget about me. I was a fool to believe that. When they realized I was continuing my research they sent a messenger to kill me."

"You're utterly insane," I said. "I should have realized. Only a madman would keep a pet fish in a dry box."

Ahab pursed his big, protruding lips. "That is not a fish. It is a Shoggolath. The Deep Ones breed them. With their arcane sciences they somehow crossed prehistoric marine reptiles with sharks and other ... unspeakable things. It was sent to destroy me. I was lucky to survive. I keep it in a box to prevent it reaching water. If it could fully rehydrate itself ... I would be doomed."

He was talking nonsense ... I didn't believe him ... but ...

I *had* seen the thing. It did look like it was part shark, part reptile, part god-knows-what. It was bone dry. It should've been dead. But I'd seen it open its eyes ... It couldn't be true ... It *couldn't* ...

We both heard a crash from the next room and looked at each other. I swallowed nervously.

"You know you've been keeping the thing in a sea-chest?" I said, "Well ... I opened it ... and ... I didn't shut it again ..."

Suddenly a terrible roaring came from the next room. There was an ear-splitting crash. Part of one wall collapsed. Ahab dived toward his whaling-axe. I struggled against my bonds, staring at ... what'd he called it? A Shoggolath? He might as well have called it a sharkasaurus for all the sense it made ...

Ahab glared at me. "You tried to kill me. By rights I should slice you in two ..."

I watched in terror as he raised his axe and brought it down in an arc toward me, sure I was about to die. But the whaling-axe cut through the rope that bound me. I gasped in relief as Ahab said, "We both have bigger problems to worry about."

A weird cry of "Tekeli-li!" sounded from somewhere close by.

Then the thing appeared through the hole in the wall. It must have found some little water, probably from where Ahab had dripped on the floor. It was bigger now. And it was still growing.

Ahab muttered, "We cannot let it reach the lake. It would become unstoppable." He hefted the whaling-axe as though it weighed nothing, swinging it backhanded at the monster's outstretched claw. The axe bit through the flesh. The limb was hewn from the Shoggolath's body. Green blood flowed from the wound. I felt sick.

Nausea became terror as I saw the severed limb begin to regenerate. Even as I watched, it was regrowing. One of the creature's tentacles shot across the floor. Ahab stamped on it. It grabbed his ankle, the suckers pulsing as the tentacle elongated, wrapping around his leg. It began to pull Ahab toward the gigantic, gaping sharklike mouth. I gazed in horror as I saw that inside the monstrous maw were row-after-row of serrated, triangular teeth. Each row was moving, the fangs rotating, like some kind of chainsaw. The monster's huge saurian claws reached out to grab Ahab, eager to feed him into the chasm-like mouth. The stump where the reptilian foreleg had been cut off began to grow, swelling, but rather than reproducing the original leg it was forming a mass of tentacles, each ending in glowing eyes and gaping mouths. From these orifices the creature screamed, "Tekeli-li! Tekeli-li!," its voices so high-pitched the sound was hideously painful. Ahab dropped his whaling-axe, covering his ears.

How could I stop the monster? Was there something special about the sea-chest I'd found it in? Was there some magic word that could control the beast long enough to shove it back inside? I'd no idea. What might kill the Shoggolath? Burning? Freezing? What else could I try? I suddenly remembered. Ahab claimed he'd developed an elixir that prevented his metamorphosis. Temporarily at least. Would this affect the Shoggolath? Perhaps stop it regenerating? Where would Ahab keep it?

Another amorphous tentacle slithered in my direction. Saurian-eyes and shark-mouths full of vicious teeth formed along its length.

I ran toward the hole smashed through the wall.

The Shoggolath grasped Ahab in its glowing embrace, his body dangling from its dinosaur-like forelimbs. The monstrosity dragged him behind as it came after me. There was only one place I could think to look. The work-table with the weird equipment on it. I jumped over the rubble into the room beyond.

Reaching the table, I'd hoped to find a bottle marked "Anti-transformation potion" or something, but was out of luck. I couldn't tell one vial of chemicals from another. As the Shoggolath approached I started throwing everything I could at it. It was awful. Part shark, part reptile, but even more like a giant tentacled-amoeba with a sickly luminescent glow. The test-tubes and jars of chemicals I threw sank into its body. Some began to react with each other. I'd no idea what they were doing. I kept throwing everything I could find. I spotted a boxful of syringes with "serum" written on them. I threw them at the Shoggolath. They spun through the air into its gelatinous body.

At last, *something* was happening. The creature was convulsing, throbbing, gyrating, its body wracked with spasms. It shook, vibrating as waves of agony shot through it. Its vast shark-mouth yawned wider. Its reptilian claws lengthened.

Then it burst.

The Shoggolath's body shattered, spinning apart to splatter into a thousand bloblike droplets. They fell to the ground and became still.

I wasn't sure if it was dead. I wasn't certain it'd ever been alive.

I heard Ahab groaning. I helped him sit. He looked at the wreckage. I could see fear in his face. If his elixir was gone ... would he succumb to the transformation and become a Deep One?

He read the question in my eyes. "All I can do is start again... and hope," he said.

I smiled at Ahab, ashamed of myself. "I can't ask you to forgive me, but I'm sorry I tried to kill you. I was desperate for money," I said. "And I'm sorry about ... who was it? Your great-grandchild? The one who lived here but left because they'd already changed too much?"

Ahab nodded. "Her name was Arabella."

"That's a coincidence," I said, staring at Ahab. "That's ... my mother's name ..."

When A Sailor Loves, He Loves So Deep

Amelia Gorman

I pulled out her teeth when I met my wife
and crushed them to bake our bread.
And I took my great white wife to altar
and then took her to bed.

    Hungry roll the briny waves
    while blood seeps up from below,
    I can't but love my gill-slit wife
    and never let her go.

Other men take mermaids,
and some fancy a fine selkie,
but the only woman I'll ever love
was born from a wolf of the sea.

    Sweetly roll the briny waves
    with thunder down below,
    I can't but love my leathery wife
    and never let her go.

We loved each other with a hungry passion,
we clasped each other tentacle tight,
while anglerfish absorbed their men,
and the grunion made love in the night.

    Darkly roll the sluggish waves
    getting greener down below,
    I can't but love my boneless wife
    and never let her go.

One day she pulled me by my soft, warm hand,
and she led me to the wine dark shore,
and ripped of my shirt with her fingers
that she learned to use like her fins before.

> *Hotly roll the sluggish waves*
> getting hotter down below,
> I can't but love my wide-eye wife
> and never let her go.

She pressed her mouth against my mouth
and I kissed her deep and true.
My tongue hit a solid barrier,
where a new set of razor teeth grew

> *Bloody roll the sluggish waves*
> as my body sinks below,
> I can't but love my cold-blood wife
> who will never let me go.

Bronson's Shark Tank

G. Arthur Brown

Bronson, the very rich American, arrived at his London flat accompanied by no fanfare after working and travelling 72 hours straight to promote his latest whatever. He was not greeted by Leeko and Kona, his sharks, who were not swimming in their shark tank. The tank, however, was not empty, but filled with a red-pink gelatin. Bronson tossed his komodo-skin briefcase (retail $25k) angrily onto his sofa ($150k).

"I'm rich," he cried out. "How are people supposed to realize that if I don't have a tank full of sharks awaiting them upon entry to my apartment?" No one answered, mostly because there was no one else within earshot, but also because the question was rhetorical. He paced back and forth momentarily before approaching the enormous tank. He leaned over at a very awkward angle to read a small, metallic label at its base. As quickly as he could, he dialed the assistance number provided on the label.

Ring, ring.

"Hello, this is Nigel speaking. How can I be of assistance today?" The tone of the Englishman's voice was pleasant even if distorted by cellular encoding and tiny speakers, which produced an effect not unlike two cans on the ends of a taut string.

"I'm having some trouble with my shark tank."

"Could you give me the model number, sir?"

He read again from the little label: "SRGST 5000."

"Ah, the Super-Rich Guy Shark Tank. Brilliant choice, sir."

"Well, I am super-rich," Bronson admitted abashedly, because this was within the dictates of the instructional book that rich Americans received upon arrival in London. Don't deny, just show some shame. "I am also American."

"Good choice on that part, too, sir. Canadian wouldn't have suited a fine gentleman like yourself. What seems to be the problem with your SRGST 5000?"

"My sharks are not in it. I came home from work, and my sharks have vanished."

"Is the tank empty then, sir?"

"No, it seems to be full of gelatin."

"Jelly is it, sir?"

Bronson pondered for a moment. "Yes … not jam. Jell-o, gelatin, jelly. Whatever you guys call it over here."

"And, if I may ask, what color is the jelly, sir?"

"Pinkish red."

"Oh, very good, sir. Sounds like it's strawberry. Wouldn't have done so well with lime, now would we? But strawberry, I think we can work with that. Allow me to consult the check list, and I'll see what I can help you with."

Bronson wondered at this. He wanted to ask, aren't we in the computer age? But he thought better of it for the sake of expediency. He was in England, after all, not the USA. He did not yet completely understand their foreign ways.

"Ah, first let me ask you, sir, did you by any chance take the sharks out, sell them off, drain the tank, and then fill it up with jelly?"

Bronson thought hard. "No, no. I would most certainly remember a thing like that."

"Quite right, sir. One does tend to remember. But, just to be safe, I thought I'd start with the first item on the checklist. Now, moving along, have you hired a person to assist in the care of your tank?"

"I've got a guy. Abdel. He does a very good job."

"Now, might this Abdel have taken the sharks out, sold them off, drained the tank, and then filled it with jelly?"

"Well, I highly doubt it. But, I'll ask him." Bronson walked over to the far wall, leaned over again at an awkward angle, and opened a small cabinet perhaps three feet in height. A short, dark man was crouched inside, motionless but open-eyed. "Abdel? Are you awake?" The man popped up, startled, banging his head on the top of the cupboard. He was apparently trying to stand before he realized he was in his sleeping room. Bronson winced. "Ouch, you okay there?"

Abdel rubbed his head and spoke in his Pakistani accent, "Yes sir, I am very fine indeed. Do you require assistance tonight? I am always glad to please."

"Abdel, you didn't happen to do anything special to the sharks today, did you?"

"Oh, no, Mr. Bronson. Today is my day off. I spent the whole day in my room."

"What about yesterday?"

"No, nothing special, Mr. Bronson. They swam around. I tested the water. I fed them only one orphan as per your instructions. Is there something that does not meet with your complete satisfaction, sir?"

"Yes. Now my sharks are gone, and there is gelatin in the tank."

"Gelatin? That is indeed alarming! Most upsetting! How much gelatin?"

"Filled to the brim, Abdel. I am not pleased."

"I can assure you that I had nothing to do with this! Woe is me! Poor Leeko and Kona! Oh, Allah!"

Bronson shut the door, muffling the cries of the servant inside. He returned to his call. "No, he had nothing to do with this."

"Says so, does he, sir?"

With a slight tone of annoyance, Bronson said, "I have absolute faith in Abdel."

"Yes, it never is numbers one or two on the list. Still, we have to be thorough, sir. It just wouldn't do to miss an obvious one. We wouldn't want that snake to bite us in the proverbial arse, now would we? Now, moving along, have you recently made enemies of your neighbors, done something they might want to get revenge for perhaps?"

"I don't know. I'm at work most of the time. I don't really spend much time in my flat, so ... I'll go with a cautious 'no,' but don't quote me on that."

"No quotes, indeed, sir. We'll rule the neighbors out. Frankly, I'll let you in on a little secret. This sort of thing happens a lot with the SRGST 5000, though we hate to admit it. Not the first time the sharks have gone missing and jelly turns up in their place. Just an engineering error, I believe."

"So, now what do I do?"

"First thing's first, we simply must get all that jelly out of the tank. No use in leaving it in, is there? Best way to do it: throw something of a soiree."

"A party?"

"Gala event, sir. Invite all your friends, especially those with a particular fondness for the eating of jelly. Serve a dish to every guest, and you'll be that much closer to a resolution."

"Is it going to be safe to eat? I mean to say, I'm not even sure that it is gelatin."

"We'll sort that straight away. Sending our agent over now."

Five seconds passed before Bronson's doorbell sounded. He opened the door, and a pygmy chimp capered in, wearing a cowboy hat and a t-shirt bearing a picture of President Bush. The caption read: "I'm the President, so kiss my ass." The chimpanzee looked up at Bronson, extended both middle fingers, and blew a rather loud raspberry, then hopped up and down, squealing in laughter.

"Uh … there's a chimp here in a cowboy hat."

"Yes, sorry about that. It's his night off, you see, but he was closer than any of our agents on duty. Might be a little bit cheeky, but he agreed to do the testing. So, simply stand aside and let get on with the task in hand would be my advice, sir. We'll cover any damages, of course."

The chimp ran down a short hall, thumping on the wall three times, until he came to the bedroom door, which he thumped on twice. He then turned around, shuffled on all fours back down the hall until he discovered the kitchen. After a short survey of his surroundings, he commenced opening each drawer and cabinet, tossing everything he found onto the floor until he held one spoon and one bowl. He tottered awkwardly on just his back legs to the living room, hopped up on the tank and spooned out a bowl of the gelatin.

"He's got a bowl of the stuff," Bronson said into his phone.

"Good. Now leave him to eat it, sir, and we'll see how he fares in a half hour's time. In the meantime, I'll recite some Blake for you if I may. *'When my mother died I was very young, / And my father sold me while yet my tongue / Could scarcely cry "Weep! weep! weep! weep!" / So your chimneys I sweep, and in soot I sleep …'"*

Bronson eyed the ape, watching for the most infinitesimal change in demeanor or breathing pattern. Nigel continued with the poetry, although he knew Bronson wasn't paying attention. He slipped in a "What light through yonder window breaks" and Bronson didn't even chuckle. Nigel did not bother to call out the American on his ignorance. This was in keeping with the lessons of his manual "How to Speak to Rich Americans over the Phone."

After twenty-nine minutes had passed, Bronson finally interrupted Nigel: "The chimp looks fine. He's hopping around on my coffee table. He tore up one of my adult magazines. I don't think he approves of smut."

"Smashing. Of course we'll reimburse you for the torn girlie mags, sir. But good news on the soiree front, what? Have your guests eat up all that jelly, then give me a call back."

"Yeah, sure. Okay. I'll do it tomorrow night. Sounds fine. Talk to you later." After hanging up, Bronson realized the chimp was still in the apartment. "Hey, you. Don't you think it's time to go?"

The chimp said nothing but cowered from Bronson's stern tone. He hung his head, picked his cowboy hat up off the floor, and left. It almost broke the rich man's heart to see the poor creature in such a dejected state. "I'll have to remember to invite him to the party."

The party was going nicely, but Bronson did overhear a particularly well-dressed socialite say to her friend, "I thought this fellow was rich. I don't even see any sharks." They muffled their laughter as he passed them, face a little red, suit a little rumpled. He hadn't been able to sleep the night before. Something about all that gelatin just made him uneasy. The guests seemed to be enjoying it though. They treated it like a cute themed affair: Jelly Night. Before too long, the entire tank had been emptied, save the usual scum that settles to the bottom. Abdel would have to take care of that in the morning.

A burly, middle-aged man with a bushy moustache approached Bronson, slapped him on the back, and said, "What an absolutely terrific place you've got here. I must say, most Americans would have something gauche, say a wide screen television, to ruin the ambience. But I like your style. Though one wonders, why keep the dessert in a shark tank? If I were you, I'd get myself a few sharks for it. Here's my card." It read:

Adrian Hawthorne
Shark Importer

It also gave the address where one could find his Fabulous Lair of Sharks. "Not just sharks, mind you," Hawthorne added. "I'm the only man in town who can set you up with proper barracuda. The other lads'll give you a dogfish with glued-on glass needles for teeth. Since I know you are a man of refined tastes, I know you wouldn't settle for that rubbish. I'll get you real barracuda, no questions asked. The other lads'll ask questions, too. 'Whatcha want with them barracuders?' they'll say. Don't take any cheek. Deal with Hawthorne. I'm your man." His spiel was much like a commercial.

Bronson waited to see if a jingle would play before saying, "Thank you, Mr. Hawthorne. I'll keep you in mind."

The party progressed well into the wee hours. Bronson was antsy and aloof, but couldn't bring himself to send his guests away. They all appeared to be having such a splendid time. Some had even fallen asleep on his sofa, in his recliners, or curled up in corners using their dinner jackets as pillows. Bronson followed precedent, and retired for the few hours of sleep he could manage before he had to get up to go promote his latest whatever.

He awoke around 6:30, stumbled out of bed and into his living room where the sleeping partygoers had all been replaced, or, rather, transformed. Large cocoons littered his rooms, smeared with gooey webs that linked them inextricably to his furniture and carpeting. "Oh, hell. What next?"

He dialed the assistance number again. *Ring, ring.* "Hello, this is Nigel speaking. How can I be of assistance today?"

"My guests have all formed cocoons."

"Ah, that's a good sign. But tell me this, did you flood your flat as soon as they fell asleep, sir?"

"Of course not, why would I do a thing like that?"

"Tisk tisk, sir. Really should have called me back like I instructed. If you had called me after they ate the jelly, I would have told you the next item on the list would be to allow them to fall asleep, then flood your flat with salt water. Won't be much good to you now as I expect they're already dead."

Bronson's heart palpitated. His palms sweated. He went to his kitchen to retrieve a very sharp Japanese steak knife and then returned to cut one of the cocoons. He peeled back the scaly husk and revealed a slimy shark in an ill-fitting tuxedo, eyes staring abnormally blankly at him, even for shark eyes. "Dead," he confirmed. "This is great. An apartment full of dead sharks."

"We'll get this settled straight away," Nigel said.

Perhaps eight seconds passed before the door bell sounded. It was the chimp again, this time in a blue jumpsuit, accompanied by several colleagues.

Bronson shrugged. "I'm sorry I forgot to invite you to the party. But from the looks of it, that mistake worked out for the best."

The chimp gave a dismissive wave. He and the other chimps scampered off to ransack the kitchen. They returned, each with a steak knife and fork in hand, teeth bared. Bronson began to worry harder.

"Yes," Nigel said, "we'll have this sorted in no time."

Old-Fashioned Farming

Emma Tonkin

The beast in the farmyard was waist-height to DCI Newman, with green scales that made him think of a lizard-cheetah hybrid. Or would have, anyway, if lizards came with a side order of focused, bitter malevolence and a perfect set of needle-sharp teeth.

Newman kept eye contact as he crossed the yard and knocked on the office door. A cloud of dried paint flakes erupted into the air.

An elderly gentleman emerged. Everything from tweed to Wellington boots shouted *farmer*. The man was maybe eight inches taller than Newman's own five-eight. He involuntarily straightened his spine.

"Come in!" said the man. "You'll be the policeman from up Wellsway, then?" He stuck his hand out. Newman shook it.

"That's right," he said. "We spoke on the phone."

"Right. Right."

Newman took a pen and notebook from his pocket. Just then, something poked him in the thigh. He gasped, recoiling. It was the lizard … no, though, it wasn't. It was *another* lizard. His farmyard friend was right where it had been, by the gate that led to the cowsheds, staring at him with distant disgust in its alien half-slit eyes.

"Mr Andrews," he said, with all the dignity he could find. "Would you mind if I came in? Perhaps we could talk? Maybe indoors?"

The farmer grinned, showing his own first-rate dental work. "Don't mind the girls," he said. "They're just being affectionate."

The lizard favoured Andrews with a broad yawn. It had *very* good teeth.

"Polly," said the farmer, "Be gone with you. Time for pheasant patrol. Take Dolly along, too."

He shut the door behind its retreating tail. "Tea?"

Newman felt a crippling rush of relief. "Mr Andrews, I'm here to talk to you about the ramblers' right of way through your land. But first, if I might just ask – what were those things?"

Andrews retreated into his office and emerged with a glossy catalogue. "Come through to the kitchen," he said.

At the big oak table, Newman examined the catalogue. *Venables'*

Bio-Farming Goods. "Trained velociraptors," he read. "Secure your game from poachers and predators with Nature's gamekeeper ... that's ridiculous!"

"Might be," said Andrews cheerfully,"but they work. And they're cheaper'n freezing your arse off at all hours standing watch with a shotgun."

"Velociraptors had feathers. Like birds."

"Yup, and they were nasty daft wee sods who'd take your hand off soon as look at you. Going green doesn't mean you have to make stupid decisions. No, my little ladies here are bred for safety."

"Really?" Newman peeked out of the window, watching the two raptors lope off into the fields, great clawed forelegs slashing idly at the air.

"Unless you've got buzzard in your family tree, lad. I've got three raptors. They're the best friends a farmer can have in this day and age. Good workers, raptors. You know how many buzzards nest here? Bloomin' things've been eating their way through my stock. Nothing like a velociraptor to frighten off yer basic bird of prey."

Newman closed the catalogue. It wasn't his job to police perfectly legal organic farming methods, he reflected, however insane they seemed. He suspected that buzzards were, properly speaking, a protected species. Then again, no pun intended, that problem wasn't his pigeon.

Toothy lizards gone, he felt his composure return. "Right, then, sir. I'd like to discuss rambler access to public paths across your land –"

The boots, carefully laced with meticulous double knots and crowned with neatly folded socks, sat forlornly by a hedgerow. A splintered bone peeked whitely from the left. Newman smelled blood and new-mown grass. He looked away, gulping involuntarily.

"Don't," said Hosein. "Bad form, puking on the evidence."

Newman stared up into her hazel eyes. He nodded carefully. Dizziness pricked at the edges of his vision. "Is this the lot?"

"Nope." She gestured into the field, where a clique of white-clad investigators poked into a scraggly heap of gorse. Newman trailed as Hosein strode towards them.

One of the forensics guys called, "There's an Ordnance Survey map here! And a compass. On a bit of string."

Newman's wife had a compass on a string lanyard, too. It was part of the British hiker's essential kit. It went with woollen socks into which trousers are tucked according to tradition, and a thin waterproof jacket in a primary colour, inevitably porous and ineffective unless repeatedly sprayed with a substance that cost more than the original garment.

His stomach gave an uncomfortable lurch. He looked away and spotted an electric gleam in a tangled nest of heather and furze.

"What's that?" He found a stick and poked at it.

"Nice find," said Hosein. "A camera."

"Map, compass and camera? Sounds like our guy's a hiker," said Newman.

"Was," said Hosein flatly. "I don't get it. There are no bears here, no wolves, no predator larger than a fox. Whatever did this had sharp teeth and strong jaws. I hope it's not a rabid suburban fox. Can you imagine what the hunt saboteurs will say if dear old foxy-woxy gets done for murder?"

Sharp teeth and strong jaws. The DCI thought of snakeskinned emerald raptors loping away into the distance, heads high and curved claws poised to slash.

"Hang about," he said. "Are we anywhere near the Andrews farm?"

Hosein stared at him. "What do you know?"

"Nothing. Not for sure. But -"

"I think maybe you do." She gestured towards the west. "That road leads to the Andrews place. It's half a mile away, if that. Why?"

The camera held a dozen photographs of velociraptors, including two selfies. The last image, probably an unintentional shutter activation, showed a blurred reptilian head and a lot of needle-sharp teeth.

They found the hiker's name by tracing the insurance provider for her camera. Flora Chantry-Wilberforce, primary-school teacher and amateur photographer, had taken the last ramble of her life.

Arresting a velociraptor turned out to be the easy part. The three creatures came tamely in response to Andrews' call. He identified them to the police ("Polly, Dolly and Molly. Molly's the one with the crooked foreclaws.")

Despite the wetness that stained the farmer's tired eyes, he seemed to understand and accept the need to cooperate with the police. He directed the reptiles into their cages. They followed his guidance tamely, if sadly. All three chirped forlornly as Andrews turned his back on the police van and walked away.

Once the animals had been impounded, the problem became legal. The velociraptor and its family, *Dromaeosauridae*, were not listed in the The Dangerous Wild Animals Act (1976). Once again, the law was lagging behind the consequences of technological change.

Another legal basis for the detention of the animals would have to be sought. Someone suggested that manslaughter charges be brought against Andrews, suggesting that the rambler's death was the result of gross negligence. The legal precedents were not encouraging for the success of the manslaughter gambit. Neither the Dangerous Dogs Act nor the Animals Act seemed to apply. The conversation went on as spring fell away under the weight of summer and the ground hardened in the heat of the sun.

Where the legal team would have arrived is anybody's guess. Eventually they might have fined the farmer under the Animal Welfare Act (2006) for unlawful employment practices and the failure to pay minimum wage. There was no legal precedent condemning the use of a team of velociraptors as gamekeepers. It could've been a test case worthy of an economy-sized bag of popcorn.

In the end, it didn't matter.

Newman stared into the girl's partially eaten face. Her nose was missing, her left cheek torn away. Her throat was an empty and twisted ruin. The green iris of her right eye looked sadly upwards into the sky. Her torn-out shoulder leaked slowly onto the bank of the quarry lake.

He swore to himself in sadness and disgust.

"Hey," said Hosein.

"Andrews must've bought himself some more raptors," he said. "If we'd acted faster – we could've –"

She shook her head. "You don't know that," she said.

"Have you ever heard of Occam's Razor?"

"Sure I have," she said. "I don't care for it. Any hypothesis that smug must have something to hide."

If the girl's broken face weren't still burnt into his mind, he might have smiled. He shuddered.

Hosein patted him on the shoulder. "Don't," she said. "We did what we could."

Leaving the forensics team to it, they walked away from the lake, up towards the fields clustered around the lane leading towards the

Andrews farm. There was nothing to hear but a deep silence interspersed with their own footsteps crunching on dried roots in the summer heat. The fields were overgrown, weed-strewn. Perhaps the farmer had given up, gone away to nurse his sorrows in a foreign land.

There were no velociraptors, either in the field or in the farmyard. There wasn't even a farm cat prowling the empty barns. The site was deserted.

"I don't understand it," said Newman. "There's nothing here." He swiped at the door-handle with the cuff of his white shirt. It came away filmed with dark dust. "This door hasn't been opened for a good long time."

Something barked in the distance. A dog, maybe, but it was frightening enough in that abandoned place. He was running before he knew it.

Hosein ran, too. She grabbed his arm and pulled, directing them towards the origin of the sound. He hadn't known whether he intended to find it, or to flee. Running, he thought of a bright green eye, vacant and dead, staring into nothing.

The source of the barking was a small, elderly Scottie dog wearing a tartan overcoat. It was currently engaged in dragging its owner from one tree stump to another, on the dirt path that ran from the Andrews farm and into the village. Hosein introduced herself to the terrier's custodian.

"Nadya Hosein, hey?" said the gentleman in the wax coat cheerfully. "Nice to meet you. I'm Matthew Holbourne. Don't meet many people down here, this time of day. Not many of us pensioners round here nowadays."

Hosein said no, she supposed not.

"I was in the first eleven, you know," Holbourne added.

She took the non sequitur in her stride. "Oh, yes?"

"Yes indeed," he said. "Almost the whole team is gone, by now. The Palmer twins left three years ago, and I think Jacob may have passed on by now, though there wasn't a funeral. I mean, what's the point? Funerals are for the living, they say. Who's left, except for me and little Biscuit here?"

The dog sat down, cocked its head to one side and whined engagingly.

"Good dog," said Holbourne vaguely.

DCI Newman cleared his throat.

"Can I do something for you, young man?" asked Holbourne.

"Well," said Newman. "I was wondering – that is, have you seen any velociraptors around here?"

The old man laughed. The terrier scratched at its nose with a hind leg and sneezed.

Newman waited.

"Bless you," said Holbourne, "hasn't been a single velociraptor here since they took away young Bennie Andrews' three back in spring."

"Are you sure?"

"Yup."

The two police officers looked at one another.

"'Course," said Holbourne, "there's always the quarry lake."

Newman blinked. "What?"

"I mean, if you're looking for dinosaurs."

Newman stared at the man, who paused to tickle Biscuit's head and fuss at the animal's tartan waistcoat.

"I wonder if you could expand on that remark?" said Hosein gently.

"It's the bloody *Tiktaalik roseae*, isn't it? Massive great sharky things, I don't know, all teeth and elbows. And feet! Fish shouldn't walk on land, say I, it ain't natural."

The old man spat reflectively onto the path. "I daresay they do everything they're supposed to do, keep down the algae, discourage poachers, frighten away herons, all that, but they've got a vicious attitude. Anyone who's ever fished in that lake knows they're bitey little buggers if you give them half a chance. They've got bloody big teeth, those things."

"You don't mean –" said Newman.

"Of course I bloody do. D'you think I live with a terrier for fun? Nah. But I can still run faster'n little Biscuit here." The pensioner tugged on the dog's lead and wandered away.

Newman and Hosein watched him leave.

"I'll get an armed unit down to the lake," said Hosein.

Newman nodded. "You do that."

There was a moment's uncomfortable silence.

"What's up?" Hosein asked.

"Oh, I don't know," Newman said. "I suppose I was just wondering whether velociraptors could sue for wrongful arrest."

Shark's Tooth

Ken Goldman

Benjamin Crabb enjoyed sweating, and today the sweat on his forehead made him feel especially alive. The salty air that swirled off Key West complemented the moisture beneath his shirt, making Benjamin feel forty years younger. To see him preparing the complex rigging of the *Sonia's Smile* was to believe that age was only a state of mind. The triangular shark's tooth around his neck glittered in the sun upon its golden chain as he stepped onto the flying bridge.

"Nella! The tanks! Would you check the hoses for me? And the pressure? And –"

"– And the six cold ones? Not to worry, Dad. Done, done, and done!"

Benjamin peeked into the cooler just to be sure. There would be one hell of a reason to celebrate his seventy-fifth birthday if he found the golden treasure he sought today. How many years had he searched for it? How often had he failed? He knew only that it was out there somewhere in the Atlantic, just about seventy nautical miles southeast of the Saddlebunch Keys.

He knew because forty-five years ago he had left it there.

He checked that the fuel supply of his twin Volvo diesels read 'full' and wiped the glass of the fathometer and radar reflector clean. His thirty-four foot trawler would not fare well if one of those freighters en route to the Gulf Stream crossed the *Sonia's* path.

Benjamin felt uncomfortable knowing the Coast Guard closely monitored the area surrounding the Keys, and getting around those maritime salvage laws was always tricky. But his age had worked in his favor the last time the USCG boys had stopped him. Three officers had smiled at the old man in the scuba gear, and one had said something under his breath about Jacques Cousteau being alive and well in Florida. Benjamin had simply smiled back at the young officer.

Behind him on Duval Street the sign to Crabb's Bait and Tackle Shop swung and squealed on its rusted hinges. Benjamin knew how much Nella hated that sound and pictured his daughter gritting her teeth with each swing. He turned to watch her through the store's huge bay window.

Nella seemed too absorbed in her *Cosmopolitan* to be giving much thought to the sign. She looked up at the old man and shrugged. The store had been open for over an hour and there had not been a single customer. She stepped out onto the pier and rolled up her *Cosmo* into a megaphone.

"Better you should be giving more thought to selling these stinking worms than going out on another one of your excursions. What is it this time? The search for Atlantis? Or maybe Jimmy Hoffa?"

The old man smiled as he watched her. His daughter seemed such a strong woman, much like her mother had been. At thirty-six, clearly Nella did not belong near the smell of any raw fish that wasn't sushi. Yet he had never heard her complain once.

"Already found Hoffa! He's in that barrel next to the blues. Makes for a good chum line!"

Benjamin's smile flickered, but only for a moment. With any luck, by next month the store sign would have another name upon it. Nella might soon be reading her *Cosmopolitan* far removed from the smell of fish parts. Of course, Nella knew nothing of this yet, but that was hardly important.

What was important waited for Benjamin Crabb somewhere deep in the Atlantic. It had been waiting for a very long time.

"Well, wherever you're headed this time, you sure picked a great day for it. Don't know why you'd want to bake in the sun out there when you can celebrate your birthday basking right here under your favorite squeaking sign."

Nella stepped aboard the *Sonia*, shielding her eyes from the bright sunlight that hit her deck. "Honest, Dad. I worry about you alone in the middle of the ocean, looking for God knows what. Unless, of course, you got something going with the marlin I don't know about."

"We're just good friends, so never mind the rumors." Benjamin's expression turned serious. He stepped off the bridge, brushed a golden curl from his daughter's forehead and cupped her face in his hands. "Nell', hear me out, will you? This time's going to be different. I can feel it. I'm going to take care of you and little Matt. You know that, don't you? This time when I return, you're going to have it all ... everything ... every damned thing you ever-"

Nella placed a finger to her father's lips. "Listen, you old coot. I've already got all the worms I can eat. What more could a girl want?" She kissed his cheek and stepped off the boat. "Okay, Popeye. Beer's in the cooler. Tanks are on board and on 'full.' Fish are jumpin' and the cotton is high. Shall I wait dinner or will you be dining with the dolphins?"

"Wait dinner!" Benjamin called out, releasing his line. "You might want to chill some champagne too!" The 55 horses inside each of the diesels kicked in with a roar. "Here's to swimmin' with bowlegged women!"

Nella stood on the pier as Benjamin steered his way out of the slip. She did not wave goodbye as the *Sonia's Smile* headed for the open sea.

Few places are more quiet than upon a calm sea, but Benjamin Crabb knew of one such place. He thought of that place often when he was alone. With the *Sonia's* engine purring at 25 knots and the La Concha Holiday Inn slipping below the horizon behind him, this moment seemed the appropriate time to think of it. Benjamin could not say whether it was the tune he hummed that had brought the thought, or the thought that had brought the tune to mind. But he hummed it with a determination that made the thought all the more vivid.

The tune formed itself as a wordless hum upon his lips, yet his mind sang the words note for note ...

*"To-morrow shall be, to-morrow shall see, the world only knows how to-morrow shall belong ... **to us!**"*

Benjamin's eyes seemed to widen with each note. His lips slowly tightened as he hummed so that his mouth seemed curled in an odd smirk.

"... this day we must wait, this night must abate, but to-morrow shall see, to-morrow shall be ..."

As he hummed, he instinctively caressed the shark's tooth that dangled around his neck. It had remained there, close to his chest, for the better part of the last fifty years.

... It even dangled around his neck that day many years ago when a young officer dropped a large chest into the Atlantic from his seventeen foot chartered skiff, a very large chest, containing riches beyond his wildest imaginings, beyond anyone's wildest dreams ...

Benjamin cut off the *Sonia's* engine and listened from the console as the water lapped against her side. He checked the compass, released the anchor, and reached into the cooler for a cold beer. In a moment he would work. He lay flat on his back upon the deck mat. As he drank, some beer dripped down his chin, but its coolness soothed him. The sun burned into his skin, and Benjamin closed his eyes to await the comforting sweat that would cover his body. The words pounded in his brain.

*"... but to-morrow shall **be**, to-morrow shall **see**, that to-morrow belongs ...*

... to us! To us!" young Officer Klaus Reichmann sang under his breath as he began his morning inspections of the camps. Mornings were always quiet. Distasteful, to be sure, this business of clean-up, yet a job not without certain rewards. The pliers in Reichmann's coat pocket would help in the attainment of those rewards.

Last night's rainfall would make this a messy business today. The resulting mud-coated pile of remains had been given a certain sameness that made the job somewhat less – could the term be applied here? – distracting. Reichmann's work moved quickly enough while he inspected the older males and females. But the younger women had the tendency to impede the officer's efficiency. There was still something so affecting in their faces ... in their sweet young, dead faces. But it was not their faces in which Officer Reichmann took so keen an interest.

It was their mouths.

He knew what they called him, and the thought made the task now, while not pleasant, at least tolerable. "There walks The Shark," and "The bite of the shark is always lethal," he would hear them whisper. The stories they told throughout the camps, while not altogether true of the young officer, had done nothing to hurt a reputation in which he took pride.

True, as a youth he had taken the tooth, which he now wore on a golden chain around his neck, from the maw of a tiger shark. No need to admit that he had found the creature washed up on a lonely Baltic shore and half-devoured by the gulls.

How appropriate that the tales they told of The Shark had so much to do with teeth. For there were other tales that were true. One had only to observe the dried blood upon Reichmann's pliers to learn how true they were.

So many with their mouths open ... So wide open ...

Dark mud clung to the young officer's boots as he inspected the muddied corpses. He wondered if their last words had been screams.

Reichmann reached into his coat pocket and felt the cold steel of his pliers. He studied the half dozen piles of muddied flesh. Today it would be difficult to distinguish the old from the young, the males from the females.

There were many piles of older ones today, and they yielded the most treasures for the simplest efforts. The younger gums, being stronger, had a tendency to resist the pliers, and often the teeth came out only when the gums came with them. This made the business of separating the tooth itself from its golden interior much more tedious, and often the younger ones possessed healthy teeth that had required no need of repair, teeth which yielded no treasures.

"Come ... come ... Out with you! No need to be so stubborn ...! "

One had to search to be certain. It was much like the process of finding pearls. One had to crack many oysters to find even a single pearl.

The Shark had come prepared to crack many such oysters today, and to crack them first. A sharp eye could detect a small golden glimmer even amid the most badly decayed molars. Some of his bounty he would report to the Offizier. He would hand him the small leather pouch and smile.

*As for the rest ... the fruits of his past efforts could be found locked in a secret chest with the initials **K.R.** beneath the floorboards of his bunker, safe and secure from the prying eyes of the other officers.*

Mud ... so much damned mud ...

Someday he would melt his gold into coins. Or perhaps he would create some bracelets and baubles for the right woman when there would be time to think of such matters. Today he must provide for that day. Tomorrow would provide time enough for the rest.

*"... tomorrow shall **be** ..."*

Reichmann hummed a verse of the song as he stepped forward. He did not cease humming as he moved through the rotting piles. His thumb and forefinger extended into the mouth of the skeletal woman at his feet.

"Mrs. Goldstein, you are not looking so well this morning. And is this your husband beside you? I cannot tell with all this mud. "

The Shark showed his teeth as he smiled ...

Benjamin Crabb awoke covered in sweat. The late afternoon sun had turned the color of burnt gold, as had the color of the old man's skin. Without checking his watch, Benjamin knew the time had come to get to work.

"Tomorrow will be ours, my sweet Nella. Just as I promised," he spoke aloud, as he watched the waves heave below him, as if each wave contained that promise. He opened the cooler and popped the top off a Heineken. He raised the can toward the sky. "And to you, my

Sonia, and to the dreams we might have shared."

He finished the beer without it leaving his lips. He held the empty can to his cheek for a moment, savoring its coolness, then allowed it to drop to his side as he sat upon the mat.

Perhaps just a moment longer. To reflect.

Benjamin reached into the cooler again. Another beer would bring the memories quickly. He caressed the can even as he drank.

The memories came …

… of his Sonia's smile, the most radiant smile Officer Klaus Reichmann had ever seen. The kind of smile meant to melt the soul as well as the heart. The kind of smile that could melt even the soul of a shark.

But that would not be necessary. The Shark was dead, as dead as those who lay in the muddied heaps of the camps. Or so the rumors had stated. Some had said the young officer had smiled as he pointed the revolver into his mouth. Others claimed his smile had remained even after he had pulled the trigger.

Reichmann himself had often smiled hearing the story of his death. He thought of it on the day he had plunged into the Atlantic, the day he had followed a large chest as it sank to the bottom. His golden treasure would wait here for him – if necessary, for years – hidden on the ocean's floor.

But it would not be Klaus Reichmann who would reclaim it. Nor would Klaus Reichmann be returning to shore on that day.

As the rumors had stated, The Shark was dead. The shark's tooth was not. From that day onward it would hang from the neck of Benjamin Crabb. Sonia had never so much as heard the name of Officer Klaus Reichmann. Benjamin had sworn to himself that she never would.

"I love you, Benjamin. I shall always love you. And shall I tell you why?"

Benjamin smiled across forty-five years with the smile that had once belonged to a young German officer.

"There is no need. I already know. It is for my strudel and cheese. I am one of your few lovers who does not give you gas."

"No, Benjamin," Sonia answered, unable to restrain her smile. "It is because you are one of my many lovers who makes me laugh. And as for your strudel …"

The soul of Klaus Reichmann had died, but the heart of Benjamin Crabb lived. It had been given life by a smile that now traveled across the years back to him.

"... to the dreams we might have shared," Benjamin whispered. He tossed the empty beer can over the side, and went below to get into his wetsuit. He imagined how ridiculous he must look struggling with the heavy air tank at his back. Nella had once told him he had looked like an aging hunchback trying to maintain his balance.

Behind the amused grin of his daughter lived the soul of her mother. The smile did not die with her. Nor had the dream died of reclaiming the treasure that the young Officer Reichmann had left behind so many years ago somewhere in these depths as a gift from the past to the future.

The past does not die, thought Benjamin as he clutched the shark's tooth in his fist. As he had done so often, he studied the chart he had marked and penciled in the day's diving location. He checked the hose assembly, bit hard on the mouthpiece and secured his face mask. Still grinning from behind it, Benjamin Crabb plunged into the sea to reclaim his gift.

The water seemed especially clear today, for there were other times when he could not see bottom until he was practically standing upon it. Today the Atlantic treated Benjamin to an underwater panorama, making the search a much simpler task. If his treasure were anywhere near, today he would surely find it. Nella had filled the tanks, and should another dive be necessary, he would have enough for over one and a half hours. The water that lay south of the Keys could be especially deep.

This was an unusually long plunge, and despite the water's clarity, Benjamin did not see bottom for several minutes. A school of rainbow darters cleared a path for him as he descended. How easy to become distracted surrounded by such beauty, but better if he were not. One had to be alert for the job at hand.

And one had to be alert for danger. The ocean's floor contained as much menace as it did beauty. One often had to choose blindness to ignore its beauty. Distraction would not do. He reached for the flashlight in his pouch and snapped it on.

The faces of the young women ... the faces ... hard to concentrate ... hard to be efficient ...

Benjamin's foot touched bottom. A swirl of mud encircled him.

Is that your husband, Mrs. Goldstein? ... So much mud ...

Where to look? Benjamin's eyes searched the floor of swirling sand. The light's beam sent a nearby school of pencil-shaped minnows skittering out of its path while a bluestripe drifted directly into it. Benjamin turned slowly, extending the flashlight. Formless shapes moved in and out of its track as he studied the sandy bottom. He could see the *Sonia's* danforth anchor as a shimmering blur resting upon a darkened pile of sand, while a curious rosefish explored it.

Foolish old man! Why are you here? The thought always came at this time. This was like searching for a lost coin in the Atlantic. And he was devoting a lifetime to the search. *Foolish ... Insane!* ... Perhaps it would be best to leave his treasure as a gift for the fish that swam at his feet.

Over forty-five years ... Buried ... Lost ... Or perhaps found by someone else ... Foolish old man ... !

Yet there was something different this time, something that was not like the other times. Something out of place.

The anchor! The darkened pile of sand upon which it rested! Quickly, Benjamin spun around and directed the light's beam at the *Sonia's* anchor. He could not make out anything but a darkened blur beneath it. He rushed toward it in an awkward motion that was neither running nor swimming, leaving a train of air bubbles and sand in his wake. The anchor rested on strangely colored sand indeed. Benjamin pushed the anchor aside and clawed at the seaweed and brine like an over-anxious child attacking the bothersome gift-wrapping that contained a precious reward.

His fingers scraped metal. Again he tore at the seaweed, ripping off clumps as he clawed. Benjamin's eyes widened. Beneath the seaweed his fingers traced the outline of a chest. He scratched at it like a cat.

The initials above the combination lock read **"K.R."**

Young Officer Klaus Reichmann lived again. The Shark lived again. Benjamin Crabb smiled for both of them. He smiled for Nella and for Sonia.

... And for the young girls, the old men and women, the rotting remains of flesh gone to dust and blown away, except for ...

... except for what waited inside the rusted chest that lay on the floor of the Atlantic at Benjamin Crabb's feet! He flung his arms around the chest in a lover's embrace.

*Open it ! Open it **now!** Just one look!*

Benjamin tore at the cheap lock, but it would not budge in spite of the thick rust that coated it. He pounded it with the butt of his flashlight, but still it would not yield.

Open! Open, damn you!

He raised his foot in an aborted attempt to kick the lock and fell backward upon the *Sonia's* anchor that lay in the sand behind him. The metal prong tore through the neoprene wet suit along his forearm, tearing the flesh beneath. A long rivulet of blood smeared the sea water around him. The old man paid no attention to it. He had only the chest to consider.

The anchor! Of course! The anchor!

Benjamin strained to lift the anchor with both arms curled in front of his chest, and brought it down heavily upon the chest's lock. The rusted lock cracked in two and the halves fell like rose petals to the ocean floor, disappearing among the surrounding flora.

Benjamin tugged at the lid, gritting his teeth against the resistance of five decades. Gouts of blood swirled from his arm, but that could be attended to later. He grasped the top with both hands and dug his feet into the sand as he strained. The lid groaned open, producing a wall of air bubbles that floated through the vapors of blood rising from Benjamin's arm.

The old man could not see clearly what lay inside, but he had waited long enough. He cupped his hands and plunged both of them deep inside the chest. Something sharp pricked his palm. He filled both hands and brought them close to his face mask to study his golden treasure. From behind his mask Benjamin's face turned white.

Impossible! Impossible! This can't be ...!

His hands were filled with small mounds of human teeth. Some were rotted black. Others were wrapped in graying flesh. Still others contained long pointed roots.

Teeth! Impossi...!

["Come ... come ... Out with you ... No need to be so stubborn."]

He threw them aside and again plunged his hands deep into the chest, upturning perhaps thousands of teeth. The chest was filled with them.

Benjamin's hands clawed through the pile, ignoring the pain caused by the teeth that tore at them. He shoved both arms deep into the pile, to his elbows. The teeth ripped the festering arm wound even wider, some embedding themselves inside it. Benjamin ignored the pain.

His hands touched something solid on the bottom of the chest. He tugged at the object that lay beneath the pile and pulled it out of the chest. Several sharp teeth clung to the loose flesh in his arm as he withdrew his hands. He held the object in front of his face to see it clearly.

Benjamin's mouth piece did not stop him from screaming.

In his hand he held Klaus Reichmann's pliers. Forty-five years beneath the sea had not washed the tool clean.

How easy to become distracted...how easy surrounded by such beauty ... and by such –

Benjamin spun around. His entire arm dripped with blood. A dim memory formed in Benjamin's brain. Something about blood ... something about blood and ... and about what is attracted to blood.

How easy to become distracted ...!

He spun around again and realized he still held the pliers. He dropped them and extended his flashlight in front of him. Dark figures, many of them, drifted into the beam. Benjamin quickly turned to look behind him, and flashed his light upon even more dark figures. The old man squinted, trying to bring them into focus. He looked up and saw more dark shadows above him, drawing nearer.

He saw them on all sides.

Something about blood and what is attracted to blood ... how easy to become distracted ... How easy ... Something about what is attracted to blood ...

Benjamin Crabb felt his free hand move instinctively toward the tooth that hung around his neck. The dark shadows seemed everywhere, and he knew what the figures were even before his light beam caught the reflections of their teeth. There were many teeth.

A ridiculous thought struck Benjamin. A trick of the eyes perhaps, or some insane sort of underwater mirage. What he saw simply was impossible.

These sharks! – Their teeth! Something is wrong with their teeth!

He was still screaming when the first one tore the flesh from his leg below the knee, and he screamed as the second severed his hand to the bone. It still held the light as he watched it sink to the sandy bottom.

Impossible! Impossible!

Even in the dark waters surrounded by his spilling blood, Benjamin Crabb could see what was so different about the sharks that drew nearer as they surrounded him.

Each shark had teeth of solid gold.

Bikini Ergo Sum

Justin Short

Samantha adjusted her bikini top and waited for the announcer to call her name.

Why do I do these stupid contests? I have a rockin' bod, sure, but is it worth the dirty jokes and creepy old men? What is life? What is existence?

She looked around at her fellow contestants. Most were fake-smiling for the middle-aged crowd. Others stretched and posed. The oiled girl in the yellow suit twerked beside the diving board.

Extra credit, Sam mused.

Without any warning, a monstrous head appeared in the center of the pool. It was arrow-shaped and dark gray, with a neck taller than a basketball goal. Before Samantha could quite register what it was, two massive flippers slapped against the surface of the water. The vibrations nearly knocked her to the ground.

She craned her neck to get a better look at it. *What is this thing…a mutant whale? A manatee with an anaconda glued to its head? An aftereffect of last night's pot?*

"Thank goodness," a spectator said. "It's just a plesiosaurus. Nothing to worry about, folks."

"All right, girls," the wrinkled judge said. "You heard the man. Back to your places."

Samantha crossed her arms. "But sir, shouldn't we try to figure out –"

The judge spat into his coffee mug. "I said *now!*"

Suddenly, a hot breath hit her face. The plesiosaurus was coughing.

She backed away from the pool, trying to avoid its –

Too late. The plesiosaurus coughed again. Spittle and phlegm and fish chunks coated her neck and chest. She bent down to wipe it off. When she lifted her head, she was face-to-face with a Tyrannosaurus Rex.

That thing must have burped him up. But then, we're all burps in the esophagus of the universe, my friend.

It was a perfect specimen. Dark eyes, sharp claws, skin like imitation leather. Much smaller than the ones from the nature shows. Probably the size of a Saint Bernard.

As Samantha waved her hand in front of her eyes, trying to decide whether or not she was still high, the T-Rex leapt through the air. It sailed over the bikini-clad contestants, touched down behind the line of plastic lounge chairs, and grabbed the judge by his jugular.

An instant later, the judge's severed head dangled between its front teeth. Blood pulsed into the crowd like drops from a sprinkler.

The dinosaur's sharp teeth made quick work of the old man's face and toupee. With a cute little squeak, the T-Rex crunched through the breastbone and proceeded to chomp his way all the way down to the man's rubber sandals.

"Poor thing was hungry," Jeanie said, applying more sunblock to her chest.

Samantha took another look at the plesiosaurus. It clapped its flippers like a trained seal. Cheering its buddy on, no doubt.

What's your game, Mr. Dinosaur? Are you testing us? Trying the limits of our belief? What's the nature of perception, anyhow?

"Excuse me," a man in a suit and tie said. "I came here for a bikini contest. So, is that still on the agenda, or am I wasting my time here?"

Bruup! Bruup!

The plesiosaurus burped up two more T-Rexes. The dinosaurs landed on the ground, shook off the saliva and chlorine, and launched themselves at the businessman. He hit the ground with a high-pitched wail. Samantha watched the little dinos rip his eyes out of their sockets, and then turned her head to let them eat in peace.

The plesiosaurus released a contented moan and ripped off another belch. A fourth T-Rex tumbled out, rose to its feet, and approached Samantha. She waited for the fear to paralyze her, but it didn't show up. Instead, the memory of a childhood puppy entered her mind. She dropped to her knees and extended her hand. The T-Rex licked her palm, its coarse tongue nearly tearing holes in her skin.

It left her side and raced along the edge of the pool, its eyes darting from spectator to spectator. It caught sight of a teenage boy and crouched.

"Whoa there," the kid said. "I'm in the prime of life, bro. I'm beggin' ya –"

The T-Rex lunged. It ripped the kid's intestines out before he finished his thought. Samantha held her hands to her lips. It was enough to make a person vomit. But at the same time, she found herself rooting for the little T-Rex.

He caught his first meal! Such a big boy!

The teenager screamed as the other T-Rexes joined the feast. The dinosaurs soon muted him.

Five minutes later, the formerly-white concrete was solid red. There weren't any corpses lying around. Just bits and pieces. A finger here, a brain stem there, a pelvis on the lounge chair over yonder.

Samantha surveyed the damage and realized she and her fellow contestants were the only survivors. Not a single spectator lived through the carnage.

We bikini, therefore we are. Thought is reality. Reality is mind.

The Tyrannosaurus Rexes stood in a line at poolside, the plesiosaurus behind them.

"What do we do now?" Chelsea asked.

Samantha shrugged. "Take our dinosaur friends and overthrow the government?"

"Geez, girl! I was thinking more like grabbing a couple drinks."

"We have time for both," Jeanie said. "It's not even dark yet."

The girls laughed and headed to the parking lot. The gang of T-Rexes squealed excitedly and ran after them. The plesiosaurus watched them leave, moaned, and dove underwater. Its thick tail hovered in the air, almost like a farewell. Then it disappeared into the depths of the pool.

Samantha shielded her eyes from the sun and looked into the distance. She smiled as she thought of the days to come, of happy hours and a dinosaur-backed oligarchy and the sweetness of existence.

The Discovery Of Loch Ness

Carissa Harwood

Usually people get something fun for their senior thesis.
I got death.
Well, academic death anyway.

Scotland is a magical place full of dreamy moors and moss-grown castles, a great place for an archeology student to study, but the Loch Ness Monster? Talk about career suicide.

The Loch Ness Monster is beyond cliché. When she had been revealed to exist, everyone in the world and their mother was now an amateur dinosaur expert, and Scotland saw record tourism that year. It was like being asked to do a thesis on the Big Mac. So what, big deal, $1.99 anywhere.

What they didn't reveal were the other discoveries in the water, the kinds that bite.

But I did it, because I was in school, and I was asked to do it and when I grumbled about it to my professor, he said to just think of a way I could look at the Loch Ness Monster in a new way. Use a new lens, he told me. No one has ever looked at the Loch Ness Monster the way you will, Teresa. Remember that. So I sucked it up and thought I'd chalk it up to paying my dues.

The University had rented a boat for me, and I found it waiting, much to the amusement of the captain. There had to be at least fifty boats just where we could see. Almost all of them tourists, all of them looking for the same thing I was. The next big discovery. Nessie had made several appearances lately, getting lots of attention, but still notoriously elusive.

Not a lot of people actually in the water, though. I didn't know if that was good or not.

The captain gave me a place to store my bag and a place to change into my wetsuit as we cruised to the middle of the lake to an area where the rest of the boats looked like little dots.

"You're still going through with this, huh?" At least that's what I heard. The accent was pretty thick. I peered up at him as I was adjusting my hair into the wetsuit. "You're really going down there?"

"Why wouldn't I?"

"You haven't heard?" He looked at me like he couldn't tell if I was messing with him or not. "When we found out our Nessie was real, we found something else." He swallowed, looking over the edge of the boat, not looking at me. "There are talks of sharks out there. Freshwater prehistoric sharks. At least, that's what they call it. Something big. Something with teeth. Lots of teeth. That's why you don't see anyone in the water. Either you come back with bites or not at all." He spit over the side of the boat, like getting a bad taste out of his mouth.

"Why wouldn't anyone tell me this?"

He shrugged. "Because everyone knows. I thought you knew. You still going?" He looked me up and down, and with that look alone, I was still determined to go.

I was already suited up. The protocol was to tie a line around me when I jumped, so he could pull me in if he had to. I wasn't entirely sure that I trusted him, but I was here, and I wasn't going to let someone's attitude stop me.

"You know, even if you dive, you won't see much, and that's if you don't get eaten. That lake water is so murky you can hardly shine a flashlight and see a few inches in front of your face. Like a good pint of beer." He laughed and shook his head. "If you make it, I'll buy ya that pint myself."

In response, I tucked my knife into a sheath by my leg, grabbed my camera, and fell backwards into the water. I didn't know or care about his reply. I was doing this. I let myself adjust to the cold, and the dark. He was right about the visibility, at least. It was grey-green, and I could hardly see in front of my face.

I don't know how long I was down there; time felt shifty and meaningless. I let my camera pan over the water, taking in full circle views, until I felt it. I felt something near me, around me right away. I couldn't tell if it was behind or underneath.

Then I felt a bump. My heart jumped into my throat, and I dropped the camera at once. *Oh my god.* It was under me. And then, I felt a tug. Something had my flipper. I pulled, and it stuck fast. Whatever it was had a good grip. I pulled hard on the line that connected me to the boat. My breathing was fast, and I tried to make myself calm down. *I can't panic in scuba gear.* This was such a stupid idea. Finally, the rope started pulling me, I was getting closer and closer to where I could almost see the underline of the boat when a large shadow cut across my vision, and I felt the line snap.

And then I felt teeth clamp down on my ankle, I could hear the crunch. Pain raced up my leg and I screamed. God, there was more than one. One cut the line while one pulled me down. I struggled, and the more I struggled, the more it held me. I fumbled for my knife and managed to pull it out of its sheath. I couldn't see it, but the pressure on my leg made me feel my foot was going to be snapped off any second. I just stabbed, slashed my way in the area around where my foot was being held. It hurt so much I didn't know what I was doing. I was hitting something, but I wasn't sure if my blows were doing anything. I could see a vague shape around my foot, large, stone-grey. I finally felt like I made an impact, I could see a small jet of blood spurt into the water, and it let go.

I looked up and I couldn't see the boat. Out of terror, I swam; I swam as much and as hard as I could and I had no idea where I was going, I just swam away, away, away, get away. It was behind me, I felt it. It was coming after me and it was so hard to swim with what was at least a broken if not almost severed foot. I could feel it flop as I tried to swim. The flipper was gone.

I was swimming blindly so I was surprised when I hit something solid. Was it a wall? A giant rock? I felt around it in the murky darkness, coming up with a plan that if I followed it towards the surface, I could maybe flag down the captain. I couldn't be that far away. Instead, my hand felt a hole, and with the thing behind me, I swam into it, thinking maybe to hide long enough for it to forget about me. I swam into the hole as far as I could. It was incredibly small and dark and I was afraid of small dark places, but not as much as getting eaten.

And then the hole opened into wide water, and I was startled because it was clear. Clear and glowing softly, I could see light on the surface above me, and that's what I swam for. My head broke the surface, and I could see a dark shore. I was inside a cave, underwater. I heaved myself onto the shore and unhooked myself, took my goggles off, and my one flipper. I rolled down the top half of my suit to feel the air. I could barely see in here, the only light came from some bioluminescent lichen. It was like trying to see by faint candlelight.

But I could see the mess that was my foot. It hurt so much, and although the light was poor, I could see a glimpse of what I thought was bone. If I didn't get help fast I might lose my foot.

A soft sigh came from behind me and I froze. I was not alone in this cave. There was no place that I could see that air was coming from, it couldn't be the wind. I turned around slowly from where I was sitting, and that's when I saw her. My heart stopped in my chest, and tears stung my eyes. She was lying with her head down and her mouth open. It reminded me of when a dog is tired and in pain. Her eyes rolled to me, as if she couldn't make her head move. She made a sound that was like a moan and cry at the same time and it raked across my heart and tore it to shreds. She was in pain, and she looked like she was dying.

I limped closer to her, trying as hard as I could to give off "I'm-safe" vibes, *I'm not going to hurt you*, my hands up. The cave was so humid; it never stopped being almost wet. My hair was plastered to my neck and the breath of the creature made it feel like the walls of the cave were moving itself. Like a beast inside a beast.

I was so close. At this moment she could probably snap my arm in two, or maybe, maybe she'd let me touch her. She was so shy, one of the shyest creatures in known history. So shy that legends were built so big around her, that no one had known if she really existed or not.

She existed, and there was nothing I could do to help her. I was earning credits on the field studies of these animals, but I wasn't a vet. I didn't know anything about what was happening to her. I had no idea why she was as sick as she was.

I was now standing within a few feet of her, trembling. I was so in awe of her presence. She was beautiful, with shimmering blue black and darkest green scales. She was slippery, like a fish. Silver flashed and caught some of the bioluminescent lichen; it was actually the only thing that helped me distinguish her shape in the wet darkness, a silvery outline of her head, neck, underbelly, flippers and tails. She leaned in to me and for a quick moment my heart sped up and a number of scenarios raced through my mind. Her large mouth, full of teeth, crunching down on my arm. Crunching like a pretzel. Like my foot. I wondered, half giddy with pain and blood loss, how I would taste with ketchup.

Ew, gross.

But there was no snacking on my arm, or violence of any kind. In fact it looked like she could barely even move her head towards me. Like it was taking all her effort. I reached out my shaking hand and let it fall on the top of her broad head. I saw her close her eyes and close her mouth for a moment. Maybe she had never been touched before. Maybe it had been eons since she'd been touched by anyone.

I started crying, and I forgot about my foot, which I could no longer feel. She was beautiful, and larger than life. A soft sigh came from her and it communicated something, it touched something down to the deepest part of my soul. I felt like this was the absolute right time and place for me to be here, and I didn't often get that kind of feeling. I was feeling that for once I was in the right place at the right time. I closed my eyes. I wanted this moment to last forever. I didn't want to forget it. I realized something of importance was being given to me, and I wanted to hold onto it. Maybe this was the reason for all of her sightings lately. She needed help; she needed someone to find her.

But my thoughts were interrupted by what sounded like chirps. Little chirps, like the kind a newborn kitten or baby bird makes. Had something gotten into the cave, injured and dying? Was this a place where things went to die? Like a death chamber?

But how would a bird or a cat get trapped in here, underwater, deep in the underground of Scottish earth? I moved slowly away from the head of Nessie – because what else could I call her – and she moved her long neck away from me, slowly, like it hurt, in the direction of the little chirps. I followed her gaze and saw that her massive body was arranged that way not because she hurt, but because she was curled around something, not favoring a flipper or an injury. Behind her slowly breathing body, I peered around her ribcage and saw that she wasn't sick, she was a mom. A very recent mom. Everyone was looking for a big discovery in Loch Ness and I just found it.

There were a bunch of cracked open white-blue shells. Amid the cracked open eggs were so many little Nessies, only a few inches big, crawling, scooting, and wriggling among the seaweed and moss that made a huge nest. She was showing me her babies. I whirled to look at Nessie's head, and she lowered her neck, letting her head rest on a stray clump of moss. The water trickled, I could hear the waves of the pool, left from primordial past. Just like Nessie herself. I felt this immense sense of responsibility. Out of all the people that had come to see her in past few decades, she chose me. I just had this feeling it wasn't an accident that I was here. But why? For what?

Me, who could hardly pay her rent. Me, who got a C in biology. But I had barely made it here on the sharp end of the paleo-sharks, proto-sharks, whatever they were. Things with big teeth that wanted to eat me. How did I get back past them, past the things that wanted to eat me? And of course, if they wanted to eat me, these little guys would probably be like snacks to them.

I watched them, thinking. There were roughly about a hundred of them. No way could I take them all with me.

What were my options?

Was there another way out of here besides the swim through the cave tunnel? I pushed myself away from the wall, using it to steady myself, and looked into the black water, faintly illuminated by underwater glowing lichen. I saw a faint light where the opening to the pool here connected to the outside, light filtering into the lake. The lake was out there, and hopefully people would have started looking for me by now. Nessie had to have gotten in here somehow, too; she couldn't have come through the narrow tunnel that I did. But I couldn't see any larger opening.

Wait for rescue? If they were combing the lake, they might think that I'm dead, devoured piranha feeding frenzy style. Was it possible to fight my way out? How could I do that? I could try to make a swim for it, but I had barely made my way here, and only by sheer chance. I didn't see a way out. I didn't have a plan. I don't know what I should do.

There was something moving on my good foot. I looked down, still expecting something with too many teeth, or something slithery with a giant mouth, with teeth on the inside of the throat, so you couldn't struggle.

But this was soft, gentle, and I probably wouldn't even have felt it if I hadn't been thinking so hard. A little Nessie was curled up on my foot. My foot apparently made an inviting little bed. My heart lurched. I mean, how can you resist a tiny little Nessie? I'm the only person I've ever known or heard about to come this close to Nessie, let alone her babies. I felt a fierce protectiveness against the thing that lurked in the deep biding its time, waiting for me, waiting for the sick Nessie, and waiting to eat her babies like popcorn. Actually, they're so small it would be more like jellybeans…I pushed the thought away.

If I understand how things work (admittedly this isn't my area of study and I'm definitely not an expert in these things), in order to make babies you need to have a mommy and daddy and, I don't know, maybe a bottle of wine? Soft music? I had a picture in my mind at the thought of a mommy and daddy Nessie, having a candlelight dinner on some secluded spot on the Lake.

Okay, I was getting a little hysterical again. Probably shock. I had to move.

I had to think, though. Nessie didn't make these babies by herself. This means a Daddy Nessie was around. Somewhere. Had to be. Was there anyway at all that I could find him, get his help?

I considered what I had with me. My scuba gear. A knife in a secure sheath at my leg. A piece of broken rope from where my tether had broken from the boat. But I was one girl, one girl with a knife against a giant beast with a mouthful, maybe several mouthfuls of teeth.

Well, what else could I do? I had to find a way out, I couldn't stay here. Who knew how long I could stay in this cave? Maybe the water was drinkable, but there was nothing else, no food and nothing to help my foot.

So, down through the water I had to go. Again. Who knows how long they'd search before giving up. The cave was so dark, the water was even darker. It could be broad daylight; it could be midnight, who knew.

Nessie knew. She knew what I had to do. I sat down to shrug the rest of my suit on from the shoulders. The back of it didn't feel quite right, but I couldn't worry about it now. I checked the oxygen in the tank. There was plenty. I hadn't been in the water long before that thing, whatever it was, the anti-Nessie, had attacked me. Before adjusting my goggles and putting my mouthpiece in, I turned to her. I reached out a gloved hand. I patted her neck, stroked the side of her face.

I'll come back. With help. I promise. I always keep my promises.

I turned to the black water lapping in the cave. I hoped I'd be able to find my way here if I needed to. I did it once. On accident, but I did it. I could do it again, right?

I took a deep breath.

I already had a threat waiting for me. I'd already given it my pound of flesh.

Let's see if it wants more. I closed my eyes. If I went into the water as a fighter, maybe I would have a better chance of coming out alive. If I made it to the surface, I would be safe. That's what I told myself. I took the knife in my hands before I jumped in.

I went out through the tunnel, trying to gauge where the thing was. I couldn't see far in the front of me, or the sides. It was a difficult swim since I couldn't move my right foot. It was too numb; I couldn't even tell it was there.

I don't know how far I got, but I could see the surface, before something hit me from the left, knocking my mouthpiece out, and clamping down on my arm at the same time. I hit it repeatedly with my knife, until it let go long enough for me to move out of its grip. I swam as hard as I could with one leg and one arm to the surface. My oxygen was gone, the back of my suit ripped. I had to get there or die.

I finally broke the surface, my torn air tank hissing and goggles destroyed. I gasped for air, knowing that I wounded but not killed thing hunting me. And my arm. My left arm was numb, too numb from the attack. Maybe it could smell blood. In that case, between my leg and my arm I was in trouble.

It was late afternoon, almost evening. I could have almost appreciated the sunset. I couldn't see anything but trees around me, but there, there in the very far distance, little white specs. Boats? Maybe, hopefully, boats looking for me? I didn't see the boat I had come in with anywhere.

I twisted around as best I could, feeling the need to hold myself together. I was shivering from the cold, seeping into my suit from the torn spots, and probably blood loss and pain. I couldn't use the air anymore, that was done, but if I could take stock of my surroundings, maybe I could remember this place. For when I came back. But this place looked like all the others. Cold grey-blue water. Tall pine trees and rocks on all sides.

How many feet was it to land? How long could I swim with one arm? I was about to find out. I tried to swim. I tried breaststroke, I tried everything. I couldn't move very far, and all I was able to do was splash around in a circle. That thing wasn't far. And it was pissed at me. I knew it was coming. I had to get out of here.

I dunked underwater, adjusting my goggles and letting my one good foot in its flipper propel me, and this worked much better than the surface method of swimming. I tried laying my injured arm flat against my body to be able to swim more streamlined. In my right hand, I clutched the knife, ready to strike if I had to.

How many more yards to shore? It never seemed so far away. I let myself come back up to the surface. There. Maybe 15, 20 yards. *I can make this. I will make this.*

I dove under the surface, and there it was. Waiting for me. I hadn't seen it or felt it. The water was so murky but the teeth came through absolutely clear. It was right under me, clouds of dirt and seaweed streaming into its gaping mouth by the force of its swimming. I kicked my legs and swam for shore. It was all I could do. I couldn't make it, there was no way. It was too big, too fast, and I was too small and injured. Even if I hadn't been injured, I still would have been at its mercy.

The shore was so far away. I stopped. I wasn't going to make it. I turned, dove under water and had my knife out. I was going to go down fighting. Torn to shreds, but fighting. So many images flashed in my head, most of them how badly getting eaten alive would hurt. I felt the rush of water, the only clue in the murky lake that it was close.

I closed my eyes. I saw its black eyes as I drew my hand back, then plunged the knife into one eye as hard as I could. I kept stabbing and stabbing until I felt the hardness of bone underneath. It could scream, a scream that sucked the sound out of my ears, and made me feel like my ear drums were bleeding. I just stabbed and stabbed until it wrested itself away from me, with my knife wedged into its skull. It disappeared, suddenly, and I had to get back to the surface again for air.

I broke the surface and gasped, breathing in so hard my lungs hurt. And I saw it. Its surface fins were coming right for me and I had nothing. Nothing to defend myself with.

Nessie and her babies came to my mind. They'd never be safe from these things.

For the final time, I gulped air and dunked under the water, looking at it coming at me from 40 feet, 35, 30. I did all I could do. I bunched my arm in a fist, my one last act of defiance. At least I'd fight. No one would know but me. No one would know what's become of me. But I'd know. At least, until I was dead.

Come, on you bastard, I thought at it. *Come and get me!*

It was maybe 10 feet away from me when something barreled into its side, driving it away from me in a rush of darkness and water so hard its wake pushed me backwards.

Something was at it. Something battling it. I didn't stop to think; I just tuned and swam, using my one leg and one arm to push me as far as they could, a million miles it seemed, until I could get to the shore.

The shore, the shore, the beautiful shore. Beautiful land, I love you. I collapsed, my flipper still on, struggling out of my now useless air tank, letting it fall to the ground, empty, broken. I saw two shapes fighting under the water, sometime the proto-shark coming to the surface and sometimes – a dark green-blue shape. It couldn't be Nessie; she was too weak to hold up her head. Was it her mate? Had to be. Unless there were more of them around than just the two of them. There was definitely more than one shark; there had to be more than one "Nessie".

I saw the head rise up, then, the head of the shark, and I saw it clamp down on the neck of the Nessie. Blood spurted out of its massive throat and the thing cried in pain. I was so helpless, on the sides. All I could do was watch. They both disappeared under the surface, the shark using its weight to hold the thing under the water.

I waited a long time after that. Nothing happened. Nothing came back to the surface. By the way the sun was heading towards setting, I knew I was a long way from the base. That was all I could do. Make my way back. I needed help. It would be a long trek, as hurt as I was.

I took off my one flipper. I left it on the shore, next to the busted air tank, so that I'd know where to come back again. Because I was coming back. I would find her again, and keep my promise. It would take me a long time to walk all the way; I might not even get there until long after dark. Just me and my wetsuit and ... something lodged inside one of the holes in my wetsuit, right in the small of my back like seaweed slipping over my skin. I squirmed to fish it out, clutching a clump of it and pulling it out, then almost dropping it in my shock.

It may have looked, and felt, like seaweed. But it wasn't. It was a small, although very tired looking, baby Nessie. I knew if she, excuse me, he, if he could survive almost getting eaten by a shark thing, and being pressed up against my lower back for who knows how long, this little guy could survive anything. We were survivors together and that made him special.

I think I should keep you a secret until I decide what to do, I thought at it. How I was going to keep him a secret, I didn't know. He was making little noises, almost like a baby bird makes, rubbing his head on the end of my thumb. Right now he was a few inches long, but eventually he'd be the same size as his parents. But for now ...

I stood up, holding him to me with my good arm in some instinctual effort to keep him warm. We'd walk back together, over a rocky shore line because I deserved, and was determined to get, that pint of beer or seven.

What happened after I got there, I had no idea. But that's life for an archaeology student, isn't it? It's all about unknowns and guessing. Just like the creature I was holding as I limped towards people and safety.

Welcome to the surface, little guy.

Somehow, The Mounting Of Dinosaurs, And Then ...

Sara Wilson

A wet release of soft eggs,
a sloughing of new thews,
a goo mixed frothy and hot,
dribbles onto dirt.

This product of obtuse thrusts,
the angles awkward and
some kind of impossible,
is strewn about the ground
in mounds, slick, sticky, amongst
the prints of roving giants.
This is the latest batch of addicts
or just a high protein meal sampled
by scavengers and heedless feet.
There is always this danger in being
beneath the tread and migration of amative beasts,
the unceasingly mounting behemoths.

So there will always be more
where those came from.
Everywhere they go, a hundred tons
of flesh smacks against another
hundred tons, a rub of pelvises
on rumps, somehow a slapping
together of soupy milt and ovum.

Hungry

Amy Fontaine

Hungry.
That is all I am: hungry.
Life is simple: emptiness yawns inside me so I seek to fill it with anything and everything around me. I swim through the endless blue, striking at whatever else does. They try to escape, always they try, but in the end I always win. When I bite it releases red, and that makes the emptiness stretch deeper. That stirs me on, so I bite and bite more, faster and harder, until I have devoured everything within my sight that I can.

And then I move on, to where it can begin again.

It is never over. I am always hungry. Big, small, hot, cold, it does not matter. I take whatever might fill the emptiness. It never does, but I always try and I always triumph. It is easy. So easy ...

And then ...

The net!

Something closes around me, something tight and impossible. I cannot breathe, I cannot bite. I thrash. It does nothing.

I feel myself rising upward against my will.

Suddenly, I have broken through the blue.

Horror of horrors! The brightness. It is not blue. It burns my eyes. It burns inside me.

I cannot swim in this space above the blue. I cannot breathe.

And it hurts!

It hurts, as if a thousand whales are pressing down on me. Yet I keep moving up with the net, up although I do not want to know this place above the blue.

We are over the side of a thing that is floating on the surface of the blue. And if I fall here, I may never return to my world. My home.

As I am lowered down toward a tiny imitation of the blue embedded in this thing, I thrash ...

And immediately a tiny sharp thing like a tooth is pushed into my soft side.

And then ...

Nothing.

After returning to the cave, the two scientists stared down at their catch, which lay motionless in the murky pool they had built into the sea cave's floor. A firm glass wall enclosed one side of this rectangular piece of water, the side that would otherwise have flowed into the sea. The other three sides were walled in naturally by the rock of the cave's floor. A pump pushed water through the shark's gills, keeping it (just barely) alive.

The men looked like malevolent angels, with their long coats white as death. Machinery stood behind them: a black screen, a large speaker with a strange dial, and a metal cap with seven ebony cords spreading from it, which looked almost like a petrified jellyfish. However, the scientists focused only on the large, gray form in the water, grim expressions on their faces.

"She's a beauty," said one quietly. Tall and wiry, he pushed his square-rimmed spectacles further up the long bridge of his nose as he examined his subject, nervously running a hand through his unkempt hair.

"Yes," agreed the other. "A beauty, and a devil." Unknowingly, the thickset man imitated the gestures of the man beside him, raising a hand to smooth hair long absent from his scalp, pushing round glasses tighter against his face. "To be honest, I can't believe we succeeded."

His thin companion nodded. "Indeed. It seemed impossible. Fantastical even. But here she is."

The bald man nodded. The two men stood in silence for a few seconds, staring at the shark.

Suddenly, small, wet footsteps resounded against the cave's stone floor. Both the scientists whirled around to face the intruder.

In the light of the cave opening stood a twelve-year-old girl.

The two men relaxed. But the girl was anything but relaxed. Rage blazed on her face. Her copper hair tossed about her like a stormy wave as she raced into the cave, glaring at the scientists.

"I saw you!" the girl cried. "I saw you, from the shore! You were fishing in my family's private cove!"

The men exchanged looks.

"Listen, little girl," began the bald man, "the ocean is everybody's ocean, all right? We can fish where we want to ..."

"No!" exclaimed the girl. "That is not all right! You didn't even ask us! And now you're loitering in a cave that is part of our property, too! You'd better –"

Before the girl could finish, her gaze fell upon the animal in the pool. She frowned in confusion.

"What ..."

The girl's voice became soft, small. Dazed. "Poor thing," she whispered, "poor thing ..."

The girl fell silent for a while. Then, trembling, she whipped around to face the scientists again. "What did you do to it?" she demanded.

The scientists looked at each other again. The wiry one released a hesitant bark of a laugh. "Do you realize," he asked the girl, "what you're talking about? That thing ... is a shark!" The two men laughed together now. When the girl's face remained unchanged, their laughter fell away.

The bald scientist added gently, "It shouldn't matter if it's a shark, should it?"

The girl's glare remained as hot as ever. "I know what it is!" she said. "I knew the moment I saw it! But you yourself said the ocean belongs to everyone. Well, then, it belongs to that shark, too. Even more than it belongs to us! You have no right to keep it in this pool!"

The wiry man looked at the girl as if she was mad.

"You don't know what you're saying, sweetheart. We have something amazing going here, something that, if successful, could change history. You don't want to interfere with that for one shark, do you?"

The girl still glared. "What are you talking about?"

The man opened his mouth to answer, but before he could a fretful stirring and sloshing sounded behind the three humans. They turned and looked down at the pool.

The shark was moving.

Where am I?

Dark place. Lone place. I am in water again, but alone.

Alone?

But am I always alone?

I breathe, but barely. I thrash, but weakly. I still feel... off.

I just try to keep breathing, and move just enough to live. It's all I can do.

I am too dazed to resist when a force above the blue slips a cool metal thing onto my head.

Black things attached to the metal spread out softly. Then suddenly they squeeze, like the tentacles of a squid, probing into me, into a part inside my head I never noticed before.

And then suddenly ... it is alive!

I am awake. It is prying, prodding, as if the touch is asking questions. I never knew of questions before today.

But now I am being asked, and I give what answers I know from my life. Hunger. Pain. Desire. But no fear, never fear. Not until I was plucked from the water.

And always, the knowing that I can eat whatever I want. And yet I will be empty afterward anyway, no matter what it is.

Conscious. I never knew what that was before, but now I do. It is a shuddering awake, as if all my life I had been living in this pool, and now suddenly I am free, free and swimming in the big blue.

But there is no big blue here. Only this murky puddle.

I am hungry. I am so hungry ... and yet ...

Is that all there is?

"Observe," said the bald scientist, gesturing at the black screen. A spectrogram danced across it, leaping up like a mountain, sloping softly like a hill, ducking deep like a valley or rolling like a choppy sea. Constantly moving, fluctuating.

"What is that?" asked the girl, her eyes wide.

"It is this shark's brain waves," explained the wiry scientist. "Using the technology we have built, we can manipulate the frequencies of these waves, of any beast's brain waves, to synchronize them with those of a human, just by adjusting this dial." To demonstrate, he gave the knob on the speaker a twist. The chart changed pace and shape, becoming something else entirely.

A soft, scratchy noise, like static on a poorly-tuned radio, had been emanating from the speaker, but now this sound distorted and became something new.

"Hungry," said a robotic voice from the speaker, repeating over and over with each dip and peak. "Hungry ... hungry ..."

"See?" the wiry scientist said to the girl. "We are hearing the shark's thoughts, translated into an understandable human language."

The girl stared. "But this," she said, gesturing to the cap on the shark's head, "is wrong. Aren't we hurting it?"

The bald man laughed softly. "No, no, little girl. If anything, we are helping it. That shark, you see ... all it can think of with a shark's 'intelligence' is how hungry it is. But, after the wires on that cap have done their work, it won't think like a shark anymore. It will think like us. So then it can focus on other things." He smiled kindly at the girl. "Isn't that better?"

The little girl had eyes only for the shark. "How would you know?" she asked. "You are not the shark."

Neither of the men answered. Like the girl, they just stared at the huge beast in the water.

The tendrils began seeping in. And the thoughts became more than 'Hungry' …

What is this feeling?

Suddenly, I am not just hungry. I am … I …

Am.

An ocean of depth rises within me, and out of the blue I realize that there is more than the restless hunger always inside me. There is *me*. I am a being; I am more than the hunger. And now there is thought, words.

I notice. I can actually see the world with my mind instead of my emptiness. Rather than being driven constantly by the ache in my belly and the need to keep moving, I can control myself, pause and look at where I am, swim because I want to swim, instead of merely being forced to because I am roaming for a meal and require oxygen. I observe the rock around me, and I sense new things. That I am not free. That three creatures are watching me.

I look up out of the water. I see them, and feel, strangely, like I know them. Like they are a part of me now in a way no other shark has ever been.

These thoughts, they are overwhelming! Sensing has become an exchange, a process, rather than just drinking it all in like water. There is something … *more* inside of me now, than there is outside. Some addition, from … my brain.

My brain. I never noticed it before. It was tiny and weak, it knew only hungry. But now there is something strong there, something that can realize and interpret for itself. Something … intelligent.

And with this new reasoning comes another new thing: reflection.

I can look back, and I realize suddenly what I am and the things I have done. I can … remember. Remember, with a clarity I had never known, up until now.

And I am terrified.

I remember, on many instances, me taking everything within my sight, tearing it apart indiscriminately, desperately trying to fill the emptiness. It never worked, but I just kept doing it.

But it never worked.

I think now. I think about those things. I think about how beautiful the silver creatures were, miniscule, scaly beings darting through the blue. And they always fled from me. Which they needed to do, because otherwise, I destroyed them. It was all I could do to interact with the life around me: consume, and destroy. It was all I knew.

Maybe that was not such a bad thing. Maybe they were as much machines as I had been.

But then again, maybe not. Maybe they could have awakened too. Maybe they already had. I would never know now. I did not ask questions then. I just ate.

Even if the silver things had been just like me, I remember other things. Worse things. I remember a plump, round, gray thing with large, sweet eyes. It had been lounging in the sun in the world above the blue and I had grabbed it, shaken it, ripped it to shreds. It was alive, and then it was not. It was so warm.

Such awakened eyes. Such conscious, knowing eyes.

And I remember taking one of the creatures on two legs, one of the beings from above the blue. He was riding on a thin, well-shaped piece of driftwood, balancing carefully as he struggled to stand, cresting a wave. He fell, and ... I took him. Without question. I spit him out later, because he didn't taste as good as the silver things or the plump thing, but by then it was too late. The water was red. That was the end of him; I could sense his life leaving, even as I left to go hunt better-tasting prey. I never thought anything of it back then. I didn't really think at all.

But those two-legged creatures, like the ones watching me now, they feel these complicated things. They think the thoughts. They are awake from the moment they are born. Now I know this.

And I know he is gone because of me.

Because of me. Because of my hunger, my yearning to fill an emptiness I never will. The satisfaction of one meal never lasts; always I have to take another. I just fight to survive, kill everything I can, and keep moving endlessly, never content. Just trying to live, just trying to be who I am. Yet somehow that feels wrong now.

And yet ... I cannot change it. There is nothing I can do about it. I am who I am, and my existence is what it is. I am a hunter, and it has always felt so natural, just doing what I was born to do. It is why I am here.

Isn't it?

"What is she doing?" cried the little girl.

The shark swam in restless circles, looking, in some odd way, like a philosopher pacing a library, an intellectual question in her mind... or else a criminal awaiting the verdict of a jury.

"We don't know," said one of the scientists. "The frequencies have gotten jumbled. We cannot read her thoughts any more."

All three humans stared at the great white, so mighty and so distraught.

I hate it. I hate detesting who I am without being able to do anything about it. I feel the suffering of every life that is now gone from the sea because I was born. I feel it all in this new mind of mine; it can comprehend the pain of all of them as well as mine. And in the midst of all this remorse, despite every new sentiment I feel for my prey, pangs the deep and desperate hunger, more urgent than ever.

And I loathe myself for it. This is a pain worse than the emptiness ever was. That was simple; this, this new wealth of understanding, is more complex and confusing than anything in the world I used to know. It contradicts itself, nature fighting nature. And it will not go away.

I chase my tail in circles, angry and despairing.

I want to die. Dying would be easy, like killing once was. So easy...

I bite myself, drawing red. And then, of course, I must draw more, and more. I cannot stop. I will surely go now, go to the place where I sent all the others. I feel a hysterical sort of delight in it, revenging upon myself ...

"Stop!" cries a soft voice.

I understand. I understand that word now. Something within my new self musters the strength to stop. I look up at the rock shelf beside the pool.

A girl is there, a young girl. She is looking at me. She meets my eyes.

Her eyes.

In her wet, blue eyes I see it, the answer, the reason this complexity to being is all worth it. Why it can be good. It is so clear, there in her eyes.

Love.

Love for me, regardless of what I am. Sorrow because of my suffering. Concern, a desire to help, to change my pain even if it means pain for her instead.

I understand.

"Let's go," she says. Her hands pry the cap off my head, letting it fall and sink into the water. The changes in my mind remain, but that is okay now.

She strokes my battered side, so gentle. Before, I probably would have tried to snap at her, even despite knowing that she and her kind do not taste very good. We great white sharks must eat almost constantly to survive; our entire existence is a life condemned to serve our own hunger. Or that's how it is … for most of us.

That's how it had been … for me. But now, I don't feel that emptiness. The emptiness has been filled by a young girl's eyes.

She clambers onto my back, weightless as a gull feather. And suddenly I know what to do. With all the strength I have left, I surge forward, ramming the glass wall in front of us again and again until at last I break through. Together, we swim out into the bright sunshine, back into the blue, with two men in white coats staring after us.

And I'm not hungry any more.

How To Make A Monster

Mary Pletsch

I run my hand over the smooth and massive skull, taking care to avoid all three rows of razor teeth. I've felt a little unhinged ever since the hot tub incident, and it makes me feel better to see my personal nemesis reduced to a cage of bones, washed up on a beach on a deserted South Pacific island, slowly bleaching in the brilliant tropical sun.

But where there's one, there's always others, so I take care to walk to the far side of the skeleton before I admire too closely. Not that it matters. We discovered, to our sorrow, that the sharks can swim on land.

Although I'm standing, once again, in the shambles of a career, I can't help but feel a little perverse admiration for nature's nightmare. If there was such a thing as God, if He'd set out to engineer a perfect killing machine, I don't see how He could have done a better job than this creature before me. In my first job I'd learned how to improve on Mother Nature, but I'd never pulled off a masterpiece like this.

I kneel down to stroke the elbows, the ankles, the claws on the toes. "So this is Sharkasaurus."

"*Squalusaurus terriblis,*" Dr. Bernard Campbell corrects me, from the other side of the bones. He flashes me a smile, his teeth even brighter against his dark skin than those of the skeleton, and I remember what I'd seen in him all those years ago, when I'd been a PhD candidate with stars in her eyes. He was the reason I finally gave up playing with temporal mechanics and devoted myself wholeheartedly to biology. I hate that he can still get this reaction from me, even after everything that's happened in the time since.

Next to him, Dr. Esker looks up from the samples she's collecting and rolls her eyes. "It should be *Pistrisaurus terriblis.* '*Squalus*' refers to a specific family of shark, namely the dogfish."

"But *squalus* is the Latin word for shark," Campbell – Bernard – argues. I don't know how to refer to him now that we're no longer either colleagues or … Well. Last night's encore for old time's sake does not equal lovers, not in my book.

Bernard looks at me, seeking an ally, and when I don't respond right away, he prods me. "Bella?"

I sigh. "The word *squalus* once applied to all sharks. *Pistris* is a more generic term for a sea monster, which can also be applied to whales or even boats of a certain type."

Esker shoots Bernard a cold look. "Does that not look like a sea monster to you?" she asks dryly, suggesting she might have a sense of humour buried underneath her wearisome pedantry.

If she has one, I'm not interested in an archaeological expedition to uncover it. My academic career is long over. Really, I have no business standing on this beach with the real scientists. My role is simply to mind *Calamari Crunch*, the boat that brought us here.

I look out to sea and spot my yacht, my one-time entertainment, now my home and source of my livelihood. She bobs at her moorings offshore, and I ought to be there with her. Besides, even though Campbell said the radioactivity was well below safe levels for exposure, I'm still not entirely certain that I believe him. Trusting other scientists – Campbell included – was how I'd lost my academic career in the first place.

The scientists could've managed the dinghy that had brought us to the island, but no, I'd insisted on rowing them myself. Why? The last vestiges of my scientific curiosity must have trumped my better judgment.

Or maybe I just wanted to face, in person, the monster that had ruined my second career.

After I got kicked out of the scientific community, I decided to live out the last twenty years of my working life as a resort manager in paradise. The tropical nation of Samiki had modern medical care and a large expatriate retirement population. If my life had gone according to plan, I would still be in my air-conditioned office at the Regent Constellation, sipping mai tais and watching middle-aged tourists in bikinis and swim trunks turn beet-red in the South Pacific sun. But all the advertising in the world couldn't have saved Samiki's tourism industry after that documentary came out, the one with blood and sea water running down the ruined streets of the capital.

The atolls to the west of Samiki are rotten with classified research labs, fallout from atomic weapons tests, and God only know what else. Islands like the one I'm standing on right now. Facilities like the one that looms over the beach to the west, a hulking morass in granite and steel that the jungle has only partially reclaimed. The remains of concrete pillars, all that are left of a long-ago dock, poke out of the water like broken teeth.

Sixty-some years ago the Americans, and the French, and the Russians, and more, decided to conduct their experiments here because it was too isolated for the rest of the world to be affected. Right. Nobody was *affected* until three years ago when the first vacationing tourists on Samiki got snapped up by Sharkasaurus.

Everyone at the Constellation had hoped that the attacks were an isolated incident–a problem that could be solved with explosives and guns as soon as we found out which big, hungry creature had overcome the ancient taboo of snacking on humans. The resorts hired locals who killed a lot of sharks, and another critter that resembled nothing so much as a big ol' gator, so far away from where any gators ought to be. My guys finally bagged the biggest shark I'd ever seen. I ordered them to drag it onto the beach in front of the hotel and pretend to try to keep the tourists away, but of course I really wanted everyone to know that there was nothing to fear any longer.

Then the Windspar up the coast lost one of its guests. A charter boat tour went out from the harbour and never came back. When my staff saw the fins in the ocean we knew that there was more than one monster out there, and we knew we had to make some permanent changes.

They weren't easy. Nobody goes on a tropical getaway with the expectation of staying out of the water. We built extra pools to give folks more places to swim and we roped off a tiny swimming area, barely knee-deep, in the ocean. Tourists complained, but we were doing okay until we found out that the next generation of Sharkasaurus could move on land.

I won't ever forget the morning I woke up early and made myself a cup of tea and went out on my balcony to watch the sun rise. Instead, I was treated to the sight of a swimming pool turned red with blood and a juvenile Sharkasaurus wallowing in the hot tub, chewing on what had once been a rather loud-mouthed middle-aged salesman from Milwaukee. Something in me snapped that day, because I couldn't help but admire the ruthless efficiency of the Sharkasaurus, even as it shredded my life's plans to bits.

That was the beginning of the end of the Regent Constellation Samiki. We weren't the only island with white beaches and clear waters and warm tropical breezes. We *were* the only island with a

Sharkasaurus infestation … at the time. But times are changing.

Regent's leading competitor, the Coastal Togi Togi, had once been so smug, even putting in their ads that they were Sharkasaurus-free. Well, until we folded and the tourists all went north. The Sharkasauruses are going north now, too, in search of prey, and it's only a matter of time before Togi Togi goes the way of Samiki. Schadenfreude aside, there's no future in the South Pacific resort business.

Then again, when had my life ever gone to plan? If I hadn't lost my first career, I'd have been the one sent out here with Dr. Campbell to investigate the Sharkasaurus, and someone else would be driving the boat. I look at Bernard, and the Sharkasaurus, and admit that there's a terrible beauty in the capacity of the past to screw over the present.

"Daylight's wasting," Campbell says. "Let's get going."

I stroke the Sharksaurus's forelimb one more time, shoulder my pack, and then climb to my feet. "Since I'm not officially part of your expedition, maybe you could tell me where we're going and what we hope to find there."

"We're investigating the origins of the, ah, 'Sharkasaurus.'"

"On land," I say dryly.

"Dr. Esker had the privilege of genetically sequencing a specimen and, well, it wasn't what we expected."

I'm not sure what the hell that's supposed to mean until I make an intuitive leap and land right on top of a crazy possibility. Could it be… *really?* "It was engineered," I guess, and I watched Campbell's face to see if I'm right. I smile when I discover that I am still capable of catching him off guard.

"We … we thought the Sharkasaurus was the result of a natural mutation, or series of mutations, facilitated by the radiation in the atoll region," he explains. "But when Esker sequenced it … I wish you could've seen it. It's a veritable genetic jigsaw. There's *dandelion* in it, and *cockroach*. The thing regenerates. It's damned near indestructible, unless you blow its brains out." His gaze drifts over to the skeleton, as does mine.

Dr. Esker sniffs. "I'm told you're the kind of person who might admire something like that, Moreau."

"It's Bella," I correct her. "Or Captain, if you want to be formal about it."

Bernard doesn't stop to stand up for me, just as he hadn't during the ethics committee hearing all those years ago, when I took the fall for the projects we did together. "So if the Sharkasaurus isn't nature's design, then it came from somewhere. We're here to find out where. We did a flight overhead in a helicopter and noted not only this carcass but also the presence of that complex over there."

"Truthfully?" Esker says, glancing over at me. "I'm still not entirely sure it isn't your doing."

So that's why they hired me. To investigate me. "I wish," I retort, and despite my ruined retirement plans, part of me actually does. Maybe it's that being so close to Bernard reminds me of my old life, my old dreams. Or maybe it's just that I wish I had a pet that could bite the sneer off Esker's face, the way the hot tub Sharkasaurus had done to our troublesome guest.

We can't get into the complex from the beach. It looks to me as though some kind of tunnel opens directly into the ocean, but Bernard is certain it's just a wastewater dumping tube and not likely to be navigable in the dinghy. I'm not so sure. I'm almost certain I see a fin come out of the tunnel and then slip beneath the surface of the water, but I keep my mouth shut. I'm just the tour guide.

We leave the beach and climb our way up a forested slope. It's easier than it should be because someone's already hacked a path through the jungle. I'm debating whether or not to tell Bernard about the fin I thought I saw, but by the time we reach the front gate, I still haven't made up my mind.

The walls topped with barbed wire would've looked imposing at one time, before they'd grown over with vines – and back when the occupants bothered keeping the front gate closed. "Are you sure we have authorization to enter this facility?" Esker asks as we walk past an empty guard hut. She's asking Campbell, but she's looking at me.

I don't condescend to answer her. I've done enough "pleasure cruises" that were definitely drug runs in order to pay my bills. It's not my place to complain if Campbell wants to do some urban exploration, at least not as long as his cheques don't bounce.

Campbell replies, "The university –and the government – want us to find out where the Sharkasaurus came from, in the hopes that we can find out how to stop them from breeding. Ergo, they want us here."

"American facility," I summarize.

The main foyer is everything I expected from a ruin: filthy with leaves and puddles of standing water, furniture rotting, windows broken. But as we walk deeper into the building, things change. Down below, where the labs are, the floors are clean, the corridors are tidy. I think I hear the thrum of distant machinery – and something else.

"Does anyone else hear that?" Esker asks, proving I'm not crazy.

I strain my ears and yeah, it's exactly what I thought it was. Somewhere in the depths of the building, Jimmy Buffett warns us about fins to the left and fins to the right.

Oh, Jimmy. I know to watch out for sharks.

Suddenly the notes of the song become weirdly stretched, just for a second, but long enough to chill my blood. Because it isn't just *a* Jimmy Buffett recording. It's *my* Jimmy Buffett recording. Specifically, the Greatest Hits cassette tape I'd kept in my office at the lab. Some kind of damage to the tape resulted in an odd sound distortion during the last verse of "Fins." I'd never bothered to exchange the tape because I'd had most of the songs on records at home.

I look over my shoulder at Bernard and find him staring right back at me. "Is that *your* Jimmy Buffett tape?" he asks with a frown, and I remember Esker's suspicions.

I'd gotten rid of most of my belongings when I moved to Samiki, but I'd kept my old Walkman because it was portable. Later I'd bought a CD player and relegated my cassettes to my boat.

I open up my pack, rummage around, and yank out the Walkman. I pop it open, pull out Jimmy Buffett's Greatest Hits, and hold the cassette up for Bernard to see. "Must be a manufacturing defect," I say, because I'm not going to admit responsibility for something I haven't done yet, and I'm not going to dignify the sign on the wall behind me that says TIME MACHINE and HABITAT with an arrow pointing forward. "Probably happened to the whole production run."

Anything else would be *crazy*. Right?

Because standing inside an abandoned secret research facility with my ex and a total stranger, because of the attack of the land sharks, isn't crazy at all.

Esker looks doubtful. I shove the Walkman and tape back into my pack and walk on in the direction of the arrow, through a set of double doors and into an area that reminds me of the zoo. It's humid and I swear I can smell animals over the heady scent of vegetation and the tang of salt water. The music's louder, coming from a door at the end of the hallway.

The right side of the corridor might be a butterfly garden. Mesh fencing, two stories tall, stretches all the way up to the roof. Thick vegetation prevents me from seeing very far into the enclosure, so I can't tell how big the room is, or what's in the cage. I think I see a pool through the undergrowth, but most of the water smell is probably coming from my left.

The left side of the corridor is the wall of a truly huge tank, the kind that reminds me of a polar bear exhibit or a performing orca show. I peer into the water, but I don't see a diving bear, a whale, or anything else. It doesn't look as though there's any kind of land in the tank, the way there would be for a bear or a seal. The water is strangely dark, murky and still. The floor isn't smooth concrete. It's silt and soft loose soil, interspersed with the long fronds of water plants that wave back and forth in the current. It's strangely hypnotic, and I find my head turning as I walk down the corridor, because out of the corner of my eye I keep seeing flickers of movement caused by leaves and tendrils and … and …

It's alive.

It moves through the murky water, and I find myself looking for the serrated fins of *Sharkasaurus apocalyptus* or whatever science will finally end up calling the beast that brought us here. Instead I see a wedge-shaped head with a square jaw and then neck. And neck. And more neck. Just when I think I'm looking at the mother of all water snakes – an anaconda, perhaps – I see shoulders.

The creature puts on a burst of speed and swims past me. Past *us*. It's not a shark. It's a fucking pleisiosaur. Nessie.

Esker's looking into the tank, and she's gone pale white. I don't know what her problem is. Part of me thinks the plesiosaur is pretty frigging awesome, even though I know damned well it's not supposed to be here.

"Oh shit," Esker whispers, "oh fuck."

I'm not going to laugh at her, even though she doesn't seem like the kind of person who'd ordinarily use that kind of language. "I think Dr. Esker is trying to point out that we're in over our heads," I say to Bernard. "This facility is in active use. There are living things here which we're not equipped to deal with. And now I'm going to make another intuitive leap and say that if the Sharkasauruses didn't escape by accident – if they were deliberately released into the wild through that tunnel that leads from this facility into the ocean – then what we're looking at might be more than just an illegal lab. It might be an act of terror."

Bernard's response is to reach into his pocket and dig out his cell phone. He leans forward and snaps a few pictures of the plesiosaur.

"Are you kidding me?" I hiss.

"Which is exactly what the head of the department, the university chair, and my contacts in the government are going to say if I tell them this story without any proof."

"Because someone revived a plesiosaur?"

"And did that to it."

I look again and oh shit, oh fuck, I can't keep the grin off my face. It's only a plesiosaur at the front.

"This can't be happening," Esker protests, and then the doors at the end of the corridor swing open.

TIME MACHINE, says the sign above the doors, and though I've never seen the person standing there, I recognize her at once, or rather, bits and pieces of her. She looks like a student, so maybe nineteen, and she's wearing a white lab coat over jeans and sneakers. I make another one of those intuitive leaps and realize that sleeping with Bernard last night is either the worst mistake of my life, or the best, and I'm about to find out which.

"Hi, Mom," she says, and she grins. Her skin's not as dark as Bernard's but her teeth are white, so white, like a shark's.

Bernard gawks at me, but Esker steps forward to face off with the stranger. "Who are you supposed to be?" Esker demands, all belligerent, though I notice her skin still looks like ash.

"I'm Doctor Bernabella," the stranger replies, and takes half a step to the left so she can wink at me over Esker's shoulder.

Bernabella. Like Sharkasaurus. Half Bella, half …

Bernard gets it too. "This can't be happening," he stammers.

Which is exactly what Esker said about the pleisio-thingy and what I said when I found a land shark in the hot tub. I've found out the hard way that those four words don't do much to bring reality back in line with rational expectations.

Esker doesn't even notice that Dr. Bernabella has my eyes and Bernard's nose, my stocky build and Bernard's tightly curled hair. "Doctor?" Esker sneers, raising an eyebrow. "You got your doctorate from … where?"

"Sorry." Her grin broadens. "Home schooled." She saunters forward, and reaches out to fiddle with a panel on the wall of the butterfly enclosure. "But I *am* a certified genius. Look at the land sharks … sorry, *Sharkasaurus*. Mom said that's what you call them. How many kids cook up something like that for their eighth grade science projects? Mom says I'm one of a kind."

"You," I splutter, "*you* let the Sharkasaurus loose?"

She smirks. "*Dentasaurus horriblis.*"

Something in me feels smug that both Bernard and Esker were wrong, and I'm *proud* of her, unspeakably proud, but another part of me rises up in anger and snaps, "You *ruined* Samiki ... ruined my career!"

"Self-preservation," Bernabella snaps back. "*Something* had to get you and Dad back together! Let's be honest, Dad preferred vacationing in the Caribbean and *you*, you were never happy at that resort no matter *how* much you tried to fool yourself. Your *paradise* is always going to be a lab full of samples and no ethics oversight, and ..." Her eyes narrow. "You wanted to know if any of that stuff you tried on rats works on humans? *Hell yes it does.*"

God help me, I thought about it. God help me, I wondered what would happen if I laced a human fetus with the genes I'd tried out on rats. I'd made them smarter. Stronger. Super-rats. Even before the ethics committee shut me down, there'd been a previous experiment that I'd shut down myself. They'd not just gotten out of the lab – they'd followed me *home*. That whole batch, they had to go.

But I remembered how I'd made them so successful.

Dandelion. And cockroach. And a few other things.

I stare at Bernabella and ask myself again, *worst or best mistake of my life?*

"I hope you're ready to spend the rest of your life in jail," Esker says coldly, and I can't tell if she means Bernabella or me.

Bernabella isn't particularly bothered. She presses a few buttons on the panel and a big hatch, like a garage door, slides open in the mesh wall. My future daughter looks at me and asks, "What should I call this one? I'm thinking *pteroctopus.*"

Dr. Esker can't resist saying, "If you were so smart, you would know that *Pteroctopus* is already the name for a genus of octopuses in the family ..."

I never find out what family they're in, because Bernabella whistles and gestures and a pteroctopus ... yeah, the name works for me ... launches itself out of one of the trees and divebombs Dr. Esker. It happens so fast–one minute she's there in front of me, and then all of a sudden she's *not*, and the other pteroctopi come fluttering out into the corridor to get a piece of the action. It takes my brain a moment to make sense of the little red bits falling down from the feeding frenzy overhead.

I try to process what I'd seen. My brain tells me no, but I insist on slow-motion replay. Reluctantly, my mind gives up a series of disjointed images. The pteroctopus descending like the judgment of an ancient god. Three long, suckered arms curling around Dr. Esker. An unnecessary close-up of one of those arms clapping over Esker's mouth, even as her one free hand claws at it. Leathery wings seeking purchase on the air. Esker budging the tentacle on her face long enough to scream, before the two around her chest cut off her air. Did I hear the snapping of ribs? I couldn't have. All the other pteroctopi flying out into the corridor and flocking around, hungry for a piece of the catch. And then ...

Make it rain.

I should be horrified, but instead I find myself choking on ugly giggles. I look over at Dr. Bernabella and splutter, "What, did you put some seagull in 'em?"

And she winks and replies, "You know I did," and she flashes me this sly little grin and suddenly we're leaning on the plesiosaur tank in hysterics together, and Bernard, Bernard is running.

I swear at him, because he's supposed to be in this with me, dammit, he's supposed to be a *father*. I start running after him, but I slip on a bit of Dr. Esker and by the time I've picked myself up again, he's got a good head start. The pteroctopi follow me as I pursue him through the complex, down the slope, and out onto the beach. By the time my feet hit the sand, Bernard is in the dinghy and paddling hard for *Calamari Crunch*.

I race across the sand, shouting and waving, but Bernard doesn't look back as he climbs up the ladder into *Calamari Crunch*. "Hey, you fucker!" I yell across the water. "Hey, asshole! *That's my boat!*"

Bernard doesn't care that he's stealing my boat. He doesn't look back as he hauls up the anchor, then runs into the wheelhouse. A few minutes later I hear the engine start. *Calamari Crunch* starts moving out to sea, and Bernard ... Bernard doesn't care about me. He doesn't think twice about leaving me behind on a deserted island with the pteroctopi flying in great circles overhead and the creator of the Sharkasaurus coming up behind me.

Bernabella sets down a tray of drinks in the sand. Then she comes up to me and throws her arm over my shoulders. "Sorry Mom," she says, with a tenderness I wouldn't have thought she could feel. "You do ... you do know he never loved us, right?"

I guess I knew. I guess I'd always known, because Bernard hadn't said or done anything before the ethics committee filed their report. If I'd made a point of not wondering how they'd gotten hold of the sensitive stuff, the stuff I only worked on at home, well, it's because my subconscious had intuited an answer my heart didn't want to confirm.

"Yeah," I choke out. I wipe away tears as she leads me back to the beach and we watch *Calamari Crunch* sail off towards the descending sun. I try to tell myself there was nothing out there for me any more anyway.

With nothing else to do, I sit on a beach at the end of the world and raise a mai tai in toast to the sunset. A daughter I've never known clinks her glass against mine and sips delicately from her straw.

I'd feel bad about drinking while pregnant except I already *know* how the baby turns out, and no, she's not fine, but all morality ever got me was shipwrecked on a deserted island with two busted careers, so I'm willing to give amorality a try. I feel the urge to make a toast.

We should never underestimate the capacity of the future to screw over the present.

I giggle hysterically because there is no way to *know*, there was no way to *ever* know about the time machine and the Sharkasaurus and my mad scientist daughter from the future who's even now in my belly and oh my god – who, sorry Bernard, oh my god-I-don't-believe-in, oh my god, Bernard, *we are the past*. We are the past screwing over the future because we thought it would be a great idea to have unprotected sex and then come to a radioactive island and you, you sailed away in my boat and now I'm *here*, marooned and pregnant and *hey*, nothing better to do than sit on the beach at the end of the world and wonder, what would happen if I mashed up a spider and a velociraptor in that lab down there?

I have nothing left to lose so I roll over on my left side and ask Bernabella what she thinks would happen and she grins and tells me that the spideraptors didn't work out so well but there's still one left, she's got a big web out in the west paddock and would I like to meet "Blue Widow" and oh god, oh yes, yes I would.

Except another thought occurs to me as I get up and sway on my feet. I'm going to be fine for the foreseeable future – at least until Bernabella's born – but ... I kinda know better, but still I've just got to ask ...

"Hey ... what about Bernard?"

She favours me with a smile. "You're afraid he's going to come back with … what? The police? The army? Whose?"

She might have a point. Samiki's army has bigger concerns. Togi Togi never had an army to begin with. The larger nations have a lot of layers of bureaucracy that will dismiss Bernard as a nut long before he'll get to someone with the power to come all the way out here and do something about a missing scientist and an expatriate sea captain. Still …

I look at Bernabella and say, "They don't come, because they didn't come, because you lived to be born. Right?"

"Nah. They don't come because … hey. You're gonna want to watch your boat so you can tell me this story when I'm born."

I turn my head, and sip my mai tai, and watch as a giant tentacle rises straight up out of the ocean and slaps down across the bow of my yacht.

"The plesiosaur."

"Plesio*squid*." She has the good graces to look regretful. "Sorry about your boat."

Calamari Crunch. My giggles return. Can I name them, or what?

The plesiosquid makes short work of *Calamari Crunch*, and Bernard. The Sharkasauruses help. First one opportunistic fin appears in the water, then another, and finally the water that laps at the beach in front of us is redder than the sunset, while the pteroctopi circle overhead and snap up the bits that float to the surface.

And I smile at Bernabella, my beautiful daughter, and I lean close to her ear and whisper to her, "I think you're the best monster I've ever made."

Waters That Sparkled So Green

Oliver Smith

She lies on the beach. He, a prince among sharks,
Steps naked from the waves showing his teeth.
She is near-blinded by the sharpness of his smile.
Her heart rolls like a drum as they lie
Radiant – clinging together
On a bed of sand and shells and seaweed.

Exhausted he crawls back to the hungry swell.

He is returning to the sea for just a day:
She spends the next hundred years waiting
In her tower counting his absence in heartbeats.
Each oscillation grows a little weaker
Than the last until she can count no more.

She extinguishes the flames of her golden lamp
That burned bright as the sun to bring him home

Through the hurricanes and night and storms.
What use a lighthouse to lead him to her arms
When willingly he rushes onto rocks
And his thunder roars across the waves?

It is not air he needs: it is the hungry
Coal-black waters – down where fish signal
In lightning flashes across a deeper cosmos.

So she flies like a gull away from her home
To meet him where the wind
Scatters stars like sea flung spray;

Where the earth clasps the ocean to its rock
Like a mother, her heavy belly a well
That draws water across new grown scales.
He lies blanketed under sleep-heavy waters:

A hundred fish slide around his silken bed
While living galaxies swirl in the ocean sky.

His palace stands on coral-encrusted ruins
 Of older worlds: Dunwich, Mu, and Lyonesse.
While half-rotted ships disgorge luminous
Treasures looted from sea – devoured Atlantis.
The now shipless crews throng like rays:

They school in the bright harbours of his abyss.

The drowned dance and sing and then lie at rest,
And dress her hair with combs of shell,
And brilliant crowns of pearl. She reaches out
For her prince's razor-kiss:
It is then she knows the deeps
Hold so much more than the heights.

Milton's Monster Menagerie!: The Micro-Sharkasaur™ Edition

Becca J. Morgan

"Mr. Thidwick–"

"It's Doctor." Milton adjusted his glasses, puffing his chest out.

The board of judges looked between themselves. They were big heads, for the most part. Scientists with failed hypothesizes or that had never gotten tenure. But this one –

"Right, yes, *Dr.* Thidwick." She had introduced herself as Joyce Barrett. No doctor or professor in front of her name. That was something Milton was not expecting. "When we posted this contest, we were looking for a marvel of science. Something that the world of genetic research has never seen before."

"Which I have delivered, yes." He gestured to the covered cage next to him.

A man, Professor Cordes, if Milton remembered, sat up. "You have to understand, son, it's just not what we're looking for."

"Don't call me son. And how isn't it what you're looking for? You said Sharkasaurus, and I delivered."

"It's rather small, isn't it?" Joyce said.

"Rather – excuse me?" Milton pushed his glasses up.

"Usually," a scrawny doctor, whose name escaped Milton, said. "when one says 'Saurus' at the end of something, they expect it to be, ahem, larger than a dog."

"I've genetically crafted the perfect hybrid between a mako and an extinct species! And you're complaining because it's *smaller than you thought?*"

"We thank you for your time, Mr–"

"Doctor!" Milton cut Cordes off before he finished.

" – Thidwick. Now, please, show yourself out?"

"That was all that happened?" Dash lounged on the couch, popping jalapeño poppers into his mouth. He watched as Milton walked into the kitchen.

"What, what do you mean *That was all that happened?* They rejected me!"

"I mean, yeah, you've mentioned. Around fifty times."

"It's bullshit! I created a genetically unique creature, just like they wanted! Do you have any beer?"

"You're underage, I can't let you drink."

Milton peeked his head out from the kitchen. His black hair dripped with water.

"I need a drink, Peterson. Don't test me."

"Did you dunk your head in the sink?"

"No, I was talking to Joey."

Dash stopped mid-popper bite. "Joey?"

"Yeah."

"You did not bring your tiny shark-rex here."

"What? Me? Here? Uhhh ..."

"Milton."

A large splash came from the kitchen. Dash let his head fall into his hands.

"I stopped here before I went home! I couldn't just leave him in the car, I'm not a savage."

With a resigned sigh, Dash heaved himself up off the couch and pushed past Milton into the kitchen. There, sitting in a moderate sized aquarium (he was convinced this was the same one previously used to try and create a living organism out of yogurt), was Joey. He scrabbled against the glass with very tiny arms, a series of bubbles coming out of a mouth full of very large teeth. Milton tried to push his way in front Dash, but was quite easily held back by the man nearly two feet taller than him.

"Milton."

"Yeah?"

"Can it breathe under water?"

Milton finally pushed his way in front of Dash. "What? Of course he can! I'm a twenty-year-old with a doctorate, I think I know what I'm doing!"

"I don't see what that at all has to do with the fact that this thing's gills might be broken, but whatever." Dash went to the fridge and grabbed a bag of chips from the top of it.

"Do you honestly think I'd make a mistake like – ?"

Some scrabbling cut Milton off, as Joey worked his way out of the aquarium and fell with a thud to the kitchen counter. The shark-mix whimpered, before letting out a low "Grrrrr ..."

"Milton –"

"Dash, don't freak out he's harmless –"

"There's a fucking shark-dinosaur-thing on my goddamn kitchen counter!"

Milton scrambled, picking Joey up in his arms. "Look, it's no problem, he's 100% harmless. Just, like, look at him!"

Dash hated to admit, but the tiny semi-shark snuggling into his friend's arms was actually a little cute. Joey had stopped growling the second Milton had took him up in his arms, and ... was that purring? No, it had to just be Dash's stomach. That was it. Shark-dino-hybrids didn't purr. Right?

"What are you going to do with him?" Dash threw more chips into his mouth. "You lost the contest, and I'm pretty sure you can't have pets at your place."

"I don't know." Milton stroked the back of Joey, scratching right behind his fins. "I was hoping to win the prize, you know? That $50k would have been nice ..."

"Well, can't help you get $50k. And you already owe me big time."

"Look, I apologized for that time you almost died, and I'll pay you back for the warehouse, once I get the money."

From the other room, the quiet droning of the TV caught Dash's ear as it switched to a very recognizable theme song. *"I wanna be the very best ..."* His eyes widened, as he glanced through the doorway, to the TV, to the tiny ... practically "pocket"-sized monster in front of him.

"I've never seen you think so hard, there, Peterson," Milton said, cocking his head. "What's up?"

"Listen, firstly, I should not be encouraging you, because you could just move on and do something fucking normal for once. But, if it'll make you happy ... and rich ... I have an idea."

"Just spit it out, what?"

"Listen, *Pokemon* is huge again, because of *Pokemon Go* and everything, and here you are ... creating something that's practically one of them. People don't want virtual reality any more, they want ... reality reality, you know?"

Milton's eyes went wide, his petting ceased. Instead of focusing on Dash, he was completely zoned into his own world.

"I mean," Dash continued. "you've already made one, making more can't be that hard?"

"I would like you to explain what I'm looking at, Dash."

Dash raised his head from his hands. He first met a pair of very disapproving blue eyes, before darting back to the computer screen in front of them.

"It's … a website I helped Milton make."

"Oh, I know, I see that. It looks like it was made by two completely inept lobsters. What I want, is you to explain why the hell this is happening."

He looked away from the computer again, meeting his other best friend's eyes. "Sara, I suggested it to him."

Sara pushed some of her light brown hair behind her ear, letting out a very frustrated sigh. "Suggested what?"

"Fuck, do you just want me to say it?"

"Yes, Dash, what do you think I'm setting you up for?"

"I suggested he sell the damn Sharkasauruses he made, okay?"

There was a long pause as Sara just blankly stared at the computer, not even turning to Dash. It sent a chill creeping down his spine. Minutes passed, as he watched her watching the childish clipart graphics flick across the monitor. *Milton's Monster Menagerie!* boasted about the creation of the Sharkasaurus (also the yogurt-ooze, and the macaroni monster, and Zack the Slime), going over every step of combining the genetics of the mako and the dinosaur of choice (Dash didn't know how to pronounce it, even after the number of times Milton had repeated it). Of course, there was the link to the videos. All of the videos of Joey in action. Him swimming, walking, roaring, learning to play dead; all of the basics that could be asked for in a pet.

Then there was the link to the purchase page, leading straight to an *Etsy* shop where a custom (within reason) Sharkasaurus could be ordered.

"Dash."

She had turned her head slightly back towards him. Her face lacked an expression, and Dash could swear his life flashed before his eyes.

"Yeah?"

"What the fuck were you thinking?"

"Well –"

"You know, actually, I know exactly what you thought. Nothing. Absolutely nothing."

"That's not –"

"You know that when Milton gets an idea–whatever idea–that he follows it until it – or someone – dies."

"*I* didn't die." Dash stood, closing the laptop in front of Sara.

Sara walked over to the couch, throwing herself on it. "Oh, yeah, you didn't. You were just covered in third degree burns and *almost* died, God forbid …"

"I've regained all the strength in my arm again."

"Dash, this is not what we're talking about! How many of those things has he sold?"

He sat down next to her. "I dunno, the site just went live."

Sara pulled out her phone, typing in the site address. "Please tell me you aren't paying for advertisement anywhere."

"I mean … *I'm* not."

She gave him another deadpan, disappointed look. "Dash Randall Peterson."

"I just … Milt made a Facebook page, and and and, that's linked on the site, and he paid for the Facebook ads, and shared it in our high school group, which I really don't understand why he did, since he was hardly ever in class because he was always in those college courses, not to mention that time he mutated half the football team …"

"Dash."

He sighed, leaning over her shoulder. "What?"

"This page has over five thousand likes already."

"… What?"

"Grab the laptop. Check the website."

"Uh …"

"Peterson!"

"Uh, yes!" Dash awkwardly leaned over Sara and grabbed the laptop off the table next to her. He opened it quickly and fumbled with the keyboard, trying to log in.

"Oh my god … so many people have commented on here …" Sara muttered.

"What are they saying?"

"Well … *I just ordered one!* and … *I just ordered three for my kids!* … oh no …"

"Sara."

"I just refreshed the page. The number doubled."

"Sara."

"What?"

The door burst open. The two jolted, looking towards it to see a very excited Milton Thidwick, glasses gleaming, smile wide, with a

Sharkasaurus tucked under his arm, run in.

"Guys! Guess who has almost a thousand orders already!"

Dash and Sara exchanged a horrified look.

"I can't believe we're watching this," Dash said.

"Shhh! It's back from commercial!" Luna Thidwick said, flopping down to his side, spilling popcorn onto his lap.

"I agree with Dash; this is just going to encourage him." Sara dug the remote out from where it had fallen between the cushions of the couch, and unmuted the TV.

"So, Mr. Thidwick –"

"It's Doctor." Dash, Sara, and Luna spoke in time with Milton on the TV.

The TV personality cleared her throat. "Of course, sorry, *Dr.* Thidwick. Now, we just got back from your demo of how you created these wonderfully cute shark-hybrids, and I just have to ask: what made you decide to market these as pets?"

"Well, after I was rejected from the Sharkasaurus contest, I hit this low of depression, because I had created something that is 100% genetically unique, with no flaws that are commonly befitting of species that are unwillingly bred. Like we see in dogs and cats that have those smushed-in faces. The Micro-Sharkasaur™ behaves well on land and in water, and the addition of limbs doesn't take away too heavily from the natural aerodynamics of the perfected shark form underwater.

"Anyway, I was inspired, with the help of my good friend Dash Peterson, of Peterson Fireworks Inc., with the rise in popularity of certain small 'pocket monsters,' if you understand my meaning."

"Yes, I think I completely understand what you mean, Doctor. And these Micro-Sharkasaurs™ have really taken America by storm. As of this show, you have sold ... over fifty thousand of these adorable pets?"

The in-studio audience cheered, as little Joey in Milton's lap perked up. Milton smiled, giving the shark a little pat on the head until he curled up and went back to sleep.

"I'm certainly very impressed by how well the Micro-Sharkasaur™ has been doing." Milton said. "I'm just happy that I could've brought something like this to the world that has really strong benefits."

"As am I. Now, your original creation, that's him right there, right?"

"Yes, this is Joey. The one I originally submitted to the contest."

"And he is so precious. Would he like a treat of any kind?"

Joey's head perked up again. "I believe he would," Milton said.

"Well, during the break, we sent out a Twitter poll about the number one treat to give your Mirco-Sharkasaur™, and we received resounding feedback about the best treat that everyone's shark seems to love. And since they're all clones of Joey here, I'm sure he'll love it to. Could we get the treat out here?"

Cheering from the in-studio audience. Milton tensed, looking nervous from Joey to the crew member walking onstage with a tray.

"Now, America! You've voted, and the number one treat to give the Mirco-Sharkasaur™ is ... *bacon*!"

The audience cheered loudly, as the crew member opened the silver tray, revealing several thick strips of fresh-off-the-grill bacon. Joey's snout twitched, as he stood up. Milton's grip tightened on the Sharkasaur™ as he paled, standing from the talk show couch.

"No." Milton's voice was barely above a whisper. The TV host turned to him, piece of bacon in hand. "No!" With that, Milton turned and ran, and the TV cut to static.

Luna, Dash, and Sara stared at the TV, blinking.

"What the fuck just happened?" Luna said, turning to Dash.

"You're asking me? Why the fuck would I know?"

"You're his partner in this," Sara said. "You helped him with literally everything."

"Partner is a strong word. I just suggested the idea, and he said he'd give the family company a shout out while he was on air! I have no idea why he ran out like a fucking weirdo!"

"You always defend him!" Luna gave Dash a tiny punch to his arm. "You even forgave him when he –"

"When he almost fucking killed me, I know! But, Sara always defends him more, because she's still in love with him!"

"Dash, for the last time, I am not still in love with him."

"Bullshit; you are." Luna said.

"This is not what we're talking about! We're talking about the fact that something totally just set off *our best friend* on national TV!"

"It was something about the treat, right?" Dash said. "That's why he ran."

"Oh. Shit."

Dash and Sara turned to Luna.

"Oh shit, what 'oh shit?'" Dash said.

"Okay, so like, you two both know that when my brother talks I never listen, right?" Luna said, standing from the couch and placing the popcorn on the coffee table. "Because he's a pretentious shit lord that thinks he's allowed to talk constantly because he's got a doctorate and is the "prodigal child" or whatever? Which makes me feel like shit, because I just want a bachelor's in studio art and to just live in a lesbian art commune or whatever. Anyway, I remember him talking my fucking ear off about the god damn shark dinos, but I definitely remember him saying that bacon does something totally weird to them, and like, fucks up the perfect system that he created? Like, the part that makes them nice caring pets instead of ravenous monstrosities?"

"Wait," Dash said. "You're saying, that the number one thing that people feed pretty much any pet ever, is the one fucking thing Milton fucking Mortimer Thidwick *designed* to cause that reaction?"

"I mean, shit, Dash, I don't listen to him. Maybe, idk."

Sara stared the ground, her head in her hands. "This is the fucking yogurt all over again."

"The yogurt had a name."

"You're not helping, Dash."

"Sorry."

The door burst open, and the three turned to it. Milton, in a very wrinkled tux, and a baby sling slung across his chest, panted in the doorway.

"Okay ... so ... we have ... a bit ... of a problem ..." he said, undoing the sling and letting Joey out onto the floor.

"Yeah, Thidwick?" Dash said, standing and crossing his arms. "Would you care to explain this fucking problem?"

"Well, uh ... Sara, I'd like to start and say that I did not mean for this to happen, and I fully understand if you're mad at me again, but this wasn't out of spite or anything," Milton started. "Not like the time I almost killed Dash. More like when I made –"

"Milton."

"Y-yeah?" He trembled as Sara stared at him.

"What does the bacon do?"

He took a breath, and pushed his way over to the couch. "Okay, so in my genetic reconstruction of everything, I found this strange ... anomaly when I mixed the mako DNA and the Tyrannosaurus. I ... it's hard to explain, because I don't really understand it, but the combination of the two species somehow created a violent ... reaction to bacon. It's not exactly allergic, but that's the best way to describe it. Once the stomach fully digests too large of a quantity of bacon ..."

"Finish what you're saying!" Dash said, throwing his arms in the air, his hands slamming into the ceiling. "Ow!"

"The niceness that is found in the Micro-Sharksaur™ reverts to the nasty common nature of the Tyrannosaurus, and starts to corrupt the mako. Also ... um ... it reverses the effect of the genetic shrinkage that I did?"

Sara let out a very loud sigh. "You're saying that if people feed your Joey-clones bacon, they will grow into giant monsters that hold no care for the human race?"

"Well, I didn't do full research into what their emotional states become and how their reactions to different humans were, I just figured 'Ooo, giant monster bad.'"

"Well, hey," muttered Luna, "at least he's finally learned *that* much."

"But," Dash said. "isn't that exactly what that contest was asking you for? And instead, you've inflicted fifty thousand people in the world with ticking monster time bombs?"

"... Shit. I could've won the Sharkasaurus contest."

"Is now really the time to lament the fact that you fucked up the contest?" Luna asked.

Silently, Milton grabbed the remote to the TV and switched it to a news station.

"–Reports are coming in from all over the country of the Micro-Sharkasaur™ pets becoming thirty-foot-tall giant monsters, now roaming city streets, destroying and killing anything in their way. Footage here shows one not-so-Micro-Sharkasaur™ growing to its full size in the middle of a family home and destroying its previous owners. Warning, the content of this video is graphic."

The screen flashed in deep blue-greys and red as the four watched. It then cut back to the newsman.

"A hunt has been put out for one Milton Mortimer Thidwick, the man responsible for unleashing these monsters onto this world in the guise of simple household pets. If you see Mr. Thidwick, please report his location to your local police immediately."

With a flicker of static, Milton turned the TV off, face blank.

"Well, Milt," Dash said.

"Yeah," Sara said. "What do you have to say for yourself?"

A long pause, Milton still blankly staring at the TV. Then, finally: "It's Doctor."

Other Oceans

Blair Frison

The public was left in the dark as long as possible to avoid mass panic. When the news finally started to leak, nobody believed it. And who could blame them? It was patently absurd.

But some of the greatest minds in the scientific community were in agreement: a huge mass, measuring tens of thousands of miles in length, was heading towards Earth at an impossible speed.

It appeared to be a living organism. A cosmic titan swimming the empyrean.

Its appearance was serpentine. It had two fins near the center of its body and was pulsating a strange, fiery glow as it sped towards the planet in an undulating pattern.

There were conflicting theories on the origin of this phenomenon, and no one could agree on almost anything about it. Except that its velocity was steadily increasing. Impact was imminent.

The skeptics were silenced when it became visible to the naked eye, a stark and solemn shape beyond the clouds. Many believed the beast to be God himself, bringing with Him His promised purge. An epidemic of suicide and madness swept the planet as the thing neared.

World leaders stayed silent on the matter and no attempt was made to restore order. Nor was any kind of offense mounted. At least, not that the public was aware of. Rumours abounded of a mass exodus from Earth by the ruling elite. Their supposed destination, if any, was unknown.

As the shape in the sky grew more rapidly, Earth was unchained from her eternal path and succumbed to the immense gravitational pull.

In no time, the beast was so close that its face spanned the entire horizon in the Western Hemisphere. The sky was a sea of eyes and teeth, a sight that brought the remnants of humanity to their knees.

The beast opened wide as the planet hurtled towards the darker black of its gaping maw. It chewed through continents ravenously, as it continued on without pause, savouring its sustenance as the Earth died screaming.

Sharkasaurus Slim

Stumpy McDurmit

I'd been working the carnie about three years when the bossman told me I'd be bein' the sharkasaurus in the sharkasaurus tank, bein' as how Melvin had got in a bad way and wasn't doin' it no more.

Me, I wasn't so sure, bein' as how old Melvin smelled kind of funny, was always making squishy sounds, and drippin' like he couldn't stop sweating or something and I didn't want no part of that. Bossman said that I could either climb in the tank and start swishing my tail, or I could take a long hike down a long road because he didn't need me any more for any thing other than swimming around, pretending like I was a shark.

I knew my work was a little not so good, as they say, whoever the hell *they* is, but I didn't think I stuck out like a thumb what's been banged by a sixteen pounder or stepped on by a triceratops, but, well, there it was. I know my thinking don't count for beans against the bossman's 'cause he's got all the money and if he don't want to, I don't get paid.

Now for them's what don't know about these things, the sharkasaurus tank – like every other sharkasaurus tank in all the other carnies – is this great big, clear sided bath tub what's about two tall guys high, ten by fifteen on the sides, and filled almost to the top the most disgusting mix of salt water and crude you can imagine, assuming your imagining doesn't come up with living in a sewer and only crawling out when the moon is full like I used to do when Arne and myself lived there for, maybe, fifteen years. The moon'd round out and he'd start growl'n and growing fur and I'd get the hell out of there so's he wouldn't think I was a chicken or something that was tasty. In fact it was a full moon when I joined the carnie 'cause it had set up near the swamp our smelly old sewer dumped itself into ...

But that's a whole other story, and I was telling you about the tank where I was supposed to swim about, pretending to be a big old sharkasaurus, and scaring all the rubes and their little kids.

Everybody knew it was fake and that the scary thing was really a guy in a rubber suit, but everybody made a big deal about bein' scared so the little kids could have a good time.

Me, I didn't know a thing about a thing about the act except'n what I'd seen from Melvin: he'd hide down in the kelp and then burst out, big old shark mouth open, lots and lots of teeth, and he'd ram the wall goin' like a bat out of wherever bats go out of, if they've got to be going real fast. Everybody would scream and knock over their chairs and then he'd swim back into the kelp, sneak over to someplace else, and do it again.

I figured it couldn't be all that hard and it would be a lot better than pounding stakes and hauling stegosaurus shit. But I was worried about bein' smelly and drippin'. But I figured that if I didn't want to go back to the sewer and take my chances with Arne, not that I thought I could find that rat hole after three years of traipsin' around the country fleecing the rubes out of all their spare nickels and dimes, well, I figured I'd better go find Melvin and find out how to do the sharkasaurus act.

So I asks the bossman where is Melvin and he says to me that Melvin's gone and it's no good looking for him. I say, okay, and then I asks him how I'm supposed to know how to work the suit if Melvin's not around. He says to go find Bessie and she'll fix me up.

Now Bessie, for those of you who don't know, and I'm pretty sure that's everybody because Bessie don't hardly ever come out where anyone but carnie folk can get a look at her because – well – because she's like that. She don't like nobody lookin' her over, which is kind'a weird bein' that Bessie's one mean mother and ugly as sin so's nobody would look at her twice.

Now that's assuming that sin is really ugly, which it can't be, bein' as how sinning is so popular and how maybe half the carnie folks around here, and I'm not sayin' this is the truth about all carnie folk everywhere, but around here it sure as hell is – about half of us makes enough of the little extra we need to keep our noses just above the crud. A fella can't get decent illegals without a little cash, if you know what I mean.

So, the short of it was, as much as I wasn't thrilled about swimming though the kelp in the sharkasaurus tank, scaring little kids, and I sure as hell didn't want nothin' to do with Bessie on account of she scared the hell out of everybody, and that would be including me, but there wasn't anything else to do. So I went to go see if I could find her and get this miserable show on the road.

The carnie's got fourteen wagons what the folk live in, and I didn't know which one belonged to Bessie. While I'm scratch'n and trying to think where to start, I sees Wanda over by her caravan, swallowing fire sticks. I don't know how she does it, but it's like she takes a big bite of raw meat and chokes it down and then she swallows a piece of burning stuff. She claims she likes to cook her meat inside. I tried it once and it hurt like hell, so I never did it again.

Anyway, I goes over to her and asks her where I can find big Bessie. She burps and I jumps back and beats the fire out of my shirt on account of I forgot it's not good to stand too close to her while she's cooking. For an answer, she just shrugs, which I take to mean that she doesn't know, which I also think is kind of strange 'cause Wanda's been with the carnie a lot longer than me and, as far as I can tell, knows everybody everywhere and who's fucking who and why and who knows and who doesn't and, best of all, which one's will pay the most to keep her from telling somebody who they wants not to know.

So if Wanda don't know where Bessie hangs her drawers, then nobody does. Except maybe the bossman, but I'd have thought he would have told me. So I decides to go and ask him why the hell he didn't.

The bossman wasn't anywhere nearby, so I thought to check down by the stegosaurus pens, knowing that the steg's were kind of pets of his. We always set up separate pens for the steg's and the tri's on account of if we don't the steg's would try to bash the hell out of the tri's with those big old, spiked tails of theirs while the tri's would run at 'em and stab them in the guts. Steg's and tri's are hard to find these days and the bossman always gave us gazoonie's hell when something like that happened.

The pen was down at the end of the alley between the two rows carny wagons. Bein' as I'd been so long with the show and I took care of the wagon wheels, I'd got so's every time I walked around I'd be checking to make sure the wheels were on tight and nothing much was broke. I must'a not been looking where I was walk'n, probably 'cause I was check'n axle bolts. I ran straight into the bossman, bounced off, and landed on my ass. Bossman is a little large, like almost twice my size and I ain't small, and nothin in that fancy ringmaster suit of his is soft.

He glared down at me and I jumps up and explains to him I can't find Bessie and I'd asked Wanda and even she didn't know where she is and I was sure he did and would he tell me please? He snorted and pointed to a caravan off by itself that I'd never seen before. The damned thing was twice as tall and twice as wide and three times as long as any other one, except the ones we put the steg's and tri's in when we were moving to another town. I guess my mouth was hang'n' open because bossman said to close it up and get my ass in gear. So I did.

Now I'm not scared of much – the bossman for sure and, of course, a 'saur in heat – but I was most absolutely, definitely most scared to hell of Bessie. I climbed the steps – all six of them – up to her caravan's back door and knocked.

Nothing happened, but then even I couldn't hear my knocks, so I tried again, just little harder. Still nothing happened, not a noise. It was quiet as death around that van, not even crickets chirped. I'd screwed up my courage to really give the door a whack and raised my paw to smack it one more time when it whipped open and there she was. I fell off the top step and landed on my ass – second time that night.

She growled and turned back inside, but left the door open. I had to replay that growl two more times before I knew that she'd said: *you're late, jackass, get your ass in here.* I jumped up and scrambled up the steps and inside into the dim light and evil smelling single room. Bessie stood at the other end, leaning over a big table working on what looked like the sharkasaurus suit.

I took a step and the door behind me slammed. I spun around. No one was there. I'd seen horror movies when I was a kid and this was the place where something bad always happened to the guys who weren't the hero. And if there's anybody who ain't a hero, that guy is me, so I wasn't much surprised when these big hairy arms wrapped around my middle and picked me off the floor. Well, the thing, whatever it was, carried me over to the table and I finally get a good look at what's on the table.

First off, it was plain as day that it was the sharkasaurus suit. But the thing that's even plainer, and something I'd not known before, is that this suit ain't made of rubber, it's a real sharkasaurus hide and the guy inside can't take it off.

Big old Bessie had just finished snipping the places where the suit's sewed to old Melvin's carcass. From the smell of him and all the ooze that was leaking out, I figured pretty quick that he was dead. I also figured how he'd been breathing under water. They'd hooked the old sharkasaurus hide's gills up to Melvin using plastic tubes. Old Bessie had just finished unhooking them old dead Melvin's lungs.

At that point I was pretty sure I'm wasn't not going to like what happened next and, prove'n I'm not completely dumb, I didn't.

Once Bessie'd finished sewing me into the suit and she and big hairy monster finished breaking my legs so's that my tail would flip right, they carried me to the sharkasaurus tank and tossed me in.

All in all, it ain't so bad a job. I don't have to haul no steg' and tri' dung and don't have to pound no posts. I never cared much what I ate, so all the fish ain't all that bad, especially when they throws in a treat – a wandering kid or two after the last Sunday show.

So, make sure to stop by the tank and see me next time the carnie's in town. I've got the slam-into-the-side down real good, better than old Melvin ever did. I've even added a jump-and-splash that'll soak your socks.

No Cure For Cancer

Paul M. Feeney

He runs, his brain pounding in tandem with his heavy footfalls. The night seems to close in around him, smothering and oppressive.

Can't breathe. Need ... air!

And it's true. Up until a minute ago, his lungs were working fine, pulling in cool, clean air, keeping his heart pumping. But now, it's as if someone has pulled a plastic bag over his head; each attempt at inhalation results only in a tiny sip of oxygen and his throat feels as if it has shrunk to the size of a thin straw.

He runs without thought or knowledge of where he is going, but even if he was aware of his rough direction, he would not be able to discern his current location; his vision is blurred to the point of uselessness. His surroundings are painted in dark smudges of unclear shades, as though he were viewing everything underwater, and so he travels blindly, at least where his vision is concerned.

His staggered gait takes him on a tangent, away from the industrial complex and toward a cultivated, garden landscape area. Beyond this is an artificially created bay which leads into the ocean. If he were able to analyze his state of mind, he might suspect that this is his intended destination, propelled instinctively by the amygdalae nestled at the centre of his brain; but as it is, he is too consumed by what is happening to his body to pay even the slightest objective attention.

He powers up a slight rise – smashing blindly through carefully and neatly planted flower-beds – and down the other side.

His whole body aches as though burning, his bones feel like they are being twisted within their fleshy sheaths, and his tendons pinch in excruciating agony as if being stretched like over-tight rubber bands. Pain flares in his neck on both sides, sending silent, white lightning exploding through his head. He slaps his hands over the skin and feels heat pulsing beneath the tissue. Through the blinding torment, on the edge of awareness, he thinks he can feel actual *movement* just under the skin.

He stumbles, nearly drops to his knees, then recovers, pushing on as his body erupts in fresh waves of agony. His spine contorts and pushes out, as if it wishes to escape its prison of flesh; his limbs feel as though they are being pulled from their sockets, stretched beyond their limits, and his whole head is now throbbing, his skull a slow-motion explosion.

His esophagus continues to constrict, and now he cannot pull even the smallest of breaths into his lungs. In addition to all the aches and pains, the various agonies which reverberate throughout his body, his head now buzzes with the quietly growing din of oxygen depletion. At least it has the effect of dimming those other torments; in a way, it is an almost welcome relief.

Through the rising white static that fills his mind, one thought bubbles up, almost calm and peaceful in its clarity: *I'm going to die. This is it. All that wasted research and for nothing. I'm dead, anyway.* He accepts this with a kind of weary resignation.

And then, on the absolute edge of his awareness, barely more than a fading dream, he feels his legs splash into water, soaking his trousers. He has reached the bay, and his body – apparently of its own accord – seems intent on taking him deeper into the water.

In moments, his entire body is submerged, and he drifts, floating slowly downward. His lungs continue to ache, burning with the need for air; several parts of him feel as though they are changing, reshaping. Yet all of this is happening at a remove. Soft, soothing white light is filling his head, and he is ready to slip away into oblivion.

But his body has no such intentions.

Sensing its imminent demise, acting purely on survival alone, his mouth opens wide and tries to take in another breath. Barely conscious, he muses with detached amusement how futile an action this is, being that even if his throat weren't closed up, fluid would fill his lungs and the result would be just the same. And that is when the water not only floods his mouth, but flows out through the slits which have grown on either side of his neck.

Cool, refreshing water washes through, revitalizing his senses and astonishing him.

The buzz of mounting unconsciousness recedes and disappears, leaving him more aware than he has been since the pain began. Not only that, but most of his agonies seem to have ended, or at least diminished.

He floats, serenely, and opens his eyes. And is amazed at the clarity his vision now possesses. Even only a few meters under the water, he would have expected everything to be dark and murky, yet it seems as though his sight has never been clearer. In addition, his sense of smell – *a sense of smell under the water!* – astonishes him; he can detect a myriad of different scents coming to him each time he 'breathes' in water, each odor creating a picture in his mind, like a three-dimensional map of the area around him. He is beginning to suspect what has happened, but for the moment, he keeps the idea at bay.

A number of muffled clicks and pops brings his attention back to his body. It would seem that his transformation – his *mutation* – is not yet complete, though he senses it is *almost* done. He holds his hands in front of his face and barely recognizes them; where he expects to see pale, pink flesh, he is instead confronted with elongated, grey-tinged limbs. Further, his fingers are growing longer and thinner as he watches, the skin between those digits flattening out like the wings of a bat. He is too amazed – and possibly shocked – to feel any fear or concern. Looking down, he sees his legs have gone through a similar process, tearing and splitting his trousers. His whole body has changed; though he cannot see every instance of mutation, he can feel it; like the weight of heavy muscle and skin on his back or the widening of his head and mouth, the growth of a snub snout. Reaching up with care, he gingerly runs a finger along crooked rows of large and very sharp teeth.

He cannot fathom how this has happened. Oh, he knows what has caused it – *that goddamn compound* – but not *how*. Yet he remains eerily calm. Perhaps it is the new DNA threading through his system, the cold blood which now fills his body. Whatever it is, it allows him to adapt very quickly to his circumstances and new environment.

Kicking his legs and swishing his hands in experiment, he is propelled swiftly through the water. Exhilaration bubbles up within, and he spends a few minutes simply testing his new ability, swimming with an ease that he has never before possessed.

Soon enough, though, the situation comes back to him and he ponders what to do and where to go.

And that's when a faint yet familiar scent comes to him. His new senses indicate the source is quite a few miles away, but in his mind, it shows as a thin, pulsing thread in the water.

Without much thought, he flicks his feet and follows the line of this enticing smell.

It began, as these things often do, with the noblest of intentions.

The Shaw Institute for Medical Advancement, on the coast of Massachusetts. Research and Development Division, specializing in incurable diseases.

Matthew Brody perched on the edge of his tall stool and pulled on the hem of his wrinkled lab coat as he waited for the latest results to come in, the computer humming as though it was actually in the process of thinking. As much as he tried not to, as much as he'd gone through the same process hundreds and hundreds of times before, he always experienced a faint whisper of hope that this time – *this time* – it would be different. Thousands of tests with minute variations in the inputting stage had produced the same negative conclusions every time.

Matt's feet tapped out a fast, impatient rhythm as he silently urged the machine to complete its calculations. He wished he had its soulless capacity for patience, its inherent lack of worry or anticipation; it simply crunched the data and spat out the end results with no judgment or disappointment. If only he were able to do the same.

A change in pitch deep in the machine's workings alerted Matt to the imminent arrival of what he waited for. For the thousandth time, he sat up straighter on the stool and stared at the computer screen, silently hoping, willing, but trying to prepare himself for yet more failure.

The pixels on the screen slowly revolved, random specks of color and shape which – Matt thought – were supposed to represent the synthetic mind deliberating. The display shut off with abrupt suddenness, causing Matt to take and hold a sharp breath. Long seconds passed agonizingly slow as his hands curled into fists, fingernails digging into his palms. The tension built within his mind, a silent scream approaching from a great distance. And then graphs and numbers coalesced on the screen and Matt let out his breath through pursed lips. Another negative. Another dead end in the maze that was shark immune-system research.

Though the myth persisted that sharks did not develop cancer, the reality was they did, though they certainly appeared to be very resistant to its effects, not to mention other ailments. Many researchers and scientists believed – and Matt and his colleagues agreed – that the key to understanding the robust nature of shark immunity lay, naturally, with their unique immune systems. Even if a cure for cancer were not possible – and since cancer was not one, single disease, this was pretty much a given – unlocking the mysteries of the shark immune system might provide leads to at least reducing the effects of some cancers. Though it had been proven years ago that shark cartilage was useless in this regard, Matt believed he was very close to a breakthrough in regards to the actual immune system of these remarkable animals; just not yet close enough.

Frustration and exasperation fizzed in his blood and he lifted his hand with the intention of slamming it down on the table, arresting the momentum just before it hit.

"Shit!"

Martina Hooper, the lab's post-graduate intern, looked up from the microscope she'd been staring into and smiled in sympathy.

"Another bust, huh?"

Matt nodded but kept his head down, not wanting to look at her, not wanting her to see the sheer desperation painted across his face, the grim agony in his eyes.

"Hey, shit, dude; sorry. Take a deep breath ... take a break, try again. We'll get there. I know it."

For once, Martina's seemingly bottomless enthusiasm didn't lift Matt's spirits; if anything, her consoling perkiness irritated him even more than he already was. He felt the sudden urge to scream at her, to tell her to *fuck off*,' but knew this was simply an aspect of his growing impatience with the whole project. His mounting bitterness needed an outlet, and that was something he'd have to keep a lid on.

So he swallowed down his frustrations and bent back to the weary task of running yet more samples through the system.

"Dad, are there real mermaids living in the sea? Like, *really* real?"

Matt leaned back against the headboard on Ben's bed and thought about how best to answer his six-year-old son.

They lay together on the tiny single bed, Ben snuggled up under Matt's right arm. The boy had insisted on being read his bedtime stories in this way, so that they could both see the pictures and read the words together in whichever book had been chosen. Lately, Ben had developed an interest in creatures of the sea, real and mythical, mermaids in particular; though obsession might have been a better word for the way the child devoured such stories. Matt couldn't blame the kid. Ever since they had moved to the beach-house provided by the TSIMA contract two years previous, Ben had fallen in love with the beach and ocean that stretched away from what was, essentially, their back lawn.

Initially, Matt had been terrified the then four-year-old would get carried off into the ocean and drown, but the child had taken to the water like a natural, showing an affinity for the ocean but also a sensible head; not venturing out too far, keeping close to his parents. It was astonishing to see, especially in one so young. Matt had – at the time, and still did on occasion – marveled at this wonderful little life, had been almost overwhelmed with the responsibility of looking after him, the sheer terror-filled joy of being a parent. He loved watching this minuscule human toddle up to the water's edge, fearless and intensely curious in his oversized swimming trunks and inflatable armbands; feeling his heart squeeze in pain as the boy splashed and yelled with pure joy in the incoming waves.

In the two years they'd been in residence, Ben had ditched the armbands and progressed to a snorkel, becoming a competent little swimmer, though never straying too far out. Matt still watched him in terrified joy, which threatened to burst his heart every time.

An impatient snort from Ben brought Matt back from his reverie. His mind stuttered, grasping for a suitable answer that would satisfy both the child's wonder and curiosity, but also Matt's determination not to outright lie to his son despite how harmless such things might seem.

"Um ... I've never seen one myself, but ... the ocean is a pretty big place. It wouldn't surprise me to find *all* kinds of fantastic creatures down there. They say we know less about the ocean than we do about space. I don't know if I believe that; I mean ... space is a very big place, but ... I get what it's trying to say."

Ben tapped his little hand on the open page of the book Matt held; the brightly colored image depicted a trio of smiling, cartoon mermaids as they sped through the ocean, schools of curious fish chasing their wake.

"I wish ... I wish *I* was a mermaid." His little finger idly traced the contours of the bubbles which trailed behind these exotic creatures.

Matt pulled his son closer. "Well, you'd be a mer*man*, or merboy, I guess, but that would be amazing, being able to swim deep under the ocean." Matt wasn't really sure what to make of his son's statement, though he knew children – and Ben was no exception – had the tendency to come out with all kinds of bizarre and fantastical pronouncements. He hoped it didn't signify some dark undercurrent in his son's young psyche, which would lead the boy to venture beyond his capabilities in the water.

Matt shook his head, and chastised himself for such grim thoughts.

You're a damned idiot, man ... he's just a kid, expressing a silly fantasy. He'll have forgotten about it next week. Don't be such a worrier; you've got enough on your plate as it is.

"Listen, buddy, I think it's probably time for you to go to sleep. We'll read the rest of the book tomorrow night, okay?"

Ben looked disappointed but nodded. "Okay. Can we go swimming tomorrow morning?"

"Sorry, buddy, I'm working again early in the morning, and I'll be there until the evening. But we'll definitely get out there at the weekend."

Matt's heart pinched at the look on his son's face; he knew he'd been working far too much recently, and too hard, leaving little time and energy to spend with Ben beyond these short, evening interludes. It wasn't enough, and he resolved to make it up to Ben, even though his son – and his desire to be there as a father – was the main driving force behind the urgency of his research.

Climbing out of the single bed, Matt tucked Ben into the duvet and kissed his son on the top of his head, blowing a raspberry into the boy's unruly mop of hair. He told him he loved him and whispered goodnight – receiving a sleepy reply in return – then turned the light off before leaving the room with the door half cracked open.

Lorraine ran her hands over Matt's shoulders and onto his chest, pressing her front against his back and hugging him close. His elbows rested on the dining table, palms flat against the smooth wood.

"I don't know what to say, babe ... maybe you just need to come at the whole thing from a fresh angle? I do know all this stress and anxiety can't be good for you. You need to try and relax more."

Matt sighed, reached one hand up to grasp Lorraine's arm. "I know, I know ... just really difficult when I feel I'm so close. As if the answer is right in front of me but I can't see it for looking too hard. It's twisting me up inside. I need this ... *we* need this."

Lorraine buried her face in his neck, nuzzling and kissing. Ordinarily, this would be enough to have both of them pawing at each other in growing arousal and attraction as they stumbled into the bedroom, but these days, Matt more often felt a kind of leaden numbness; a lethargy of the soul that he found difficult to shift. He still managed to take small comfort from his wife's ministrations, though.

As he sat there, with the warm pressure of Lorraine leaning into him, and the light above the table glaring down in harsh brightness, Matt thought he could actually feel the cancer moving in his body, spreading its insidious, corrupting tendrils through his very fibers. Though Dr. Quint had reassured him that the tumor was in the early stages and that she had every confidence he would respond positively to treatment, Matt couldn't help but feel that she had been soft-pedaling his prognosis somewhat, trying to soften the blow. He'd read up on thyroid cancer, and though it seemed that his early diagnosis coupled with it being the more common form of an admittedly rare cancer, it had all been enough to worry him that he might not live to see his son's next birthday.

He ruminated again on the bitter irony of developing the very disease he was attempting to find a cure for.

Lorraine spoke against the back of his neck, her words muffled. "I know, baby, I know ... but we also need *you*. Ben needs you to be a father, to be there for him. I'm not trying to make you feel guilty or anything, but if you closet yourself away and don't spend any time with him and ... and ..." But the words wouldn't come, were choked off. Instead, Matt felt warm tears slip down the skin of his neck, felt Lorraine's body convulse against him as she tried to stifle her sobs.

He swallowed, an action which resulted in a now familiar discomfort; but added to the pain caused by the malignant lump which nestled at the base of his jaw line, was the ache of bitter sadness. His own tears prickled the corner of his eyes and streamed down his face as he squeezed the lids shut.

Matt grabbed onto Lorraine's arms with both of his hands, held on tightly and wished – not for the first or last time – that this whole situation was somehow some horrible mistake.

Three weeks later, Matt let himself into the Institute and headed toward the research labs; trying to look casual and unconcerned, but painfully aware he was failing, knowing that every movement he made telegraphed suspicion and guilt.

Sweat trickled down his forehead, stinging his eyes; he blinked rapidly and swiped an arm across his face. He could feel it forming rivulets down his back too, and hoped it wasn't soaking through his t-shirt and creating a sweat patch on his jacket. His heart thumped rapid and hard. He knew he shouldn't feel this way, that he had every right to be in the building at this time, and wasn't committing any transgressions; at least, not yet. But the knowledge of what he was here for, what he intended to do, caused guilt to flood through his body. Matt was reasonably sure the place would be empty at this time, anyway – the place was mostly locked up outside daytime working hours and had no serious security staff on site – but if not, if a colleague happened to bump into him and if they happened to ask what he was doing there so late, he would have to simply try and convince them he was picking up some documents that he wanted to work on at home. As for his appearance; well, perhaps he could explain it away as the onset of illness. After all, that wasn't far from the truth at all. His gray, sweat-slicked skin, drastic weight loss, and hollow, sunken eyes were the result of more than simple nerves at being caught. He was scheduled to go in for an operation at the end of the month – two weeks away – and a short while after that the chemotherapy would begin. But he couldn't wait that long as his cancer had decided to take a huge downturn in the last few days, and Matt feared that if he didn't do *something*, he wouldn't last much longer.

He tottered down corridors half-lit only with power-saving emergency lighting, his hand clenching and unclenching continuously on the bunch of keys he'd used to unlock the doors.

Matt managed to reach his labs without encountering anybody else, offering up a silent thanks in relief.

And now came the point of decision.

Though he had already made the effort of coming to the labs after hours, though he was already filled with the intent to do what he felt he had to do, there was still a chance for him to change his mind, to walk away. He was about to commit possibly the greatest professional transgression a researcher could, and possible side-effects of using the solution would be the least of his worries if he were to be discovered.

A myriad of scenarios washed through his mind in flashes and fragments: losing his job; the condemnation of colleagues; prosecution. But swimming above all of this was the image of Ben's face, his sad eyes brimming with tears as he watched his father succumb to the fatal ravages of the cancer. It was this above all else which had motivated Matt to make the desperate decision to do something drastic.

Trying to ignore the heavy hush of the deserted lab, the way the oppressive silence tugged at his nerves, Matt went over to the refrigerated compartments and unlocked the doors with a key from his bunch. He reached in and took out a tray containing a dozen or so phials of clear liquid. These were the latest compounds synthesized from enzymes located within the immune systems of great white sharks. The last two weeks had seen significant leaps forward in their research, the computer algorithms indicating great promise; not necessarily that they were on the *right* path, but were on *a* path that might lead to a breakthrough. The next step was animal testing on mice, but Matt could not wait on that painstakingly slow process.

He carefully slid the tray onto a workbench – his hands shaking so much, he was convinced he was going to drop it – and took off his jacket. He rummaged around in one of the cupboards until he found what he was looking for: hypodermic syringes and needles sealed in their packaging. Bursting items from the plastic, he threaded a needle onto a syringe, then stuck it into the top of a phial and siphoned the liquid into the receptacle.

Once full, he held the syringe up to his eyes and contemplated what he was about to do.

Before he could change his mind, he slid the thin needle into the flesh beneath his jaw, using the reflection in the storage cupboard's glass door for guidance. He hissed, winced; the pain bit deep but he had to deliver the solution straight into the cancer's location. The next part was worse as he squeezed the cold liquid into his neck, taking three steadying breaths before he did so.

Two more doses and he was done.

Matt leaned over the table, hands braced and arms locked as he steadied himself and his thumping heart.

Well, that's it. Just have to wait and see. Could be weeks. It might not even do anything, but I –

And then the agony exploded under his jaw, like a tiny, localised bomb going off.

Matt reared back and collided with the cabinets behind, glass smashing under the force. He slipped on the shards and fell, landing on his side, barely feeling the impact as he writhed in pain, grunting and wheezing. The pain spread, encompassing his whole body, as though he were burning from the inside out.

And then he screamed, bolted to his feet and ran from the facility, out into the night.

He propels himself through the water with ease, rejoicing in this new form.

Thoughts of his recent former existence continually try to bubble up to the surface of his mind, to gain his attention, but are swept away by both his new-found exhilaration and the strange nature of his human-shark hybrid brain.

He still follows the enticing and strangely familiar scent through the water, though he is constantly distracted and tempted by other scents and sights; at one point, he almost succumbs to the nearly overpowering urge to chase after a school of fish, as they dart through the ocean dozens of meters away, glinting and winking silver as they go. But his remaining humanity manages to restrain the compulsion.

Though Matt still retains most of his personality and memories, it all seems inconsequential and distant, like a dream. Instead, he has never felt more alive than he does now, and the more he explores his new body and abilities, the more he comes to inhabit it; and it, he.

Yet one thing from his past keeps recurring to him and that is the face of Ben; his little boy, his son, is not something he can easily forget, even as transformed as he is, and perhaps that one specific memory refuses to allow him complete submission to the hybrid animal he has become.

But it is a tenuous bond, and Matt's slowly sinking consciousness, his human mind, feels – though with little in the way of concern – that it will not be long before even that one link is gone.

His body continues to change, though the manipulations and reshapings are no longer painful, and the whole process seems almost complete. His body is now far longer than it used to be, more flexible, facilitating swift movement through the water. The musculature in his shoulders and back has grown massively, accommodating a large fin that has sprouted between his shoulder-blades. His senses continue to evolve, to sharpen.

He cuts through the water at speed, and before long, arrives at the source of that enticing, intoxicating smell. A few dozen meters away is a small figure paddling through the now shallow water, its feet pumping in – to hybrid-Matt's new perspective – ungainly and energy-wasting fashion, its head at the surface, snorkel protruding up.

Matt holds himself in the water, little flicks of his hands to keep him stationary, and watches this tiny form with fascination.

A name floats up from the depths of his dissembling humanity, from the core of his human consciousness which is slowly being subsumed and surrounded by new instincts and impulses.

The name is Ben.

Hybrid-Matt recognizes – in the most vague and remote way – his son, as fragmented images flit through his mind like tattered strips of paper in a storm: holding a blood-slicked baby fresh from birth; watching with painful joy at Ben's first tentative steps; picking the boy up after falling from his first bike, scraping his knee; sitting with him in the evening, flicking through children's books filled with mermaids and other strange and wonderful creatures of the deep. All of these memories pass through hybrid-Matt's mind in moments, and then are gone.

With a slight kick of his feet, the strange shark-human thing that used to be Matthew Brody swims closer to little Ben. The child's scent is almost overpowering now, a fresh, meaty, vibrant odour; and it causes a new sensation within hybrid-Matt's body. A gnawing pit of hunger opens inside his stomach.

And then Ben spots him.

The child seems frozen for a moment, then swims closer. Ben's face shows no fear or surprise, and his heart rate – which hybrid-Matt can feel pulsing through the water – remains calm. Instead, he appears to be curious, even fascinated.

Hybrid-Matt swims closer again, and now there is only a few meters between the two.

They hold like that for a few long seconds, then Ben reaches out a hand toward hybrid-Matt, a huge grin on his little face.

Hybrid-Matt opens his own mouth in return, in what might be mistaken for a huge smile, as that aching hunger grows within.

It is only when they are a few feet apart that Ben's expression changes to one of concern and worry, but by then, it is far, far too late.

Shark Infested Custard

Richard Leavesley

It's sweet and yellow,
with dangerous bits in.
Beneath its gloopy dairy surface
lurking dangers swim.
This creamy smooth confection
hides the deadliest deception.
It's a glorious dairy snack
that's going to bite you back!
The surprise beneath is totally nothing
like a slice of pie or toffee pudding.
Just look at it, you fool, for goodness sake!
It's sweet vanilla charm is totally fake.
See it moving? Slowly churning?
See those angry circles turning?
That's no cake in there and no bananas;
just fish that want your guts for garters!
This sweet isn't sweet and far from nice!
It's full of angry sharks that bite!
No! Don't try to taste it, you stupid fool!
Stop it now! Put down that spoon!
You swallowed it, you prat, and now you're done!
There's nowhere for you to run
and there will be no way of fighting
when the jaws inside your guts start biting!
And then you'll scream and then you'll shout,
as your pudding eats your insides out...

The Life You Want, But With Sharks

Leslie Anderson and Evan Dicken

The human race, in general, was doomed, but no particular human more so than Captain Duke Masterson.

"They're at the Oprah Memorial!" He crouched behind a ragged slab of concrete, shouting into the handset, the smells of oil and burning rubber thick in the air. Nearby, the chatter of machinegun fire gave way to the high, teeth-on-a-blackboard screeches of makos. Now, Duke's company was the only thing that stood between the Sharks and the stream of panicked refugees fleeing Washington, D.C.

"Where are the dinosaurs? We need support out here!"

"Thank you for calling Command and Control." The recorded voice crackled over the command channel. "All our logistics oviraptorosauria are currently assisting other commanders. Wait time is currently: COUNTLESS minutes, please remain on the –"

Duke threw the handset into the rubble. By Oprah, sometimes dinosaur bureaucracy could be worse than the Sharks.

Another wave of spike landers streaked from the clouds with a bone-rattling boom. An anemic salvo of anti-aircraft fire made smudged fireworks of some, but most came sweeping down, row after row like the serrated teeth of a great ocean predator closing on the broken concrete of the National Mall.

"Sir? Sir!" Sergeant Elisabeth Singh's shout cut through the ringing in Duke's ears. "We can't let them take Oprah!"

Duke looked up at her, blinked. "Too many Sharks, Liz. It's lost."

Singh started to turn away, shaking her head, but Duke caught her arm.

"We *have* to keep them away from the refugees." Duke fought to keep his voice level. Oprah the Redeemer was more than a national hero. Her role in establishing human-dino relations had taken on almost mythical proportions in the history of the New Mesozoic Republic. Losing the statue would be like losing humanity's soul.

Duke looked across the ruined National Mall, almost unrecognizable, now. The great bronze statue of President Oprah stood amidst a nest of twisted rebar, golden sword raised, her expression determined and proud. Duke glanced back at the refugee column – too slow.

"Hold the line. The dinos won't abandon us," Duke said. "The Sharks can't be allowed to take the column."

"And if they do?" Singh asked.

Duke glanced down at the detonator clamped to his belt, then at explosives planted around the National Mall. "The Sharks *can't* be allowed to take the column."

Singh nodded, then turned away, already shouting orders.

The call went down the line, grim-faced men and women shouldering up to the ragged wall of concrete barriers, the flash of their laser rifles a thin, glittering arc against the flood of makos.

But there were too many, always too many.

Void Sharks, apex predators of the vast, unfathomable darkness between the stars. Since the dinosaurs first returned to Earth they had spoken of the great Permian wars. Ancient battles that had left Mars a scoured ruin and almost extinguished life in the solar system. All the might of the vast, intergalactic dinosaur civilization had been barely enough to hold back the Void Sharks the first time. Now, the dinos were beset on all fronts, and humanity so, so *small*.

A mako leapt over the barricade in front of Duke, claws reaching for his face, its mouth open to reveal row-upon-row of serrated fangs.

Duke swung his rifle, cursing as the mako ripped it from his hands. The thing was fast and strong, deadly as only an intergalactic apex predator could be. He flinched back just in time to avoid the mako tearing out his throat. Duke drew his machete, bringing his blade up to meet the mako's next strike.

Salty blood spattered across his face as two-feet of sharpened steel carved into the mako's rough, gray flesh. The thing hissed, snapping at Duke's face. If it felt any pain, there was no sign and the spark of cold hunger never left its flat, obsidian eyes.

Duke backpedaled, hacking down. His blade lodged in the cartilage of the mako's shoulder and Duke was forced to grapple with the thing. He dragged it to the ground, fumbling at his belt knife as the mako screamed and spit. It tore at his body armor, claws shredding Kevlar and shrieking across the ceramic plates that covered Duke's vital organs.

He stabbed the mako in the chest, then the neck, and still it fought. Only when Duke buried his knife in the thing's eye did it finally stop.

He pushed to his feet, blood pounding in his ears. The line

swarmed with makos. Here and there a knot of soldiers struggled against the tide. Sergeant Singh stood atop of one of the barricades, a machete in each hand, slashing at the howling mass, her face a mask of fury and determination.

Oprah would've be proud.

Duke's throat was dry and tight as he watched the makos carry off scores of wounded soldiers. Poor bastards. He'd heard the stories – people dragged off to vivisectoriums and flesh reefs on the great megalodreadnaughts of the Void Shark harvester fleet. He'd seen what the Sharks did to their prisoners – bodies fused into mangled titans of bone, fins, and quivering flesh, their minds twisted into constellations of shrieking rage.

Better death than that, better almost anything.

He fell to his knees by a nearby puddle, regarding himself in the muddy water. Years of battle had battered his face into unrecognizable geometries. The proud regional manager whose pet supply stores routinely earned highest sale awards was gone, replaced by a red-eyed hollow of a man, bent beneath the weight of fear and loss.

The detonator felt surprisingly light in his hand. Gritting his teeth, he keyed in the command override, set his thumb on the activator, and –

The water in the puddle rippled again. And again.

At first, Duke mistook the low rumble for the funereal thud of more spike landers, but the beat was too slow, too regular. He gaped at the great shadows through the pall of smoke. Ranks of duck-billed gryposauruses drove the makos back with flame and cannon fire from shoulder-mounted heavy weapons as squads of smaller combat raptors advanced to reinforce those human soldiers who were still fighting. Explosions tore through the back ranks of the makos, missiles and rockets streaking up to fill the sky with fire. Duke turned to see a pair of mountainous, four-legged dinosaurs, long-necked and fierce, their heavy, armored bodies bristling with artillery and anti-aircraft emplacements.

He smiled. *Apatosaurus Sapiens Sapiens*.

The cavalry had arrived.

"Real integrity is doing the right thing, knowing that nobody's going to know whether you did it or not."
-Oprah Gail Winfrey

Project Manager First Class Chrotchaomi drummed her claws on the desk. She glanced at the chaos unfolding on the screens in front of her. There were 78 screens, a dinosaur for every six, watching battles on eight different worlds.

If she went down the hall she would pass 32 rooms just like this filled with dinosaur bureaucrats, directing their little teams, trying to turn the tide against the Sharks, defend the universe, reverse the great sins of the Dark Behind All Moons. Or so they said, but she knew the truth. They worshiped promotions and tiny nods from their superiors, hoping that even if they were bonitasuara or gryposaurus or even lowly oviraptorosauria like her, they might one day be a supervisor, or even an assistant supervisor.

It depressed her.

There was a time she too worshiped Stone In The Sky and despised Dark Behind All, but since she'd come to Earth she'd tried to open herself up to new experiences. She'd tried Chicago Style Pizza, which had been a mistake. She'd gone in on an apartment in Little New Jersey and ridden a roller coaster – also mistakes. She'd also gone with one of her few human neighbors to the Church of Oprah The Redeemer and that had not been a mistake. Chrot found in the stained glass windows and adoring face of the human saint a peace she had never felt before. Now, she kept a small Oprah medal hidden under her feathers. When she was assigned a portion of Earth she knew she had been chosen by the Redeemer, even as the styracosauruses chuckled that it was a 3rd class mission, at best.

But they were losing. The battalion that was supposed to be assisting the humans had gone missing. Worse, her reinforcements kept being reassigned and her work orders ignored. Chrot had lost enough battles to know this one was almost over, but she couldn't abandon the humans.

They were Oprah's people.

The door at the end of the room opened and Supervisor Bax entered, late, as usual, and with Starbucks. Chrot never could quite figure how he still got the stuff, what with Earth almost completely overrun. Bax nodded at them each in turn down the line. Chrot's colleagues turned and nodded back, giving little, submissive head bobs, swishing their tails politely. She fiddled with her keys, switching between cameras, even though she knew exactly what each one showed. Death, death, death. She made herself stand as Bax reached her.

"Supervisor Bax, I wondered if you had a chance to review my work order."

Everyone froze, the clicking of claws on keys falling silent, tails still on the tile floor. Chrot felt cold all over, but she didn't lower her head. She could even feel her back feathers raising. She took a deep breath. It wouldn't do to appear too aggressive.

"Ah, Project Manager ...?" Bax paused.

"Chrotchaomi," said Chrot; Bax never remembered her name. "I need that work assignment approved or the Earth Capital is lost."

"Then we lose it. We're already missing a battalion, I won't throw a regiment away, too." Bax leaned down. He could have swallowed her in two bites, and might have in a less civilized age. They said that in the Jurassictown slums oviraptors were still hunted in the dark and no one spoke of it. She swallowed.

"Sir, please, I know the humans aren't our highest priority, but I really think we shouldn't give up on them. I don't need a large contingent, and, well, Earth is –"

"Just *one* world, and a *small* one, at that. I get it Chrot, I really do ... you spend all day in front of the screens, you start to identify with the little monkey men. They're small and weak, *you're* small and weak ..." Bax loomed over her, all sharp teeth and coffee breath.

"I was, I mean ... if you'd just approve my work order ... there's a strike force in position to –"

"Yes, and their commanders have all been routed to Gamma for the next three months for teambuilding exercises. Do you want to send our troops out with no leaders? Do you?"

"No, I –" Chrot felt panic skitter up her neck.

"Well that's settled, then." Bax nodded at her and continued down the line, toward his office. Unconsciously, she tapped the little silver medal hanging under her feathers.

"Supervisor, please!" She started after him.

"ENOUGH!" Bax roared loud enough to cause several of Chrot's more excitable coworkers to bolt from their seats. "*Sit. Back. Down.*"

Chrot wanted to stand up to him, but oviraptors weren't fighters, they were runners – fast and quick. Her traitor legs carried her back to her chair, back to the wall of death.

"Good. Now get back to work." Bax stormed into his office, slamming the door. Several workers yipped and there was a clatter as they made grabs for their coffee as the cups almost jumped off the table.

Chrotchoami stared at the screens, watching helpless as the humans fought and died to protect their people, their savior. On screen four, the statue of Oprah stood untouched by the chaos, one hand pressed to her heart, the other raised high, her sword bright and gleaming. It was as if she were staring right at Chrot – questioning, judging.

Chrot brought up the work order on her monitor – an entire regiment of dinosaurs, enough to turn the battle. All it needed was Bax's signature.

A quick tap of the keyboard brought up an old order, signed and sealed. Not quite believing what she was doing, Chrot clipped the signature and superimposed it over the blank space on the deployment order. She changed a few titles here, removed the commanding officers so the order wouldn't trigger any red flags and–

She paused. Who *would* command?

Like she was watching herself in a dream Chrot typed her own name. She'd managed hundreds of battles, would it be different to command them in the field?

Her claws hovered over the execute button. This would be the end of her career for certain, maybe even the end of her life – deploying soldiers under false pretenses *was* treason, after all. Questions flashed through her thoughts: Did she really think no one would notice? Could she pretend to be a Commander? How could she even be considering this?

She took a slow breath, gripping her medallion so tightly she could feel the edges dig into the flesh of her palm. So many questions, but only one really mattered:

What would Oprah do?

"Where there is no struggle, there is no strength."
-Oprah Gail Winfrey

Duke stared up at the oviraptor who stepped over the tangle of human and mako bodies. He knew enough about plumage to guess the dino's sex, but not much else.

The dinosaur cocked her head, then gave a little flick of her feathers as swarms of commando raptors advanced under covering fire from weapons mounted on the backs of the larger dinosaurs.

"Sorry for the delay. There was a battalion enroute, but ..." The dinosaur commander tilted her head to regard him with one eye, then the other. "Captain …?"

"Masterson, ma'am, but call me Duke."

"I'm Project –" The dinosaur's feathers flattened, then abruptly straightened. " – Project Commander Chrotchaomi."

Duke chewed his lip, he'd never heard that title before. Still, didn't really matter what she called herself, she was here, and she was fighting.

"Commander Crotchamam –"

"*Chrot*. Commander Chrot."

"Commander Chrot." Duke saluted. He'd seen dino regiments before, but never one headed by an oviraptor. Species hierarchy was big among the dinos. Still, best not to look a gift raptor in the mouth. He grinned, then remembered the dinos considered it rude to show teeth and settled for a tight smile. "Thank Oprah you came when you did, those toothy bastards were about to –"

A shockwave knocked them from their feet.

Duke came up shouting, the screams of humans and dinosaurs barely audible over the ringing in his ears. His arms and legs felt loose like someone had greased all the joints. Swearing, he scrambled to where Commander Chrot lay, throwing himself down next to her. "What the hell was that?"

Duke could hear the chatter from Commander Chrot's headset – soldiers and non-coms shouting for orders. Slowly, she sat, then stood, scorched feathers fanned out behind her. Ash and dust swirled around them, the aimless chatter of rifle fire a grim counterpoint to the cries of the wounded, the dying. In the distance, an apatosaurus bellowed once, then fell silent.

"Oprah deliver us." One of Chrot's hands went to her chest, scrabbling at the plates of her armor as if she was searching for something. She scanned the ground. "Where is it?"

"Get down, Commander. There could be more of whatever that was." Duke tugged at Chrot's arm, then realized she probably weighed close to a ton. Fortunately, she slumped back behind the barricade.

Duke peered over the ragged concrete. Much of the debris had fallen back to earth, and he could just make out the edges of the scorched and blackened circle of rubble that marked the edges of where the Shark weapon had impacted.

"Was that a mass driver?" Duke glanced back to Chrot – the dinos had been fighting the Sharks for millennia – she had to have an idea what happened, at least. "Are they starting an orbital bombardment?"

She shook her head, frowning. "None of the Megalodreds are close enough, and besides, scorched earth leaves no food, no captive biomass for the flesh reefs. Invasions always go the same way – spike landers with waves of makos, hammerheads, or blacktips."

"You've *never* seen this before?" Duke asked.

"The Dark Behind All Moons only cares about consumption, they'd never destroy food." Chrot paused. "Unless ... no. I'd always thought saurians were immune."

"Unless what? Immune to what?"

Chrot started shouting into her headset.

"Unless *what*?!"

The Commander waved a claw at the destruction. "Unless *that* wasn't a weapon."

Rubble shifted in the center of the circle, the shriek of tortured steel echoed by a far more primal scream.

A huge shape rose from the debris. Assembled from what must have been hundreds dinosaurs, its hunched frame was covered by a patchwork of mottled skin. Several heads sat amidst a mane of thrashing tails, and its long arms were studded with talons that twitched as if to shred the very air. Its scales were cracked and scabbed, a greenish-yellow glow seeping from within as if the creature were full of radioactive magma.

The thing stepped from the crater. Makos, blacktips, and hammerheads boiled up behind it like an angry flood, tearing toward the thin line of men and dinosaurs.

Rockets rained down on the abomination, but it simply shouldered through the barrage, swatting at the explosions as if they were mere bug bites. It kicked a hole in the barricades, scattering humans and dinosaurs alike. There were calls coming in on all channels now, screams, howls.

"Commander, what do we do?" Duke's voice cracked.

"I – we ..."

"Commander!?"

She glanced down at him, her expression pained. "I'm not –"

With a teeth-gritting howl, the abomination reared back, the glow inside its body growing suddenly brighter. It threw back its many arms to send the sickly brightness sheeting forth.

Duke shielded his eyes. There was a flash, then nothing.

He realized the coms had gone silent, as had the weapons fire. He could still see soldiers all around, struggling with laser rifles gone cold and dead, shouting into headsets that were little more than powered-down lumps of plastic and steel.

Somehow, the Sharks had managed to grow an electromagnetic pulse generator.

The thing roared again, echoed by its smaller brethren as they scrambled over the rubble, desperate to get to grips with soldiers reduced to fighting with blade and claw. There was a moment of indrawn breath, wincing expectation stretched tight as a drumhead.

"Shit," Duke said.

"Shit," Chrot agreed.

And the Sharks came screaming in.

"Doing the best at this moment puts you in the best place for the next moment."

-Oprah Gail Winfrey

In the beginning there was Home and The Stone in the Sky and The Darkness Behind All Moons and war. There was always war. Only on Alpha did the dinosaurs live in peace. That was a lie, of course. The larger dinosaurs lived in peace and ate the smaller ones, broke their bones in their teeth as they died screaming, but the sermons on Clawday didn't mention that. It was a struggle to realize they actually glossed over a lot of things, and once Chrot did there was nothing left to do but lose faith.

"Commander!" Duke yelled, "Commander you have to do something!"

Her troops were holding the line, if barely – human and dinosaur fighting side-by-side as Oprah intended. Chrot felt a surge of pride for them followed by horrible, mashing guilt.

"I'm not a Commander," she said.

"What?" Duke yelled, but she realized he wasn't astonished. He hadn't heard her.

"I'm not a Commander. I'm a Project Manager. I'm … I'm a tech," she dropped her head, "I watch videos of battles."

Duke crumpled. He was shaking with anger, or maybe it was the blood loss. It was so hard to tell with humans. They were, in many ways, so much bigger than her – overblown with their goals and their gestures. They charged when it was time to retreat. They held the line even when reinforcements would never arrive. Perhaps that is why the Church of Oprah used that word so often – *hope*. She wanted her medal, lost somewhere in a puddle of blood and sludge now. That medal gave her hope.

"That's it, then." Duke said, drawing a small keypad from his belt. The look on his face made Chrot sick to see.

"What's that?" She nodded at the keypad.

"Detonator," Duke said as if the word caused him physical pain, then nodded at a backpack-sized black box on one of the nearby barricades. "The whole Mall is rigged with explosives. But they're useless, now." He shook the detonator. "Damn thing is electric."

Chrot wanted to say something, anything, but the scream of teeth and steel made her look up. An apatosaurus was being torn in two by the massive Shark abomination. Chrot made herself watch. This was her fault. Bax had been right. All she'd done was waste dinosaur lives.

"Can we detonate the explosives manually?" She asked.

"Maybe one at a time." Duke shook his head.

Chrot reached for her medal again and remembered it was gone. All around her, humans and dinosaurs fell, clawing and struggling as they were dragged away. The abomination staggered forward slowly, painfully, an unbalanced mess of screaming mouths and gnashing teeth. It threw back its arms to unleash another electromagnetic pulse, almost toppling over.

Chrot shielded her eyes, then looked back. So much power. That thing would need to be a walking nuclear reactor to generate so much energy. It was only a few hundred yards from the statue. Even dwarfed by the thing's massive bulk, Oprah seemed to stand tall and undaunted, her sword raised as if to pierce the abomination's huge, glowing bulk.

An idea began to form in Chrot's mind. She felt something grow in her chest, a strange feeling, one she hadn't felt in a long time. She shouted at her surviving troops to fall back quickly and take as many humans as they could.

"Duke," she said. "Can you set the explosives on a manual timer?"

He looked up, frowned. "Yes, but they're spread out. I can't detonate enough for it to matter."

Chrot bobbed her head. "Leave that to me."

She knelt. "Get on."

He stared at her.

"*Get. On.*"

Slowly, Duke threw a leg over her back, grasping the feathers along her spine. Chrot stood, shifting to adjust his weight on her back. It wasn't comfortable, but she could manage.

"We need as many bombs as we can get."

"What?"

Chrot jerked her head at the abomination. "We're gonna knock that thing down."

"Yes, ma'am, I –"

Chrot was already running. Millions of years of fleeing from larger predators had made oviraptors sleek, and swift, leaving them perfectly designed for speed. And Chrot was faster than most.

She sprinted across the rubble, dodging around broken barriers, leaping over piles of debris.

"There!" Duke shouted, and she skewed to the side, ducking so he could reach down and snag the explosive. A half-dozen makos came screaming over the barricade, but Chrot slipped to one side, weaving through the flailing arms, the clutching claws.

And she was off again.

Chrot sped over the cracked tiles of the National Mall, wind and ash blowing through her feathers. One, two, three, Duke leaned down to snatch the explosives from their nests amidst the rubble. Soon they had a half-dozen of the packs. And still Chrot ran, skewing around packs of ravening makos and blacktips, towards the gigantic creature.

She spared one look back at the thin line of humans and dinosaurs fleeing toward the waiting transports. She only hoped they could get far enough away.

Chrot's ankle caught on a piece of twisted rebar and she almost fell. The pain was like something gnawing on her leg, biting deep with every staggering step. There were perhaps a hundred makos chasing her, now, mouths hanging open in anticipation, a terrible hunger in their matte black eyes. Her breath came ragged, every step an agony, fear growing in her chest. Millions of years of evolution told her to run away, to hide.

The abomination loomed above her, and just beyond, sword raised, Oprah stood firm.

The thing's leg was a mass of flesh and feather and scale. Chrot leaped, claws sinking into the rough flesh. She tore down, as, on her back, Duke leaned in to stuff the explosives into the ragged wound.

Darkness ate at the edges of Chrot's vision, pain and exhaustion almost causing her to lose her grip. But she held on, teeth gritted, until Duke had placed the last explosive.

Then she fell.

The ground took the wind from her. Duke was shouting again, his arms over her head, shielding her. Beyond, the thing lumbered away, not even seeming to notice them. What were tiny claws and tiny teeth to a creature made from pain?

Sighing, Chrot closed her eyes. She could have stayed on Alpha. She could have stayed in the video room. What brought her here, to die? It was that thing – that thing that made humans so brave and stupid – that made them run toward their fears rather than away. And now that she found it, who would tell her she wasn't human?

The bombs detonated.

One of the abomination's legs buckled, and it toppled, falling slowly like one of the great, broadleaf trees on Alpha. It hit the ground with a thunderous boom. For a moment, Chrot thought it would heave itself back upright, but then she saw Oprah.

The creature had impaled itself on the statue. Oprah seemed to rise from the thing's back, covered in blood and viscera, her sword bent but unbroken. Otherworldly green pulsed from the abomination, lighting Oprah's brave, proud face, and for a moment she seemed to smile at Chrot.

There was a flash of verdant brightness, and then black. And cold.

"You become what you believe, not what you think or what you want."
-Oprah Gail Winfrey

"I'll eat her *myself.*" A familiar voice echoed through Chrot's fevered dreams.

She clawed her way back to consciousness, head aching like it was about to burst. Dull sunlight filtered through the canvas overhead. She was in a big tent. The air smelled of blood and antiseptic and coffee breath.

"Ah, the traitor's awake." Supervisor Bax grinned down at her. "I'm glad – takes all the fun out of it when they don't scream."

Chrot tried to move, hissing as pain shot up her side.

"Ah, but let's make this all nice and legal." Bax drew a small dataslate from his pocket, keyed a few commands, then turned it around to show her. "Project Manager First Class Chrotchoami. You've been stripped of your position and your charter, Inter-species

Treaty regulations no longer apply." He grinned. "You're an outlaw, Chrot, you're *prey*."

Chrot knew she should be afraid, but strangely, she found herself laughing.

"What's so funny?" Bax asked.

"You remembered my name."

He scowled, shaking his head. "By the Stone, I'm gonna enjoy eat–"

"Stop!"

Painfully, Chrot turned her head to see Duke enter the tent along with a score of other humans, all armed.

Bax snarled. "You have no authority –"

"I think, Supervisor, you'll find we do." Duke limped up to the large carnosaur, glaring as if Bax couldn't have swallowed him whole. He held up a small datapad, wincing as the move stretched the bandages on his arm.

Gingerly, Bax took the pad, holding it close to read the tiny human font.

"I think you'll find all the paperwork in order." Duke said, then turned to offer Chrot a rough salute. "Ma'am."

She cocked her head.

"Pursuant to NMR regulation J808.3 governing the wartime conscription of civilians and J412.9 detailing battlefield promotions, I hereby enlist you in the Earth Armed Forces and confer upon you the rank of acting Commander."

"I'm sorry, mammal," Bax said. "But this a saurian matter, as a government contractor, Project Manager Chrotchaomi isn't bound by–"

"Normally, yes, but *you* just stripped her of her charter," Masterson said with a smirk. "Scroll down, you'll find Commander Chrot's petition for asylum, which the NMR is *delighted* to grant. She is, after all, a national hero."

Chrot couldn't believe it, her throat was thick, her vision swimming with tears. She'd never felt so much acceptance, so much *hope*.

"Commander." Duke offered a ragged salute. "You're to be put in command of the first mixed human-saurian battalion. It seems that your bravery inspired quite a few dinos to resign in favor of joining the NMR. This war hasn't had many heroes. We're all hungry for them."

"This is an outrage," Bax sputtered. "Expect a formal inquiry when I return to Alpha."

"Feel free." Duke shrugged. "I'm sure something will come of it – dinosaur bureaucracy *is* known for its speed and efficiency."

Bax roared, causing the humans to unshoulder their rifles. For a moment Chrot thought Bax was about to lunge at Duke, but the Supervisor paused as an apatosaurus snaked its massive head into the tent.

"Everything okay in here, Commander?"

With a start, Chrot realized it was talking to her.

"Yes, yes. Bax was just leaving," she said with a pointed look at the Supervisor.

He snorted, teeth bared as he stalked from the tent. She heard his footsteps fade like a thunderstorm.

"I think that went well," Duke said.

"He won't let this go."

"Does it matter? By the time he finishes the paperwork, the war will be won." Duke held out his hand. In it glittered a small silver medallion. "Oprah willing."

Chrot took the medallion, paused, then pressed it back into Duke's hands. "You keep it. I don't need it anymore."

He seemed about to speak, but just nodded, eyes shimmering. They sat for a while, Duke's small, human hand clasped in Chrot's large, scaled one. Human and dinosaur together at last.

Just as Oprah intended.

About the Contributors

Jarod Anderson

Jarod K. Anderson is afraid of sharks. He understands that they are beautiful, misunderstood animals that need our protection. He also understands that they are apex predators who can sense your blood from miles away and never stop growing new rows of teeth. Happily, Jarod lives in landlocked Ohio where he will be safe so long as sharks never learn to swim through corn. His work has appeared in *Apex Magazine*, *Daily Science Fiction*, *Escape Pod*, and elsewhere. Jarod's work is forthcoming from *Asimov's* and *Pseudopod*. Find him online at: www.jarodkanderson.com

Leslie Anderson and Evan Dicken

Evan Dicken and Leslie J. Anderson's writing has appeared in *Analog, Asimov's, Apex,* and *Beneath Ceaseless Skies* to name a few. By day Evan studies old Japanese maps and crunches data for all manner of fascinating medical experiments at Ohio State University, while Leslie J. Anderson coordinates marketing for a financial consulting firm and draws comics about hats. By night they fight crime, write, and/or obsess over small dogs. They also, occasionally, collaborate on short stories. See more of their writing at evandicken.com and lesliejanderson.com.

David W. Barbee

David W. Barbee is an author of bizarro fiction, the weirdest fiction on the planet. He's written five very weird books and many short stories published online and in print. He lives in Central Georgia, but you can find him on the internet in places like facebook, twitter, and wordpress. He's still never watched any of the Jaws movies, and he'd like to take this opportunity to apologize.

Jeffrey Blevins

Always viewing life through the vines of death, I pay the utmost attention to those looking back. I hope my son Malachai enjoys this story more than I enjoy corn on macabre.

G. Arthur Brown

G. Arthur Brown is unable to be biographied for reasons literary science has yet to explain. His name is inscribed as author on such works as *Kitten*, *I Like Turtles*, *Governor of the Homeless*, and *The Long Night of the Eternal Korean War*, but little else can be verified. Rumor has it he took a CHEMTRAIL at Taco Bell and now he dead. <sic>

Jonah Buck

Jonah Buck wanted to study eldritch knowledge and commune with pale, semi-human creatures that flit across the sunless landscape to terrorize the living, so he became an Oregon attorney. His interests include history, exotic poultry, paleontology, monster movies, and professional stage magic. He is also the author of *Carrion Safari*. Special thanks to Dave Frohnmayer.

Sara Codair

Sara Codair lives in a world of words: she writes fiction whenever she has a free moment, teaches writing at a community college and is known to binge read fantasy novels. When she manages to pry herself away from the words, she can often be found hiking, swimming, gardening or telling people to save the bees. Find her online at https://saracodair.com/.

Gary Couzens

Gary Couzens has had stories published in *F & SF, Interzone, Black Static, Crimewave, The Third Alternative, Midnight Street* and other magazines amd anthologies. His collection *Second Contact and Other Stories* was published in 2003 by Elastic Press and a second collection, *Out Stack and Other Places*, was published in 2015 by Midnight Street Publications. He edited *Extended Play: The Elastic Book of Music* (2006) which won the British Fantasy Award for Best Anthology.

Jennifer Crow

Shy and nocturnal, Jennifer Crow has rarely been photographed in the wild, but it's rumored that she lives near a waterfall in western New York. You can find her poetry on several websites, including Goblin Fruit, Uncanny, Mythic Delirium, Eye to the Telescope, and Mithila Review. She's always happy to connect with readers on her Facebook author page or on twitter @writerjencrow.

Courtney Cullinan

Courtney Cullinan lives in Jacksonville, Florida, where she writes stories about existential terror and magical talking horses. In addition to writing, she enjoys listening to the *Hamilton* soundtrack on constant repeat and watching campy movies with her boyfriend and their cat.

Em Dehaney

Em Dehaney is a mother of two, a writer of fantasy and a drinker of tea. Born in Gravesend, England, her writing is inspired by the dark and decadent history of her home town. She is made of tea, cake, blood and

urban magic. You can find her at www.emdehaney
.com or lurking about on Facebook.com/emdehaney posting pictures of
witches.

Amber Fallon

Amber Fallon, formerly known as Alyn Day, lives in a small town
outside Boston, Massachusetts that she shares with her husband and
their two dogs. A techie by day and a horror writer by night, Mrs. Fallon
has also spent time as a bank manager, motivational speaker, produce
wrangler, and apprentice butcher. Her obsessions with sushi, glittery
nail polish, and sharp objects have made her a recognized figure around
the community. Amber's publications include *The Terminal, Daughters
of Inanna, So Long and Thanks for All the Brains, Daily Frights 2012,
Women of the Living Dead, Zombie Tales, Here Be Clowns, Horror on the
Installment Plan, Zombies For a Cure, Quick Bites of Flesh, Daily Frights
2013, Mirror, Mirror, Operation Ice Bat, Painted Mayhem*, and *Return to
Deathlehem.* Tweet her @Z0mbiegrl or visit her blog at
www.amberfallon.net and listen to her podcast, It Cooks, on Project
iRadio!

Paul M. Feeney

Paul M. Feeney, a lifelong reader of genre, it took until 2011 for him
to realise he wanted to write. Since then, he has had a number of short
stories published in various anthologies (through Sirens Call
Publications, April Moon Books, and others), and two novellas – *The
Last Bus* through Crowded Quarantine Publications (a limited edition
paperback only), and *Kids* through Dark Minds Press. He is currently
working on his third novella, *Reflections*, and hopes to start his first
novel soon. He also has a number of other projects due for release in
2017. You can find him on Amazon.

G.H. Finn

G. H. Finn is the pen-name of someone you are very unlikely to have
heard of but who keeps his real identity secret anyway, possibly in the
forlorn hope of being mistaken for a superhero. He is of mixed European
& Native American (Cherokee-Choctaw) ancestry and for many years
lived on one of the remote Isles of Orkney, off the Northern tip of the
Scottish mainland. G. H. Finn has been an amateur strongman, a breeder
of rare & endangered birds, a professional martial-arts instructor, a
teacher of Northern European mythology, a bodyguard, a deep-sea
diver, a computer programmer, a performance poet, a coach to world-
record-breaking athletes, a singer in a punk band, a massage therapist, a
champion needleworker, an international currency smuggler, a

consulting sorcerer and an elephant keeper. Three of these are total lies, the others are all true, but you'll have to guess for yourself which is which.

Amy Fontaine

As a wildlife biologist, Amy Fontaine has studied all kinds of creatures, from wolves and hyenas to honey bees. She has collected raccoon tracks in charcoal and followed whales and sea lions on the open ocean. The wonders of nature never fail to inspire her. Amy's writings tend to be on the speculative side. She enjoys seeing the world, not only as it is, but as it could be. You can find more of Amy's published work, including short stories, poems, and a novel or two, through her website: https://amyfontaine.wordpress.com. Amy loves both sharks and dinosaurs!

Blair Frison

Blair Frison lives on the beautiful island of Cape Breton in Nova Scotia. He spends his free time reading, writing, and watching an unhealthy amount of horror movies – usually with his equally horror-obsessed daughter. He has a passion for the outdoors and hopes to get over his fear of flying someday. His writing has appeared, or will appear, on sites such as *Deadman's Tome, Boxing 24/7, Haunt of Horrors,* and *Polar Borealis.* He is currently working on a collection of short stories.

T.W. Garland

T.W. Garland has a stack of Victorian novels that taunt him with their unbroken spines. He has published stories containing monster hunters, supernatural creatures, steampunk adventurers, aberrations of nature, crazed criminals and psychic detectives. He buys more books than he could hope to read and is glad not to have been born in the nineteenth century or in a novel by Dickens. One day he hopes to live in the real world. For now, he hangs out at his blog: http://twgarland.wordpress.com. Drop in when you have a moment.

Kenneth Goldman

Ken Goldman is a former Philadelphia teacher of English and Film Studies, and he has taught courses on Horror and Science Fiction in Film & Literature. An affiliate member of the Horror Writers Association, Ken has homes on the Main Line in Pennsylvania and at the Jersey shore depending upon the track of the sun and his need for a tan. His stories appear in over 830 independent press publications in the U.S., Canada, the UK, and Australia, and over thirty of Ken's tales are due for publication in 2017. Since 1993 his stories have received seven honorable mentions in The Year's Best Fantasy & Horror. He has written five books: his anthologies of short stories, YOU HAD ME AT ARRGH!! (Sam's Dot Publishers), DONNY DOESN'T LIVE HERE ANYMORE (A/A Publishers), plus an e-book, STAR CROSSED (Vampires 2 Publications); and a novella, DESIREE, (Damnation Books). His novel, OF A FEATHER, was published by Horrific Tales Publications (UK) in January 2014, and his upcoming novel, SINKHOLE, is due late summer 2017 by Bloodshot Books. Ken's stories haven't made him famous yet. He expects that to happen posthumously, after which universities worldwide will make GOLDMAN 101 a mandatory course for future writers. For now, you may find many of Ken's stories online and at Amazon.com. Stop by and scream hello.

Amelia Gorman

Amelia Gorman is one of the world's leading expert in shark selkie biology. You can read other poems by her about strange creatures of lake and sea in *Winter Tales* from Fox Spirit Books and *Fossil Lake III: Unicornado.*

Carissa Harwood

Carissa Harwood earned her MFA from UNLV in Playwrighting (yes, it's spelled correctly!) in 2007. You can visit her at http://:3500wordsperpound.blogspot.com. She lives, writes, and teachers in rural Nevada.

Kevin Holton

Kevin Holton's poetry and prose has appeared with companies like Siren's Call Publications, James Ward Kirk Fiction, and Crystal Lake Publishing. When not writing, he's the North American Representative at www.gametimereviews.com. He is also a student, voice actor, and amateur Batman who can be found at www.kevinholton.com.

Richard Leavesley

First published in 1991, English writer Richard Leavesley has contributed numerous sarcastic poems and weird stories in multiple forms of media on subjects varying from belly buttons to man-eating vaginas. His first Kindle book *Intravenous Flytrap,* an anthology of his first published work from the nineties, is now available at Amazon. "Shark-Infested Custard" is his second visit to the shores of Fossil Lake.

Stumpy McDurmit

When I tried to pass your bio request on to on to Stumpy, I couldn't find him. The circus has been having problems with some animal rights activists over their treatment of prehistoric creatures and unknown monsters. They seem to have fled the country. I'll keep trying in case he comes back, but I'm not optimistic. It's too bad. I kind of miss him even though he's pretty short and kind of ugly. I'll keep looking if you want. -- Mike Howard.

Tim Meyer

Tim Meyer dwells in a dark cave near the Jersey Shore. He's an author, husband, father, podcast host, blogger, coffee connoisseur, beer enthusiast, and explorer of worlds. He writes horror, mysteries, science fiction, and thrillers, although he prefers to blur genres and let the stories fall where they may. You can follow Tim on his blog @ timmeyerwrites.com OR like his Facebook page here: http://www.facebook.com/authortimmeyer OR on Amazon: https://www.amazon.com/Tim-Meyer/e/B009ISFTZ6

Becca J. Morgan

Becca Jaenyth Morgan is a playwright, prop designer, stage manager, and occasional author, mostly due to the insistence of her mother. Aside from torturing herself in the world of theatre, Becca enjoys trying to win the love of stray cats and buying literally anything with a crustacean on it. She can be found on Twitter at "BexZombie" and someday maybe might have an official website.

Sheryl Normandeau

Sheryl Normandeau is a Calgary-based writer who spends an inordinate amount of time at the public library (mostly because she works there). Her stories have appeared in several anthologies and magazines, including *Ficta Fabula, Different Dragons, Weirder Science, The Dragon's Hoard,* and *Universe Horribilis.* She is a shortlisted author for the 2015 Howard O'Hagan Award for Short Stories.

Richard King Perkins III

Richard King Perkins II is a state-sponsored advocate for residents in long-term care facilities. He lives in Crystal Lake, IL, USA with his wife, Vickie and daughter, Sage. He is a three-time Pushcart, Best of the Net and Best of the Web nominee whose work has appeared in more than a thousand publications including *The Louisiana Review, Plainsongs, Texas Review, Hawai'i Review, Roanoke Review, Sugar House Review* and *The William and Mary Review.* His poem "Grease Poet" was a recent prize winner of the Woodrow Hall award for enduring excellence in poetry. His poem "Nemesis" recently won the Songs Of Eretz Editor's Choice award.

Mary Pletsch

Mary Pletsch is a Parrothead who's had a few Changes in Latitudes, Changes in Attitudes before settling down in One Particular Harbour near Margaritaville, just under the Volcano. She's a Brown Eyed Girl who won't give her age, but let's just say sometimes A Pirate Looks at Forty. She ate the Last Mango in Paris, was found innocent of The Great Filling Station Holdup and could really use a few more Boat Drinks. She'd like to send her readers a postcard. On the front, there's a Cheeseburger in Paradise and the legend "The Weather is Here, Wish You Were Beautiful." On the back it says: Keep an eye on those Fins, but remember the things you really need to be afraid of are Vampires, Mummies and the Holy Ghost.

Frank Roger

Frank Roger was born in 1957 in Ghent, Belgium. His first story appeared in 1975. Since then his stories appear in an increasing number of languages in all sorts of magazines and anthologies, and since 2000, story collections are published, also in various languages. Apart from fiction, he also produces collages and graphic work in a surrealist and satirical tradition. They have appeared in various magazines and books. By now he has a few hundred short stories to his credit, published in more than 40 languages. Find out more at www.frankroger.be.

Justin Short

Justin's fiction has previously appeared in places like *Perihelion*, *Broken Pencil*, and *Dear Abby*.

Oliver Smith

Oliver Smith is a visual artist and writer from Cheltenham, UK. His writing developed from an interest in surrealism and as a result his stories and poems generally involve the weird, fantastic, and speculative: a mermaid in the bath, pickled brains plotting in the pantry, and a green man who has lost his head and isn't going to take it lying down. His writing has been described as "literary splatter-horror, and wild-conceited ironic fantasy to die for." (D F Lewis), "richly textured and shaded through a dark and subtle palette" and "hauntingly poetic" (Amazon reviews). Much of his previously published short fiction and poetry is now collected together in the book *Basilisk Soup & Other Fantasies,* this and other publications can be viewed on his Amazon author page.

Trevor Tolliver

Trevor Tolliver is a professor of English and Developmental Composition at Mount San Antonio College and is the author of the musical biography *You Don't Own Me: The Life and Times of Lesley Gore*. He lives in southern California where he shares his home with his husband, their four adopted sons, three fish, two walking-stick bugs, a pair of guinea pigs, an anti-social hamster, and a perpetually angry gecko. Included in the menagerie is a shark that may or may not exist in the family swimming pool.

Emma Tonkin

Emma Tonkin is a researcher working in the South of England. Having recently given in to the desire to write SF, she has written for various anthologies and magazines, including the *Mad Scientist Journal* and the anthologies *Visions IV: Deep Space* and *Singular Irregularity.*

Mike West

Mike West is a writer and musician from Rock Ferry, England. Influenced by Lovecraft, Poe, King and Harris he loves Horror tinged with Sci-fi, Universal Monsters and anything cryptozoological or unexplained. A writer of comics, short stories and flash fiction, he wears his influences on his sleeves and strives to add his own unique perspective to his work. He can be found on Facebook at https://www.facebook.com/mikewest333

Sara Wilson

Sara Wilson is a graduate of Vancouver Island University, earning her BA with a major in Creative Writing. Her poems have appeared in *Portal, Dinosaur Porn, Slim Volume*, and *White Stag*, with more poetry slated for publication in a number of literary magazines and anthologies. Stay up to date by visiting sarawilsonpoet.wordpress.com and following her on twitter @SaraWilsonPoet.